W9-CGM-596

The Reindeer Hunters

Also by Lars Mytting in English translation

FICTION

The Sixteen Trees of the Somme (2017)
The Bell in the Lake: The Sister Bells Trilogy I (2020)

NON-FICTION

*Norwegian Wood: Chopping, Stacking, and
Drying Wood the Scandinavian Way* (2015)
The Norwegian Wood Activity Book (2016)

Lars Mytting

The
Reindeer Hunters

Translated from the Norwegian by
Deborah Dawkin

MACLEHOSE PRESS
QUERCUS · LONDON

First published as *Hekneveven* by Gyldendal Norsk Forlag AS
in Oslo, Norway, 2020

First published in Great Britain in 2022 by MacLehose Press

This paperback edition published in 2022 by

MacLehose Press
An imprint of Quercus Publishing Ltd
Carmelite House
50 Victoria Embankment
London EC4Y 0DZ

An Hachette UK company

Copyright © Gyldendal Norsk Forlag AS, Oslo 2020
English translation copyright © 2022 by Deborah Dawkin

This translation has been published with the financial support of NORLA

The moral right of Lars Mytting to be identified as the author of this work has been
asserted in accordance with the Copyright, Designs and Patents Act, 1988.

Deborah Dawkin asserts her moral right to be identified as the translator of the work.

All rights reserved. No part of this publication may be reproduced
or transmitted in any form or by any means, electronic or mechanical,
including photocopy, recording, or any information storage and
retrieval system, without permission in writing from the publisher.

A CIP catalogue record for this book is available from the British Library.

ISBN (MMP) 978 1 52941 608 4
ISBN (Ebook) 978 1 52941 609 1

This book is a work of fiction. Names, characters, organisations, places and events are
either the product of the author's imagination or are used fictitiously. Any resemblance
to actual persons, living or dead, events or particular places is entirely coincidental.

3   5   7   9   10   8   6   4

Designed and typeset in Adobe Caslon by Patty Rennie
Printed and bound in Great Britain by Clays Ltd, Elcograf S.p.A.

Papers used by MacLehose Press are from well-managed
forests and other responsible sources.

"For there is nothing covered, that shall not be revealed; neither hid, that shall not be known. Therefore whatsoever ye have spoken in darkness shall be heard in the light."

LUKE THE EVANGELIST

"Some place in the Hekne Weave yer face too shall appear."

ASTRID HEKNE

Contents

A Forgotten Event

1611–1613

Forged by Dwarves

THE RIVER LAUGEN WAS FROZEN AND THE WEATHER WAS perfect for travelling by sledge, so it would take Eirik Hekne and his daughters just three days to get from Butangen to Dovre. The year was 1611 and only the roughest cart roads ran through the valley, but when the river was iced over these trips were made easier and even invigorating. Folk whose paths they crossed in the snowstorm thought the two sisters sat so close under their reindeer skin to keep warm, but they never ventured down from the sleigh when the horses stopped to rest, and when asked how old they were, they answered that they were both born in 1595, but that Halfrid was born in the summer and Gunhild closer to Christmas, and as these over-inquisitive folk gawped after them, the girls and their father travelled on, bursting into laughter as soon as their sledge was out of earshot. It was a laugh with a dual clang, absolute abandon around a core of self-denial, but containing less hurt than the mean snicker when one sister wanted something and the other told her she could "go fetch it" herself.

They headed on northwards and as darkness fell they stopped at a farm in Sel, where the Heknes had acquaintances. Here the two girls twisted themselves out of the sledge and four feet landed on the ground at once. Then the first thing they did was to tighten their apron – so wide it went round both their waists – before they limped into a log cabin with an uncommonly wide bed.

Next morning they were up with the sun, though it vanished the instant they entered the Rosten Gorge, where everything lay in shade and the mountain walls were so jagged they might have been hacked out by an angry, slighted giant. The sun never reached the valley floor, and it was said that a summer's day was no warmer than an October night, and that the only creatures to live here were those who neither needed, nor tolerated, the light. All about them the mountains plunged into the seething river below, where the waters that never froze were visible only as foam. Eirik Hekne chivvied the horses up steep slopes, through deep snow and between fallen rocks. Father, horses, daughters, sledge and all went white with rime from the spray of the river, whose roar was so loud that nothing could be heard, and there was no need to say anything, as the only thing on anyone's mind in the Rosten Gorge was how much further it went.

Then the terrain flattened out, the sun reappeared, and the mood of both horses and travellers lightened as they reached Lie farm and were welcomed by the girls' aunt. She had been present for their protracted birth, which had resulted in her sister's death, when the womenfolk had flocked to see the marvel that had been squirming in Astrid Hekne's womb: two baby girls joined at the hip.

They were sixteen years old now and going to stay in a cabin on the slopes opposite Lie, suitably remote from prying folk, on a cart road few ever used. Newly built, just for them, it was a fine, wind-tight log cabin, with smoothly hewn inner walls that gleamed yellow and smelled of fresh-cut pine, one room to sleep in and another to work in. And they saw to their own needs, making the usual jokes, as when Halfrid asked Gunhild to put on more logs and she replied: "Aye, if ye go 'n' fetch the water."

From a very young age the twins had astonished and delighted the Hekne family with their elaborate weaves. But the folk of Butangen and the surrounding villages kept to simple, homely designs, and Eirik wanted to give his daughters the centuries-old skills he knew still existed further north. Living with their aunt, they could meet the oldest mistresses of the craft, from Bøverdalen to Lesja and the villages between. Usually old maids, bent-backed and a little grouchy, muttering and exacting, these were the bearers of hundreds of years of knowledge about wool, plant dyes and patterns that would come to be known by names such as *skybragd* – cloudburst – and *lynild* – lightning fire – made in ways that could not be conveyed in either the spoken or the written word, but only by sitting close and watching for weeks on end, and then repeating them over and over.

Unbeknown to themselves, many of the North Gudbrands-dal womenfolk were among the most skilful weavers in all Europe. They sat, day in and day out, at their upright looms, warp threads dangling in bundles from their stone weights. In other lands across Europe what the Døla folk called Smettvev – glide weaves – were called Flemish tapestries, and their production was governed by rules and laws, and regarded as the sole preserve of men. But opinions held elsewhere were no more interesting to them than what happened on the moon, and if anyone had voiced any objection, they'd soon have learned that the womenfolk of Gudbrandsdal, rich or poor, had no tradition of servility and could make a veritable hell for even the most placid man.

Month after month the Hekne sisters were visited by their teachers. The daylight hours were used for weaving, the evenings for spinning before the fireplace because the warmth softened the grease in the wool. The girls were taught the rarest methods of plant-dyeing, and then in the half-light they were shown – so it was said – weaves from pre-Christian times, pictures that depicted ancient Norse legends through mysterious symbols and the figures of shape-shifters and creatures that were half beast and half human.

But these lessons belonged to the night, and in the morning light the girls sat ready once more to weave pictures of the stories of Christendom, side by side as always, with that wide, beautifully embroidered apron covering their laps, their nimble-fingeredness already manifest in the myriad hair braids they had made for each other in the dawn, and the sadness they had to bear was not yet mature or was something they had already accepted.

The old women soon discovered how quickly and precisely the two worked. With their unique four-handed method the sisters could make the shuttle glide faster than anyone, and all who saw them understood why the word *vevkjerring* also meant 'spider'. Their teachers noticed the peculiar connection they shared. Their reflexes in tight synchrony, their every thought as tangible as a shadow passing across the other, when one had an idea, the other was instantly there to help realise it. But when they were at odds, everything stopped and they worked against each other, so that one sister could do nothing without the other immediately blocking or wrecking it, and, each being able to predict the other's countermoves and plan her own, there was never any resolution or outlet for their anger, just a stalemate, a violent tussle of hands and arms that the old women had to avert if the beginnings of a beautiful weave would not be spoiled.

The sisters rarely worked their own designs. The mysterious images for which they would later find fame, and which would reach perfection in the Hekne Weave, their depiction of Skråpånatta – the Night of the Scourge, when the earth would be scoured bare and both the living and dead swept to their doom – had not yet entered their imagination. All winter they wove the three kings and the wise and unwise virgins, and rejoiced when the spring of 1612 came, followed by a summer that was still at its height one Sunday in late August.

A Sunday that was to be etched in history. If it had been a

Saturday, everything would have been different, since it was on Sundays that the villagers gathered in the church. Everyone except the two sisters, who because of their defect avoided any public gathering.

Which was why they were unaware that the sheriff of Dovre had done the unthinkable: he had marched in and interrupted Mass, and not just that, he had not left his battleaxe in the weapons porch, but had taken it up to the pulpit and struck the floor three times with its shaft, and declared that Norway was at war. From that very moment.

Several hundred Scottish mercenaries had come ashore in Romsdalen and had passed the villages of Lesja on their way to Dovre. The sheriff told them that message batons – *bud-stikker* – had been sent north and south in the valley and along the side-valleys to rally the menfolk in defence of their land. The pastor declared Mass over and the church was emptied. As the day progressed each farm contributed one fighter, and down in the valley farm after farm was abandoned as folk fled to the *seters* – the upland dairy farms – often leaving behind a lonely tethered calf in the yard. Folk knew that soldiers always expropriated what they needed of food, shelter and women, but rumour spread that these Scots were in league with the devil himself, that they slaughtered anyone in their path and burned all the houses, and had dogs that tore runaways to pieces, and cut off the hooves of the milking cows and let them stumble about bleeding just for fun, which was why it was best to tether a calf in the yard and leave all the doors open, in the hope there would be enough food and space for them to spare the farm itself.

The Hekne girls stayed, however. Whether to protect a valuable weave, or because being so slow-moving they would make easy prey if the enemy followed them to the *seters*, or perhaps because they secretly had no *wish* to flee, nobody was well enough acquainted with them to know.

7

Next day a rowdy troop of more than three hundred soldiers passed through Dovre. The dogs first, then officers on horseback, wearing helmets, pistols and swords, the rest a motley crew of press-ganged foot soldiers and young boys, followed by a few women, gunsmiths and saddlers, and a rearguard of seasoned veterans who chivvied any stragglers on.

The soldiers chose a little cart road some way up the valley, and soon they were marching directly outside the Hekne sisters' cabin. They must have heard the tramping of soldiers and horses and the general hum of talking. Almost the entire line of soldiers had gone past when an officer stopped his horse and issued an order. Two young men were given swords, and stepping out of line they approached the log cabin while the rearguard looked on.

They entered without knocking.

Stayed inside for a remarkably long time.

So long that the officer was about to send some men after them, but then they emerged with swords lowered and two leather bags filled with drinking water.

What was said between those four in the cabin that day, only they would know. What is almost certain is that, like most young soldiers, they were probably very nervous and easily scared, and they might have wondered at first if they had stumbled upon the mythical Norns sitting at their loom – the mythical sisters of fate who spun, wove and cut the thread of each human being's life. After all, the old Norse legends were still very much alive on the islands from which they hailed.

The four of them might also have been astonished that they understood each other's language. The officers were from the Scottish mainland, but their men were from the Orkneys and Shetland, which had been inhabited by Norwegians for more than six hundred years, and where the Norse dialect still prevailed even though the islands were now under Scottish rule.

The army travelled on, and set up camp that evening at Kråkvolden, an hour's march south of the Hekne cabin, and they lit campfires and settled into drinking and wrestling, customs inherited from their Norwegian ancestors.

What the Norwegians did not know was that these soldiers had no plans to conquer Norway. They were headed for Sweden to serve as mercenaries to the Swedish king in the Kalmar War. They had not burned any farms or slaughtered folk on their way, but rumours of their wickedness had served them well. Particularly since almost all the soldiers were unarmed and few had ever seen combat before; indeed, most were poor youngsters recruited under duress, some bought out of jail, some simply press-ganged.

Colonel Ramsay was commander of the forces, and serving under him was Lieutenant-Colonel Sinclair, who burned gunpowder in his palm each morning and read the smoke to see what dangers the day would bring. Not that they feared the Norwegians. They were marching across Norway because it was less risky than taking ships through the Skagerrak. Norway was a poor and wretched land, a barren wilderness whose malnourished inhabitants melted away at the mere sight of strangers – wasn't that what their journey had proved thus far? Not an enemy in sight!

But news spread slowly then, and what Ramsay and Sinclair did not know was that King Christian of Denmark had lost faith in the use of mercenaries to defend this cold and rugged land in the north, and had imposed order just eight years previously, by issuing a *leidang*, which not only made the local farmers duty-bound to provide soldiers but required each farm to own a gun. Calls to arms were carried by *budstikker* along strictly defined routes. Also known as *hærpiler*, or war-arrows, these message batons were scorched at one end and marked with a hangman's loop at the other, a reminder that any farmer who failed to uphold the *leidang* would be hanged from the roof beam of his own house, while it and his entire farm were set ablaze around him.

The men gathered.

By Tuesday the *hærpiler* had reached the remotest corners of Gudbrandsdal, and five hundred peasant soldiers were at Kringen, just a day's march south for the Scots. Here, the mountains plunged straight down into the River Laugen and a small, crooked path was their only way through. When the Scots reached it on Wednesday, it proved so narrow they were forced to march single file, and as their army stretched to its full length, a shot rang out and Lieutenant-Colonel Sinclair fell. The shot that hit him in the forehead that day was a jacket button of heirloom silver, chewed into a bullet shape and fired from a two-metre-long wheel-lock rifle by a huntsman from Ringebu, who knew that only silver could kill a man in league with the devil. The only consolation for Sinclair was that for centuries he would be considered the leader of the Scots because he rode at the front.

The Scots were attacked from above with rifles, spears, long axes and scythes. Three hours later, half the mercenaries were dead. Only a few Norwegians fell. The survivors were taken south and imprisoned in a large barn. The sheriffs ordered that they be taken to Akershus Fortress in Kristiania and handed over to the king's men. But it was August, the busiest month of the harvest, so as the liquor was passed around that night there were mutterings, since to accompany the prisoners that far would require a large contingent of guards and supplies, and would take so long that the grain and hay would rot in the fields back at home and lead to winter famine, and was that really all the thanks they could expect from the king for defending the land?

Next morning began with various escape attempts and quarrels between guards and prisoners, then quarrels between the guards themselves, and culminated with the prisoners being led out of the barn two by two and executed. Either shot or speared.

In the silence afterwards came the terror and shame.

God, help us. What have we done. Almighty God. What have we done?

An internalised horror. Over the brutality that was within them.

That we could do this. Even I. Even you.

Eighteen men escaped death. Three were taken to Akershus, where the incident was recorded by the governor general and the file duly closed. It was a military triumph followed by a massacre, and nobody liked to be reminded of the bloodbath that had taken place outside the barn. Eighty years passed before anything more was written about the Scottish invasion. It was then given fresh life in poetry and song, depicted as a wholly heroic deed. In one song however, which was quickly forgotten because it told of the massacre, there was a verse which described a young boy who had been spared. He had broken free, and, running towards the spear of his own accord, he had said in Norwegian:

When God gathers and reckons the dead, then count me a friend of Halfrid Hekne.

It is just possible that this was the selfsame boy who came north to Lie a few days after the battle. He had a bad knife wound and offered to work for free in exchange for food and lodgings. His brother had been killed at Kringen, they were farmhands from the Hebrides who had sought work in Hjaltland when the officers came and press-ganged some of the local youngsters, which they had no legal right to do, but they were armed, which the boys were not. The sisters believed his story, and let him go about with a scythe and an axe and a hoe and a shovel. Each day he carried water and firewood and food up to the cabin. But exactly what happened early next summer was never divulged. The girls' aunt managed to keep the incident hidden from the local gossips, and the only person beyond Norddalen to be told what had happened was Eirik Hekne, when he arrived that Christmas to take his girls home, and by then their wounds were almost healed. Those that could bleed, that is.

The aunt reported that screams had come from the Hekne cabin, screams from both girls, so shrill and intense that they could be heard from down at the farm. They had run up and discovered the twin sisters bloodied and in a state of terror. But neither would say what had happened, only that they had cut themselves and that nobody else was to blame. There was a huge to-do and the wound was difficult to dress, and it was late afternoon before folk noticed that the Scots boy had vanished, having sneaked enough food to get him to the coast. But even stranger were the telltale signs that he had actually returned to the *stabbur* – the farm's old two-storey food storehouse – and replaced some of the food. This was taken as proof that he had originally packed for two, but had then abandoned the plan and his fellow runaway.

The wound turned nasty and the sisters were struck down with a fever, which they only survived, so their aunt believed, because they had cut themselves with the knife they used for their weaving. This knife had been given them by a woman from Bøverdalen, and was said to have special powers. Not only was the knife *jordfunnet* – that is, lost on snow-free ground and rediscovered after having been long forgotten – but it was sharp enough to be *dvergsmidd* – forged by the magical dwarf blacksmiths deep in their underground caves. Knives of this sort were found in every village and passed from farm to farm to heal sick animals and folk, and it was these magical healing properties which the aunt believed had saved the girls.

A new silence entered between the sisters after this episode.

They began, for the first time ever, to work on separate weaves, the first two of which were said to depict the things they'd seen when they were delirious with fever. Some folk reckoned the boy had returned to them one night, leaving something behind for Halfrid, something she later held dearer than all else, though nobody ever found out what it was. Their father took them home, and beneath the ice on which they travelled, the River Laugen streamed towards the sea with yet another secret from Gudbrandsdal.

Back home again in Butangen, they moved into the newly built farmhouse at Hekne. They had an extra loom installed in the room for a work that would occupy them for the rest of their lives. The Hekne Weave was given to the church when they died and was the most elaborate and enigmatic of all their works. Later, after the Sister Bells were cast and named in their memory, the villagers began to realise the power of their inseparability, for just as the girls had been inseparable, so too were the bells. But the wanderlust that lurked below the surface of this inseparability was nigh on invisible to anyone not privy to what happened in Norddalen. Likewise, there were few who had any notion of the powers that were unleashed at the sisters' deathbed, when Gunhild folded Halfrid's hands in her own, and said:

"*Ye shall shuttle wide, and I shall shuttle close, and when the weave be woven we two shall both return.*"

First Story

Children of the Silver Winter

The Thistle

SOME HUMAN BEINGS ARE AS INFLUENTIAL IN DEATH as in life.

Kai Schweigaard knelt down and rested his knee on his Bible. He did not usually tend her grave in his cassock, but a thistle had been carried here on the wind, and lay in the bed of heather and buttercups. It was a mystery to him how it could have blown this far, since they generally only grew on the other side of the cemetery wall, around the old, unmarked gravestones of outlaws and those who had hanged themselves.

It was beautiful, this thistle. Lifeless, but still beautiful with its deep-green leaves and sharp thorns.

Like her in so many ways.

He made a hole in the earth, scattered some of its seeds and patted them down. Got up and brushed his Bible clean of grass and soil.

There were those who said one should move on.

But they did not have the death of another person on their conscience. Or two or even three, when he was hardest on himself. Without a doubt, Gerhard Schönauer's, but also perhaps Astrid Hekne's. And one of their twin sons, Edgar, who lay in an unmarked grave somewhere in Kristiania.

Far below him, on the surface of Lake Løsnes, the breeze inscribed itself in tremors across the water before it reached up to him. It was a hot August day, and it blew from the south and bore within it the smells of the Løsnes Marshes. A burst of the same breath that blew the thistle here to Astrid's grave.

Now and then he had a feeling something was happening. That his feet were somehow heavier as he stood here in the graveyard. That somebody was calling out to him. Though when he turned, there was no-one to be seen. No-one to be seen, but something to mark, just as the villagers claimed to have done through the years, when they said they heard the church bell ring from the depths of Lake Løsnes, calling out to her sister.

The cemetery gate creaked over by the church. It was Oddny Spangrud. Still known as the *new* midwife, despite having been here in Butangen for eighteen years, she was clearly come with a purpose.

She gathered up her apron and nodded. "Herr Pastor?"

"Yes?"

"I am come with a message from the old midwife. Widow Framstad. She says there be sommat the pastor mun know, but she be too feeble to come down here herself."

Schweigaard nodded and said he could go later that day or the next. Oddny Spangrud thanked him and left.

She was a good midwife. Knowledgeable. No doubt she had inherited Widow Framstad's old iron forceps, the tool that midwives were not formally permitted to use, but to which the local doctor wisely turned a blind eye.

Kai Schweigaard braced himself and walked back up to the parsonage. He was met by the smell of Oldfrue Bressum's cooking, and decided there and then to head straight for Widow Framstad's. The hour's walk each way would be good, *hunger* being a prerequisite if you had to down any of Oldfrue's meals these days.

The year was 1903, nonetheless Kai Schweigaard's appearance had changed surprisingly little since the day of his arrival in the spring of 1879. Still straight-backed and robust, not burly like a farmer, but keen-eyed and resolute like a falcon. A touch of grey at the temples, a furrowed brow, suited to his life's work as a hammer forged to the perfect weight. After Astrid's death, his brusque and uncompromising nature had mellowed, and his obsession with rules had been replaced with an open-mindedness. But he could still, without warning, slam his fist into a table and admonish hard-drinking fathers or slippery quack doctors. He generally worked in his office from early till late, with only a break for supper, a supper which, since he couldn't bring himself to sack Oldfrue Bressum, was generally over-salted or tasteless.

She was a legacy from the previous pastor's household, and for the first decade she had been both short-tempered and obstinate, but these characteristics were now replaced with total muddle-headedness. She rarely knew what year it was, and for long periods she lived utterly in the past, calling Schweigaard the *new* pastor. During the archdeacon's official visit to Butangen six years earlier, fresh liver-patties had been on the menu. But to save money Bressum had obtained some sharks' livers, suitable only for the extraction of fish-liver oil. To cap it all, they were rancid, and had, as Schweigaard realised with his second mouthful, been rancid for some time.

That had been the last time the parsonage saw anything resembling a social event.

Years had passed. With hymn-singing, harmonium-playing, baptisms and deaths. Coughs and colds dogged him from November to March, and his joints and neck ached after sitting at his paperwork and writing his sermons in his draughty office. Such were the occupational hazards of a village pastor.

But then came the summers. The long, hot Gudbrandsdal summers, when the heat shimmered between the valley walls and insects hovered over the sedge grass. And he would go out in the priest-boat trolling every other evening, the stiffness of winter melting from his shoulders with each pull on the oars. He often visited Astrid's grave on his way down, and always on his way home if he caught a big trout.

And there he would linger. Before the only person to whom he could present his catch.

Back in the spring of 1881, at the Birthing Institute in Kristiania, he had scorned God and turned his back on Him. Later, he and the Almighty had come to an agreement of sorts, that they would speak again in forty years. Then, if Astrid Hekne's death was revealed to have some greater meaning, he would become a man of faith once again. Meanwhile he would oversee Butangen as he saw fit, here in this secluded backwater, which God might not have forgotten but which He had leased out with no particular qualms.

Life in the first year after Astrid's death had been dark and meaningless; work dragged and everything he did seemed futile. At first he could be in such a daze that he forgot she was dead, and when he saw something beautiful, he felt the urge to tell her, only to realise that she wasn't there and would never be there again.

Bitterness dominated him in the years that followed, and he often let his anguish flood out in full force, from behind a dam he only ever half-heartedly repaired when it burst. The anguish of that winter, which the villagers called the Silver Winter. The winter when the Sister Bells disappeared – Halfrid to Germany and Gunhild to the depths of Lake Løsnes.

He had brought her home in a coffin, but he also brought home a burden of duty that lent him new strength and direction. Sitting in his lap on the sledge trip back was Jehans, dressed in the woollen jacket that Astrid had knitted in the months before his birth, a little bundle he had promised to protect, a little boy he had tried to provide with schooling and a good upbringing, both of which he had managed for years.

Jehans belonged to the Hekne family and should rightfully have grown up on the farm, but the family had fallen out over Astrid and her wilfulness, a falling out that marked their treatment of Jehans, raised on the finest goat's milk but never allowed to sit on anyone's lap. On his second birthday he had been sent to live at Halvfarelia, one of the Heknes' tied smallholdings, where the elderly tenants cared for him like their own.

Schweigaard kept a watchful eye on Jehans' progress through the years. It was arranged that the boy spend his weekends at the parsonage, during which Schweigaard managed to cultivate the strengths and talents he could see in him. But the bonds between them were sadly severed when the youngster turned fifteen.

It came in flashes now, the sorrow. His memories no longer brought the same swingeing pain. He liked to sit before the fireplace in the drawing room, smoking and reading, preferably with an open window, so as to feel both the heat from the open fire and the refreshing evening chill. And sometimes she came to him, Astrid, a thickening in the shadows, a shift in the curtains, and he talked with her when things were tough or when he was happy, and sometimes she whispered to him, and other times she was dead. He knew he ought to have put his grief behind him long ago. But the priesthood is the worst profession imaginable for a troubled man. His graveside eulogies were famed for their wisdom and urgent sincerity. Reason being, each coffin he lowered was Astrid Hekne's coffin. With every speech about the resurrection, Astrid Hekne rose again. And when each funeral was over he was always more drained than he let his parishioners see. He sat down on his own and breathed out and was still, and then, come wind or shine, walked out into the orchard and looked out over the place that had become home, with a gaze that scanned for changes, but also sought reassurance in the things that remained unaltered.

*

He changed into a woollen sweater, breeches and narrow-brimmed hat. He liked to visit the humbler folk in the village, and seldom, except when he needed to display his full authority to some big landowner, did he arrive by horse and carriage. A confident stride and firm speech were his hallmarks, and a modesty that resembled the parsonage itself. The parsonage was essentially two farms in one. First, the large, white-painted house in which he lived, a two-hundred-year-old building with too many empty rooms, with its flagpole, an orchard and spacious courtyard with a few smaller buildings. But then, second, behind a screen of pussy willow, was a working farm, whose sole task was to provide the pastor's family with food and transport. It was here that the stables, carriage shed, barns and tied cottage were found, and it was from here that the smell of cow dung and horses wafted up to the house, along with the clucking of hens and mumbling of farm folk.

The villagers had been generous when Christianity came to Norway, as evidenced by the parsonage's fine location, situated on a broad slope of arable and pasture land that stretched all the way down to Lake Løsnes. The terrain might be steep, but it was even, and it was here that Butangen's largest farms were situated. But today Kai Schweigaard set out on the stony road that wound alongside the River Breia, where small log cabins and cottars' farms perched at the top of near-barren fields that led straight down to the river, often so steep that the farmers could only work with their arses turned downhill.

This was Butangen. These were its folk.

And they each had a lifespan, as the plough and roundpole fence have theirs.

He stopped at the stream where the cart road split into two. One path led past the very smallest and poorest cabins in the village, among them Halvfarelia, where Jehans lived with Adolf and Ingeborg, his foster parents, and then headed further up towards the *seters*. But the path Schweigaard took now was narrower and surrounded by spruce forest. Towards a hidden house on a hidden mission.

He filled a hip flask from the stream and drank. From here he got a last view over the village, and as always when looking at it from afar he felt a sort of demand, an expectation, laid upon him by this place where he lived. It was as though the Silver Winter had left an imprint on Butangen. As though the trees, the cairns, the fields and the river all knew something about him, and had a claim on him, and the authority to redeem this claim.

Doubtless this was because the village itself had been marked by *his* past deeds. There on the slope between the parsonage and Lake Løsnes stood the ancient stave church, there as only a memory now, having been replaced by the new, white church, which would never be anything but the New Church, as nondescript as the prairie churches in America. He had had more success with the bell tower, a two-storey tower without windows that he had erected to house the Sister Bells. It also served as the village mortuary over the winter, housing its dead, row upon row of coffins in the dark, waiting for the frost to loosen its iron grip on the earth in the spring to allow graves to be dug.

But no bells hung in the bell tower as he had promised Astrid they would, and the view that demanded most from him was that of Lake Løsnes. Just as this stretch of water marked the village's border with the outside world, so it was *his* border too. So long and so narrow it was impossible to see its beginning or end from the parsonage. In the evenings Lake Løsnes lay dark and glassy below the forest-clad shore on the opposite side, at least when it did not take on the shape of the wind and warn of coming storms.

The knowledge of what lay at the bottom of the lake dragged at him like a powerful undercurrent. Sometimes he thought that if only he could bring up the bell from her resting place there, he could make up for everything. Others had come here to look for her. Jehans had built a raft when he was only twelve years old, and, together with a friend, he had tried to find the bell and bring her up. That was long ago. Before he had bid a wordless farewell to the boy.

Years ago some young Germans had come here on the same quest, presumably because a bounty had been offered in Dresden to anyone who could reunite the Sister Bells.

So many had tried, so many had failed, that the explanation had to lie in the old legend: that only chain-brothers – brothers born without any sister between – would be able to raise Gunhild and thus take the first step to reuniting the Sister Bells.

He crossed the Breia now, on the bridge that withstood spring floods and heavily loaded drays, and as he embarked on the final stretch of his walk to Widow Framstad's cottage, he suddenly remembered his other promise to Astrid. When they had torn down the old church, he had promised to look for the Hekne Weave.

The weave was said to depict doomsday. Creatures that were half bird and half human, spat flames and set fire to everything beneath them. And it was also thought to warn the villagers of avalanches and plagues, floods and forest fires.

Schweigaard did not believe in such things, although many events in Butangen had put his powers of reason and theology to the test. Yet the *possibility* itself thrilled him, forcing him into the twilight beyond the usual paths of thought. How might it have been to receive a warning about the future when life was at its toughest? Would he have believed such signs in 1880, when he had taken such a wrong turn?

It was said that the Hekne Weave had vanished from the church through locked doors, but such vague, semi-occult fantasies drove him to find out what had actually happened. That was, at least, what he had told himself all those years ago when he had first begun to look for it.

In every corner.

He had started by rifling through every floor and every basement in every building in the parsonage grounds. He crawled under the *stabbur*, climbed into attics, rummaged through cubbyholes and slithered under floorboards. His only rewards were a few threadbare horse blankets, a musty odour on his clothes, and woodlice and centipedes down his collar.

But a promise was a promise. And promises to the dead have a habit of becoming obsessions.

Every time he visited another farm he tried, not always with equal elegance, to turn the conversation onto the subject of ancient weaves. Once he forgot his manners altogether, as he stood in a dining room transfixed by a wall hanging that might resemble the Hekne Weave, depicting, as it did, six gigantic birds with outstretched wings. None of them spat fire or had human faces, yet he stood staring at it, hoping to discover something new, until three recently bereaved daughters coughed politely and said they were ready, and had been for ages, to discuss their father's eulogy.

On another farm he lifted a shroud to peer under it, thinking he had glimpsed an embroidery on the other side, only to find he was mistaken.

The dead man said nothing. But may have had an opinion on the matter.

Gossip soon spread that the pastor was interested in weaves, and he was soon being offered – and for politeness' sake buying – all sorts of threadbare furniture coverings and wall hangings, which he hung on his living room walls.

The only farm he did not visit was Hekne. But it was unlikely to be there, or Astrid would have found it.

Calling upon the logician in himself, he narrowed down his

search to the most likely year for the weave to have disappeared. It was a simple enough matter to get an overview of Butangen's previous pastors, but it was quite another to interpret their imprecise records, written in showy but untidy Gothic script, often with extensive gaps between one entry and the next. After he had spent many hours in the bishop's archives, two snippets of information stood out for him.

One was that the pastor who served Butangen during the Hekne sisters' lifetime was called Sigvard C. Krafft. He was in Butangen from 1591 until 1620, when he set out on a mission to Nordland, leaving no papers behind him, and despite Schweigaard sending several earnest letters of enquiry to the bishop up there, Schweigaard could find out no more about him. He seemed to have evaporated without trace, just as the Hekne Weave would a couple of centuries later.

The other man to attract Schweigaard's attention was a certain Ørnulf Nilssøn. Butangen's pastor for just three years, from 1813 to 1816, he seemed an uncompromising, duty-driven man. One document in Bishop Hamar's archives – so dusty that Schweigaard could barely stop sneezing – revealed him to have come to Butangen with the same unshakeable determination as the young Schweigaard, *immediately* being his favourite word:

> *It was incumbent upon me to Repair this barren and soul-less Parish, and to this end I immediately drew up a List of Beneficial Undertakings, the which I planned to execute.*
> *1. To immediately Order the Cleaning of Church Properties, including making good the flaked Paintwork on the Pulpit.*
> *2. To immediately Burn the Pagan Weave which perverts True Faith and frightens young Recruits from Serving as Soldiers, for they imagine they will meet these monstrous Fire-Birds.*
> *3. To end the Practice, forbidden for years already, of Burying the Dead beneath the Church floor. 4. To School the ignorant*

Farmers in the benefits of the potato plant. 5. To Acquire a new Chasuble lined with Reindeer Pelt, to warm my frozen Joints in this insufferably cold Church. 6. To Provide better-quality Silverware, including Chalices and Candlesticks, the old ones being too small, dented from use, and in all probability Counterfeit. 7. In some Years' Time: to Build a new Church.

With some regret, Schweigaard recognised his younger self in this man's plans. But this was no time for soul-searching: he had found both a year and a reasonable explanation. He was bemused that men would be frightened from being soldiers by the *monstrous fire-birds* – it sounded like an excuse the villagers might give a naive pastor – but that the weave itself might inspire fear did not surprise him. As late as 1879, when Schweigaard himself had arrived in Butangen, superstition had been rife. In the early 1800s beliefs and customs must have been positively medieval. And in a year like 1813, the worst for generations, with famine and impending war, folklore would doubtless have taken greater hold than ever, as hunger and fear drove the villagers to look everywhere for guidance and signs.

It was in such a year, then, that Pastor Nilssøn had come and ordered the burning of the Hekne Weave. The villagers must have protested loudly. But what had actually happened? He found nothing more. Nothing except that by 1816 Nilssøn was defeated by the village's lack of soul and his *frozen joints* and had gone on his way.

Six years later, and Schweigaard had been forced to give up his search. All the farms had been scoured and the bishop's clerks were tired of him digging in their archives. He put his obsession with the Hekne Weave to rest, just as the bell was at rest in Lake Løsnes, and had not thought about Nilssøn for years. Until today, as he stood gazing over the village on his way to Widow Framstad's.

You clearly had your faults, Pastor Nilssøn. But I? I stayed. And here I am, looking out over the very same village you left, and the same Lake Løsnes.

Here I am, gazing over it. Here I am. Knowing it.

As one who stayed, and can look out over my mistakes.

"I shall die in twelve days," she said.

Widow Framstad had grown very old. Wrinkled and crooked, a true ancient. The wood burner was lit and from it came the smell of coffee. She was sitting in a rocking chair in a corner. He took a stool and drew it close. A tiny flame glowed through the damper in the burner. The room was so dark he could not see into the corners.

"Now. There be two matters. First, this place. This cottage and plot o' land. The church may take it if the church do want it. Put it t' good use. For the poor or the old."

Schweigaard said it was a most generous and useful gift, and that they would be wise in its disposal. When the time came.

"Second be the flower-meadow just above the rhubarb patch. I did bury them there. Every one."

A solemnity filled the room as he realised who she was talking about.

"Those I were obliged to take. Those that couldna pull through. Those I mun take home wi' me in my midwifery bag. Naebody ever saw them. Two hundred 'n' three, all told. In two score 'n' fifteen year. I kept count. Gave each a name and a ceremony o' sorts."

Those I were obliged to take. Stillborn children, and those she had dismembered in the womb in a bid to save their mothers' lives. The ways of the ancient midwives. To act promptly, leaving no room for questions or doubt over the necessity. These children were unbaptised and were not buried in the churchyard, since they were not become the Children of God. Though what else they might be, nobody seemed able to say.

"Just so ye knows about it," she said. "So ye can take partic'lar care o' that meadow, leastways not set potatoes or turnips there. Ye shall know it when ye see it."

Kai Schweigaard nodded. A deep pastorly nod. Head bowed, pausing before he slowly raised his gaze again, as though lifting his face to the world after a moment's silent contemplation. He knew it. The darkness such memories held for parents, when joy was extinguished on a day of such hope. The despair that never quite burned out.

He had wondered where they ended up, Butangen's stillborn children. According to new rules they were to be swaddled, then laid in the bottom of a newly opened grave in the morning before the burial of an adult, whose coffin would then rest over the child. But this was impossible in smaller villages without daily burials, and privately he had thought midwives must have their own solutions, and now he had found out what one of those was, and he suspected that the new midwife also had a flower-meadow.

Clearing his throat, Schweigaard said he would have it fenced. "I shall take care of it."

"I know."

They sat in silence.

She said: "Ye were a fine pastor. Though it be 'twixt 'n' 'tween wi' your faith."

He said nothing to this, but asked what made her think she only had twelve days left.

"I saw it. The sign."

When he asked her what the sign was, she took his hand and squeezed it.

"Ye shall live long. But ye too shall see the sign. Ye, in partic'lar, Pastor. And ye shall see it in good time."

She let go his hand and he cleared his throat and asked no more. Widow Framstad rose stiffly to her feet, fetched the pot from the burner and they drank their coffee. Lying on a small table was a pile of white linen with a needle and thread, and he understood that she, like many old folk in Butangen, was following tradition by sewing her own shroud. He did not experience all this as macabre, since the old midwife sat slurping her coffee, wholly at ease and untroubled.

"I can't find your entry in the *kirkebok*," he said. "So I don't know whether you have any other names, or your exact date of birth."

She chuckled. "The pastor were well brought up." She provided him with her first name. "I were a love-begot child. Given away by my mammy and grew up in Framstad. There were no calendars down there. Happen I arrived in about 1810, and I reckons I could walk by then. Herr Pastor may plump upon a date that suits."

Widow Framstad chuckled.

"'Tis like that old joke. Which came first, the midwife or the babbie? Happen I were never born at all. Happen I came awalking on my own two feet. Haha! Nay, I canna' tell, I were too little."

She put down her coffee cup and grabbed his wrist.

"Herr Pastor. The Hekne girl. I know ye were fond o' her."
Fond.

"She knew. She knew it were dangerous to travel away to have her babbies. Had she given birth wi' me in the old way she'd have lived. But nae the bairns. I would have had to take them. They would be lying up by the rhubarb now. But her? She would have been here in Butangen and given birth to other littl' uns. Maybe yours. Likely yours. That were the old way. Nae messin'. And so she did it. Travelled to the city to give birth. Had to. To see them live. Happen because I felt her belly and knew it would be too hard for her to get them out."

"She told me that," Schweigaard said. "That she had been here and had a vision. That she saw her children."

"Saw that there would be two. Two boys. Saw them walk down the path right here, heading down from the mountain. But I reckon she saw sommat that frightened her too. She didna' wish to tell me what. But I knew there were sommat."

"One of the boys died," Schweigaard said.

Widow Framstad seemed to be searching for something up on the ceiling.

"I heard that too. But I canna' creed it. She visited me later that winter, and I felt them stir in her belly. Both were equally good 'n' stout. Life can be unjust, but 'tis never that unjust. Think o' the bell that lies in the lake. The one that only chain-brothers can raise. There mun be two o' them. Nay one and nay three. Two chain-brothers, just as there be two church bells. Just as there were two Hekne sisters."

Her saying that they were *equally good 'n' stout* aroused an old sense of uneasiness in him. He had never been given a straight answer about what had gone wrong during the birth. But a newer curiosity was now aroused in him too, by her mention of the Hekne sisters.

"You were a child in the early 1800s," he said. "Did you perhaps see the Hekne Weave?"

"I canna' recall it. Though a woman in Framstad did. She said it were gigantic and strange. And that she didna' dare look long upon it. There were birds in it, she said, that scared her. As though they drew her in."

He asked if the villagers talked much about it and its history.

"Aye, they talked alright. Some said *Everyone shall see their faces in the Hekne Weave*. But they wove so much, and folk said so much. 'Tis strange how all the sisters' weaves are now gone. I heard they wove with warp yarns o' nettle, and they lasted well. But in some weaves they did sommat strange with the warp, so it would rot after a certain time, and the whole weave would turn to dust. For they didna' want it to last longer. It had done what it were meant to do."

"Do you know what happened to it?" Schweigaard asked. "To the Hekne Weave? Whether it was hidden or burned?"

"It was na' burned. That be all I have heard. But it vanished alright. I met a woman once knew where it went. But she be long dead. She said it had na' floated far. That folk could see it wi'out seeing it. That it were so close that it were impossible to see. She didna' care to say more, for the Hekne Weave would come t'sight when the time were right."

"And – would that be a long time away?"

"Some while before Skråpånatta, so it were said. And the sisters would return. When the weave be woven."

"And what did that mean?" Schweigaard said. "Or, what do you think it meant?"

She shook her head. "Hard to say. Happen they shall return. But not perhaps in a way folk might usually understand."

He bid her farewell and stood outside the door looking at her large vegetable plot. She must have weeded it just before his arrival, for the soil was black and newly turned around the carrots, cabbages and potatoes. Through the window he saw her standing by the basin, washing the coffee cup he had used.

The treetops swayed gently in the breeze, and all that could be heard was the burbling of the brook further down. Schweigaard walked up to the rhubarb patch and had the strong feeling he was in the right place. Just as he could always feel someone's presence in a house whether or not they were actually there.

They were at rest here. All around him. Down in the bumpy ground. Each beneath a little boulder, probably from the River Breia, placed at regular intervals between the flowers and long grasses. Here they were. The little ones that death had cut down in their very first step. All those who ought to have had breast milk and food and learned to crawl and eventually walk. This was where they would have been, Edgar and Jehans. Had Astrid not made the greatest sacrifice.

Fewer newborns died now, and far fewer mothers. Some years ago, a doctor named Sänger had found a way of performing Caesareans that was far safer for mothers, his discovery being that the womb had to be stitched with silver thread, a discovery that earned Sänger the Order of St Olav.

He took out his Bible and said: "I declare this a consecrated ground and a blessed resting place for the bodies of these sleeping children. May the Lord let his peace rest upon this place of the dead until the day of resurrection."

Twelve days later Widow Framstad died, and now he was holding her funeral. For once, the church was completely full. Almost every adult in Butangen had come into the world in her hands, and many a husband had thanked her for conveying his wife safely back to him.

Kai Schweigaard could not say he was satisfied with his sermon. He never was these days. He felt that they all took on the shape of the new church. It might reach heavenwards, but its spire was short and blunt. Inside, it was too well lit, with no dark nooks or crannies, as though insisting he could illuminate everything in the human soul. Only the sound of the harmonium was unpredictable. He longed for the old stave church, for the deeper mysteries it concealed, for its resonance with other forces, for the smell of tar and a bygone time. The stave church had been so dark that it proclaimed how little of life was ever fully comprehensible. But the new church tried to shine light on everything, making the inadequacy of his services all too clear, and his words seem farcical as they echoed from the walls.

But things could not be reversed. He had ordered the demolition of the stave church himself, and now here he stood, listening to his own voice as it rang out from the new pulpit. The sharp light made each face instantly recognisable, and Schweigaard scanned the pews, looking for him. For Jehans. But, as usual, he was nowhere to be seen, not in the church nor anywhere else. He was probably up in the mountains hunting again.

Outside, the sight of the lowered coffin was enough. The smell of the damp earth as it slammed against the lid. Her words came back.

Ye too shall see the sign. Ye, in partic'lar, Pastor.

She had died precisely twelve days later, making it harder for him to dismiss the rest of what she had said.

Schweigaard bid farewell to each of the many funeral attendees, including Oddny Spangrud, who, from today, would be called simply *the midwife.* Then he was left to ruminate. He felt anxious that time was running out, a feeling that was out of place in a cemetery, the ultimate viewing point of eternity.

She said it had nae floated far. That folk could see it wi'out seeing it.

He walked over to an unmarked grave just above the church. He searched with the tip of his shoe, leaned down and pushed aside the long grass to reveal a fist-sized lump of quartz, white and glittery-black. It was to this place, in 1880, that they had transferred the coffins that lay beneath the floor of the old stave church. They had all been grey and half-rotten, some had split open so that skulls and bones could be seen between the planks.

But one had been completely different from the rest. Made of solid ore pine. More square in shape, without any distinct head or foot, and when it was shifted, there was no rattle of bones. Which was why he had marked this place with a quartz stone.

His old sense of unease was rekindled. And with it his strong urge for action. The urge that had driven him once to reform the local funeral customs, the paupers' relief and the school in Butangen.

His walk of penance had surely gone on long enough.

This silent coffin. What if it did not contain a human being at all, but the weave of all weaves?

Could it be that it had never left the church? That someone had slyly – not unthinkable here in the village – put it in a coffin under the floor? So that it might still be within the church, and so continue to wield its power along with the other forces that lived and breathed in the stave church? Perhaps a piece of old, threadbare weave might, in some way, help him reach out to Jehans again?

Kai Schweigaard rushed back up and yelled out to Oldfrue Bressum that she must prepare a late supper for himself and Røhme, the churchwarden. No, not now, a *late* supper. At about seven. Yes, fish would be perfect! The trout I caught last night! He dashed up the stairs to the attic room and knocked.

"Y-yes?" answered the warden, and opened the door.

"Herr Røhme. Change into your work clothes. There's something we must – must carry out."

The other man nodded. Schweigaard explained what he had planned, but Røhme swallowed hard a few times and shook his head.

"Calm down," Schweigaard said. "It's a cemetery. Everyone's used to the earth being dug up. What they're less used to are coffins being dug up. And we'll keep that part a secret. As best we can."

The Chamber Charger

The reindeer descended the mountainside like the French cavalry, but prouder and faster and in tighter formation. Newly exposed antlers glistened with blood, like sabres fresh from battle, the difference being that these were not just the survivors or the chosen few, they were all here – calves, youngsters, females, adolescent and full-grown bulls, the entire entourage, springing, one and all, from the first matriarch in ancient times. Their antlers were broad and tall, with branches long and pointed enough to strike any wolverine or wolf in the heart, and, in the rutting season, each other. They had been rewarded with this weapon after millennia spent out on the bare mountains, where there was nothing to restrict them, where their antlers were free to grow wider and larger than those of the elk and deer, their relatives who did not dare roam in the open, but were content to hide deep in the forest.

There must have been four hundred of them. They had survived the frosts, the storms and the rain in the mountains, come through the winter, kicking at the snow till they found moss, the females heavy with calf, who in the springtime gave birth in that same moss and suckled their young before nudging them into feeding themselves. And thus they went on, fattening themselves up through the summer, scattered in little groups until the larger bulls separated from the herd and started to fight over the females, and then mate. Later the herd would gather again to meet its enemies and the winter, forming long columns that followed the mountain's contours like flowing water. Close up, you might spot some antlers waving high above the backs of the younger animals and females. These were the older, bigger bulls, the genetic material so aged the shaggy fur under their necks swept towards the ground, and on sight of an enemy they could crowd round and stab and stamp on anything that ventured too close.

But generally they just vanished. They came from nothing and returned to nothing.

For two days Jehans had followed them, though that was a word he would never use, it being impossible to *follow* a herd of reindeer. But for two whole days he had felt their proximity, he had lain in their tracks and felt the wind, looked down on the terrain from mountains with forbidding names: Jammerdalshøgda, Kleberkakken, Gråhøgda. Crossed wet marshlands where he hoped to find them, did as the reindeer would have done, thinking all the while: If *they* were hunting for me, I'd be dead within the hour.

It was unusual for so many animals to be herded together at this time of year. But all he could know for sure about reindeer was that he could never know anything for sure. He remembered every reindeer he had shot, yet the circumstances under which he had shot them were never identical.

He lay flat and followed them with his eyes.

The herd had settled far away on a stretch of marsh. A mirage rising from the damp and heat caused the animals to constantly change shape.

A small group separated from the main herd and came nearer, a procession of shaggy grey pelts, long legs and buckled antlers. Jehans stayed low on his haunches until the animals knelt and lay down. One or two antlers were visible through the heather, then they too disappeared.

But the matriarch stayed on her feet.

The ever-vigilant guard. The old matriarch who could no longer bear calves, who had seen all there was to see and survived all she had seen, and who now guarded and warned the young.

He lay on his belly, aware that as long as he could not see her, she could not see him. He spied a thicket further ahead and dragged himself towards it, his rifle rocking in the crooks of his arms. The barrel was newly cleaned and the lock oiled, but it had unquestionably seen better days.

A chamber charger, it was stamped with the maker's name, Kongsberg Våpenfabrikk, and the year 1848. Adolf had found it under strange circumstances some forty years ago. It had been a lean year when they had nothing to feed the cows but forest fodder, and he was out collecting moss and twigs when he came across it leaning upside down against a pine tree. Its stock was mildewy, there was an ant sitting on the trigger, and the metal was rust-speckled. The only explanation Adolf could think of was that some soldiers had stayed there in a bivouac, and that one of them had deserted or simply left without his gun.

Whoever it was must have kept his rifle well oiled, since the mechanism still opened smoothly. It was slim for a black-powder gun that used seventeen-millimetre bullets, but it had been designed for the kinds of tactics used in the Napoleonic Wars, was almost three cubits long with a bayonet, and was as much a spear as a firearm. It fired cylindrical bullets of around forty grams, and though every gun had its day, the chamber charger had last been described as "modern" back when most people were still using muzzle-loaders. Added to which, after being left outside for years, it was never reliable or accurate. No matter how steady Jehans' aim, the furthest he could shoot with accuracy was sixty metres. Later, he and Adolf had cut the bay-onet in two and forged it into new knives, leaving a long enough spike on the gun to sever a reindeer's cervical vertebrae. He had slain several animals this way, just as hunters had done in these mountains for thousands of years.

But at least it was a rifle, and for years Jehans had been proud to carry it. With it he was richer than anyone, and a grown-up man. He shot his first reindeer calf at the age of eleven, and Adolf carried it down to Halvfarelia while Jehans was allowed to carry the rifle, as he would do from that day forwards. Then, after eight years of their hunting together in the mountains, Adolf declared he had nothing more to teach Jehans and that the rifle was his.

The herd was still calm. Jehans inched his way forwards, on his belly, making swimming-like strokes with his elbows and knees.

A stream ran before him. It was impossible for him to straddle it, as the matriarch was sure to be standing and on the lookout. He shunted his body round until he lay parallel to the stream, rolled calmly into it, and felt his homespun trousers grow heavy with water. Holding his rifle and powder pouch high in the air, he edged his way to the other side as more water flowed under his collar. His clothes seemed to get pulled back into the stream as he flung himself out again, and his trousers got caught up again and again, as if every twig wanted to drag them off. He had lost weight during the hunt and they were loose; he grabbed the waistband and tugged it into place. His trousers were already quite threadbare and now he tore them, but he was unfazed, the terrain here was perfect, the stream had created a dip which hid him from sight, and he knew that when he crept up to the edge he would find a solid rest for his gun and a good view of the reindeer.

He took his rifle, got into position and peered carefully over the top.

They were still lying down.

But they know. They know I'm here, he said to himself. Somehow they know.

The matriarch was standing there with her back to him, rest-less, and a young buck was about to get up. He staggered to his feet and shook himself. Jehans felt the blood tingling in his fore-arms. The buck was majestic and shaggy, but his antlers had not yet come through. Nonetheless he sniffed at the rear end of a cow, bothering her so much that she stood up. He was unsure if the buck could be shot, for if he was in rut the meat would be rendered inedible and not satisfy his dues to Osvald Hekne that summer.

It was an entangled deal. For decades Adolf and Ingeborg had been exempt from offering their labour on the farm with the other Hekne tenants. Instead Adolf had delivered meat to the Heknes in lieu of rent, including one good reindeer in the summer, and any grouse and other game he managed to trap in the winter. The contract was still valid, but Jehans was being called upon increasingly often nowadays to offer his labour in the middle of the week, Osvald's repeated excuse being that he was getting off too lightly.

According to Adolf, things had been very different at Hekne in the old days. They'd always stood strong by what they called the *Hekne Way*. It was characterised by a deep sense of justice, but also by an inclination for great and reckless deeds, as when Eirik Hekne had ordered ordered the Sister Bells cast, at such huge cost that the farm almost went bankrupt. The fact was that Osvald's older brother, Emort, had been meant to take over the farm. Jehans barely remembered him. A gentle, rather timid voice, a hand on his shoulder, a shock of brown hair under a flat cap. But Emort lacked any aptitude for farming, or simply had no interest. So he had handed over his inheritance to Osvald and left for America with a younger brother.

Jehans craned his neck.

The bull must be ninety kilos, perhaps more. But was he in rut or not?

He lay on his back and pulled the lever back a semicircle, releasing a hollow cylinder from the lock. Hanging from a leather thong about his neck was a watertight box made of birch bark, a little masterpiece that had taken Ingeborg many evenings to make, and from which he fished out a paper bag of gunpowder and bit it open. He sprinkled the gunpowder down into the cylinder, and, after pressing a lead bullet into place, took one of the small, round percussion caps and wedged it onto a pin under the cylinder. The weapon was ready to fire.

He eased the gun forward, turned and rested it on a rock.

Several of the herd had got up now.

A two-year-old buck was well in range. Too young to be in rut, a fine animal. Separate from the others, quite far away, but not impossible. A kill large enough to cover Adolf's dues that summer. And if he was quick to reload, he might even manage to shoot another one, then they would have food for much of the winter at home in Halvfarelia too.

The young buck stood with his flank facing him. This had to be the one.

He breathed in, centred the sight needle and fired.

A metallic click sounded as the cock struck the percussion cap.

Then nothing.

The matriarch turned towards him and several more animals got up. He cocked the gun again, took aim, and again the gun let out a click. He tore open the cylinder, took out a new percussion cap and fixed it in place, but then he heard the clank of antlers knocking against antlers and realised that the herd was on the move. A female lingered behind, and he kept her in the sight. He was hoping against hope that she did not have a calf, but then he saw her retrieve a calf that had gone astray. Adolf had told him on their very first hunt, all those years ago, *We never shoot a mother with a calf that be suckling*, and he now took aim at the calf instead, but by then the pair were trotting off with their rear ends towards him, setting the main herd in motion. He would never know whether the shot would have hit its target, for he never released it.

He rose onto his knees and gazed after them until they were gone.

Meat enough to feed all of Butangen.

He pulled out the percussion cap and looked at it. It was impossible to know if it was working or not. All hope drained away, and he knew he would blame himself for the rest of the day for all the things he might have done differently.

What kinda dunce be ye, Jehans Hekne? After all the finger exercises ye have done so as to load up fast. Ye ought to have had a second percussion cap ready in your fist! Ye ought not to have wafted your gun so when ye changed it!

He said this out loud.

It had all gone so well until it went wrong, now everything was ruined and he started to doubt if he was really cut out for hunting, despite the many reindeer he had shot before. When a shot was bodged, there was nothing more desolate or unforgiving than the Gudbrandsdal mountains.

It was impossible to feel more alone. Those who died up here were rarely found, and when they were it was as a curled-up skeleton that bore witness to how they had slowly frozen, fully conscious of what was to come.

Jehans got up and tugged his wet trousers into place. Deep down he knew that hope would rise in him again with the dawn, or maybe even tonight if luck was on his side. A fleeting glimpse of something out on a marsh, antlers swaying behind a rock.

That was how it was and always would be. "The reindeer in our mountains be so wary," Adolf had once said, "that ye mun have eight chances to every beast ye hit." Adolf estimated that four of these chances were wasted on poor shots, lousy gunpowder or faulty percussion caps. The only thing they had any real control over was to get better at spotting the reindeer. Observing tiny variations of colour in the landscape, looking for dots out on the marshes and waiting to see if they disappeared again, dots as small as the full stops in Schweigaard's books. He could stand and stare at a mountainside for hours before a patch would seem to lift away, quite suddenly, then move and become a reindeer herd on the run, and all they left in their wake were footprints that resembled two half-moons. Thus with each step the reindeer marked the stamp of the moon on the Earth with their hooves, and like the moon they too were pale and unattainable.

Yet this hope . . .

He had felt so rich in that first year, walking here in the mountains alone with this rifle. He had been beholden to nobody, everyone was equal, there were no fine folk to step aside for, no hierarchy or smug uncle by the name of Osvald Hekne to sneer and pass judgement, and however much he froze in the mountains, it was never with the same resentment he felt in his ice-cold bed in Halvfarelia, and when he was hungry here, it was not an angry hunger. He would often take his six-section fly-fishing rod, which he had inherited from his father. A rod with no equal, just as his father had had no equal, the German architecture student who had overseen the demolition of the stave church in the village, and he fixed a worm hook to his line, and fished trout from rivers that nobody could own.

But now, when the front-heavy rifle had merely clicked, he felt overwhelmed by the weight of poverty.

He remembered the day that he had polished his boots and put on his best clothes, walked all the way down to the train, bought a ticket to just the next stop, but stayed on all the way to Lillehammer, and walked into Helleberg's sporting and hunting shop, where he saw a Krag-Jørgensen.

The Krag had been patented in 1894 by Colonel Krag and Gunsmith Jørgensen, and was manufactured by Kongsberg Våpenfabrikk just as the chamber charger had been, though a sea of craftsmanship and technical advancements separated the two. The Krag had attracted attention around the globe as the world's most advanced and precise rifle, and it was Norwegian.

The projectiles were amazingly long and just 6.5 millimetres in diameter, with a muzzle velocity of an unbelievable 770 metres per second, so there was nothing on this Earth that moved faster than the bullets shot from a Krag, and it was said to be able to kill from a distance of 600 metres. All the bother of preparing the chamber charger to fire was eliminated with a little water-proof cartridge, and not just that: the Krag could take up to *six* cartridges at once! He had studied the mechanism closely and thought he glimpsed the workings of its maker's mind, and the two parts of him – the engineer he had once wanted to be and the hunter he already was – began to daydream.

Everything came together in the Krag, all that Kai Schwei-gaard, Adolf and Ingeborg had taught him. The pastor through his long evenings of physics and mechanics, his foster parents through the days and weeks spent in the forest and mountains. Engineering and nature, brought together in an elegantly bal-anced masterpiece of wood and steel, where a single millimetre of movement on the trigger would start a technical miracle of physics and ballistics that lasted a hundredth of a second and killed the prey safely and quickly, which had been every hunter's wish since the Stone Age.

The price tag dangled on a thin bit of twine tied around the trigger. But when he turned it over and saw the price in pencil – fifty-four kroner and sixty øre – his heart sank. He had worn the same pair of shoes for six years now, because new ones were so costly. A second-hand Krag was rarely to be found, and was so sought after it was unlikely to be much cheaper.

He released the price tag so it swung like a pendulum, and turned away before it stopped. He felt a twinge of sadness and rancour, knowing that Kai Schweigaard would have given him all the money and education he might need to become a man worthy of a Krag. But he had turned his back on the pastor's offer long ago and become who he was: a young man who bought percussion caps for an old chamber charger.

He crept back to the stream and drank. He took off his clothes and wrung them out, but they were so caked with leaves and moss that they needed to be soaked. He pinned his braces down with rocks, and waded downstream, naked and shivering, to a pool where he could wash. He had a tiny scrap of soap with him, which, beside his gun, knife, axe, back frame and water bottle, was pretty much all he ever carried. Soap was as vital as gunpowder. Sweat had to be removed every day, as did the odour of shit, otherwise the reindeer would catch the smell of human being.

He sat in the evening sun and stared before him. He sometimes felt that the reindeer could smell his very thoughts. That was fine by him. In such moments, alone in the mountains, he often allowed himself to think of his mother and brother. His father had died in Germany, and, although he now owned his fishing rod, it was his mother who always felt closer, because she had lived at Hekne and it was easier for him to imagine what she might have been like. Easier to picture what his life might have been like, if she and his brother had survived the birth. They would almost certainly have lived at Hekne, so that Hekne itself would have been entirely different. But he was here now, and must live for all three, and he was never quite certain they were satisfied with him.

As he sat drying in the last of the sun, he spotted the herd silhouetted against the sky. They were heading in the direction of Jammerdalshøgda, and he was instantly reinvigorated. One glimpse was enough, like a mix of blood poisoning and love. His whole body wanted to follow the reindeer, but he wouldn't survive the night if he set off without food. He let his gaze wander from the reindeer and started to pick and eat handfuls of crow-berries. There was no wind, so his clothes were still damp as the evening closed in, but at least it wasn't cold. He set off in the direction of the herd, and by dusk he had reached Jammer-dalshøgda. He found some huge boulders, and in their shelter made himself a nest of moss, then covered himself with twigs, over which he laid his damp clothes, and fell asleep. His dreams were filled with glimpses of antlers against the sky, constant wandering and cairns on mountain tops, but the mountains had no names and all the reindeer were identical.

Later that night he noticed that the wind had changed, and long before dawn he sat with one hand on his rifle, gazing out into the distance. The landscape stepped out of the darkness and acquired contours and shapes, and soon the horizon emerged and the mountains grew discernible, though colourless. Then, with the first shafts of sunlight, the land took on shades of grey and green and brown, and the colours grew stronger, a signal that the sun would soon be fully risen.

There were no reindeer to be seen. It was futile to try to track them like this, for reindeer were always somewhere other than the place they went towards.

Thirst and the need to look for water interrupted his scouting for the herd. He spotted a stream a little way off and climbed carefully down to it. When he was close enough to hear the bur-bling of water, he stopped.

His attention was drawn to something moving in a willow thicket beyond the stream. He stood in complete silence, gaze fixed. When no new movement followed, he quietly lowered himself onto his haunches.

Was that an antler he had seen moving? Or just a branch?

The wind direction was perfect, blowing into his face, so that he could get up close to the animal, if it was an animal, without it catching his scent. He wanted to move forwards as fast as possible, but forced himself to take a drink first, he barely had two hundred metres to cover, but it might be an hour or two before the opportunity came to shoot an animal. It was vital he choose the best approach. He could walk straight ahead and go down into a dip, but the rocks there tended to clatter, so he decided to crawl in a wide semicircle, which took a little eternity.

He came over a ridge and looked to the thicket again.

Nothing. Had he spent an entire hour creeping up on something that would prove to be a dry twig?

He waited and waited and grew thirsty again. He had almost lost hope when he heard another rustling in the thicket.

Yes. There it was. A pair of antlers.

Enormous. With branch upon branch springing out from two mighty stems. Curling proudly towards the sky, like a pair of longbows drawn, declaring war on the sun. The reindeer itself was invisible in the thicket, but it had to be a mature bull on his own. And since the velvet was not yet shed from his antlers, he was not in rut. Such beasts wandered about occasionally. Lone emperors.

Or he could be what they called a *returbukk* – an old bull whose strength was fading, and who had lost his fights over the females. These old males used all their energy in vain to build a magnificent set of antlers while their bodies grew increasingly emaciated. And when they were finally cornered by their predators, who ripped at their Achilles tendons and sank their teeth into their necks, never to release them, their huge antlers were left as a memorial to the monarch of the mountains.

The antlers sank down into the thicket again and disappeared. Nothing moved. He was about sixty metres away.

The wind had picked up again, and as he loaded the rifle Jehans had to be careful not to let his gunpowder blow away.

The bull moved again. More rustling in the thicket. Jehans

could hear the sound of munching, chewing, belching. He took out a percussion cap, held it between his fingers, fingers that were now shaking. He opened the lock once more and leaned over it to prepare the rifle for firing.

A drop of sweat dripped from his forehead onto the percussion cap.

In the thicket he heard the rasping of branches against antlers and fur. The bull was getting up.

Jehans trembled and dropped the wet percussion cap into the heather. He wiped his fingers dry on his sleeve, took out a new cap and looked at it.

Come now, he thought to himself. D'nae fail me now.

The bull rose from the thicket while the rifle's lock was still open. He was big, more than big, certainly no *returbukk*, he was a giant, a colossus, and then he grew even larger, since he had been on his knees and now got to his feet, revealing himelf to be what Adolf would have called an *Imsdalsprest* – an Imsdalen priest. With a long, white beard hanging over his chest, shaggy grey flanks, antlers so curled that they were almost circular, and more points than all the knives kept on a big farm, he suddenly burst out of the thicket and turned towards Jehans. The two of them stared each other in the eye. Jehans snapped the lock shut, set the rifle against his cheek, found the reindeer in the sights, aimed for his heart and fired. He vanished in a cloud of black smoke. The echo rang in Jehans' ears. Through the haze he watched the bull thrashing and flaying and knew he had hit his target.

Yet something wasn't quite right.

The shot had sounded odd, louder than usual and too shrill, with a strange ringing sound over the familiar boom, similar in tone but more intense. Jehans feared that the chamber had burst, and that he had been so badly injured that he felt no pain. He looked down at his hands, but there was no blood on his fingers, he touched his temple and felt it was wet, but again his hand had no blood on it. Then a sudden gust of wind dispersed the dark, powdery cloud, and there before him, clear as day, he saw the huge reindeer bucking towards the sky. His front hooves thundered into the ground, so that he heard and felt it, then he took one step forward and turned and Jehans got up and faced the animal. They looked at each other until the bull came crashing down and lay still.

He walked slowly forwards, knowing he would remember this moment as long as he lived. There was no joy in killing an animal. But there was a kind of joy in being the one to hold an animal in your memory. Some of them for the rest of your life, and with each return to the site of the event, the animal would come back to life, and from there it would run immortal into the mountains.

He saw a movement in the corner of his eye. A man holding a rifle rose from the heather, and then two others appeared some way behind him.

All three men stepped forward, steady, decisive. The closest was young and bareheaded, with a mop of dark, curly hair and dressed in a grey tweed shooting jacket with breeches to match. A pair of shiny lace-up boots reached over his calves, and his rifle gleamed with blued steel and red-brown wood.

He locked eyes with Jehans, picking up speed as he walked towards him. His movements were lightning-fast, the man bristled with wits and resourcefulness.

He was angry, but said nothing.

Jehans was standing between him and the bull. In the right hand of each man was a rifle, each weapon still emitting the smell of gunpowder, as though it were gauging the other's strength and purpose, as though their barrels were clashing together, and the sound of steel weapon against steel weapon hung in the air.

The stranger was a little shorter than Jehans, with sour breath, brown eyes and heavy eyebrows. They stood staring at each other without being able to say anything. Soon the other two men had appeared on either side of Jehans. They were both much older and kitted out like mountain guides.

"It was our man's shot and his reindeer," one of them said. A pair of binoculars dangled from a cord around his neck.

"Can he na' speak for himself?" said Jehans, still staring the younger stranger straight in the eye and ignoring the others.

"You'd be ill-advised to quarrel with us. This man is a sportsman from England, and I'm his interpreter. You've been following us, haven't you? You watched us creeping up on the reindeer?"

"Who'd do such a thing?" Jehans said.

"Someone like you!" hissed the man. He spoke with a city dialect. "I know your type alright. Our client has travelled all the way from England to hunt reindeer. And you come along and try to shoot the reindeer we spotted first? As if you could hit anything with that old musket! Get on your way now! And I mean now!"

The man grabbed him by the arm, but Jehans wrenched himself free.

"Happen we take a look at the reindeer," Jehans said. "If your man hit it too, there mun be two bullet holes."

The two guides refused to listen, and when Jehans altered his grip on his rifle, they tried to grab it from him. The Englishman raised his hand and addressed them in his native tongue.

"Gentlemen, gentlemen!" he said. "I'm sure we can deal with this rather more amicably."

"But you can't let this ruffian get away with this," said one guide.

"He's trying to claim your kill," added the other.

It was at this point, to the astonishment of all three strangers, that Jehans piped up in almost perfect English.

"And I have every right to do so! And I would suggest," he

continued, turning to the bull, "that the reindeer itself may be the best judge of our shots."

Glances all round. Unsure of his English, Jehans half expected the strangers to laugh at him. But then he thought he felt Schweigaard's steady hand on his shoulder, and he was back in the parsonage with his English textbook open in front of him. *You're doing fine, Jehans. "Judge" is an excellent word.*

The Englishman smiled. As though he was relieved in some way, as though this was very different from what he had wanted, but was somehow to his liking.

"Leave us alone for a minute," he said. The two mountain guides turned and sat at a distance.

The stranger stretched out his hand and introduced himself, in a rather stiff Norwegian, as Victor Harrison.

Jehans shook his hand and offered him his name too.

"You can speak Norwegian?" Jehans asked.

"*Ja, litt.* I had a *Norske barnepike* – or, as we call it, a nanny."

The Englishman swapped his rifle to his other hand, and, with its barrel pointed down, pulled back the lever. Jehans briefly caught sight of a shiny brass cartridge in a fine mechanism of blued steel. Victor looked over at him for a moment, pressed the cartridge down into the magazine, pushed the bolt forward so that the weapon was locked with an empty chamber, and laid it down. It had an elegant recoil pad of a burnt-orange colour that stood out against the green and purple heather on which it now lay. Jehans placed his chamber charger alongside it, and the difference between the two weapons reflected the differences between the two men. They knelt down before the reindeer, and, searching with their fingers, found two gunshot wounds very close to each other. Sitting in silence, they felt the animal's warmth and let the sights and smells sink in and take hold. The reindeer's eye was still glassy-clear, and in the reflection Jehans could see that Victor's admiration for this beast was equal to his own.

Victor Harrison grabbed the bull's hooves and straightened its legs to grant it more dignity. The movement must have torn its shot-spattered heart and blood started to seep into the fur from the two gunshot wounds. It spread slowly until the two bloodstains flowed into one another, and it was no longer possible to know which blood trickled from which wound, only that the blood flowed from the same heart.

The Torn Cassock

The digging continued steadily. Behind them stood the new white church, too naive and juvenile to understand the gravity of what it witnessed. It was half past four in the morning, the air was raw and neither man had wanted breakfast.

Suddenly their excavations took on a different tone. The shovel hit something softer than rock but harder than earth.

"Impossible to see what 'tis," Røhme said, climbing back up the ladder to go and fetch the paraffin lamps.

Schweigaard leaned over the edge. It was pitch black below. The sunrise, he thought to himself, has never reached, and can never reach, down into the depths of a grave.

Schweigaard's heart sank as Røhme walked back, a figure now rendered unrecognisable in the morning mist. The pale-yellow flames seemed to hover above the grass and tombstones, and set Schweigaard thinking all sorts of bizarre thoughts, among them that if these lamps could light up the ground beneath them, they would have seen a swarm of dead people.

The day before, Schweigaard had been determined that the grave-opening should not turn into some ghoulish event, with dangling paraffin lamps glowing through the damp morning fog. But such works could never look seemly. There they stood, among the crooked gravestones in a churchyard in twilight, both appropriately bareheaded and dressed for the task, Herr Røhme in his best overalls and he in his cassock, the one with a shovel and the other with a Bible.

"Hand them to me," Schweigaard whispered, reaching out for the lamps. "I'll hold them while you dig."

More digging. Loose soil thrown into the air from the darkness below. Schweigaard sat on his haunches and watched.

Despite the odd fault, Kåre Røhme had proved the perfect choice for the job of churchwarden. Born in Hamar, the only son of a widow who ran the village hardware store, he had been twenty-one when Schweigaard had discovered him; now twenty-six, he had in those years proved a loyal and versatile helper. When he was freshly shaven and in his black suit, distributing the hymn books, he was also decidedly *handsome*, and church attendance among young unmarried women had risen steeply since his arrival.

But Herr Røhme had one debilitating defect, which meant he rarely held eye contact with anyone besides Schweigaard. He was a *stammerer*. An impediment so crippling he had found it easier as a child to pretend he was a mute, and failed to finish elementary school. His stammer made him painfully shy, and Schweigaard had thought when he met him: Røhme was born to be a churchwarden. At funerals, during Mass, at baptisms and weddings – in the numerous tasks assigned to a warden – it is *best* to hold your peace. This young man has manners, a good physique, can manage on a slim salary and would never stoop to gossip.

Never before had this last quality been more vital. Herr Røhme stopped digging and declared that the coffin was now, at last, freed from the earth. He climbed up and cast an expectant look at the pastor.

Kai Schweigaard tucked his robes around his knees, clamped his Bible firmly under his chin and stepped out onto the ladder. He was never quite sure what the smell of an open grave meant to him. It had a despair and helplessness in it, yet there was something fresh, somehow *obliging*, about the odour of the earth in its readiness to receive seeds and moisture, warmth and new life.

It was ice-cold there in the grave. He went down on his knees, turned up the wick on the lamp, and ran his fingers over a smooth dark surface.

Yes. This was it. The casket they had lowered in the summer of 1880. Rather smaller than he remembered. Nonetheless, he thought, caskets that lie side by side with coffins tend to be coffins too.

He brushed the earth away and saw a carved H emerge beneath his fingers. An H that had haunted him throughout his life. An H for Hekne.

"Have we f-f-found it?" Røhme whispered. Schweigaard turned and nodded. Far above him, at the top of the shaft's steep walls, the sky seemed amazingly wide and bright. This, he thought, is the view of the dead as they lie here, before the earth is scattered upon them.

Two swallows sailed past. He turned, put the Bible on the coffin and whispered, "I must take you up into the daylight. For a little while. Forgive me. But you must meet the day once more."

Røhme came down again and they slipped two hemp ropes under the coffin. As they climbed back up, Schweigaard was so on edge he tore his cassock on a nail in the ladder.

"Quickly," he said. "Hurry, before someone comes!"

They grabbed the ropes. Røhme stood hunched over, ready to lift, but hesitated. He was staring in the direction of the cart road. A man was walking there. He stopped. Approached the iron gate and stood gawping at them.

The problem in Butangen was that folk were never in a hurry!

Schweigaard got up and gathered the folds of his cassock. And now, in the stronger morning light, he could see that it was even muddier and more torn than he had feared.

At last the man continued down to Lake Løsnes.

They gripped the ropes. The coffin swayed, knocking from side to side as it came to the surface. Earth cascaded into the depths. They still had no real idea what might be about to emerge from the darkness. Then the coffin appeared over the edge, and gained form and colour.

The coffin was very mouldy after twenty-three years in the earth. Now it stood on the wooden floor in the middle of the sacristy. A dark, rectangular block that emitted a chill and the smell of the earth.

Once again, just as in 1880, they had heard no rattling in the coffin. Nonetheless, Schweigaard still thought it more likely he would find a skeleton than the Hekne Weave. Skulls and bones. Brownish dried skin, mouths without lips. If he found *two* skulls, then he *would* know it was them. Not that this would result in anything other than an even worse night's sleep.

He cleaned the swollen wood with a shoe brush, looking for the join between the lid and the casket itself. Finally, when he rubbed the edge with a rag, a row of wooden nails came into view. He seized the mallet Røhme had laid out and prepared to make the first blow, but stopped.

He was momentarily gripped by images of the ancient Norse faith, in which the coffin was a means of transport, equipped with everything its owner needed for their journey through the kingdom of the dead. And he wondered what course he might obstruct were he to tear the coffin open now and cast daylight down upon a secret required by the dead.

Stop it now! he said to himself. Get a hold of yourself, Kai Schweigaard!

He drew the paraffin lamp closer and brought the hammer down. The lid refused to budge. He grasped the coffin and shook it. Nothing had loosened inside.

More blows. Echoes bouncing from the sacristy walls. He walked around it and hit it harder still, and then – then a different sound rang out. A gap came into view. Putting his knee against the lid, he tugged at it, tearing his cassock even more. Dry, crumbly soil spilled out about him and shrieking sounds were heard as the timbers gave way. He was kneeling as though in prayer. Mumbled some words and pushed the lid aside.

Even after so many years, he was prepared for a stench, a smell with the power to shock him like hartshorn. Or for something large and hazy and grey to rise from the coffin. Something solid or otherwise.

Instead, there was nothing but peace down in the coffin. A peaceful calm and the smell of ancient times.

And between its greying, swollen timber walls lay two pillows. Side by side.

As though the girls had just got up that morning and stepped out into the world, each leaving an impression of their head on one of the pillows.

And Schweigaard asked himself: If they weren't buried under the church floor, as folklore says, where are they? He lifted the paraffin lamp to see better. Each pillow was wedged between thin wooden bars, like a matchstick house, that prevented it from touching the walls or bottom or lid of the coffin, thus protecting it from water or other damage.

Each pillow was covered in a woven fabric in a large chequered pattern. He ran his fingers over both, and was surprised at how rough one of them was, how scratchy. Made of raw yarn in soft browns and greys and patches of sea-green, its pattern reminded him of his old Scottish travel blanket. The other cover was in a softer yarn, better suited to a pillow. The pattern was similar again, but the checks were red and dark green, similar to the skirts he had seen worn by women in Norddalen.

A stronger light was now streaming in through the sacristy windows, and he could see the details better. The girls must have lived longer than legend had it. Such wear and tear could only come from many years of use. There was a shiny dip in each pillow where their heads had rested. But each imprint was quite distinct. The coarsely woven pillow seemed to bear heavier traces of moisture from a cheek, or even tears. Evidence he recognised from his own pillow.

Kai Schweigaard ran his fingertips over its surface again. It was hard to think that one of the sisters would have laid her cheek on anything so rough and unyielding. In particular, one of *these* girls? When they were among the valley's best weavers, wouldn't they have been more meticulous when making something for themselves?

Carefully he eased the pillow out. A sharp smell reached his nostrils, subtle and faint. He carried it over to a table by the window to view it in full daylight, avoiding any sudden or rough movements, in case it had been woven as Widow Framstad had described, in a fabric designed to disintegrate after a certain time. He lifted it up slowly to see the reverse side.

Yes.

Look at that.

The back showed a completely different world. As dazzling as any queen's gown. Glowing patterns on a gorgeous, deep-red background. A circle with animal motifs, a myriad of intricate figures in bright yellow ochre, moss green and burnt orange. Birds and reindeer, cows and oxen. In shades more beautiful than anything he'd ever seen before, either here in the valley or in Kristiania's high streets.

He lifted the other pillow and turned it over. It too had intricate figures that spun round in a circle, reminding him of the mythological creatures on the stave church portal. They too were woven in the same fabulous, glowing colours, but set against a lighter, almost silvery background.

As he lifted the pillow, there was a clattering sound. He stopped in his tracks. An object that must have lain between the pillows fell to the bottom of the coffin. And as he reached out to grasp it, blood started to run from his fingertips.

There at the bottom of the coffin was a knife. Or a cutting tool of some kind. Without a shaft and curved in shape. Black and crudely forged, but with an edge shiny and sharp enough to greet an incautious priest.

He wiped the blood on his cassock and in that moment he felt that the ancient beliefs and new beliefs met and greeted each other, but he instantly let the thought slip away, entranced as he was by the images on the two pillows.

Mountains and lakes, animals and birds. Some of these creatures seemed to leap from one pillow to the other, but since they ran in circles, it was impossible to tell which was the first picture and which the second.

Might this have some meaning? Or was it just meant to be decorative?

The sisters had been two but simultaneously *one*. If any stories were being told through these pillows, it was impossible for him to know where they began and ended.

Other than that they were two narratives divided by a knife.

Fifty-Four Kroner and Sixty Øre

"Well. Fair's fair. There are *two* bullet holes here," Victor Harrison said. They spoke in English now, as Jehans was clearly the more proficient linguist of the two.

They had sat in silence for a long time. Kneeling side by side before the reindeer. Letting their hands turn blood-red as they stroked its pelt around the gunshot wounds. The bullet from the Englishman's small-bore gun had left a neat hole, while the huge bullet from the chamber charger had dragged fur and membranes with it, leaving a far coarser wound. Behind them in the heather lay their rifles, their barrels now cold.

Steam and blood had continued to issue from the half-open mouth, but this had now stopped and the reindeer's eyes were glazing over. Jehans watched as the stranger pushed its lower jaw into place so its tongue wasn't left hanging out, and brushed off some blood-soaked lichen. Both men found it difficult to end the moment.

"Where are you from, Mr Harrison?" Jehans asked. "He said you were an Englishman. From London?"

Victor paused. "No, I come from the north of England. Northumberland. Close to the Scottish border. Feel more Scottish than English, actually. But, yes, I'm an Englishman, I suppose."

"So what is the custom there?"

Victor seemed confused by the question.

"The kill. Who does it belong to? To the huntsman who sees the prey first or the one who fires first?"

"To the one who fires first," Victor said. "If his shot hits and kills the target."

"And we can see that this one did," Jehans said, pointing to the smaller gunshot wound. Then he pointed at the other man's

59

rifle, and said, "Your gun uses modern gunpowder? Yes? Less smoke?"

"Yes, it's smokeless. A Rigby, as you can probably see. The bullets leave the muzzle at more than 2,400 feet per second. Or that's what the salesman said."

"There's black gunpowder in mine."

"So I saw. Quite a cloud of gun smoke!"

"So this is *your* reindeer," Jehans said, getting up. "My gun is slower, and it was your bullet that reached it first and your bullet that killed it."

A look of confusion crossed the Englishman's face, which turned quickly into a look of suspicion as he wondered if Jehans was out to trick him in some way.

"Well, there can't even have been a half-second's difference," he said.

"No, probably less."

Jehans turned away, grabbed his chamber charger and hooked it over his shoulder. His hands felt dry and crusty with congealed blood. Victor stood watching him, and seemed reluctant to say goodbye.

"Stop a moment," he said. "Where I come from we talk a lot about fair play and good sportsmanship – *god sportslighet*. When you said that the reindeer was mine because my bullet hit it first – well, that has to be the best example of good sportsmanship I've ever seen. You're a true gentleman – *en virkelig edel mann*. You didn't even point out the advantage – the unfair help – that my gun gave me. An advantage that can be bought."

Jehans stroked the barrel of the chamber charger. "*Takk.* Thank you," he said. "But it is the most sensible solution. When one thinks about it."

"Yes, *if* one thinks about it," Victor said. "But not everybody does."

"One has much time to think when one walks here alone."

The wind had dropped now and the mountains were peaceful and green. The guides started towards them, but Victor motioned for them to wait. He took the reindeer by its antlers, rocked them gently and said: "This is the first reindeer I have shot. If I did indeed shoot it."

"You shot it," Jehans said.

"You must have shot a great many?"

"Sixteen with this one. This is the biggest."

"You hunt for food?"

"Is there anything else to hunt for?"

"To sell, perhaps?"

"I must kill one large reindeer every year. As a kind of rent. If I shoot more, I sell the meat."

Victor Harrison cleared his throat. "I've a suggestion – *et forslag*. It's only the antlers – the horns – that interest me. And the reindeer's head. I want to have it stuffed. How about I take the whole animal and pay you – *betaler* – for the meat? We've a packhorse on its way, and it can carry it down the valley. And these fellows," he said, indicating the two men behind him, "will do the work of gutting and skinning it."

But Jehans' mind was suddenly wandering. Not only was he finding Victor's English difficult to follow, but there was something oddly familiar about this stranger. Had he appeared in the newspapers? Jehans felt sure he had seen a photograph of him, although it was very unlikely, since the man was barely any older than him, and it was a long time since he had read Schweigaard's newspapers.

"Let me repeat," said the Englishman. "What sort of price were you hoping for? *Din pris?*"

"For the meat?" Jehans said, coming to again.

"Yes."

"Fifty-four kroner and sixty øre."

*

It was dark when he came down from the mountains and stopped for a moment to look up at the night sky. Each star was a clear, pure-white point against a blue-black infinity, and it was thanks to them that he had navigated his way down to the village. Jehans knew that some folk thought they could predict a person's future by the position of the stars in the heavens, but he had been brought up to read the signs of the forest and the weather and farm animals. If the stars bore any message for him, he had a feeling it would be short and simple: Where 'er ye be in the world, ye shall always turn back here, to Butangen.

He stood for a moment and looked out over the landscape, framed by the valley sides. By daylight the village was visible from here, now he could barely make out Lake Løsnes far below. There were no buildings to be seen, just little yellow flecks in the dark, trembling lights in the windows, candles and paraffin lamps in one or another farmhouse. Butangen was as dark, he thought, as it had been when his mother was alive and through the many centuries of his forefathers, so ancient they were no longer remembered by name. But then again. He would never have thought of the dark as dark had it not been possible to desire the light.

He found the path through the birch forest and followed it to Halvfarelia. He walked past the sheep byre and leaned his rifle against the timber shack in which he lived. Then he slipped quietly into the log cabin, and heard Adolf clearing his throat in the bedroom, as he always did in pretence of just having woken up, although Jehans knew that the old man always lay awake when he was late getting back from a hunting trip.

"Did ye get a reindeer?" whispered Adolf.

"In a way," Jehans said.

He was up at first light. The air was damp and a morning mist lay over the potato field and vegetable patch. Carefully tended, as always among the poorest folk, because everything they would and could live on grew there.

Sunbeam must have heard him close the shack door behind him, since she bellowed loudly in the yard as he left. Walking past the parsonage, he felt he ought to go up and see the man who had meant as much to him for the first fifteen years of his life as Adolf and Ingeborg. But whenever he met Schweigaard he turned back into an angry boy.

He decided instead to borrow the priest-boat. Schweigaard had said he could borrow it whenever he needed, but he never had. Thus the pastor would see that he had accepted something from him for once, and that would have to be a sufficient greeting this time.

Midway across Lake Løsnes he slowed. Slipped quietly through the water as droplets fell from the oars. He looked up the slope, past the new church and towards Hekne with its green fields and handsome black log houses with white-painted windowsills.

The water was utterly still. A crane flew above him in the direction of the Løsnes Marshes.

He rowed to the southern end of the lake. Drew the boat alongside the large spruce trees that grew by the shore. The raft should be under a tree where the branches hung over the water's edge. No. It wasn't there. The trees had grown since he was here last.

Just as he had grown.

He found it a little further down. Darkened, waterlogged logs lashed together with hemp rope. It lay heavy in the water and was covered with moss, algae and pine cones.

He had built the raft when he was twelve years old, together with his friend Fløtersønnen. Out on the lake night after night, they let everyone think they were out with their lamps and leisters to catch trout, when they were really searching for a church bell that could ring from twelve metres under. They had worked systematically, scanning the bottom of the lake with a grapnel hook and pulling up anything it got caught on. In the centre of the raft was a wooden frame over a large hole, and their plan was to borrow the hoist from a stump-puller and drag up the bell. Jehans fantasised about it being hung in the bell tower. Unlike the other children who feared the tower, and terrified each other with stories of being locked in it all winter with the dead bodies, he would not be scared, and the bell would ring so loud that even his mother would be able to hear it from the grave.

But the only things that ever got stuck in the grapnel were roots and rotten twigs and grasses, and two summers later they realised that the legend was stronger than them.

Fløtersønnen – the Logger's Son – had got his nickname on account of his father drowning in a logging accident on the River Laugen in the spring when he was born. Raised by the Paupers' Association, he was one of the gifted children to whom Schweigaard had given extra tuition. Under Schweigaard, Sunday School consisted of a very swift grace before Bressum set to fattening the scrawniest children with fried liver or pork knuckles. Jehans had spent all his weekends at the parsonage, but the others had never eaten from porcelain before. Fløtersønnen was so anxious that Schweigaard had to give him a wooden dish before he would eat. They then received a reasonably liberal education in Norwegian, German, English and history, with excursions into letter-writing, world news, medicine and the sciences. Jehans and Fløtersønnen were both fascinated by electricity, and Schweigaard took them to a lecture and demonstration in Vålebrua, where they saw an electric light bulb and a motor that went round. On their way back home in the horse-drawn carriage, the two boys chatted away about all the possibilities, practically ignoring Schweigaard, noticing only that he occasionally smiled to himself. Not until their return did he reveal that he had bought them a model electric motor that could be driven by an accumulator with zinc and copper plates dipped in acid. The two boys devoured Dietrichson's *Physics Textbook* and Corneliussen's *Inventions*, which described everything from torpedoes to hydraulic pumps. They felt invincible and wanted to be engineers.

The two of them had had equal prospects. Fløtersønnen went on to a secondary school and was then accepted on a course with Norges Statsbaner; he was now the telegraph operator at the recently opened Vålebrua train station. Meanwhile, Schweigaard had told Jehans that he was willing to pay, out of his own pocket, for him to go to a college in Kristiania.

This had somehow come to Osvald Hekne's attention. One week after his confirmation, Jehans was called to Hekne. He had not been there since he was small. A maid pointed the way up the stairs, he knocked on the door of the office where he assumed Osvald must be, and waited an age before a voice shouted for him to enter. There he sat. A big and broad-shouldered man, sitting in a high-backed chair, surrounded by maps of his properties and a photograph of himself with his wife and six children. Osvald pointed up at the birch rod that hung on the wall. He had, he said, raised six children with it, while Jehans had been spared it, and with that any proper upbringing. But more regrettably, he had been spared an important truth about Pastor Schweigaard.

"It were the pastor that fixed things so the Sister Bells disappeared and yer father died. He lied to them, this pastor o' yorn, and your father overturned the bells into Lake Løsnes so as to hide them. Happen the pastor has na' told thee? How he was blind wi' love for yer mother? And betrayed them both?"

Jehans felt his knees go weak.

"Nay. I thought not. Ye have let yerseln be duped by the very man who sent yer father to his death. All this engineering non-sense, Jehans, 'tis just sommat the pastor says so as to soothe his own bad conscience. To make up for the harm he caused. 'Tis *he* wants the bell up from the lake, while ye reckon 'tis thee. That raft down there, Jehans, 'tis the raft of a fool."

The newly confirmed Jehans ran home to Halvfarelia filled with confusion. He sat on his bed, stroked the electromagnetic coil the pastor had given him and watched the light skitter on the beautiful, orange-red wires. Sprinkled some iron filings onto some paper and guided a horseshoe-magnet under it, as Schweigaard had done.

Observed the fan shape of these invisible forces.

Schweigaard came to ask him why he had been absent from class, which was when everything exploded. There in that poverty-stricken farmyard, grazed bare by the only cow they owned, standing next to the ramshackle woodshed, with Adolf and Ingeborg sitting inside with their heads hanging in shame, he let all the resentment and anger that he had unknowingly stored up inside him gush out of him like water from behind a dam as he harangued the pastor for hiding the truth.

"Ye only helped me because ye regret what ye did," Jehans screamed.

"Many a good deed has been born of a bad conscience," Schweigaard ventured, instantly realising that such talk might be acceptable from the pulpit, but not in a humble cottar's home, in the face of the man most affected by his actions.

"Ye lied to my mother about the bells. 'Tis your fault the bells left the village. 'Tis your fault my father froze and died with lung sickness. I have nowt more to learn from thee!"

"Jehans," the pastor said, "don't throw everything away. Your talent. Your abilities. Take what I'm offering now. I shan't ever ask any thanks from you. Forget me afterwards, but venture forth into the wider world."

"Venture forth! Pah!"

"Yes, you need to venture forth if you're to learn anything! The school isn't here! There's nothing here in Butangen!"

"Look at yerseln!" Jehans said. "Ye be here!"

"I meant to tell you everything, Jehans. Really, I did. When you were old enough. But I never found the right time. It's hard to find the right time to say these things. And it wasn't all beneficial for you to hear."

"And that were for ye to decide?" Jehans yelled.

The pastor turned to go, but stopped. "Before she died, your mother asked me to help you. I have lived my whole life trying to fulfil that wish. I'll never be ashamed of that. Come to me any time, Jehans. Any time at all."

He left, and Jehans never went back to the parsonage. Never went back to collect his things. He preferred to depend upon a chamber charger and a scythe.

But today, out in the priest-boat, with the thick envelope of money in his inside pocket, Jehans noticed a change in himself. Something had affected him the previous day. Fair was fair. He would never have been able to deal with a wealthy foreigner with such confidence had it not been for Kai Schweigaard. Or dare to demand many times over the normal price for such a reindeer. And then *accept* the money because he felt he deserved it.

Jehans rowed to where he thought the church bell lay, and let the boat rock to and fro. He had come to this place so often as a child, trying to feel something, to get a sign. The place had always been as silent as his mother's grave.

But today Jehans felt something. Anger towards Osvald. The man who governed Hekne. Who had clearly taken such pleasure in sowing discord between himself and the pastor. Anger at Osvald's way of measuring greatness and success in the numbers of workers or dairy cows he owned. In the height of a rye field or the cutting tone of a voice. The level of pressure he exerted on the cottars to work harder and for longer hours.

But should he really spend all this money? There were so many things they needed, back in Halvfarelia. Saw blades and rope and knitting wool and nails. Ingeborg's old potato-kettle was so leaky that it left moisture on the hotplate. But what was the point of patching up life as it was? He needed to make his way up.

The boat started to sway. As though a hand was reaching up from the depths and rocking the keel. He lifted the oars and looked around. It seemed a kindly embrace. Like lying in a lap, being rocked. No sound accompanied it, just a tremor that rose from the bottom of the lake and up through the water and into the boat, through the oars and his body, gradually growing in force, shaking so that anything loose or corrupt fell away, and anything useful and right would remain. And he sensed that his ancestors' silver lay twelve metres deep and wanted to come up to him, and with it, the ancient Hekne ways. All the things Eirik Hekne had known when he threw his silver into the cauldron.

And this much was clear. Great deeds were never accomplished by folk who asked others for advice.

He rowed into land and set off for Lillehammer.

Closest to Our Dreams

The priest-boat was gone.

Kai Schweigaard walked across the garden, over to the bench with a full view, and noticed that his boat was moored on the other side. Nobody in Butangen ever borrowed a boat without asking, since all the villagers would witness them out on the water.

Conclusion?

It could only be Jehans.

Schweigaard felt joy. A deep, tingling joy. Some kind of acceptance, at last. After all these years. A rather meagre form of greeting, perhaps, but a greeting nonetheless, and a public statement too, since the entire village would see that Jehans was using his boat.

He went back into the parsonage, through the living room, crept up the stairs into his office, and locked the door behind him. He felt more vigorous than he had in years.

He had been studying the pillows since the previous morning. Walking around them as the dawn light and midday sun and the afternoon gloom and evening darkness invoked their various shifts in colour and texture.

They had been mistresses of their craft. In inspiration and execution. That much he knew from all the weaves he had studied. And all the sisters had at their disposal were sheep's wool, foraged plants and tools made of bone and wood. They had worked day after day to ensure the yarn held these glowing colours. The wool had to be sorted and carded, spun, and dyed in a decoction of plants and bark. Then there was day after day of intricate craftsmanship.

It was impossible to know whether the animal figures should be viewed in a certain order, running as they did in unbroken circles. If this had any meaning, it evaded him like animals hiding in the forest. Perhaps the circles were the sun and moon. Was the action meant to run from the red pillow to the silvery one, as though the animals leaped between the sun and the moon? Or were dreams meant to flow between those who slept upon the pillows?

He studied the motifs one by one. A reindeer crashing to the ground. An ox with only one horn, legs astride, strangely angular in shape. Two calves sniffing at a dead reindeer. A pale-yellow bird in flight. Two reindeer bulls with golden eyes, stepping down into a lake. The same two beasts resurfacing, metamorphosed into a bird and an ox, with the same luminous golden eyes. A cow with two huge calves. A bird lifting an ox. The ox was apparently dead, for its head and legs hung limp as the bird with outstretched wings carried it over the surface of the lake they had previously stepped down into and up from.

Mere ornament or not, it was unlike anything he had seen before. Most of the weaves on the farms round here were limited to the borders of table linen, the only pictorial images being pious depictions of the Christian message. The three kings, the wise and foolish virgins, exotic tales from the Bible lands. But what he was looking at here sprang from a different tradition entirely. These weaves were the product of an altogether different imagination.

What was that? Oh heck! There she was. On her way up the stairs. As always she tugged on the door handle without knocking, and when she found it locked piped out that his porridge was hot *now*.

"Alright!" he shouted.

She began muttering outside the door.

"Yes, yes!" he answered.

More muttering.

Yes! I'll be there soon! My dear Bressum. It's been porridgetime at twelve o'clock for twenty years! I'll be right down when I've finished writing these letters!

His thoughts did not stop. Could these pillows lead him to the Hekne Weave? He looked out of the window. The priestboat was still on the other side. There really weren't *that* many generations between the Hekne sisters and Jehans and his dead brother.

Schweigaard suddenly had an idea. There *was* someone who could help him. Right now. Today. But only as long as the priest-boat was moored on the other side of the lake.

Soon he was standing in Halvfarelia.

Years had passed since he was here last. But as he entered the cottar's yard, it all came back to him. The gut-wrenching day when Jehans had poured his anger out on him. Schweigaard shook off the memories, knocked on the door and said he needed help with something. Adolf and Ingeborg thought he was asking where Jehans was and told him they had no idea; he had returned late from hunting and had left again early that morning.

"No, I'm here about something else," he said, nodding towards the sheep byre that had once concealed a stave church portal.

Herr Pastor could, of course, come in, though they didn't have much to offer him.

"I . . . I'm trying to get to know some of the old stories from hereabouts. It's become something of a hobby of mine. I've found some – old sketches."

Kai Schweigaard took out a notebook in which he had made some sketches of the various animals on the pillows. Saw that the ox's shape was rather imprecise, and with a pencil drew it again, but before he was done, Adolf said:

"Ah! That be Lynstuten!"

"Lynstuten?"

"Aye. The ancient Hekne mark."

"A family crest? Lightning Horn, you say? Because of its horn?"

"Indeed," Adolf said.

There was a silence. Ingeborg gave him a little nudge. "Go on, tell the pastor!"

Adolf said that he didn't know how old the crest was, but that the Heknes had had it carved on their gateposts long ago. And that they also branded their livestock and tools with it.

"Aye, but Herr Pastor mun be wondering who Lynstuten were," Ingeborg said.

"Oh, 'tis a tale from of old. Lynstuten were a young ox that were pushed out by his herd. So he could na' mate. But, unlike the other oxen, Lynstuten were not afraid o' lightning. One day, a thunderstorm came, and the others hid on the edges o' the forest. But this ox went into the middle of a field. The rain were clashin' down 'n' the thunder were raging. And he were struck by lightning and it glittered 'n' glished all around him, as the heavens blasted and clashed above him. And a heifer, she came and gave herseln to him, and later she gave birth to a pair o' fine calves. And from these the Heknes bred many a cow. 'Twere said they had the lightning in them. Our own Sunbeam belongs to this line. Lynstuten lived some months more, but died afore the calves came. So that be the story o' the Hekne mark. An ox wi' a lightning-shaped horn, like the one ye have drawn right there."

There was another silence. It was as if the very silence in the room took solid form and asked if they would talk about Jehans.

All three cleared their throats.

"And what about these birds?" Schweigaard said, turning back to his notebook. They shook their heads and studied his drawings. If only Gerhard Schönauer had made this sketch, Schweigaard thought with a hint of his old jealousy, they might have recognised them.

"But," said Ingeborg, "there were hundreds o' stories about birds. Folk saw them as signs. Strong signs. The owl most of all. And the raven, or *hræfn* as was. For it circles over injured animals and half-dead folk up in the mountains. I recall my grandmother talked o' the Golden Raven. A lad found a tiny little grimy-yellow bird. He thought at first it were a hawk fallen from its nest, and carried it home. The bird recovered and grew, and then they saw it were a raven of a rare, bright colour. Doubtless nebbed out o' the nest for being so strange. One day the Golden Raven flapped away, never to be seen again. The lad grew up and lived to a great age, and when they buried him a Golden Raven came and sat on the stave church roof. But naebody knows if it were the same raven or not."

On his way back down to the parsonage Kai Schweigaard almost resigned himself to the idea that the creatures on the pillows must have leaped out of ancient Butangen legends. Neither Adolf nor Ingeborg had known any specific stories about the chequered fabrics. Ingeborg had said they were quite commonplace, the womenfolk wove in checks because it was the pattern that best disguised any unevenness in the dye. And added with a smile that when the world began again after Skråpånatta, and was peopled by folk without history, it would not be long before they began to weave in checks again.

Hours passed. The priest-boat was still on the other side of the lake.

He told Røhme to refill the grave and move the coffin from the sacristy up to his study. *Yes, as discreetly as possible, Herr Røhme.* He could see from the warden's expression that he had no wish to know more about its contents.

Sitting at supper that evening, he pondered again where the Hekne sisters might actually be buried. He would probably never find out, unless he found Sigvard Krafft's old *kirkebok*. He barely noticed how salty the pork knuckles were and that Old-frue Bressum had served him rhubarb instead of leeks. When his coffee finally arrived, he put the saucer on top of his cup to avoid spillage and hurried up the stairs, where he locked himself in his study.

They were still there. Colours and riddles and all. It was as though the mystery of the patterns played and laughed at his logic.

If these figures led him to the Hekne Weave itself, he would have no chance. And if he found it, he would still have no chance, for if it was woven in the same fashion, he wouldn't understand a thing.

Kai Schweigaard glanced down at his fingertips. He had forgotten how badly he had cut himself. There wasn't a single mark left on his skin now. Finger cuts usually hurt for two to three days, but his skin was completely healed. Not a single mark.

He went over to the mouldy coffin and took out the knife. Shaped much like a Stone Age tool. Curved, broad, no tang to which to attach a handle, so he had to grab it round the middle. He felt the rough iron against his fingers, blackened with grave-rust, a narrow, razor-sharp edge being the only part that glinted.

Never had he felt closer to the Hekne sisters than now, when he held a tool they must have used every day. He had often pictured them, but now he saw them as two individuals. He had a sense of two lives, two stories that wanted to go their separate ways but could not be parted. A few years ago, after much letter-writing, he had obtained a small American book on the life story of two conjoined brothers from the Kingdom of Siam. Their chests were connected by a ligament that resembled a short tube but was flexible enough for them to turn, and without any pain. They toured the world with various freak shows and amassed a large fortune from their ticket sales. On the posters for their performances they were introduced as "The Siamese Twins", a term that was soon adopted across the English-speaking world for all conjoined children.

But the thing that stayed with Schweigaard most from his reading was that the twin brothers had the same capacity for love as anyone else. They fell in love several times and eventually married two sisters and fathered many children before dying at the age of sixty-three.

He swapped the pillows over and asked himself which had belonged to Halfrid and which to Gunhild.

What had their life been like? How did it feel to walk like that? To be only partly able to turn away? To be a drag on the other's will all the time? Never to be alone, not even for a second? To know that their twin could see into their thoughts, doubts, irritations – irritations that were instantly mirrored because they saw both each other and themselves?

He shrugged at the labyrinthine patterns and turned the pillows over so that the chequered sides faced upwards. And as he looked at the shiny, worn dips in each pillow, where the girls had laid their heads, he wondered if an even greater riddle might be hidden in this utterly mundane detail.

Why had one of the girls laid her cheek against such a coarse and scratchy fabric?

Here was a trail he could follow. A trail to which he could relate. For if there was one thing Kai Schweigaard understood, it was that a pillow is the object that is closest to a lonely being's dreams.

The Hekne Krag

The shop assistant in Helleberg's was very attentive, but cast a critical glance at his pitch-seamed boots, yellowing linen shirt, and misshapen, homespun trousers. He, by contrast, was sporting a black waistcoat and freshly ironed white shirt, had pencils

75

stuck in a garter strap around his arm, and liked to balance on his toes with his hands behind his back.

There were three rifles on display in the glass cabinet. Two long Krags and one cavalry carbine, and – Jehans let out a sigh – the prices had not changed. The long Krags still cost fifty-four kroner and sixty øre. The carbine still cost forty-eight. They had lost none of their allure. The Krag was still an exquisite jewel of brown beechwood and blued steel from the Kongsberg Våpenfabrikk. A technical marvel of four and a half kilos, perfectly balanced throughout its entire length of one metre and twenty-four centimetres.

"That would indeed be something!" said the assistant, making no move to unlock the cabinet.

Jehans said he was there to buy.

The Krag. Aye. Today.

The assistant measured him up again. Said very well and took out the cavalry carbine.

"There's no great difference between them," he said, "if you want to save money. The carbine is lighter and more convenient for hunting. It kills just as efficiently."

"Happen so. But I reckon the stock in't so fine. Nor the sight."

"Yes. The Krag sight has a range of two thousand metres. But that's superfluous till we start aiming at the Swedes."

"So what be the carbine's range?" Jehans said. "In truth?"

"I've heard of huntsmen bringing game down at nearly four hundred metres. But that's from lying down. With the barrel resting on a rucksack. And a target that's stock-still. With a good shot, and no wind, the rest is luck. The bullets kill alright at that distance, but the animal is a tiny speck in the viewer! Though I do know that plenty of reindeer have been taken down at two hundred metres."

"Aye, but still," Jehans said. "Ye need only show me the two long Krags."

"They're precisely alike."

"Nay two firearms be alike," Jehans said.

The serial number of one of the Krags ended with a four. The other with a seven. He placed one of the rifles against his cheek and aimed it at a timber knot on a wall, closed his eyes, pulled the bolt open and heard the dry, glass-like tone of hardened steel glide against hardened steel. Then he pushed the bolt forward so it was locked, and in this movement, which pulled the spring around the firing pin to full tension, in this subtle turn, he noted how exquisite the mechanism was. He had tried a German Mauser once, it had clanked and clattered when loaded, it was formidably sturdy and strong, but the loading motion felt as though it was running over gravel, whereas the Krag's loading motion was as smooth and effortless as the movements of a seasoned swimmer in calm waters.

He rested his finger on it, ran it gently over the trigger and pictured himself in the mountains with the rifle ready to fire. Opening the lid to the magazine, he caught a glimpse of the polished mechanism within. What a genius had constructed this. Suddenly he was back in Schweigaard's office, as the boy he once was, thrilled by the exploded-view drawings that showed the insides of a steam engine, by the diagrams with arrows that illustrated the principles of electromagnetism, and it was as though he could see the Krag on the drawing board, a sketch in crisp, newly sharpened pencil strokes on a scale of 1:4, and then the drawing seemed to evaporate, and for the first time he felt the weight of a dream that might become reality, and as he opened and closed the magazine several times more, he observed the mechanism that slid back in and hid each time the lid opened, making it visible for only a brief moment, no matter how slowly he opened the magazine, as though it went into hiding to wait for the gleaming brass cartridges.

"May I pull the trigger?"

"Go ahead."

He checked again that the gun was unloaded, aimed the barrel at the ceiling, put his ear close to the firing pin, squeezed gently and felt for any creep in the trigger. He repeated this with the other Krag and then placed them side by side on the glass counter.

"Have they been tested?"

The assistant nodded. "Certainly. We insist on that, unlike with the military rifles. And they fine-tune the sights at the same time. Let me show you."

He got out two small paper targets. Pencilled in the corners were the serial numbers of each rifle. Each bullet hole was no bigger than a twenty-five øre coin.

"And these were from fifty metres?" Jehans said.

"A hundred!"

"A marvel, t' be sure."

Jehans checked the movement of the bolt again. The two guns were exactly alike, but he knew he wanted the one with the serial number ending in seven, the one with long, dark streaks in the wood of the stock, the signature of a very old tree that would now accompany him for a lifetime, which, no matter what age he reached, would be less than the time it had taken the tree to grow.

"And it comes with its own cleaning equipment," the assistant said, pointing to the cap on the butt-plate. "You tip it up like this, yes, it's meant to sit tightly – but here: it shakes out. Then this string has a weight at one end and a brush at the other – and here, in this neat little flask, is some oil. Do you need a case?"

Jehans shook his head.

"So, all you need now are cartridges. Lead-tipped, I assume?" The assistant opened a metal cabinet. He took out some little packages wrapped in grey wax paper, neatly bound with twine and stamped RØDFOS PATRONFABRIK. Hunting cartridges were expensive, and Jehans asked for fifteen.

"Fifteen? It'll have to be twenty. Can't divide the pack. Not allowed."

Jehans totted it all up in his head. He had every krone he possessed with him, including a few he had earned the previous winter from logging for a farmer in Romsås in deep snow, and on the sale of thirty snared grouse to the same gourmand. He already had his train ticket home, but had promised himself that he would buy Ingeborg some coffee beans.

He had pictured the scene. He would stride into the colonial store on the quay, run by a local merchant known affectionately as Herr Posekremmeren – Herr Paper Cone – because he wrapped everything he sold in newspaper cones. The bell would ring over the shop door, and he would lean his new Krag near the entrance and buy a generous portion of coffee and still have a couple of kroner left over. Posekremmeren would pack it as only he could, so tightly that the knobbly beans bulged through the newspaper. And back home, Jehans would give it to Ingeborg and then show off his new rifle: a good wodge of gratitude worthy of twenty years' care, followed by the new start that the Krag represented.

But it was as it was. They could not divide the packs of cartridges. Meaning, less coffee.

The sales assistant began writing out the receipt. He asked what kind of hunting Jehans did, and when Jehans answered that he hunted reindeer, he asked what kind of binoculars he used.

"I do na' have binoculars."

The assistant did not reply. He checked for someone in the back room and lowered his voice. "Normally I could give you a two-kroner reduction on the Krag. But the deal's done now."

"Oh? Happen I should have known that sooner."

"I want to show you some binoculars by Gulbransen. Best instrument maker in Kristiania. He supplied Roald Amundsen and Fridtjof Nansen. Makes compasses too."

The assistant took a leather case from a drawer, and out came a gleaming pair of binoculars. He took Jehans over to the window.

"Oh!" exclaimed Jehans.

He was suddenly a hawk. Able to see each and every roof tile on houses hundreds of metres away. To see all the way over to a hayfield on the other side of the valley, and the farmhands, some swinging scythes and the others raking the hay. He had never seen anything like it. What a difference this would make on a hunt.

"Well? What do you say?" said the assistant. "It's dangerous to look through very good lenses. You'll never be content with anything mediocre afterwards."

He could have them for eighteen kroner.

"Thanking thee. But 'tis more than I can truly afford with the Krag," Jehans said, and asked what time it was.

"Understood. But wait. I'm saddened by that rejection."

The assistant took out some slightly battered-looking brass binoculars.

"These are a good forty years old and have been used at sea, so they're a bit misty. And there's a scratch on one lens. But you can have them for four kroner."

Jehans looked through the binoculars and shook his head. He took out the envelope the Englishman had given him. Five ten-kroner banknotes, blue on the front and yellow on the back, from the new series without the head of the Swedish king, but with Tordenskiold and the President of the Storting instead. Freshly printed, and smelling like fresh mushrooms. A blue five-kroner note, paper so stiff it crackled.

More money than he would ever see again. An annual salary, for anyone who got such a thing.

The assistant entered his name in a ledger alongside the Krag's serial number. Still busy writing, he asked if this would be the first Krag in the house, Jehans said yes, and the assistant tore off the receipt from the block and handed it to him, saying that the rifle could now be considered the Hekne Krag, and if he and his descendants cleaned it after each hunt, it would last for at least four generations.

The binoculars were still on the counter. They were certainly functional. A Krag *and* a pair of binoculars? The very thought made him tremble, just as when he knew a potential kill was nearby. It was impossible not to think how this would change the hunt. He could scan the mountains as a bird of prey could scan the mountains and see animals from hundreds of metres away.

Coffee for Ingeborg. Mun bring coffee for Ingeborg.

"Can I have the binoculars for three kroner and thirty-two øre?" he said. "'Tis all I have left. Look."

Even as the shop bell rang for a second time, he regretted it.

It was late in the evening when he glimpsed Lake Løsnes, and dark with a grey moon when he moored the priest-boat in the gently lapping shallows and started walking towards Halvfarelia with the Krag in his hand. He hadn't a crumb left to eat. On the train home he had sat in the gangway next to an old lady from Hundorp, the Krag clamped between his knees, and at each station more folk came over to take a look, all wanting to see if the magazine really flipped open as they had heard, and if the mechanism was really as smooth as everyone said, and it was "fired" in the gangway, and the old woman said if they could make something that fine here in Norway, there were no limits to what the country could do when they got rid of the Swedes.

And Jehans realised that he'd never had anything before that folk were interested in seeing, or explained anything new that strangers were interested in hearing about, and that he'd like to do more of it.

But he felt no joy. The moment was spoiled, and *he* had spoiled it. He showed the binoculars to nobody, as he was convinced everyone would see right through him and say he should have bought coffee instead. He dawdled on his way home, and now, on the slope up from Lake Løsnes, the church spire was the only thing that stood out against the night sky. And he stopped outside the cemetery.

He had not visited her grave since the previous year.

If she were alive, would she have liked what she saw? A young man with the most expensive firearm in Butangen?

He put the Krag inside the cemetery wall, opened the gate and walked in, over to her grave. The inscription on the stone was just about legible in the half-dark.

ASTRID HEKNE
1860–1881

"I do nay know what to say to thee," he said. "'Tis as though ye did nay lie here. As though ye were some place else."

He had no idea where to put his hands and backed away. Further up in the cemetery he saw a newly refilled grave.

Black earth, darkness in the dark. Too many strange impressions.

There was light in the pastor's study window. Jehans imagined that his mother was sitting up there, an image that often came to him as a boy when he stayed at the parsonage for the weekend. He had scampered from room to room upstairs then, convinced he might find her. But with each door he opened, his hopes sank a little more, until they hid completely in a knot in his stomach, and then he would sit in some room all alone, until Schweigaard found him and coaxed him out with a book or science experiment.

Jehans walked out of the gate and swung the Krag onto his shoulder. Adjusting the strap, he wondered if he should go up and see Schweigaard. Oldfrue Bressum was so hard of hearing now that she'd never know there was anyone in the hallway. He could sneak upstairs, knock on the study door, tell him that, yes, he had borrowed the priest-boat. To buy a Krag. Schweigaard was curious about anything new, probably even a gun, Jehans might perhaps spend the night in his old room, have some coffee that wasn't made of boiled-up grounds, and maybe an egg.

But no. Not for a man who squandered money on binoculars.

As always, it was the mountains he would depend on. He would head for them at first light. Spend a morning hour with Adolf and Ingeborg. Then set off to find the reindeer.

He hurried along. The spruce trees were very dense along the cart road to Halvfarelia, but Jehans was not afraid of the dark, not when he was carrying a gun at least. As he entered the forest he felt a blast from ancient times assert itself, almost like a change of wind, and then he was finally back home, and went to bed in his shack. He was woken in the morning by Ingeborg standing before him and saying that a message had come from Osvald Hekne on the previous day. A message of the sternest kind.

Botulven

An old couple sat in a cold and damp log cabin and stared at a brand-new rifle. They had raised him as their own, but in that moment it was all too apparent he was not theirs. They could not interfere in his affairs, but nor did they have to applaud him, and they certainly did not. They did not even ask what the rifle had cost. Fifty-five kroner would have been enough to better their lives hugely, but instead a Krag-Jørgensen lay on the table and nothing else.

Jehans told them about the reindeer and the man who had given him money, and Ingeborg said that nobody ever gave anything away without wanting something in return, now or later.

"We mun spend money to make money," Jehans said, though he knew there was no place for such ideas in their minds. They had always worked, just as their parents had always worked, and their parents before them. Everything was limited to what their hands could carry and a Døla horse could pull.

"I shall head for the mountains now," Jehans said. "I shall render our dues to Osvald with my first kill. The second I shall sell. We shall have money."

He still hadn't asked what Osvald wanted from him. But something had happened. Something they found painful to say.

He gazed about the kitchen. He remembered it from a time when he was too small to understand that they were poor. The cracked iron stove, the potato-kettle, the iron pot and frying pan. The wooden spoons, ladles and scoops that Adolf had whittled. The water pails by the stove that they had to break the ice on each morning when the winter was coldest.

And there it hung. Over the stove.

The coffee roaster.

Her most prized possession. A small, enclosed pan with a long handle and a paddle that pushed the beans around. She would boil the grounds again and again until the coffee had barely any colour and a faint aroma was the only reminder of what coffee could be. Only then would she decide to roast a handful of fresh coffee beans, the first cup from which they generally drank on a Sunday. He loved watching her as she opened the lid of the roaster and dropped in a handful of pale-green coffee beans. He delighted in the little cracking sounds they made as they swelled. The way they grew oily and dark as she cooled them, and how the room burst with an exhilarating burnt fragrance that hushed them all. A fragrance that gained even more layers when she threw the beans into the grinder and crunching sounds rapped on the walls. And while all this was happening, the aspen logs burned in the stove and the water boiled, fresh water from the River Breia that everyone in Butangen took for granted, until they travelled beyond the village and tasted water from a well. And finally into this water she poured the coffee and silence reigned until they filled their cups and drank and smacked their lips and Halvfarelia was as rich as any grand farmstead.

Ingeborg brushed her skirts, though there was nothing to brush away.

"Jehans," she said, "'tis nay the Krag and yer buying it troubles us now. But the message that came here from Hekne yestereve. They wants a farmhand for the haymaking."

"A farmhand? From Halvfarelia?"

He glanced over at the pegs by the front door, where his hunting knife and packframe hung. The sun was not yet quite up. It was *now* that the wind was right, *now* that the reindeer would be up in the mountains.

"Aye. Today."

"Today? For how long?"

"Till the haymaking be done," Adolf said.

"He canna' demand that. One big reindeer or two small. And nay labour during the hunting season. That be the contract."

"Happen Osvald spied thee early yestermorn. When ye rowed over in the priest-boat. And left the village."

"I may leave the village as I please," Jehans said.

"Indeed so," said Adolf. "But I may not. Not without permission from Osvald. And he counts thee as a stand-in for me. He has na' received his reindeer, and 'tis far into the hunt season. So now he has called thee to join the haymaking. And – it seems he wants more labour out of thee too. So there be nay more hunting a good while."

He headed straight down to Hekne, but left his scythe behind, causing Adolf to follow him closely with his eyes. The farm was already abuzz with dozens of farmhands. Girls with pitchforks, men with scythes, children. All ready to set about with their regular, allotted tasks. Outside the blacksmith's the grindstone was turning, pulled by children who took turns to crank it. Three old men were on their way to the fields, slow and stooped. Doubtless heading for Storjordet – Big Field – where a narrower strip of field, which Osvald had won recently at poker, had been joined with old Øverjordet – Upper Field. The day after the poker game, Osvald had sent his men up to clear the small trees dividing the two fields, so that everyone would see who was the master.

Jehans looked across the land. He had participated in the first haymaking in early July, but it was unusual for the second round to be as plenteous as this, some farms never got a second crop at all and were forced to fetch more hay from the rough grasslands and marshes up in the mountains. But the grass in this particular field had grown long again in just eight weeks, waving luxuriantly in the breeze. And Jehans knew why: it was down to the new fertiliser.

It was Osvald's idea. He could think big, although in count-less ways he was stubbornly old-fashioned. He had scattered the field with raw phosphate, resulting in a crop that was almost double the size of the previous year's, but since he had refused to buy a harvester and the number of cottars remained the same, the mowing took much longer. And no matter whether Osvald was forward-thinking or old-fashioned, he was as despotic as any landowner from the 1700s. Alongside any new innovations, he revelled in setting his workers utterly futile and time-consuming tasks.

"Storjordet mun be covered with muck," he declared that spring, "and I have charged ye with that task, Jehans."

This *task* entailed standing in the chicken pen, all on his own, hacking at the trampled-down chickenshit while the hens clucked frantically all around him. Always on his own, even though it was not as efficient with only one man, and went more than twice as fast with two.

Osvald reputedly ate four eggs for breakfast and his sons three. Not that Jehans ever saw what they ate, the nearest he ever came to their meals was this crusty layer of chickenshit. It was fermented and some sort of gas lay under the surface, and by the time he had loaded the first wheelbarrow, he felt faint and unsteady on his feet. But he kept at it without whining about the dangers of handling chickenshit; work was not work unless it was dangerous, so there *was* only dangerous work, oh aye, go tell a lumberjack that his work be dangerous, would have been Osvald's terse response.

It was pointless. There he was, carrying chickenshit to the top of the field, only for Osvald to immediately spread artificial fer-tiliser on the selfsame spot. It would have been better to use it on the vegetable field. But Osvald wanted him to take it all the way up there, alone, in a wheelbarrow. In the end the muck was cleared, the fertiliser spread, and the hens were left clucking on a clean, dry floor. That was just the way of it, and each man in the village had something in his life that was *just the way of it.*

Jehans walked towards the scythemen. Most wearing black, homespun trousers and loose, creamy-white burlap shirts. Their jackets hung from the pegs by the tool shed, since it promised to be a hot day. Standing to one side were the women. All wearing scarves, all carrying wide, long-handled pitchforks. Hekne had eight cottars' holdings under its control now, and they all seemed to have been ordered to come today. Jehans greeted those he knew best, folk from Arnestua and Gardbogen and Hekneøygarden. The widow from Solfritt was here too, her smallholding so barren and dark it was barely possible to scrape a living from it. And Ada Borgen was here, a young girl with a bastard child of just a few months, firmly swaddled against her chest in a shawl.

Until now he had heard a general muttering buzz between the timber walls and rocky slopes. A little too quiet. It was usual to hear laughter before the start of work, folk would play the fool, pull each other by the braces, safe in the knowledge that when work began, their good spirits would transfer into strength.

But now it was altogether too muted, and silence signalled either concentration or dissatisfaction, and in this instant he saw it was the latter.

He overheard one of the cottars say, "We labour till late, one and all. Happen he thinks we do nowt but idle our time away till the order comes for us to work down here."

Typical, thought Jehans. Osvald was obsessed with working in dry weather. The scythes cut well enough in rain, but he was convinced he got more out of the workday in fine weather and often sent the cottars home when it rained, only to call them back just as they'd started work on their own land.

As Jehans walked among them, the muttering stopped. That

was nothing new to him. They did not know where they had him, he was the son of the Silver Winter and Osvald Hekne's nephew, and they probably wondered if he might snitch on them to Osvald if they complained.

Jehans walked over to Torger, Hekneøygarden's cottar. "Did ye all get his bidding so late?" he asked.

The cottar looked at him. "Yesternight."

He said nothing more.

"We mun have better warning," Jehans said. "I too thought my time were my own now."

They nodded, but seemed unsure what to think of him.

There were rowdy voices coming from the *stabbur*. Children were scrambling under it, into the shadowy gap between the raised wooden floor and the ground, dragging out the metal racks for the hay-drying and loading them onto a cart. Two old men emerged from the blacksmith's with coils of precious steel wire which they piled into wheelbarrows. It was then that Jehans caught sight of Osvald, doubtless busy counting them.

Osvald was also among the first in Butangen to use the new racks, after he realised that the galvanised steel wire was, simple as it might seem, a little miracle. Stronger than any rope of the same thickness, it remained tight regardless of temperature or moisture, never splintered, could be bent, spliced and reused, year after year. Osvald had travelled all the way to Gjøvik to buy the steel wire straight from Mustad's factory, apparently buying eight thousand metres of it, so that his racks, five rungs tall, could stand even thicker than the racks on Gildevollen, the biggest farm in the village, where until last year they had kept to the old-fashioned way of leaving the hay to dry on the ground, meaning it had to be turned with pitchforks every day to prevent it going mouldy.

Osvald came down towards them with a digging bar in one hand and a scythe in the other. Presumably to see where the first hay-rack would stand, and then take his place at the head of the field as the *førstekar*, the man who would lead the scythemen and make the first cut, the wordless ceremony they called the *release of the scythes.*

Jehans walked towards him. Osvald refused to meet his gaze until he was up close, and even then Jehans had to put himself directly in his path to get him to stop.

Everyone stared, but turned away when Osvald looked at them.

"Ay ay," said Osvald. "And ye, Jehans Half-Way. Where be yer scythe?"

Osvald was in the habit of calling him Half-Way, or sometimes Schönauer or Skjønnhaugen, or even Skjøn-bower.

"Hekne be as much my name as yours," Jehans said.

Osvald did not answer.

"My scythe be back in Halvfarelia. Where it ought."

"So ye have a reindeer kill for me?" Osvald said, spitting on the grass.

"Ye shall have yer reindeer. In accordance wi' the contract."

Osvald thrust his digging pole into the ground. "We be far into the month o' August now, and I have yet to receive any kill from thee. 'Tis warm down here in the village and we can mow a second crop o' hay from this field. And with it being dry, I intend for the work to be done now. Take a look at the other farms, 'tis the same story there. Folk are at work, nay gadding about in the mountains. I hear ye were gone from the village all yesterday. I want ye working here, nay wafting about in mockery of our contract."

"The wind hasna' been right. 'Tis only now the reindeer have gone up in the mountains. And I have bought myself a better rifle."

"Better rifle. Wind here. Wind there. Wind 'n' rifles here, there and everywhere. Always some excuse, Jehans. Ye be so flyaway. Lies and more lies. I canna' treat thee differently to my other tenants. Or they shall all go off hunting and trapping or do as they will. And then how would things look here? So this year ye shall mow. *If* ye can mow."

"Ye know I can."

"I have nay bothered to watch thee, Jehans. Adolf were never a good scytheman. That architect father o' yorn hardly knew one end o' a scythe from t'other. So ye better show me ye can mow. Go up to the tool shed and borrow a scythe. But we shall start *now*, so ye mun come after. Ye can start at the bottom o' the field with the ancients, and it would be best for ye that ye mow as well as they."

Osvald picked up the digging pole and lunged at him. "Get to it now!"

"This in't right," Jehans said.

"Right? The world in't much bothered wi' what is *right*, but what *happens*. Emort would surely ha' let ye play wi' yer toys here still. But he has gone. So ye be here now, and ye shall mow Storjordet. I shall accompany thee myseln, so ye canna go off dreaming like yer mother. What ye mun learn, Jehans Schönauer, and I have said it afore, is that whether ye lived at Hekne or at Halvfarelia ye would have had to work. It were yer mother who reckoned it were just t' run off t' Germany, and then she could swan about all day in a fancy frock. Ha! Fru Architect! Imagine that!"

"Hush yer gob 'bout my mother."

"Ha! If ye just had the merest inkling o' how she were. I *knew* her. Saw her close. Year upon year. Making plans that led nowhere. Ye have the same tendency, Jehans, and ye mun better it. Go in now and fetch a scythe. And sharpen it well. Or as well as ye *can*. Ye mun try, but I'll nay suffer shoddy workmanship. There'll not be one tuft o' grass in your lane. We shall walk across the field together after, thee and me, and ye shall bend down and cut every blade o' grass left standing wi' your hunting knife."

The haymaking team headed off, and Jehans was left alone. The door to the farmhouse opened and a young girl came out. He could see into the hallway, a pale-blue bench and a cupboard decorated with bright painted flowers, traditional *rosemaling*. His grandmother must be somewhere in there. He had a few vague memories of her, a figure in a doorway, a face that was always high up, leading him to conclude that she had never bent down to him.

He went into the tool shed, and stood in the dappled light that shone through the old plank walls. Hanging from the wall were some old scythes, one was loose in its handle and another had loose rivets, and he became aware of one that hung very high up, so high he had to grab onto a timber strut and pull himself up to reach.

It was old and very lightweight. Adolf might have called it a *ljåspik*, as it had been sharpened so often that its blade was like the slimmest new moon. It had been repaired many times, hammered and soldered and rebent. Its shaft was made of goat willow that somebody must have searched for long and hard, since it had a natural curve and sat so well in his hand.

He swung it. It would not be easy to cut with, the blade was terribly long and stood almost at a right angle to the shaft. Meaning it would bite the hay greedily, but could easily get stuck in the ground. The blade sat firm, without any wobble. Someone had once bound the blade with soaked willow roots, which, when left to dry in the sun, shrank and locked the iron and wood together so tightly it never came loose. All this told Jehans that someone had cared for it, year after year, never wanting to replace it.

He sharpened the scythe and hurried up to the field. Everyone

was mowing in the usual way, the way that had proved most efficient and had thus become routine: eight scythemen each in
their respective lane, a fixed track they had to follow. To ensure
no scythe struck at the feet of the next man, the fastest scytheman always kept to the left, so that within minutes a diagonal of
skill and speed was formed, with the young boys and old men
at the very bottom to the right. If someone proved faster than
the formation suggested, the men would swap places to maintain the diagonal. Thus the field was a visual ranking of men's age
and skill that regulated itself, through the day and year by year.

They had left the last lane for Jehans. Even the old men
must have been going at a good pace, since they were already
quite far up the field. Behind them the women gathered the cut
grass and carried it to where the hay-racks would stand. Some of
the youngsters glowered at Jehans and asked why he had come
so late.

Broad pitchforks, large scythes. Men and women, steel and
wood. Soil, grass and sunlight.

And there, to the far left at the very top, was Osvald. With
a good grip on his scythe, he cut through the hay swiftly and
precisely, turning now and then to observe the progress behind
him.

Chief Man of the field. Chief Man of Hekne.

Jehans set to work. It should have been the Krag he was wield-
ing now. A weapon with a wide view and long range. Instead it
was this scythe, shaped so it locked his right and left arms in an
unbreakable pendulum swing, the semicircle of work.

Just as the Krag was good, so too was the scythe. Difficult to
handle, but good. It was unforgiving of any foolish error, and
demanded to follow a fixed path. But in return it cut cleanly
through everything in that path. The grass fell back from the
blade, without a twist or a hitch.

Ada Borgen was raking the hay, close behind Jehans. She could be no more than fifteen years old, and her baby was lying at the edge of the field. She moved it along as they worked their way up. The baby cried. She laid her pitchfork aside and sat down to put it to her breast. But the child refused to settle. She laid it back down, picked up her pitchfork and went back to work, looking back all the while at her little one, who continued to howl.

Jehans was mowing faster than Ada could rake, and he caught up with the old men and said he wanted to pass them. The elders gave way to him, they had nothing to prove. They had shown their capabilities from decade to decade, and preferred to work three abreast, maintaining their dogged rhythm. And at the close of day they would have accomplished as much as the hotheads who had exhausted themselves before the morning break.

The scytheman to Jehans' left stopped and took out his whetstone. The sun was warming up fast and the fragrance of the freshly scythed grass now rose behind them. Jehans stopped to whet his scythe too, and they exchanged glances. The three old men came up alongside him, scythes slicing through the air, with sure and steady blows that brought the grass swishing to the ground. As Jehans hitched his whetstone back onto his belt, he heard one of them say to his neighbour:

"Did ye see that?"

Jehans lowered his scythe and began work again, but kept his ears open to hear what came next.

"He be usin' Botulven."

Botulven.

For a moment the word buzzed in his ears. Then he remembered a local story Adolf had once told him. Many years ago there had been an unusually skilled scytheman in Butangen. He was a free man, but was hired on farms, and even when he was old, he was so fast that he was always appointed the Chief Man. His scythe, just like his clothes, was fixed and mended year upon year, and the locals named it Botulven – the Patched Wolf – conjuring images of a battle-worn old wolf, with sharp gnashing teeth. Over time, the scytheman's own name was forgotten, and he too came to be known as Botulven. And it was said of Botulven that he worked right until his heart stopped beating, that he dropped dead out in the field because he did not want to surrender his position as the best scytheman in Butangen.

Jehans went on. This grizzled old scythe had a bite like nothing he had ever known. It was useless to try to discipline it. Jehans might lead the dance, but it would unfold as the scythe willed it. He worked his way up the field, finding his own pace with pauses to wipe his sweat and whet his blade, and as the rhythm settled his thoughts returned to what Osvald had said about his mother.

The anger started to flow out of his arms and into Botulven, and there was plenty more anger where that came from. He swung the old scythe faster and faster and caught up with another scytheman, who again stepped aside for him. Each man's lane was slightly narrower than the reach of his scythe, for otherwise a strip of grass would be left standing between each, and now that they were so close, their scythes went dangerously near each other's Achilles heels. Jehans took a broad swing with Botulven and closed in on the next man. This time it was Torger from Hekneøygarden. But even he showed no anger at being overtaken; on the contrary, he gave Jehans a knowing nod, took out his whetstone and let him pass.

There was just one scytheman now between Jehans and Osvald, and that was Amund, the smallholder from Gardbogen, who maintained a good pace and did not look back. They had been working for hours now, and the sun blazed hot above them. The calluses on their hands stung. Amund's shirt was dark with sweat, and he had wedged an aspen branch between his buttocks to prevent his skin getting sore from the repeated swinging action. This, and his position so high in the line, told Jehans that here was a scytheman of rank, probably faster than Osvald, though he maintained a respectful distance from the landowner.

Jehans had closed in on Amund, but was careful not to let the scythe go near his heels. But the same thing happened: Amund Gardbogen stepped aside for him and said softly: "Go to it, lad!"

Jehans was now in the same lane as Osvald, who did not look back, but seemed aware of what was happening, because he quickened his pace. Osvald was very skilled with the scythe, strong, precise, swift, and without making one error he continued on in the place of honour at the top of the diagonal.

The scythes began to slow among the team of mowers, and an increasing number of pitch forks were pointed skywards, as it became obvious that trouble was brewing. Osvald raised his tempo, determined not to let Jehans close in on him, and with their scythes singing the two men pulled away from the others. This was no longer a matter of haymaking. It was a full-blown contest.

It was then that the word began to spread in the field, for there was a word in the Døla dialect for such a contest. A word born of itchy homespun garments and prickly timothy grasses against sweaty skin, born of blistered palms and steep fields. It was usually only said in jest, but they now saw the word itself and the raw madness that lay behind it.

That word was *skårjage*.

A scythe chase, or hunt. A word that described exactly what was happening here. The one man chasing or hunting down the other. And everyone saw now that the scythe was more than a tool to provide fodder and safe passage through the barren winter; there slumbered an anger within the scythe because it was kin to the sword.

When such a contest was declared and a scytheman refused to stand aside, other rules took over. The accepted order was upturned and all lanes were locked. When a scytheman lost and was forced to admit defeat, he was not allowed to slip quietly back into his previous position, he had to go to the very bottom of the field.

Skårjage was a contest between males. Blind, stupid and savage, it turned men back into beasts. It was a hunt like that of the wild predators, with the heel as target. Just as the wolf sank its teeth into the elk's heels to bring it to the ground, so a scythe could bring a man crashing down, mutilated and limping for life.

But it never came to that, men were so worried for their heels that even the most arrogant would step aside, and on the rare occasions when a challenge to a *skårjage* was accepted, one of them always ended up backing down, exhausted and embarrassed. Then he would stumble down the line with tears in the corners of his eyes, particularly if he was old, since it was age that had defeated him and another battle was looming in which death would wield the scythe.

Jehans came after Osvald as their scythes sang. Their shirts, which at the start of the day had hung loosely from their shoulders and been the colour of parchment, were now glued to their backs and darkened. Sweat dripped from their brows and into their eyes.

For Osvald was no ordinary man who would back down. He was the lord and master of Hekne.

But Botulven began to dull, and Jehans had to swing it increasingly hard to cut the grass evenly. No! No! He slammed the scythe into a rock, and then stumbled, having put his entire weight behind it. Sparks flew. He tried the scythe again, but it no longer made the right swishing noise, the grass just sprang back up, and below him he saw the next scytheman closing in.

Osvald continued on, without scorning or scolding. Jehans took his whetstone and spat on it, but his mouth was dry and nothing came, so he dry-whetted the scythe while he worked his gums to produce some saliva, before he finally licked the whetstone to finish his sharpening, and then he was off again, but it was going to take fifteen minutes for him to make up Osvald's advantage.

But now Osvald's scythe needed sharpening, for the grass had to be cut evenly and cleanly, the battle was lost if their work was shoddy. Metre by metre Jehans was catching up, but then Osvald was off again. And Jehans shook the sweat from his hair, moved in and sent the scythe right under his shoe. Osvald turned and snarled, sweat dripping from his brow, and Jehans saw the powerful back muscles through his shirt and continued, relentless and resolute as a workhorse. Osvald held his lead for the next few swings, but Jehans was moving in on him fast, and he both steered and held back, slashing out so that Osvald only just managed to escape, and thus he dominated and controlled him. But Osvald did not cower. Suddenly everything went black for Jehans, and he lifted the scythe at an angle, flung his arms out and was poised to bring it down into Osvald's foot.

Then the food bell rang.

Jehans stopped the scythe in mid-air. Osvald took another step and they both stood hunched over, gasping for breath as the bell rang out in the yard. They stood like that until the bell stopped, without turning. Sweat dripped from their hair and arms and down into the grass, and the haymakers stood below, looking on.

"Such oafish conduct, Jehans. Nay better than a simpleton. A disgrace."

Still gasping for breath, Jehans could not answer.

"'Tis a devilish mess ye have made here," Osvald began. "Like the devil ye be. *Skårjage!* Try to chase and humiliate a man on his own land. With folk ogling on."

Osvald spoke almost calmly as the sweat trickled down his sunburned face. Jehans dared not even wipe his face, and his eyes stung.

"Earlier today," Osvald said, "I were close to letting thee go. Letting thee wander off into the mountains, against thee bringing me two reindeer next year. With that rifle ye went and got yerseln, somehow or other. But not now."

Jehans was still unable to answer.

"Thought ye could take me down, eh?" Osvald said. "Never."

Jehans straightened up. Perspiration ran from his fringe, and he saw his uncle's face through a single droplet, distorted and bloated.

Suddenly they saw right into each other. Jehans knew then how like his mother he must look, and he spied in Osvald an old animosity, and knew that the person who had actually challenged Osvald that day was Astrid Hekne.

"Idiot," repeated his uncle. "Ye ought to thank me. Thank me for not shaming thee outright. If yer scythe had left one scratch on my skin, I'd have had the sheriff come for thee. I'd have had all three o' thee thrown out. Come the fourteenth of October Adolf 'n' Ingeborg would be homeless and penniless. I could have had thee jailed. I know every word o' that contract by heart, and so should ye, a lad who has spent so many years learning to read."

Osvald came closer and, doing his best to sound like a city gentleman, said: "The cottar must be subservient and obedient to the landowner and be loyal to him in both word and deed."

He stepped back. "Makes no odds how much ye call yerseln *Hekne*, for 'twas *thee* Adolf sent in his place, and 'tis *he* mun answer for yer folly."

Jehans swallowed hard. "That were never in the contract, Osvald. Never."

"From today on, 'tis over with any reindeer payments in kind. Ye shall work at all times, haymaking and harvest and potato-lifting. Called at a moment's notice. Half day Saturdays and free on Sundays, fair being fair. And since ye have worked yer way up to head scytheman, ye can take the place of honour at the top o' the field. And when the mood takes me some day, I shall join the mowing, and it'll be ye who mun watch yer back. And besides—"

It was then it happened.

Until now, the scythemen and hay-rakers had been standing there gawping. They had continued with their mowing and raking, mainly for appearance's sake, but no more hay-racks had been set up after the *skårjage* had begun. Now it was as if the haymaking team fell apart. Everyone turned towards the farmhouse. The pitchforks came upright in their hands, the scythes were laid down, they wiped their foreheads and brushed down their clothes.

Osvald and Jehans stood there open-mouthed. For one fleeting moment the two men had something in common.

Because it was only *now* that the food bell rang down at Hekne.

The New Cassock

"Hold your arm up, sir. This safety pin needs to – there. Now, what were you saying?"

"Placing textiles. Is it possible? To find out where they come from?"

"Well, it's not always easy. If a pattern relates to a certain fashion or era, then – hold on. Lift your chin, Herr Schweigaard. The collar. Is it still too tight?"

"I'm afraid so. Just a bit."

Tailor Konow put down his tape measure. "You seem a little distracted!" he said. "At what should be a celebratory moment for us all. Is something weighing on your mind? No? Well, anyway. The neckline has to be like that. Or it looks sloppy."

"Couldn't you loosen it just a little? Please! This is, after all – my workwear."

"Workwear? Now I'm offended, Herr Schweigaard. These are clerical robes! I'm a professional and I can't just agree to anything when I'm making official garments, but then again – well – just a little. Hold your arms out. This textile of yours. What colour is it? What pattern?"

"A Scottish tartan. Soft colours. I've got them with me. In the cases over there."

"Oh, so that's *why* you keep turning away from the mirror? Relax, Herr Schweigaard. Cases don't tend to get stolen from here, and with only two of us in the room – well. Now, let's check the length of those sleeves again. Stretch them out like this. And just a couple more minutes with the measuring tape, and I'll have all I need for your breeches and shirts too. Oh – and did you decide on the Borsalino hat?"

"Yes. I'll take it. But I don't want the breeches so tight."

"My dear Herr Schweigaard. That's how they're worn these days. Those celebrity photographs of Herr Nansen changed everything."

"I've no desire to look like someone else. Add a few centimetres above – well, below the hips. At least. I need to be able to move. And four shirts as usual."

"Very well. Four. Wait, let me write that down . . . Hmm!"

"What?"

"I'm comparing your measurements. Forgive my being personal, but I've been your tailor for twenty years. You're keeping very trim, I must say. Same waist measurement for the last eight years. Muscles like a gymnast. *But* you're terribly hard on your clothes. It's only two years since I made your last cassock, and I refuse to patch up that tear. Anyone would think you were doing *carpentry* in your robes. Oh, well. We're done!"

Kai Schweigaard brushed the tailor's chalk from his skin, straightened himself up in his underclothes and put on his wool sweater. On the table, between the rolls of black cloth, lay two grey cardboard cases and his brown leather travel bag. He undid the clasps on one of the cases and beckoned the tailor over.

"It's fragile, so I don't want to take it out."

Konow bent down and studied the pillow closely. He was quiet for a moment before he said:

"Well, it's a *tartan* alright."

"And?"

"It's no ordinary plaid. Tartans are woven like a mirrored reflection around a centre thread or area. As with this one. Quite common in North Gudbrandsdalen, but you may already be familiar with that. Common in Scotland too, of course. But nothing moves as fast between countries as the patterns on textiles. This has been true for thousands of years. Unusual colours though. Must be very old?"

Schweigaard opened the second case to let him see the pattern on the other pillow.

"Yes, red and dark green, that's more common. It's a lovely, dense weave! But I've not seen this sea-green colour before. The colours used often vary from country to country, according to which plants grow in each latitude."

"So this one might be of foreign origin?"

"Very possibly. Do they originate from the same place? Do they belong together in some way?"

"It seems so."

"Well, I'm hardly an expert. I just like making elegant clothes. But I doubt the fabric on this one, the coarse one, was originally woven for a cushion. And certainly not a pillow. One wouldn't want to sleep on it! In fact, it seems more like a remnant. The pattern doesn't relate to the shape of the pillow, the squares are too big and they don't line up with the edges. But how about the back – can I see—"

Schweigaard grabbed his wrist. "Don't touch it. It's extremely fragile."

"Ouch! My dear sir!" Konow said, shaking his hand free, and sounding rather put out. "All I was trying to say is that this must be some sort of outdoor wear. If it's not Norwegian, it may have been a Scottish kilt. Something I actually know a bit about. They're so wonderfully flattering to a man's calves. How old do you think this fabric is?"

"Very old. From around 1600, plus or minus fifty years."

"Ah, that old! Then it can't be a kilt. They wore *belted plaids* back then. Is that how one pronounces it? In proper *Oxford English*?"

"Never having been to Oxford myself, Herr Konow, I'll testify to that being the finest Oxford English I've ever heard. But what is a belted . . . ?"

"A simple but very functional garment. A long piece of heavy woollen cloth, about a yard wide, and between five and eight yards long, depending on what someone could afford. Worn in various ways according to the weather – hot or cold. In the summer they wrapped the entire length round the waist and fixed it with a belt, but then when it was cold they draped it around the upper body too. And at night they rolled themselves up in it to sleep. Norway's King Magnus Barefoot, for example, or Barelegs, wore a belted plaid to show his strong calves. This evolved into the kilt. Which, by the way, is a Norwegian word;

I remember my great-grandmother saying she 'kilted' material when she folded it."

Schweigaard thanked the tailor, closed the two cases, paid his advance, and then waited expectantly for Konow to help him on with his overcoat, made two years ago at a very steep price. But Konow just lit a cigarillo, as was the fashion among Lillehammer's businessmen, and said:

"I might know somebody who would be interested in seeing those pillows. Or even perhaps buying them."

Schweigaard turned. "You do?"

Konow puffed on his cigarillo, waving his arm exaggeratedly in the air.

"Come now, Herr Konow! I apologise for being so tetchy just now."

"Well, alright. She's one of those rebellious females who are fighting for the dissolution of the Union. She and others are working on some folk costumes, what they call the Bunad. I have a fair bit to do with them, because I sell sewing machines. A year ago she wanted to try a Gritzner Model R, and she brought a piece of fabric with her, not unlike the red and deep-green fabric you have in the case there. These costumes or *national* costumes – as they so brazenly call them – have their origins, according to them, in some sort of rural tradition. She claims, for example, that the tartan pattern in Gudbrandsdalen originated from the battle of Kringen when three hundred Scottish soldiers were killed. You know the story?"

"Of course. The battle of 1612. This all sounds very promising, Konow. What's her name?"

Konow blew a few smoke rings, before replying: "Jenny Stueflaaten. One of the richest women in the Dovre area. Widow. Runs the farm herself. A city lady originally. Widely known as the owner of Norddalen's largest collection of tapestries. One of Norway's staunchest opponents to the Union and advocates of the Bunad. I think she's even visited Scotland."

"Oh, I think I might have met her. Or at least seen her. At a lecture."

"I doubt it. You'd have remembered, if you had."

The Woman Who Knew

"First, I want to know where you stand," said Widow Stue-flaaten. "Whether you're a patriot or not. It wasn't obvious from your letters."

"I've been flying the 'pure' flag for six years now," Kai Schwei-gaard said.

"Really?"

"Yes, I inherited a Union flag, but in 1897 I got my tailor to sew us a new one without the 'herring salad'!"

"Yes," she said. "I did the same. Only I did it back in 1893. Sewed it myself and hoisted it up the next morning. I had to fly it at half-mast in 1899. In case you wondered."

He offered his condolences and she accepted. Widow Stue-flaaten was a handsome woman in her forties, with greying hair worn up, and a burgundy dress with silver buttons that ran all the way up to her chin.

He had arrived with his churchwarden, Røhme, late that evening, after taking the train as far as Sel, the last station on the Otta Line. Work had begun on extending the line further north, but it was a massive task. Calculations showed that it would take five hundred men five or six years to lay the tracks to Dombås. The toughest area to negotiate was the Rosten Gorge, which consisted almost entirely of sheer drops and areas of loose rock, and would require thirty to forty man-days to lay each metre of rail track.

Herr Røhme had driven them through this territory in a rickety hired wagon with poorly shod horses, and both men were hungry and cold now. But the widow seemed in no hurry to offer them food. She had the aristocratic air that Schweigaard had observed among those from grander farms in the valley, a coolness and distance, a calculated slowness in her answers, as though she were taking his measure sentence by sentence, assessing whether it was worth her time to answer. There was no hint of the local dialect in her voice, rather she spoke in a sharp and occasionally uvular city dialect that he thought he recognised from Skillebekk in Kristiania, where he knew the well-heeled had a tradition of employing nannies from Bergen.

After discretely issuing orders to her various servants, and making sure Herr Røhme was seen to, she ushered her guest through winding corridors. Green tallow candles flickered in their sconces as they walked past. She had dismissed the idea of a chaperone; why would she need such a thing in her own home? Soon they were sitting at a very long table in a very large room in the glow of a paraffin lamp, a table so long in a room so large that he could barely see the end of it before it faded into darkness. He could just about see that the ceiling was adorned with a mural, that the cupboards were decorated with *rosemaling*, and that the walls were covered with numerous paintings and tapestries. She seemed on edge as they sat down, a little troubled even, and he wondered if she was suspicious of his motives for coming.

He cleared his throat. "I understand you've been to Scotland?"

"I have, indeed. Twice. Their national dress was banned for a long time. Because it inspired a sense of Scottish pride. It's now central to their national identity. The Scots are an example to us. They put a lot of work into establishing set standards of colour and style. I'm certain the Bunad will do the same for us when we emerge from this suffocating Union. Forgive me, Herr Schwei-gaard, if I seem a little heated about this, but the study of local folk costumes has been my life's work since my husband died."

"We can all get a little heated when it comes to the Union," Schweigaard said.

"It's not just the Union! I'm angry with all the people who want to make a laughing stock of our work with national dress! The snobs, the reactionaries, the Unionists who say we're just aping others and that we'll never create a truly *Norwegian* costume."

Schweigaard made no sign of opposition, but Jenny Stuef-laaten launched into all the arguments she had doubtless crushed many opponents with. She ranted against those who thought Norwegian costumes were mere imitations of other countries' styles, and had some fruity words to say about those who claimed that the *skybragd* – the cloudburst – was just an imitation of the French fleur-de-lis.

"A silly and tiresome objection! But, sadly, one that takes suc-cour from the narrow-mindedness that dominates Kristiania!" The truth was, she said, that no *one* country could lay sole claim to anything, since patterns and designs had travelled between lands for centuries. Indeed the fleur-de-lis resembled ancient Babylonian and Egyptian designs.

"That's why we make it our business," she continued, tapping the tabletop, "not only to find the oldest costume designs across rural Norway, but what *lies behind* the colours and shapes. Pat-terns always attract interpretation, not that they have to *mean* anything, but they often have a clear narrative behind them, and that's what we want to tap into. That's how we can integrate our history, our land and our people. Showing our local histories. The Bunad will be a flag our people can wear!"

Kai Schweigaard liked what she said. Liked it so much he failed to register when she had finished.

"What?"

"The pillow. I asked you about the pillow you mentioned in your letter."

He was careful not to make any grand, theatrical gestures as he lifted the two cardboard cases onto the table and opened the clasps.

"Ah, yes! There it is! Our national folk costume," she said, pointing at the pillow made in the softer wool. "The red and dark-green tartan."

"And this one?" Schweigaard said, pointing to the pillow with the deep dip and coarsely woven cover.

She turned up the wick on the paraffin lamp, stroked the pillow and examined it from various angles.

"This is woven in goat's hair. The same wool as we use for winter socks. It withstands just about anything, but the surface gets very scratchy. A peculiar choice for a pillow!"

She fell into thought. Took the lamp over to her writing bureau. Sitting in darkness, he heard her leafing through papers. When she eventually returned with the lamp, she said that the cover had most likely been woven in Scotland.

"Because of the pattern?"

"Because of these," she said, pointing to the areas of sea-green. "There's no plant in Norway from which you can produce this dye. Nothing, at least, which grows in any profusion. But it's a popular colour in the Hebrides and Shetland. It comes from a fern root that's so delicate that the entire plant gets torn up in the wind. It spreads easily enough, but can't survive this far north. Do you know when these pillows were made?"

"Sometime between 1610 and 1630, I think. In Butangen."

"Did they belong to someone in your family?"

He shook his head. "To the family of somebody I once knew. What I wonder is why anyone would use such coarse fabric for a pillow."

A change came over Jenny Stueflaaten. She got up and opened a door. He heard a muted exchange of words, and then she was back.

"One thing puzzled me from the moment I first read your letter. Why, I asked myself, would a man travel all this way to show me two pillows? But I can now tell you that your journey was not in vain. Neither for you nor for me. This one, this piece of fabric here, must have been an off-cut from one of the tartans left behind by the Scottish soldiers in 1612. War booty."

"War booty? Didn't they prefer swords and helmets?"

She shook her head. "Not at all. Clothing could be equally valuable. Maybe more. The making of cloth was very labour-intensive. Remember, knitting wasn't common in Norway until well into the 1700s. After the Battle of Kringen, the Norwegians were left with the corpses of at least three hundred men. They must have been dressed in something, and we know that tartans were quite common in Scotland in 1612. Follow my logic now, Herr Schweigaard. Let's say, to err on the conservative side, that only a third of the soldiers wore belted plaids, and that they were of the shorter variety; that gives us a total of four hundred and fifty metres of fabric. *But*, if we say that two-thirds of the soldiers had the most common length of about seven metres, well, then our peasant army were left with *one and a half kilometres* of tartan. Good, warm woollen fabric, in lengths that could be sewn into whatever you wanted. Without any trouser legs or sleeves or collars to remind them of the dead men who had once worn it."

"It must have been an appalling spectacle. That morning as they pulled the clothes off the dead."

"Times change, and with them what's thought right and proper. Would we have thrown away hundreds of metres of woollen cloth if winter was coming, and if the only clothes we owned had to be painstakingly spun from the wool from our own sheep? People literally froze to death then. Naturally they took the clothes. To do anything else would be like killing an animal and not using the hide and meat. It's almost a way of honouring the dead."

Schweigaard nodded. She lifted the lamp and studied the pillows again from various angles.

"I'm certain this particular tartan came to the valley in 1612," she said. "Although there are those who say it was used here as far back as Norse times. That the Norwegians were the ones who introduced it to Scotland when we colonised the islands, but then forgot it back in Norway. Many women violently disagree with me, but I think the pattern we see in our local folk costume is a legacy from the Battle of Kringen. Because it differs so greatly from most patterns elsewhere in the country. Our pattern is a *tartan*. A distinct weaving method. Mirrored around a central thread. And this is found only in the folk costumes of Gudbrandsdalen and Romsdalen, the exact same places where the Scots came. Ours is red and dark green, perhaps to symbolise the blood that was spilled."

"Hmm."

"What?"

"Something – something makes me doubt that this is booty. That doesn't really fit."

"Then you must tell me what this *something* is. Although I think I already know what it is. It's the design on the back of the pillows."

He swallowed hard. It was late now and the house had fallen silent around them. His hand went towards the lid of the case, but then he pulled back.

"I see. I'm not allowed to look at the pillows from the back. Ah well. That tells me a great deal. Not about the pillows. But about you."

"Widow Stueflaaten. I didn't come all this way to be put under a microscope, but to have this pillow investigated."

"Well, I'm sorry, but you won't get away without a woman giving you her thoughts. The first thing that struck me when you opened those cases was that there was something significant on the reverse. Something you were reluctant to show me. Something of such a personal nature, you feel I've come too close. But I probably sound cold-hearted and inquisitive. Please don't think that of me. I believe I can see into the shadows, and what I see are the contours of a woman."

She fell silent again.

Finally Schweigaard said:

"And if there *were* a woman standing in the shadows?"

"Then I imagine she's been there for a long time. A very long time perhaps. And that she might want to come out."

"She'll never come out of the shadows."

"No?"

"She died."

"Recently?"

"Not if *recently* is measured in years."

"You're a loyal man, *Pastor*, but there's really no danger in telling me that these pillows are the work of the Hekne sisters."

He froze. And when she spoke again it was with greater familiarity.

"You didn't reveal your profession in your letter. But you *are* a priest."

Schweigaard looked down at himself, at his plain breeches, light shirt and waistcoat, all slightly worn, but neutral enough, and his slim tie which bore none of the colours of the church year.

"I can tell by the way you walk into a room," she said. "My uncle was a priest. He bowed his head low before the Lord but commanded respect from his congregation. And his hands were like yours. Restless when he had no Bible to hold. Your letter was postmarked Butangen, and the pastor is the only official there. You're well dressed but have no wedding ring, and that shirt wasn't ironed by any Fru Pastor, it wasn't done with any love. So, you're the unmarried pastor of a parish where the most famous weavers in Gudbrandsdal once lived. You've listened to me talking about wool and plant dyes and Scottish soldiers for well over an hour. You've a knowledge of weaving, a subject that barely one man in a thousand has any interest in. You're a bachelor, yet you say this pillow belonged to a relative of somebody you once knew. All of which suggests to me that the woman standing in the shadows is related to the women who made these. And since you've come here with *two* pillows, I can only assume they belonged to the Hekne sisters and that the woman you can't let go of was also a Hekne."

His head was reeling as she spoke, and not until long after she had fallen silent did he answer.

"I'm not ashamed of it. You're quite right in what you say. She never gives me peace, but nor do I want peace. I have her, after all. What I've really been searching for is the Hekne Weave. The tapestry that disappeared from the church. In my search I found these pillows. And you're right. I was reluctant to show you the underside because I didn't want rumour spreading that I'd found something made by the Hekne sisters. And also because the underside is so markedly different from the simple pattern we see here."

Jenny Stueflaaten turned down the wicks on the lamps. The light grew softer, smoothing her skin and making her cheekbones and brow more defined.

She got up and, lifting them from their cases, she placed the pillows gently on the table, without turning them.

"Did you stop at Lie on your way here? The farm an hour away from here?"

He shook his head, and said they had come straight here.

"They lived there for two or three years. The twins."

"What? The Hekne sisters?"

"Indeed. They learned their craft here in Dovre. In a little cabin right above Lie. Where their aunt lived."

"Nobody ever told me that!"

"Perhaps you haven't had too many people to ask. But there are numerous stories about the Hekne sisters up here, and I think I probably know them all. The cabin they lived in is still standing. For now, at least. The railway line is due to run through there, so it'll be torn down soon. But it won't be torn down tonight."

"Tonight?"

"It's going to be a very long night, Herr Schweigaard. After we've eaten, I shall tell you everything I know about the sisters, in exchange for seeing the back of the pillows. Just so I can touch something made by them again."

"I must say, Jenny Stueflaaten, that you have a great talent for speaking in riddles. What do you mean 'again'?"

He saw a smile emerge in the semi-darkness.

"I owned a Hekne Weave myself once. Oh yes, many a businessman has been tricked into buying a fake Hekne Weave because the twins never marked their work. But mine was absolutely genuine. Unquestionably. For it was woven in accordance with the ancient Norse tradition. Which was a well-kept secret at the time, but which I *know* they learned here. My tapestry was such. Woven as in pre-Christian times. Before any priests like you came to this land."

Kai Schweigaard was starving hungry now, and increasingly light-headed. She was clearly playing with him, a game aimed at changing his antipathy towards her turning the pillows into a desire, a desire so intense that he would beg her to turn the pillows.

"So – what does your tapestry show?"

"It *showed* a shape-shifter clad in deep red. The slender body of a woman with the head of an owl. Her arms outstretched. Two spiders pulling at the threads from her sleeves. When they had finished pulling at them, she would be naked. Or perhaps she was gathering the spiders' threads for her dress, so that the spiders, nature's master weavers, were, in fact, dressing her. I was never quite certain, and that was perhaps the point."

"You said 'showed'. Don't you have it anymore?"

"It fell apart. Quite suddenly. It hung on the wall by that window for years and was in immaculate condition. But on the day I came back from Scotland the maids were airing the house for my return. There was a strong wind outside, and as I opened the front door it caused a through-draught, and the weave turned into a heap of loose threads before my very eyes. I keep its remains in a box, but there's nothing to see."

Widow Stueflaaten said that before she looked at the pillows they ought to have a bite to eat. "And that, Herr Schweigaard, is a prospect to relish. Besides running a profitable farm I have the village's best cook. Young, rather shy, but exceptionally gifted."

He got up. "That reminds me, I really must check on my driver. See that he's got what he needs. He has a stammer. So he's a bit reserved and shy."

"Yes, handsome fellow! Don't worry. I instructed the maids to look after him. I'm sure he's sitting at the kitchen table with them right now. Come along now, Herr Schweigaard. No, this way, the dining room is here on the left. By the way, I asked them to prepare bedrooms for the two of you. It's going to be a late night."

Kai Schweigaard grabbed onto the side of the wagon and pulled himself up. The September morning air was still crisp as he put the two cardboard cases on his lap, raised his hat and waved goodbye to Jenny Stueflaaten. One of the maids was standing near the barn door. Her hair was such a shiny blonde, it was almost luminous against the dark log wall. The horses were eager, and trotted around the white boulder in the middle of the courtyard and down towards the gates. Røhme was fidgety, as though his clothes were too itchy, then he suddenly relaxed and turned to wave at the maid.

Schweigaard said nothing. They came to the gates and Røhme asked: "Down to Dovre?"

"Yes. Towards Dovre. To the Lie Farm."

"Very well, Pastor."

It was a gentle downhill slope. The road was dry so they were travelling at quite a speed. Every now and then Schweigaard threw a side glance at Røhme.

"I understand we've been given a picnic lunch?"

"We have indeed. 'Tis there in my knapsack."

They drove on.

"We were treated to some excellent food last night," Schweigaard said. "I hear you had the same? Including the appetiser! The *rømmegrøt* with speke ham?"

"Aye."

"Very good *rømmegrøt*, Herr Røhme. Marvellous. And the potato salad was excellent too. And the roast mutton."

"Indeed, Pastor. It were excellent *rømmegrøt*. And roast mutton. Aye."

"Røhme?"

"Herr Pastor?"

"Have you lost your stammer?"

Røhme cleared his throat. And then cleared it again.

The carriage was unsprung and Schweigaard turned back and let his body go with the irregularities of the terrain. Herr Røhme looked extremely tired, and he himself felt as though he'd been tossed about mentally and physically. Not only had he been subjected to the entire history of weaving on an empty stomach, but he had also experienced, for the first time in years, the effect a woman could have on him.

She had turned the pillows over slowly, inspected the animal figures and said that there was no doubt at all. They were the handiwork of the Hekne sisters, made in the tradition of the pre-Christian weaves, which told stories through animals and shape-shifters. A relic from a time when few people could read or write, in a country where the art of drawing was not widespread and paper too fragile anyway. "But a weave was hard-wearing. It could be rolled up for storage and then taken out for display, year upon year. A transportable, almost nomadic historical record." These tapestries told the stories of families and villages, and, not least, they described the deeds of great men, who in those times had to travel far and wide to maintain their reputation and power. The kings' men brought tapestries with them to display at their banquets, and poets used them as prompts before they began their storytelling.

"But these animals?" Schweigaard had asked. "Why these strange animals?"

In ancient times, she explained, people believed that every human being possessed a helpful spirit in the form of an animal. Their own guide. Animals were not subordinate to humans in Viking culture. On the contrary. They had qualities a warrior might want for himself. "Who, Herr Schweigaard, in a battle, wouldn't wish they could change into a mighty bear or a quick-witted wolf? Or a raven or an eagle that can fly high into the sky and see where the enemy is hiding? And they used the characteristics of animals to describe human abilities. It was only with the introduction of Christianity, Herr Schweigaard, that animals became subordinate to humans. And from then on tapestries depicted almost nothing but Bible stories."

It sounded like a rebuke of his office, and she had a point. It was a paradox he confronted on a weekly basis, when he had to pay out the bounties to trappers and huntsmen. He had often quoted Moses' Law, saying that *go forth and multiply* applied only to humans and not to the predators they killed. Yes, they were creatures of God, but they must be kept down, and thus with the Bible in his hand, he had actively upheld this shift in respect for the animals.

He told her Adolf and Ingeborg's stories about the Lightning Horn and Golden Raven. "Do you know if these creatures might mean – something more?"

Widow Stueflaaten shook her head. "It's hard to say. They probably just represent something that happened on the farm. Something that was significant to them. To understand them better, Herr Schweigaard, perhaps we need to understand the animal within ourselves better?"

She leaned back in her chair, and the lamplight made the buttons on her dress sparkle. Night had long since fallen, and she shifted her gaze between him and the tapestries and back again and said they were masterpieces. Utterly unique. And worth a fortune, if he ever wanted to sell them. But her eyes rested on them less and less, and more and more on him.

Until she rose and walked slowly to his side of the table.

They reached Lie and had the way pointed out to them by the farmer, but he and his family had only owned the farm since 1772, so all he knew about the Hekne cabin was that there had been a smallholding here since time immemorial, and that it was due for demolition now because they had surrendered the land to the railway company.

Schweigaard battled his way up an overgrown path and brushed his clothes. Yellowing leaves floated down from the trees, and he could see clearings in the terrain, probably the remains of an old cart road. Far ahead he saw a tall, red-painted bamboo stick, and running from it a cleared path marked with more bamboo sticks lined up between tree stumps.

He took off his hat, wiped his brow and followed the path of the future Dovre railway line. Coming to a stream he crossed it, and then looked further into the distance.

There it was. A small log cabin beneath a mountain ridge.

He hurried on towards it, painfully aware of how ridiculous he must look. A sweaty, respectably dressed man, in this impassable territory, clutching two cardboard cases. But there was nobody around to see. He was benefiting from the same seclusion that the sisters had once enjoyed up here. And the sense he had now of being different, his aversion to being seen and his obscure mission – all seemed to bring him closer to them. When he reached the cabin, his heart was pounding with anticipation rather than exertion.

The roof had collapsed long ago, the door was gone, but the log walls were still standing, proud, grey, cracked with age. Inside them, raspberry bushes and nettles grew between fallen slates and rotten floorboards. It smelled of earth and autumn, but what *he* tried to smell his way to was the year 1611, when the cabin's first newly notched pine logs had been laid.

Because they had lived here. Unquestionably. He was looking at the very same view as they had. He closed his eyes and let them ask: *What d'ye want from us, Kai Schweigaard?*

He took the pillows out of their cases and laid each on a rock. And sat on his haunches.

Jenny Stueflaaten had studied them minutely before deciding that the sisters must have used rare plants to dye the yarn. She thought the red colour came from madder roots and the yellow from wolf lichen, which only grew to the north of the valley, but even she had no idea how they had produced the silvery colour.

Kai Schweigaard tried to imagine the girls as they spun and

dyed this wool almost three hundred years ago. Let me come close, he whispered. Close enough to understand what you want of me. And why you allowed me to find these two pillows. Tell me what tears of grief stained them. Tell me. Through me, you will never be completely dead.

He waited.

But all around was only silence and emptiness.

Through the doorway he saw the slopes running down towards the river and the farms along it. Soon the train would rattle – several times a day, even – over this patch of land. Perhaps the tracks would give the train a little jolt right here, as if the land wanted something to be remembered.

Something he must not allow to be forgotten.

Jenny had told him about the Hekne sisters' study time here. Many things were unclear, but he gave credence to her version as it made no attempt at completeness. It did not leach into the legends he had heard elsewhere, and it had no clear ending or point; a Scottish boy had simply visited the Hekne cabin after the Battle of Kringen, a boy who had later disappeared, and the sisters had suffered a serious wound, whose cause was kept secret.

Schweigaard pictured the mercenaries. The route they had followed was well known, and they had set up camp at Kråkvolden, just a few kilometres from here. He could hardly claim to be a military strategist, but it seemed likely that they had come this way rather than along the river below. That way they could hold their elevated position in the terrain, move quickly and avoid the enemy. Yes, he thought, this was where they had marched. Just below the Hekne cabin. A long column of soldiers, with horses and clanking equipment. Some dressed in plaid like the one he had brought back into the light of day. Curiously enough, the railway went right over the place where their bodies were buried, some kilometres south of here.

119

Schweigaard turned to the pillows. Closed his eyes and waited. But the past still refused to answer. The two pillows were nothing but wool on cold rock.

Back outside, he studied the outer walls. There must have been countless inhabitants since 1613, for the log walls were crammed with carved initials and dates. The traditional way for countryfolk to thank their houses. He ran his hand along the timbers, in the hope that an even older hope might answer his touch, two girls' hope of not being forgotten. He searched the scarred logs one by one and soon came to an abrupt halt.

HEH–GEH 1611–1613

Two girls. A hyphen to connect them as cartilage and skin had bound them together.

Halfrid Eiriksdatter Hekne. Gunhild Eiriksdatter Hekne.

He moved his arms up and down in an effort to estimate how tall they might have been, concluding they must have been about one metre sixty, surprisingly tall. Halfrid's initials were carved a little more roughly and deeply. Evidence perhaps of a stronger will. And, he decided that if the girls had turned round now and met him face to face, Gunhild would be on the left and Halfrid on the right.

High in a birch tree chirped a thrush that was invisible to him. Far below in the valley, equally hidden from view, he heard one or more horses on the cart road.

It was in just such a way that they seemed present. The Hekne sisters. It felt as though they disliked him treading so close, or the way he measured them up. As though they were parts of something he was not mature enough to understand. Or that they were pointing to something he *should* understand. Then he noticed another inscription, just above their names. So faint that he initially took it to be an irregularity in the wood itself.

He went to the stream, filled his hat with water and wetted the timber, so the letters came clearer.

frjá nauð, frjá dauðr 1613

It was in old Norse, but meant nothing to him. Jenny Stue-flaaten had said that inscriptions of the period often caused confusion. It was common for weavers to copy the work of others, but because many of them were illiterate, they also copied the initials and dates, leaving posterity to wonder. He also knew from his student days that the concept of spelling, the very idea of there being a right or wrong way to write a word, had come long after 1613.

Was this the case with this inscription? That it did not conform to any written tradition, because it was written by somebody who – who couldn't write?

He wetted the inscription again. It seemed to have been carved by somebody else, somebody other than the girls. And whoever it was must have been quite tall, since it was on a log just below the eaves.

Schweigaard looked around. He would have liked to wrench the whole log loose and carry it away over his shoulder. Instead he tore a sheet out from his notebook and took a pencil rubbing of the inscription. When he saw the words, as though lit up in graphite shadow, the pencil seemed to jerk in his hand, as though it wanted to correct something, to reshape the letters, make them legible. Might this be an ancient adage – written in the old Norse dialect from the Orkneys and Shetland, which the boy and two sisters had all understood?

Kai Schweigaard had to stretch his imagination to breaking point. If he accepted that *frjá* meant friendship, this could be a saying with words that were once common in Norwegian and English, but which had now gone separate ways in the two languages and ended up in two sayings with slightly different meanings. One that in English contented itself with embracing earthly life: *A friend in need is a friend indeed*. And another that in Norwegian extended to the hereafter: *A friend in need, a friend in death*.

As soon as they were back in Butangen he looked it up in Fritzner's Old Norse dictionary and discovered that *frjá* did not necessarily mean "friend".

In an even older sense it meant "to love".

A capacity for which, he now knew, still existed within him.

Jenny Stueflaaten had come over to his side of the table late that night, taken his hand and wished him luck. She had not withdrawn her hand, but waited for his Adam's apple to bob up and down before she kissed him lightly on the cheek and said it *really* was very late, and time to give up while the going was good, *very* good in fact, Schweigaard, I'll see you early in the morning and you must make sure to write to me about your findings.

He felt content as he retired to his bedroom. Lay alone, his body tingling, thinking of her. Perhaps she too left the signature of longing in her pillow.

Two people each in their own room. Where passions perhaps slumbered, but could still be reawakened to rejoin the game. To become like the beasts in the forest once more.

Like two shape-shifters.

His human brain was proud that he had kept himself pure and avoided the shame and remorse of giving way. His animal body trembled and sent pride packing, pride out on the floorboards, before he finally dozed off, and both his body and brain wondered whose footsteps he had heard out in the hallway.

Now, back in Butangen, he pinched the corners of his eyes. Rose from his chair and went to the window. It was the deep of night. He could only see light in the windows of a few farms, the light of oil lamps or flickering fireplaces.

But he always knew which farm was which. He knew their names, who lived there, what they looked like. If he ventured out into the night, he could find his way from one to the other; he might stumble, but the path was always there even if he could not see it. Just as he had found the glow of oil lamps in a distant darkened time, facts of a long-ago night that fell over Dovre in 1612. He knew so little for certain. The location of a log cabin, the course of an overgrown path, the scene of a battlefield, a wound the sisters refused to talk about, an inscription about love in death.

It was said that the twins were joined from the hip down. But how could folk know that for sure? They probably wore long skirts and aprons, and the only clue would be in their gait. What if they were only connected by cartilage? Besides which – he had often heard that the sisters had fallen ill before adulthood. But it seemed that they had lived much longer. Perhaps they had just inflicted a terrible wound on themselves at the time?

He pictured one sister. Desperately in love with a boy from Scotland. The kind of love felt only in youth. A plan to run away together. Two girls in a time without skilled doctors, linked together by cartilage in which they felt no pain.

Schweigaard went to the coffin and took out the knife. Tested it against his fingertip. He, for one, would have been willing to sacrifice an arm and a leg to get Astrid Hekne back.

He felt the weight of the black, rough-hammered blade with its glinting edge. There could only be one reason for it to lie beside the pillows.

The girls had attempted to cut themselves free from each other.

The boy must have heard their screams. Realised what had happened and been overwhelmed by her willingness to sacrifice herself. Must have realised they could never have each other. Left her a small memento. A fragment of tartan woven in goat's hair. The only thing he owned. Later she made it into a pillow. And slept on it for the rest of her life.

But before that was the septic fever. The images on the reverse of the pillows perhaps being what they saw in their delirium.

It was probably Halfrid who had had the pillow with the Scottish tartan. The sister who in death would *shuttle wide*, and now he had a feeling where. To the land of the tartan and thistle.

The Monarch of the Norwegian Mountains

"How about there?" his father said.

"There?" said Victor. "Perhaps."

"We can move the buffalo to the left and swap the reindeer and kudu around."

"Let's try it," said Victor. "Kumara?"

Kumara nodded, and with the help of the Wilkins boy he rolled the little crane back against the wall and started to swap the hunting trophies. Made of beautifully joined ash, it might, with a little imagination, look like a miniature Eiffel Tower. It had been Victor's favourite plaything as a child, although its real purpose was to move sculptures and heavy, hardwood cupboards. The ash had been treated with linseed oil and gave off a unique fragrance that hinted at endeavour and change, which Victor inhaled now as Wilkins set up a ladder and secured the lifting hook. Kumara began to swing it, and the rope tightened as it took the weight. The crane creaked as a buffalo head was lowered.

"Gently, Kumara!" said Victor's father.

"Yes. Yes. Gently. Trying."

Written on a plaque under the buffalo head was the name ROBERT HARRISON together with the year 1875. It had been shot by Victor's father in Rhodesia, and now that it had been removed, a pale oval shape appeared in the wallpaper. Working with the crane and the ladder in tandem, Kumara and the Wilkins boy began to move the antlers and animal heads, an arduous but relatively simple operation, since each wall mount was identical: three heavy bolts placed nine inches apart in a triangle. Fifteen minutes later the buffalo, the reindeer and the kudu had all changed places, and it was decided that the head of the wild boar, which his father had shot at a friend's place in France, must go into the attic.

"What do *you* think, Kumara?" Victor said.

Kumara looked sceptically around the room. A Tamil, Kumara had worked as the foreman on the Harrison plantation for twelve years before coming to England last summer for medical treatment, after battling with an infection none of the doctors in Ceylon could treat. He had adapted well to life in Northumberland; even the dreary climate did not seem to affect him adversely. He continued to go about barefoot as he had back at home, despite the floors being so cold here at Finlaggan. Victor never said so to Kumara, but this always aroused admiration in him. The man had even gone without shoes in London, for God's sake!

Kumara shook his head. "No. Still not good, Mr Victor."

"Hmm," said Victor's father, leaning against the weapons cabinet with folded arms. Victor observed his profile reflected in the glass doors and the array of weapons behind him. His father might give him a jovial slap on the back now and then, but the two men generally maintained a respectful distance.

"Hmm," Victor said, stepping back and knocking into the

graveyard of honour, the walnut cabinet where they kept their old, worn-out fishing reels. He leaned against it and gazed around, joining the search for a suitable place among the stuffed animal heads.

"Are you thinking what I'm thinking?" said his father.

"Probably," Victor said. "But it has to be your decision."

"We'll do it. Absolutely, we will. It's a remarkable beast. And it's about time."

They went out for half an hour and on their return Kumara seemed to have declared himself satisfied, since the crane and ladder had been put in the corner, the floor was swept and the reindeer's head was displayed in place of honour over the grand double doors that connected the gunroom with the living room. Despite the mahogany doors with their frosted glass inserts, the luxurious, deep-red wallpaper and golden-brown wainscotting, the monarch of the Norwegian highlands did not seem out of keeping; on the contrary, it looked quite at home among the various trophies the Harrisons had collected and admired for two centuries, with its huge antlers that unfurled in magnificent curved branches and tines. The taxidermist was a Scotsman with a certificate from the Maison Verreaux in Paris, and the reindeer had been cut generously so that its shaggy neck and handsome white beard were still intact.

Standing in the centre of the room was a solid table with a padded leather top. It was here that they disassembled their rifles for cleaning and oiling. The leather was a deep black after decades of little spillages of anti-rust and Rangoon oil. It exuded an oily vapour, which with the smells of the taxidermist's powder and dried animal heads created the room's unique odour. Walking over to the table, father and son turned to look at the trophy that had been obliged to make way for the reindeer: a red stag, shot in 1849 by Victor's grandfather on the Isle of Islay. It hung on the opposite wall, in a less showy position, but certainly not in bad company – hanging below it was a kudu with exquisitely twisted horns that his father had shot in the Transvaal in 1874, and alongside that a long, wooden plaque with a carved profile of a forty-three and a half pound salmon that his father had caught in Lærdal when Victor was eight.

His father opened a glass cabinet and took out his big game rifle, a heavy, scratched Gibbs .450/400 Nitro Express. "Strange. That winter, when I came back from the Transvaal with the kudu, your grandfather and I did almost the same thing."

"The same?"

"As you and I have done. Made room for my trophy."

"And what did you take away?"

"A lion that he'd once shot. Badly stuffed, but a jolly good hunting story."

"The lion that got into a tent and tore a man's cheek off?"

"That's the one. Though it was a woman. The lion ripped the tent open and sank its teeth into her as she nursed her baby. She curled up around the baby as the lion dragged her out. Your grandfather shot it in the dim light of a dying campfire. The child was unharmed. The mother was taken to Nairobi, where they did what they could for her. She survived. But your reindeer may have to move aside one day too. For another hunting story. For an animal shot by *your* son."

His father gazed up at the reindeer again. He shook his head and exclaimed: "I shan't ever tire of hearing it. Tell me about that morning in Norway again!"

It was time to eat and Victor glanced around the room. The red stag and the reindeer now hung on opposite walls. Two animals shot by a grandfather and grandson, both named Victor Harrison, stared at each other from either side of the room. He met the glassy gaze of his grandfather's red deer, yet felt the reindeer's eyes on his back.

*

After supper he felt he had been deceitful.

He had described the reindeer hunt to the last detail, but had omitted to mention the Norwegian.

Not because he wanted to claim all the honour for himself. The story would not lose anything if he told it all. On the contrary. Two shots that hit the same prey simultaneously, his own shot and a round bullet from an old black-powder gun fired by a huntsman so close to nature that he might have been a shape-shifting reindeer in the guise of a human being, a hunter who named his oddly specific price and then vanished into the mountains. Such details would not have reduced the impact of his hunting story; indeed they would have served as proof that the Harrison family were keen to share honour where honour should be shared.

But something kept Victor from telling it all. It was as if this trip to Norway had cracked something open in him, allowed him to see into something hazy which he did not understand. He had been brought up to show the utmost honesty and openness, not about his feelings, but about the *facts* of a situation. Now he felt a small knot in his stomach: not only had he concealed something from his own father, there was more.

A lie had been sown there in Norway. Without him knowing what the lie was.

Other than that it had something to do with Ragna. But how could Ragna, honesty itself, be connected to a lie?

In the evening he pulled on his tall boots and went out. With the grass beneath his feet, the evening air in his lungs, treetops on the horizon. Lucy scampered, tail wagging, over the gentle slopes where his mother had liked to ride, back when she still rode.

Lucy was his third dog; the first had been Pidge. She had followed him about from when he was five until he was sixteen and was what his grandfather called *the dog of a lifetime*. Marlow had succeeded her and now Lucy. They were Welsh springers too and wonderful dogs, their only fault being that they were not Pidge.

Victor took out his pocket watch. It was seven o'clock and he turned to watch the lamps being lit within the house. He never tired of looking at Finlaggan. The house had been named after a Scottish loch with which the family had connections. It was at its most beautiful at this time of day, with enough light from the evening sun to illuminate the deep red of the brickwork, but dark enough for the lamps to glow yellow inside the rows of windows. A generously proportioned house, completed in 1793, with three storeys, a veranda at the front, covered with a sprawling Virginia creeper. Beautiful without being ostentatious, solid and unassuming.

Rather like the Harrison family themselves. Well ordered, taciturn, landowners with an income from the colonies. They felt more at home in Edinburgh than London, and kept a simple, rather dusty apartment there. The family had an entry in *Burke's Landed Gentry*, which recorded that his great-grandfather had served in the Madras Horse Artillery. And the Harrison entry always ended with the felicitous phrase: *And was succeeded by his eldest son*. Every other year they ventured abroad with their double-barrelled rifles and chequebooks. The family legends were filled with near-calamities in salmon rivers, shots at long range and falling rubber prices.

Now another legend was to be added to the family history: a reindeer bull lit by an electric lamp in the gunroom. With just one problem: the light shone on a half-truth.

It had been his idea to install electricity; as usual his father had balked at the cost involved. But Victor had heard that some engineers were installing it on the neighbouring estate and enquired if they might extend the cable to Finlaggan. Yes, right away. No point in waiting!

He always seemed to brim with new plans, wherever he went. Just an hour's horse ride away from the house there were neglected pastures, with a fine view of the Cheviot Hills. They had been over-grazed, but if he burned the heather it would promote plant growth and possibly even tempt grouse to nest there, since there was quartz in the ground, and where there was quartz grouse liked to settle, and he made a sketch for a small cottage that would suit. But most of the working drawings that filled his head were for their plantation in Ceylon. In just a couple of months, he and Kumara would be back in Nuwara Eliya, with its green hills, red mud and ice-cold mornings, to install a brand-new cylinder dryer and start cultivating a new area that his father had deemed unusable.

They had an old bungalow in Ceylon, and yes, it smelled musty indoors and the veranda was ramshackle, but the mornings there were beyond compare. They would sit outside the bungalow, he and his father and Kumara, as the sun warmed up and the mist parted like theatre curtains, opening onto the forests and valley below. And in the evenings, after a hard day's work, they would sit there again, preferably in the company of the Scots who owned the neighbouring plantations. It was a men-only veranda and nobody ever changed for the evening.

They had given houseroom once to some Belgians who had got lost. Their guests had assumed a plantation would be a place of luxury, and were surprised to find Victor with scratched hands and covered with a rash and mosquito bites. It was something he often noticed among other Europeans – all the finery and manners that the British surrounded themselves with made others see them as one homogeneous people. It was a minority that bothered to get to the marrow of who they really were.

The Belgians might well have made similar assumptions about Finlaggan had they seen it. But looks can deceive. Truth was, the place had fallen into terrible disrepair. Henderson had not been replaced with a new butler, the cook had to weed the vegetable garden, and Kumara and the Wilkins boy had an all-day battle with leaking pipes and crumbling window putty.

Victor sat and watched as the darkness descended around him. And as the estate disappeared into the night, his self-examination grew. What was it about this day? This sudden sense of longing that he felt, a longing for something *more*? It was not the longing for romantic love, he had been gripped by that twice now, first with Frances McNoughton and last year with Evelyn Percy. No, it was something else.

There were times when he felt like a stranger, a stranger to the life that went on behind the windows of this house. He had always been at odds with the family's slow, inflexible views on life. For him the greatest joys came at you in a rush. Unexpected opportunities had to be seized, like rare birds that fluttered up and were visible for just a few seconds. Yes, he felt like a stranger, like a book that was impossible to shelve neatly, a book of awkward dimensions, too tall to put on the usual shelf and too small to put alongside the atlases. No matter what, it always stuck out.

But many people must have something similar inside. Something that never quite fitted. He had always liked to keep a careful tally of his experiences, and when he ran through his memories he found pleasure in most of them.

He had been brought up as most children of the Empire were. Ragna had looked after him from dawn to dusk until he was four and old enough to have a tutor, then he was sent away to school at the age of ten. Even as a young child he would accompany his father or grandfather for long days out in the rain without complaint, eating politely from a tin plate as they squatted around a campfire, studiously unaffected by the coarse exchanges of the work-weary menfolk around him. Indoors, his grandmother impressed upon him the refined manners needed by the heir of Finlaggan, including the most difficult manoeuvre of all: surviving a formal dinner party.

"The first thing, Victor my dear, is that you must never be late. Never! Not only do you keep the company waiting, but you give them a chance to gossip about you."

So no, he never came to the dinner table late, was the perfect guest, gracious and attentive, he never laughed too loudly, never started a boring conversation when there were ladies around, and soon after his voice broke he acquired the self-assured, patriarchal diction of his father and grandfather.

But he had never really felt comfortable at such gatherings. He always wanted to be *outside*, exploring a new forest, a new fishing river, another country, preferably by ship, and aged just seven he made his first trip to Ceylon. His father said this urge to travel had been inherited from the grandfather he was named after. As a boy Victor had been wide-eyed with admiration when Victor Senior was visited by some old fellow war veterans, loud-voiced and stone-deaf from all the gunfire and cannon bombardments, he still remembered their weathered faces and impressive sideburns, the clouds of cigar smoke and rich Latakia pipe tobacco, the clinking of glasses accompanied by cursing and wry laughter, the place names that he looked up in his atlas and which had an aura of adventure: Cawnpore, Matabeleland, Baluchistan.

As he pondered these memories he felt a growing sense of disquiet.

He rose abruptly, whistled for Lucy to follow him home. He knew there was something he was failing to look at head-on, and that was intolerable. He detested those moments when his own actions sprang from sources he could not see or comprehend.

Looking up at the house again his gaze was drawn to Ragna's window. It was dark now, of course, but for one moment he believed it might be lit up.

A door within him slid open, and he remembered what he did not want to remember. The precise starting point of the lie.

He had told the Norwegian stranger that he had a Norwegian nanny. But not that he had a Norwegian mother.

He had been rendered so naked in Norway. He had even unconsciously admitted that he felt more affection for Ragna than for his own mother. And it was *this* he had been ashamed of without remembering it. So that what was honesty in Norway had become a lie back at Finlaggan.

Ragna had always been there. Her place in the household was a little vague, but she had probably been a maid in his mother's family in Norway and was his mother's travel companion when she returned to England pregnant, a trip that concluded with his birth on board the ship.

Ragna talked to him in both Norwegian and English, although he realised later that she spoke her mother tongue when she felt homesick. She seemed a solitary creature within the household, without any real place in the servants' hierarchy. Later, he concluded that Ragna had been brought along to provide his mother with a link to her homeland, so she had someone to speak Norwegian with, or even confide in, but his sympathies were always with Ragna, not his mother, particularly when she was set unnecessary tasks or sent out in all weathers to post a letter or pick up something his mother had no real need for.

What he remembered most about Ragna was her softness. And the impossibility of placing her. She brought him his food, and tended his cuts and grazes after a day's play. She made sure he slept when he said he would, and he sometimes mistook what he thought he should feel for his mother for what he actually felt for Ragna. He had distorted memories of running after his mother, but as he wrapped his arms about her, there was nothing there and he tumbled over and found himself back in Ragna's warm lap.

Things were different with Joseph.

He was born when Victor was seven. Until then his mother wandered about the house as though she were charged with an impossible burden, in contrast to his father, who always chuckled at the morning papers and flung his arms about her several times a day. She went to a clinic in London to give birth, and when they returned with Joseph, she had become utterly unapproachable. And the infant who had come out of her seemed to glare back at the world with the same unapproachable gaze. His mother sat for hours with Joseph, breastfed him herself, cradled him in her lap, stared into his baby eyes.

Victor had assumed that Ragna would look after Joseph, too. But no. His mother looked after the new baby herself, in her own bedroom. Later, Victor believed that this endless pampering was meant to console Joseph, because he did not stand to inherit Finlaggan. He wondered if she had ever sat like that with *him*, but suspected not, as he had no memory of being cuddled or held by anyone other than Ragna.

Now, as an adult, he understood that his mother was not the person she had hoped she would be.

Exotic, admired and adored, a rose-cheeked beauty from the Norwegian coast, the judge's daughter who realised she could not withstand the rain and tedium.

She was offered a choice, and she took it.

It wasn't long before the trips to warmer climes began, away from the dismal Northumberland autumns. Then a Christmas came when she was gone and he barely noticed any difference. She stayed longer and longer in Florence and had Joseph start at the English School there. His father had taken Victor to visit them a few times, but the apartment was cramped and the only thing Victor remembered was that his younger brother had written a poem in Italian, which he refused to read aloud.

It was completely dark as he reached the house. The light from the windows spilled out across the lawn and the trees, and standing behind one he could see his father.

He went down to the servants' quarters and knocked on Kumara's door. Kumara generally cooked for himself in the evening.

"What have you made today, Kumara?"

"Kerala stew, Mr Victor."

"Mmm. May I have a taste?"

It was a breach of etiquette to sit down here in the servants' quarters, unthinkable had his grandmother still been alive, but the two men had a quiet understanding, and Kumara always made a double portion.

They ate without saying much. Victor liked the way Kumara seemed to see through his Britishness and right into *him*. But as they ate together that day, it struck him that another man had looked at him with the same gaze. A gaze that scraped out his innermost core. The ragtag man in Norway.

He had not been an Englishman in his eyes, but a reindeer hunter.

Their supper over, Victor let himself out and went along the corridors. It was time for bed, he had a long day with the forest manager before him. The Wilkins boy had turned off all the lights, apart from in the entrance hall and up the stairs, and he went back into the gunroom, so dark now that the animals in there looked as animals do in the night. As a child, he had been frightened to go in here. Frightened that he might never kill any big game and live up to his ancestors. Now he stood there, gazing up at the reindeer once more.

He had nurtured the dream of hunting reindeer in Norway

since boyhood. It had been planted in him one morning in spring, the season when Finlaggan breathed slowest. His mother and father had gone away on a long trip, fewer rooms were heated, the servants slacked on the silver-polishing and carpet-beating and weeks of boredom stretched out, without a visit, playing with the gardener's sons, even though it was not the done thing.

Generally, however, he followed his grandmother's edicts. It was only when the postman came that he really broke the rules. He became his own father. Went into his study, climbed up onto the chair, leaned on the mahogany desk and felt like a grown-up as he dangled his legs and opened his father's correspondence. Not the business letters from tea houses and lawyers and banks, they were boring and the few he opened he stuck back down, but all the big envelopes, those that contained price lists for fishing gear and mountaineering equipment, and not least the hefty, annual catalogues from the gunsmiths. On that spring day his favourite journal, *The Field*, had arrived and he lost himself in a vivid account of two Scots who had travelled to Norway, enduring shipwrecks, hazardously narrow cart roads, tempests, rugged mountains and Norwegian food, since according to the article Norwegians ate nothing that hadn't been buried in the earth or allowed to rot beyond recognition. Having arrived at their destination, they went on a hunt so exhilarating, so challenging, so pure, that nothing they had ever done could compare. *It was just us, the bare mountains and the rain, and after six days we too became creatures of the mountains and rain, and only then were we worthy to lay our eyes upon them – the proud Norwegian reindeer.*

He took the magazine to Ragna and asked her if Norway really *was* like that, and she said it was, except the food bit, which was wildly exaggerated, but both her brothers hunted on the Hardanger Plateau, they never missed an autumn, however heavily it rained and however tough it was, because the reindeer hunt was an obsession that never faded. He sat there in her room, and she gave him a hug, even though he was really too big, and when he was in the doorway, she cleared her throat and fell into the sing-song dialect of her home:

"But if ye truly wish t' hunt the reindeer, the wild reindeer, then ye mun go to the middle of Gudbrandsdal. To the mountains around Butangen. And there ye shall find him, the reindeer that can ne'er be tamed. So I have heard. Butangen."

He had never forgotten this. Mainly because she had said it so strangely. Not secretively, but as though she was saying something she ought not to say. As though she had promised someone never to give away the location of a prime hunting ground. As though it were a secret even among Norwegians. Reading the article in *The Field* again, he saw there was a breed of wild reindeer in these mountains that had never been diluted with domestic reindeer, so that all their Stone Age instincts were still intact. They were faster, stronger, shyer than any others, and from then on the dream of hunting in Norway burned in him, and this year he had at last made the dream a reality.

He wanted to go back. To feel what he felt when he was alone there. The wind from the north, the icy chill from the earth, the rain and the sky.

The house was dark and quiet now, and he liked to wander about and imagine everything that had happened there before his time. He often smiled to himself when he reached the staircase where all the family portraits hung; the *ancestors' gallery*, as his grandmother had called it, had been the most frightening place in the house when he was a child. The oldest portraits were darkened with age, so that strange handlebar mustachios loomed from the shadows. Stern-looking men and the occasional woman filled the walls all the way up the stairs from the banister to the ceiling. Now, as an adult who had frequented London's and Edinburgh's art dealers, Victor saw how uneven the quality of these paintings was, some even bordered on the amateurish,

though both his father's and grandfather's portraits were skil-
fully executed, as was his own. Victor's great-grandfather had
initiated a new tradition, commissioning a portrait of his heir
at the age of fifteen standing in his favourite place on the Finlaggan estate. His father's portrait, painted in 1855, depicted
him in a shady grove with his horse. Victor himself had chosen
to stand by one of the estate's lakes with his fishing rod, just as
his grandfather had in 1830.

Victor looked up now, and met his own fifteen-year-old gaze.

It was not a particularly good likeness. Just as with the eyes
of the red stag and reindeer. Both had glass eyes, but only the
reindeer actually seemed to stare at him.

He opened the door to Ragna's old room.

It had been like this since she left. The fireplace was swept
clean, the bed made. The cupboard empty, no carpets on the
floor.

She was probably still alive. Somewhere in Norway.

Was he eight when he realised she was about to leave them?
Nine?

There had been such an unusual sharpness in Ragna that
day, an anger towards his parents, at odds with the blind loyalty
she had always shown towards his mother. He assumed it must
be the sadness of parting that made her that way. But that
afternoon, after she had spent her best years in a grey Northumberland and was too old to have her own children, he saw
the resentment in her. A strange anger that couldn't be mistaken
for the melancholy of parting. Victor went into her room as
she stood packing her things, everything fitting into two carpet
bags, and he perched on a chair and could not comprehend that
she was abandoning him.

On emptying her cupboard, she had found a tiny knitted jacket, with a distinctive pattern that he had assumed was

Norwegian. He remembered nothing more about it apart from its deep yellow colour.

He had always thought that Ragna had knitted it herself, but now, as she laid it on the bed, she said something in the same voice as when she had described the reindeer in Butangen.

A strange remark that he never forgot although the jacket was tidied away.

"Your mother wanted thee to have this."

A Breeze from the South-East

Saturday came, the cottars were ready to start work at first light. Little was said, as everyone knew what needed doing. They must get to it swiftly with their scythes and rakes now, so they could go home in the afternoon and see to their own fields. Attend to the pigs and to their potatoes, cabbages and carrots, all the food that they and their children would depend upon through the winter, work they had always been given time for in past years. No matter how busy it got down at Hekne, the cottars had always been given Monday off and half of Saturday for their own use, and Sunday too, of course, when things were difficult and the pastor turned a blind eye, as Schweigaard had done since 1881.

But today, right before the morning porridge break, Osvald announced that there would be *no* time off that afternoon, and that they'd be expected to work the next day too.

One man shifted his scythe to his other hand. Nobody moved. Nobody nodded.

"Tomorrow be Sunday," said one.

"We mun get this finished," Osvald said. "This field. In't much left. Sometime tomorrow afternoon it will be ready mowed 'n' stacked. Then ye may wend your ways home."

"The pastor has sommat to say 'bout Sunday work," said one.

"The pastor doesna' rule over the haymakin' at Hekne," Osvald said.

There was nothing else for it but to obey. They worked on, quickly, but not too quickly, maintaining pride in the agility of their scythe-strokes and hay-raking, but muttering that the cottars' contracts, which had previously been fair, were no longer fair and were getting worse.

But although Osvald was right that the pastor had no say over the haymaking at Hekne, he was wrong to assume that the pastor's wrath might not be enforced by a higher power.

That evening the clouds darkened as the haymakers made their way home. And towards nightfall the rain began to pour. From time immemorial the cottars had been told that there was no need to go down to the farm when the weather was bad, scant comfort when the weather made it just as hard to work their own land.

On Sunday, nobody came from the cottars' cottages. Only two young farmhands and girls with rakes turned up at Hekne in the rain that morning, asking if there was anything they could do to earn a day's pay. One was Ada Borgen, still with her baby bound to her chest. Osvald saw them from his window and sent out a servant boy to tell them that there was of course no work since it was raining, and there was nothing else they could start on, so there would be no pay.

Jehans did not go down to the farm. He had managed to shake off the motion of the scythe during the night, the awkward twist in the body, the pressure in the shoulders and hands and forearms that felt like a clamp over his arms, and now refreshed, he headed for the mountains. He held the butt of his Krag so the wood would not be scuffed by his packframe, and he had never carried a gun with more pride.

There was a breeze coming in from the south-east, nothing could be better, it was with this airstream that the reindeer came to those places he knew best. He was so eager and walking so fast that it was still dark when he reached the mountains, and when it began to get light he barely noticed because the sky was so leaden. It would be impossible to see the reindeer from any distance now, so he followed their old migratory routes, carefully picking his way towards the remains of old trapping pits and what Adolf called *bågåsteller*, stone rings where in a forgotten age folk had lain in wait with bows and arrows and shot at the herd as it passed. Throughout his life, Adolf had noted the location of these traps, for together they formed a map of the reindeer's migration routes. Hunters had discovered their migratory routes thousands of years ago, and, just as the reindeer had continued to follow them, so Jehans followed them now. But he did not see a single animal, he only heard the ravens chattering as he passed the hut at Saubua that provided shelter for shepherds and hunters.

The weather lifted for a moment. He scanned the terrain for cairns and other landmarks, and when he spotted the Suleberg Maidens, three tall rocks standing on a mountain ridge, he knew where he was.

The mist settled again and he walked on, listening out for the trickle of drinking water as he wandered about in a damp, milky-white space with no height or width. Suddenly the ground began to heave beneath him and his boots squelched. He realised he was on a marsh. Crouching down, he saw large golden droplets scattered before him, in increasing numbers the lower he crouched.

Cloudberries. Cloudberries everywhere.

He moved through the mist, picking and eating, with one hand on his rifle so as not to lose it. Later into the afternoon he was still surrounded by fog and had not seen any reindeer, but was certain that the reindeer had seen him. He climbed high up onto the slopes, and, as the weather lifted again, he thought he saw a calf go over the brow of a little hill and disappear. Jehans continued up the hill until he was level with it, and sat down with his binoculars. A gust of wind ruffled his hair and lapels. He felt some distaste for this contraption. Perhaps it was the work of an illusionist. Entire chunks of the mountainside seemed to be torn off and brought closer to him in a display created entirely for him that was gone as soon as he lowered the binoculars, and returned when he looked through them again. The view of the mountain was yellowing and blurred at the edges, and the crack in the lens distorted half the image.

But everything was drawn closer. Everything was in view. As though he himself was bigger. As though he was looking through the eyes of an ancient giant.

The reindeer were probably close by. Jehans assumed the calf had been a straggler from a larger herd, and he walked against the wind up towards Kvia, the three great mountains that plunged down into Imsdalen. Most of the slopes were so steep that only birds could settle on them, but in better weather it was possible to find paths that led down towards the farmsteads.

He walked on. Thought he glimpsed the herd, lifted the binoculars and saw what looked like movement through the fog, wondered whether his eyes or perhaps the binoculars were deceiving him. He walked on. It was getting late, and he had already gone rather too far, there were no shelters here in which to spend a night. Suddenly a gust of wind drove away the fog, and he found himself looking straight at a beautiful young reindeer bull. It disappeared again and he walked on. He was *determined* to fire the Krag today, *determined* to shoot a reindeer.

Finally, far ahead, he thought he saw a female, but in seconds she had merged into the mountainside. He put away the binoculars and continued in the old way, walking against the wind and spending the whole evening closing in. He had no idea where he was when he finally got the young bull in shooting range.

Jehans raised the Krag. Drew a line from his eye to the bull's heart and released the shot. He heard the bang, and felt the short, hard push as the gun recoiled. Over the Krag's barrel, far ahead, he saw the reindeer stagger and keel over, then rise again before it collapsed and lay motionless. The rest of the herd ran on a short way before they stopped in amazement at this thing that had happened, and which they could not understand.

Jehans went over to the young bull, put the Krag in the heather and knelt down.

He sat there for a long time, the shot ringing in his ears. And in that moment – when the bull's eyes went dull and had no delineated pupils, nothing but a blue-grey depth, an opaque form that could not be compared to anything – it felt as though it knew something about him. As though in this moment the two of them came into a wisdom that was infinite in time and space, where the animal was no longer limited to eating grass or stabbing its foe, but belonged to a shared realm of animals and humans with mutually intelligible thoughts. This was not true while the reindeer lived, then each moved in their own reality, but during these few minutes he felt he could see the reindeer sink back into a terrain of its own far away, one he could vaguely see into and hear from, but neither understand nor interpret.

He managed to gut the reindeer before nightfall. He warmed his hands on its entrails, but was soon so cold that his teeth began to chatter. He got some warmth by lying next to the reindeer, and would have liked to skin it in the dark and wrap himself in the hide, but feared that he would end up cutting himself badly, which was more dangerous than the cold.

It was just as Adolf had said. It takes a second to shoot a reindeer and two days to carry it home.

He had done almost everything Adolf had warned him against: shot an animal late at night, without quite knowing where he was, so deep in the mountains that it was impossible to carry his kill home in the time that was left.

It was night. He realised that he could not hold out in the wind and rain. If he waited any longer, the reindeer would be completely cold and it would be harder to tear the skin off. Groping his way forward he managed to skin it in the dark. Or rather, he waved the knife about and managed to cut the hide free so it hung together here and there.

He took off his wet clothes, wrapped himself in the hide, wrung out his clothes and put them back on. Then he sat like that, unable to see his Krag or his bag or the reindeer carcass. Feeling his way forward again, he ate tiny pieces of raw meat, and when morning finally came, it only brought more rain and no sun to give warmth. The carcass and hide were a mess from his attempt at skinning it in the dark. The meat looked as though it had torn at by a wolverine, the hide lay in shreds.

It was no good.

Exhausted, wet and hungry, he lacked the strength to carry it. In the pale morning light he pinned the kill down with rocks. Then, taking strips of linen from his rucksack, he fixed them to the top of the pile of rocks so they fluttered, since he had no idea where he was, and it would be nearly impossible to find it again. He was so cold his whole body was shaking as he walked haphazardly along the slope and looked out over the landscape. Somewhere below him was Imsdal, although it was little help to know that, since Imsdal was huge, as was the distance between each farm. The rocks slipped from under him as he struggled down the scree slope. His rifle butt suffered its first scratches, and that grieved him. The only viable plan was to get down into the valley in the hope that he would meet somebody. He followed the slopes, so exhausted and cold he had lost any sense of direction. But he stopped at the vegetation line.

Smoke.

He sniffed it. The smoke bore a minute hint of pitch, indicating that it came from a chimney rather than a bonfire. It was birch wood and he could smell that it was good and dry, since it had a light spicy aroma, not a sour or heavy smell, telling him that there was a *seter* with a stove nearby, which was all that was needed for his survival.

Jehans pushed on through the wet birch thicket, the smell of smoke coming at him in bursts, he tried to hurry because whoever it was out there must have lit up for the morning, and when the stove got really hot it would no longer smell of smoke and he might lose his way. And then he reached it, the *seter*, a rain-sodden meadow in front of a cabin and a long barn. He opened the door without knocking. The cabin was empty, and he staggered towards the roaring stove.

Thank You, But No Thank You

The morning light shone in through the buckled glass in the small windows. In the corner was an unmade plank bed, and over the kitchen counter coffee cups hung crookedly from their handles alongside wooden spoons and ladles. A pale-green tin dish contained freshly roasted coffee beans, oily and glistening, and the thought of a hot drink made him greedy and faint. He was shivering too much to sit down and he took off his outer clothes, grabbed a sheepskin from the bed and flung it around

145

him. Removed the bolt from his Krag to show it was not ready to fire, stood it in a corner and hurried back to the hearth. His hands trembled over the glowing hot cast-iron stove, and he thought he was hallucinating when a young girl wearing a blue apron came in.

She put two buckets of water on the floor and sighed. His teeth were chattering and he was unable to explain himself. The girl went out again, to get other folk he presumed. He heard the bellowing of cows outside, and moments later she came back in, but alone. She tugged at his arm and told him to come with her outside. He gathered himself and begged to be allowed to sit just a while longer to warm up. "Then I shall be on my way."

"Ye shall come with me. Now."

He padded barefoot after her through the grass and over to a tiny *jordgamme*. Three wooden planks covered the entrance of this earth cabin, and there inside he saw a glowing pile of fist-sized rocks. She said she had taken the embers from under the cheesemaking pan, that it wasn't as hot as it should be, but it would have to do. He should take off his clothes, yes, all of them, and pour on the water from the bucket there. Then she left, closing the hatch behind her. It was dark around him except for the glowing rocks that smouldered and some light from the hole that the smoke had been drawn through. The *jordgamme* barely housed more than himself and the rocks, and he sat huddled over them before taking off his clothes and hurriedly putting them outside. Sitting naked on a sheepskin, he raked some of the rocks away from the pile, poured water on them and let them steam, then washed himself with the cloth in the bucket. The steam penetrated his skin and he came to slowly, like a fly on a windowsill in the spring. His fingers and toes soon pricked and his lips and earlobes burned. He sat there until the glow grew weak and the heat ebbed. Outside he was dazzled by the light and autumn cold. His clothes were gone and he held his hands over his crotch, looked in all directions and hurried over to the cabin. She was not there, but his trousers hung on a cord over the black stove, which burned fiercely, and his jacket was over a chair. He lay on the bed, pulled a sheepskin over him and only vaguely noticed her scent on the pillow and the sound of water droplets fizzing on the stove.

He woke to the smell of porridge.

She had seated herself with her back to the wall so that the table stood between them, and on it a small axe lay crosswise like a dessert spoon. He gazed at her through half-open eyes. He had never seen a girl eat so quickly, yet so nicely. When her porridge bowl was half-eaten she rose, taking the axe.

He raised his head, thanked her and apologised for the bother.

"Happen I've nowt better to do than tend to a daftish reindeer hunter."

"How d'ye know I be a reindeer hunter?"

"From all that blood on your arms."

"Oh."

"An' I can tell ye be daftish when ye shoot so late in the night that ye canna' get down from the mountain."

Daftish. That was not something he had heard very often.

"I were over keen," he said. "Didna' think."

"Aye, just like I said. Daftish. Nay need to tell me that ye didna' think!"

She told him to sit up in bed, and, still holding the axe, she handed him his bowl of porridge and the wooden spoon she had eaten with herself. Then, pulling a stool into the middle of the room, she gathered her skirts and sat with the axe handle resting on her thigh. He mustn't get any ideas, she had a nigh on spotless reputation to protect, and if the other milkmaid came back and found a naked man in her bed, folk would dish out gossip like freshly soured cream, and she wasn't about to sacrifice her honour for some reindeer hunter. Especially one so daftish.

"Aye, well," he said. "But that earth mound. That cabin. With the hot rocks? What kind of a thing is that?"

"We calls it a *finlands-bu*. Rids thee o' lice."

He swallowed hard and said, "Lice? I do nay have lice."

"Not anymore. Nay."

He ate and ate. Was tired. He fell back and nodded off. Was woken by a thunderous noise. She was churning butter.

"Are ye doin' that in here?" he said.

"Aye. Ye had all my hot embers from the dairy hut."

Over by the black stove, his clothes had stopped dripping. She was standing by the wooden churn that reached her waist, plunging the stick up and down, beating and beating, without pause. She peered inside the barrel and continued.

"'Tis mighty stubborn. And that be good," she said.

"How can *that* be good?"

"'Tis good *today*. For else I mun wed thee. And naebody wants to wed a foolish reindeer hunter."

He laughed and felt connected with her. He and the other young folk in Butangen also joked about the old customs. Folk had thought, actually *believed*, that if a boy came to the *seter* just as the cream turned to butter, this was the boy the dairymaid would marry.

"But this here is stubborn and will nay turn. And 'tis well."

"Aye, ye said so."

"Aye, I said so."

She was younger than him, but how much younger was impossible to tell, for as she toiled over the butter she was as fierce as all the farmers' wives he had ever known, and only when she occasionally stopped to look at him did her face soften.

It was raining again, and she bustled back and forth constantly, refusing any help and talking as though she wanted him gone. When she finally left the cabin to see to the cows, he forced himself up and put on his thick homespun trousers and jacket. They were damp and stuck to his skin, but warm, and he got his boots on, swung his Krag over his shoulder and went out into the rain.

He found the path through the birch forest and set out on the slope up to the mountains. Visibility was poor. He covered the distance in long strides, but could not find the reindeer carcass. With the wind beating against him, he searched and searched among the rocks before he suddenly heard the squawk of a raven, and following the sound he glimpsed the strips of white linen. He did not recognise this place at all. But this was unquestionably it. There was the hide, ripped to pieces, and the raven had been here, and pecked at the flesh.

The kill must have weighed nearly sixty kilos, and though he could just about lift it, it was always the last ten kilos that ruined folks' backs. He hacked off its haunches and the best cuts from its back and lashed them to his packframe. Lifted the loaded frame onto his back and started walking.

Two hours later he was down at the *seter* again, and this time there was smoke rising from the dairy hut. He hung up the haunches and shoulders in the woodshed before going in to her. This time she said nothing, just looked up from the butter churn, and as he went closer, he saw that the cream had just turned into butter.

"This meat," she said. "All o' this meat?"

"'Tis a gift."

"A gift?"

"Aye, for thee and the farm too. As a thank you. I'd have met my end w'out thee."

"Thanking thee kindly. But ye mun carry it home. Or go down to Imsdalen and try to sell it there. This *seter* doesna' belong to my family. I be nowt more than a *hired* dairymaid, and I have nay wish to explain how fifty kilos o' reindeer meat

149

came to hang i' the woodshed, or that there were a man here this night, and, worse still, that he paid for himseln! Be this your first try at butchering?"

"Nay. But I skinned it in the dark and wrapped myself in its skin so as not to freeze to death."

"Happen ye put on its antlers too?"

She turned back to her work. He observed that she was using old tools, and she told him that the farmer had promised her a milk separator, but whether he'd not bought it, or bought it then lost it at poker, there was no separator, leastways she could not see one, could he? In earlier years, she'd had a crank churn, which even a foolish reindeer hunter could have cranked, but the farmer's wife had taken it back down to the village, and all she had now was this unwieldy old churn.

She paid him scant attention. He was grudgingly allowed to go out for water and juniper twigs, which she boiled up to make wash water, so its smell filled the hut together with the smell of butter. There was a dead fly in the water, so she fetched the next bucketful herself, since she would use it to cool the butter which she then rolled in a cloth and squeezed before she kneaded and salted it, patted it into a hexagonal mould and cut crosses on the top to keep the butter free of any odious or evil power. Later she said she did not believe in these old superstitions, and only did it in honour of the two old women from whom she had learned the skills of the *seter*, but he wasn't wholly convinced when she took the time to strain all the milk through a bear's skull to keep rogue bears away from the cows.

He eventually nagged her into letting him help by chopping and splitting the wood, which was brought up from the village to the *seter* in triple lengths for ease of transport. He kept himself to himself in the woodshed, since sawing and chopping was all she would let him do, while she continued to stoke the fire, cook, clean and churn, with her front door open. At last she stopped, wiped away the sweat with her forearm, looked out at the weather, and said: "'Tis clearing up now, so ye mun go home. For I shall make *feitost* tomorrow, and that be fiddliest of all."

Her name was Kristine Messelt and she had been coming up to this *seter* every summer from the age of six, and since the age of fourteen had been the sole dairymaid employed here. The *seter* was part of the Messelt farmstead in Østerdalen, and owned by a distant branch of her family, whose lives were as different from hers as their wallets. Her ancestors had been bear hunters and wanderers, but her great-grandfather had cleared a small land-holding in Imsdal, which the local bailiff rented out to him for an annual payment of twenty-eight skilling. She was the young-est of eight and had been sent to work on one of the Imsdal farms that hired dairymaids.

"We should have been two dairymaids up here," she said, leaving Jehans to wonder what had become of the second. But whatever the case, she was alone up here, and he really ought to introduce himself now.

"Hekne?" she exclaimed. "So, 'tis a fine man I have visiting me? And I thought the Hekne *odelsgut* were a mere stripling?"

It was something he had encountered before. Girls who heard his name and presumed he was the Hekne *odelsgut* – the young heir and future master of Hekne. They had a certain look in their eyes, these girls; acquisitive, yet keenly flirtatious. A secure future. Whether the boy was an idiot or dribbled when he ate mattered not a jot. It was the *farm* these girls were marrying.

But Kristine Messelt had only asked him because she felt that an *odelsgut* was beyond her reach. Something he could cer-tainly relate to, since an *odelsgut* could not be further from what he actually was. And this was now being turned on its head into an advantage.

He was *not* beyond her reach.

"I were born out o' the family," he said. "My mother were the oldest Hekne girl, but she died when I were born."

It was like pulling a tooth and poking at the edges of the hole. He told her that he had lived briefly at Hekne as a small child. That the farm was now run by his uncle, that a lot had changed after his grandfather had died, but he had been too young to understand, and it was irrelevant to him anyway, since he was living at Halvfarelia by then.

"How did he die? Your grandfather?"

"He were kicked by a horse at Stav Market."

"Ought not t' be allowed to take a rutting stallion to Stav."

"How did ye know it were a rutting stallion?"

"Cos he kicked. And cos ye be o' *fine* folk."

"But I told thee, I am not o' fine folk."

"Ye be o' fine folk because ye shun talk o' stallions with womenfolk at table. Fine folk d' nay have to be grand folk. But tell me about the others down at Hekna."

"I remember Emort best. My uncle. He came to see us a few times at Halvfarelia. And I think my grandfather were there too. But he went to America with his brother, Laurits."

"And your grandmother?"

"Happen she mostly sits indoors and gives orders."

She nodded towards the rifle and asked if he had stolen or borrowed it, and he told her about the reindeer hunt and the Englishman and what had happened afterwards.

"So," Kristine said, "ye shoot the biggest bull reindeer ever seen in these mountains, sell it to a foreigner who has shot it too, buy yerseln a hunting rifle worth a year's wage o' a free worker, and the next day ye threaten yer uncle with a scythe-chase and forfeit the agreement that permits thee time to use yer new gun."

"Aye, that's about it."

"Dear Lord! I knew ye were daftish, but I mun find another word for thee now. Harum-scarum, that's what ye be."

She had twelve cows to milk and the milk of twelve cows to make into cheese and butter and sour cream, and she measured her breaks by the shafts of sunlight on her window ledge, as the shadow from a muntin hit the notches cut into it to mark each hour. The shadow had slipped past one of these notches. The sun was shining, the grass was steaming in the heat, and he could get to Saubua comfortably before dark. He asked if he might make himself some food, cook some of the meat, he would need something now and for the trip if he was to make it in the mountains with his loaded packframe, and he'd be happy to cook for her too. She went to the dairy hut to boil up some water and wash the wooden troughs and the milk pails.

Jehans had spotted some yellow mushrooms in the birch forest and went to pick them. She had a patch of mountain potatoes beyond the woodshed, there was a hoe sticking up in the ground and he continued in the furrow she had been digging. The potatoes were small but golden, perfectly oval and firm, he washed them in the stream and in the cabin he boiled them in water with nothing floating in it.

He cut two fine backstrap fillets from along the reindeer's spine, laid them out on the pine bench and pounded them with a stripped log. He found a pat of butter in the cupboard, as golden as only butter from cows that had grazed on summer pastures could be, and wondered if this was the butter she had been churning when he came down with the meat that he was about to carry back up.

When the cast-iron pan was piping hot, he melted the butter and fried the meat just as he used to in the mountains, but there the wind carried the smells away. What spread in the cabin now was the fragrance of the mountains and farm and autumn, but also the domestic smells of everything that the cows, the earth, the wild game around them gave – meat, potatoes and sour cream – and of floors scrubbed with gravel from the stream and wooden ladles washed in juniper.

He fried the mushrooms and tossed the potatoes in the frying pan until they were glossy and brown, put the pan on the table and found the sour cream, filled two glasses with stream water and held them up to the window to make sure there were no flies in them, and finally wiped the hunting knife with which he had prepared the food and stuck it in its sheath before going outside to shout that it was ready when she was.

Butter, meat, mushrooms, potatoes. Hope on a plate.

She came in and looked at the table. Gathered her skirts and sat with her back to the wall.

Jehans looked at the windowsill where his Krag stood, and through the window he saw the meadows and mountains into which he would soon walk and disappear. She followed his gaze and they saw the same things.

A barn, a mountain and a Krag.

Glory be!

She Were So Bonny

It was an ordinary Thursday evening in January 1904. Uneventful and quiet, silhouetted in the blue darkness stood the parsonage, its usual white-painted self, with a neat snow-cleared courtyard and lamplight flickering behind the occasional window. Supper was out of Oldfrue's dullest repertoire – a pallid-looking soup made with a suspiciously meatless pork knuckle. Later in the evening the youngest daughter of the parsonage's farmer brought the supplies of milk and eggs into the kitchen, Herr Røhme carried in water and firewood, and Schweigaard sat in front of a hearty fire in the sitting room. The parsonage was terribly cold and draughty, but the walls in here were painted red, making the room feel warmer. In his lap was a novel by Kinck. He had nearly finished the first chapter when the silence – which he had felt all winter had a strange underlying murmur – was broken by voices in the hallway.

A night visitor.

Probably a death. With it being so late. Or an illness. Certainly nothing good.

He put down his book and listened. Wrenched his feet away from the footstool, reluctant to abandon a brilliant opening chapter. But nobody knocked on the sitting room door. Instead he heard Oldfrue calling for Herr Røhme, then footsteps and voices fading down the hallway towards the other wing.

Schweigaard returned to his book and was well into the next chapter when he heard Røhme's familiar knock on the door – two sharp raps with his middle knuckle and a long pause between – in contrast to Bressum's slap-dash banging with her fist.

Røhme was there in the doorway, but did not come in. In the darkness behind him, Schweigaard thought he glimpsed a stranger, but it turned out to be Oldfrue Bressum trying to see what was going on.

"S-sommat has happened," said Røhme.

"Oh? Who was that?"

Røhme stepped inside, shut the door on Bressum and stared at the floor.

"Her. Her f-from Dovre."

"Dovre? Widow Stueflaaten?"

Schweigaard was uncomprehending.

"Nay," Røhme said, "her maid."

"Her *maid*? She's here?"

"In m-my room. She be bursting wi' shame."

Kai Schweigaard got up. "I see. This isn't good."

"Nay."

"So something happened in Dovre that night?"

"Aye. Sh-she were so b-bonny."

"Oh, but really, Røhme!"

"S-sorry! But I d-do na' want to go. I want to stay. As church-warden. With thee. But I canna' stay now. Not after I have been so wicked."

"This girl. Do you like her?"

"I wrote her a letter. But got no answer. So I reckoned nowt would come of it. That she weren't fond of me."

"A letter?"

"Aye. Two long letters."

Schweigaard began to pace the room. Hands behind his back.

"S-seems she canna' read nor write," Røhme continued. "Told me so just now. But there be nowt else wrong wi' her. She has the whole kitchen rulebook here – in her head."

Schweigaard stopped suddenly. "The sour cream porridge? The roast mutton? Were they her doing?"

"Aye."

"And the delicious lunch we were given for our journey home? Her doing?"

"Aye."

"What's her name?"

"Lilleseter. Gyda Lilleseter."

Schweigaard pretended to be mulling things over, but was really just stretching time so it looked as though he was having trouble knowing how best to advise Røhme in such a situation.

"The reading and writing may reflect nothing but poor teaching. Besides, we must consider your child now, Røhme. And Frøken Lilleseter. And your position here as churchwarden."

"Aye."

"Wait here, Røhme. Keep the fire going."

Schweigaard popped his head round the kitchen door and asked Oldfrue to heat up a large cup of cocoa. He crossed the hallway in rather a hurry, but slowed down as he approached the other wing, so his footsteps would sound more amiable and less threatening. He knocked, and recognised the maid from Stueflaaten immediately he opened the door. She was sitting with her head in her hands. Shiny, corn-gold tresses flowed between her fingers. She was dissolved, with shame, tears and exhaustion from the long journey.

"Hello and welcome, Frøken Lilleseter."

Probably not quite the right thing to say in the circumstances. He cleared his throat and sat down on a stool. "My dear. I can see that this has all been very sudden. As it often is for many people. You did right to come here."

"I'm not a bad girl," she sobbed.

"No, of course not – things just run away with us at times. Tell me. Do you still work for Widow Stueflaaten?"

"I do *now*," she sniffed. "But – with a misbegotten babby – as ye know – it in't proper."

"Come now. Listen to me. I'll arrange a room so you can stay here tonight. I'll give Herr Røhme some time off tomorrow, so the two of you can have – a conversation."

"A conversation?"

"Yes. The two of you need to decide what to do. Although it's actually very simple. When two people like each other and make a child together, they get married."

"But I can never be wed!"

"What?"

"I were never confirmed. That be the nub o' my misfortune. I canna' read my letters. I can see them alright, but they mean sommat different depending on how I look at them. So our

157

pastor didna' even let me take the public test. I be daft-headed! Daft-headed in *that* way. The worst way o' all."

Schweigaard comforted her and calmed her. "The law has changed, Frøken Lilleseter. Besides which, I can probably teach you to read, a little at least. There's been more than one private confirmation carried out at the parsonage here."

Hearing Oldfrue Bressum in the hallway, he went out and took the cup from her before shooing her away. As Gyda Lilleseter drank her cocoa she collected herself, lifted her head and met his gaze.

"Forgive me," she said. "I be all of a tumble. This in't my usual self. Father boasts about how hardy I be. 'Tis just this business o' reading. It addles me. And it makes me so chary. And then along comes this Røhme fellow, and he were a bit strange too like me, not a dullard, no, just a bit like me. And it just happened. It were my first time. The pastor mun believe me. I in't a bad girl. But I felt so warm inside. Not like that, though aye, like that too . . ."

She burst into tears again. "And now I shall give birth to a bairn who can neither read nor talk properly."

"No, not at all. Such shortcomings are rarely inherited. But it's natural for parents to worry."

"It just happened! He were so – bonny."

"Yes, he said the same about you."

"He did?"

"Indeed. Listen. This is all very sudden for you both, but I sense a real love here. These things generally end in a lifelong, happy marriage. Now, now, stop crying. I have more than twenty years' experience as a pastor and some insight. And I can certainly vouch for Herr Røhme being a kind, hardworking and honest man. I don't want to lose him, but neither can I have a warden who doesn't live according to the Bible."

"We were so smitten!"

"Yes. I can see that. And I have a suggestion, Frøken Lilleseter. Marry Herr Røhme and move in here."

"Here? At the parsonage?"

"Yes. A post has recently come vacant – for a new oldfrue. You'd have full responsibility for the kitchen and meals here. One of the wings of this house has been empty for over twenty years. You can have three rooms there in part payment of your salary. A sitting room, a nursery and a bedroom. With a lick of bright paint, it'll make a – a pleasant enough home. Truth is I've craved a little bit more life, especially the sight of children here in the parsonage."

"But what about your old cook? Oldfrue who let me in?"

"I won't throw her out. Of course not. She'll keep her room. There'll probably be the odd skirmish, but I'll get her to take a pension. No, I suspect it'll be harder to smooth your mistress's feathers. After all, Frue Stueflaaten will lose her best cook."

Reindeer Are Never Where They Were

The next summer was an agony for Jehans. Osvald decided that the old barn should be demolished and the roof slates salvaged, so two men would have to go up onto the roof and one of them had to be Jehans, since Osvald needed someone he could trust, he had said laughing. Adolf had trouble walking these days, and Ingeborg had started to have dizzy spells, so that Jehans had to look after Halvfarelia on his own. Meanwhile, the Krag hung unused from the coat hook in the shed.

Then came the rain. Too much and for too long. The grass lay flat and the earth squelched wherever he walked. Ingeborg stood in the potato field and said it was going to rot. The hay-making was delayed, and after Jehans had worked from dawn to dusk nonstop for three weeks, Osvald finally let himself be persuaded into giving him two days off to go hunting. That same night, while Adolf and Ingeborg slept, he walked out into the dewy autumn grass and up to the birch-belt. He was carrying the Krag and his father's fishing rod. He walked over to the *seter*, but Kristine seemed uneasy and strange. He had visited her that spring and one Sunday in June. It was an eight-hour walk to the *seter* from Butangen, but the days were long and he had arrived by moonlight and left by moonlight and had never felt lighter or stronger.

But now he realised she was not alone. "Be things the same?" he said, with a pang of jealousy. "'Twixt us?"

She said it was. There was a clanking sound near the dairy hut, and Jehans saw it was the farmer, and understood, from what the man said, that Kristine now had help from another dairymaid.

Kristine said she would rather be alone, with double the work and Jehans to slow her down. "I should much rather have it so," she said, straightening her apron. "Much rather."

"To have a place of yer own," he said, changing the Krag to his other hand. "However small."

"However small," she replied. "But yer own. Do ye recall the meal ye made us that day? Do ye recall that, Jehans?"

They managed a kiss behind a sun-baked wall, and some hours later he was up by Saubua without having seen a single reindeer, but he did not get a wink of sleep though the morrow would be his last hunting day.

Kristine had slipped him some potato pancakes, cheese and butter tied up in a cloth. He had never tasted anything so good. As though their flavour was infused with the sun's warmth, the babbling brook, the lush grass and mountain air, and the slow amble of cows. The cheese and sour cream were made according to the recipes and methods of the old wives who had taught her, but she had added little touches of her own over time.

Yet everything she made was taken down from the *seter* and sold by the kilo with the farmer's mark, so that nobody who ate her sour cream or her butter or cheese ever knew the name Kristine Messelt.

He could get two or three kroner for a big reindeer. A fairly good price for fine meat, but loose change compared to what he and Kristine would need to get a farm of their own.

It was all so impossible. So damned oppressive. The whole world felt like one huge storm-laden sky that filled with thunder and lightning the instant he tried to break free. Censure in everything, pain and anger in everything. A high fence around a place from which they could never escape. He had nothing to offer her and all that awaited him was work and more work. Shouldn't it offer *more*, this life of theirs? The Krag had been supposed to change everything, but had not. Where had it gone, the spark he had as a child, when he was excited by his science books, or fired up for days after a lecture about electric coils and magnets? When he had built his raft and dreamed of raising the bell?

It was one thing to challenge a legend. It was quite another to challenge reality.

He was only half aware of his surroundings and careless of the hunger that was gnawing at him, a similar hunger to that which he had felt on the morning he had shot the reindeer bull under Jammerdalshøgda.

The day rolled on.

All about him the mountains stood grey and brown, the weather did not shift, neither did the colours, and still the mountains were empty. His mind wandered on to the Englishman, and he decided to find the place where the reindeer bull had fallen. He had been walking for some hours, when he caught sight of four grey tents, and there, at the end of the southernmost Breitjønnet, he saw a man crouched by the water. Three other men and a packhorse were leaving the camp.

He lifted his binoculars. The damage to the lens meant that only half the image was sharp, the rest was broken up and twisted into the colours of the rainbow. It was as though he was watching another human being in another world. Yet it seemed this man sensed that somebody was close, since he kept looking up as he filled his kettle.

Was it him? *Him?* This year again?

Jehans stood up so he could be seen, and then, so as to be heard, he kicked a pebble so it clattered loudly. The man got up and grabbed the binoculars that hung round his neck. But then the impulse seemed to fade, and he let go of the binoculars before he had lifted them to his eyes. Jehans recognised himself in this action, he too found it ill-mannered to look at another man through binoculars when he had already made eye contact.

The Englishman walked towards him. He was carrying the same rifle as before, but was wearing new hunting clothes, grey breeches and a darker, half-length jacket with big external pockets.

Jehans held out his hand in greeting and the Englishman took it in his, placing his other hand on Jehans' shoulder.

"Is it really you, Herr Hekne?" he said, in confident Norwegian. "You may remember my name? Harrison?"

"I remember," Jehans said. "*Victor* Harrison."

"I see you've got a different rifle this year?"

Jehans lifted the Krag from his shoulder and said he had. And that it had cost fifty-four kroner and sixty øre.

They found it easier to understand each other this year. Victor explained that he'd stayed in Kristiania for a few days to purchase some equipment and revive the language he had mastered as a child. He'd planned to go hunting alone, but had bumped into two Englishmen at the hotel with fishing rods and rifles, and it had been hard to say no when they suggested taking the train up north together. Hence the three tents.

"We got hold of a packhorse in Ringebu and a guide," said Victor. "Though I'm not sure how good a guide he really is. The others have gone to look for reindeer. I preferred to stay behind and fish. And I've my rifle at hand just on the off-chance."

"Canny," Jehans said. "They can be there mighty sudden. These reindeer."

"Well, I've not caught any fish here, so I was thinking of going over to the other lake," Victor said, nodding towards the hill behind them. "Any in that one?"

"There be fish in them all," Jehans said. "But ye may not *find* fish in them all."

"And the reindeer?"

"Not here in the mountains now. The wind hasna' been right for them."

"Ah. So they might be anywhere."

"Nay, not anywhere," said Jehans. "There be one stead only a reindeer can be and that be where it be."

The Englishman turned this over in his mind and smiled. He got up and went into his tent to fetch something. Came back out and saw to the campfire.

They must have brought the firewood with the packhorse, because the logs were of lowland birch rather than the moss-covered mountain birch, they burned easily and cleanly and soon the water in the sooty kettle had come to the boil. Victor fetched a small brown pot out of which he scraped some wet grains before rinsing it out with hot water and pouring in a dry, grainy substance, coarser than coffee. When his back was turned, Jehans scooped up the discarded grains from the moss and put them in his pocket, thinking they might retain some flavour.

Victor said something about tea and its coming from their own plantation, but immediately realising that the word was unknown to Jehans, and not wanting him to feel awkward, he rattled on about "fields", "crops" and "harvest".

"I know nowt about tea," Jehans said. "But 'tis a welcome sup now."

Tea drunk, they started to compare guns. Jehans observed the similarity between the way they both sat, each man with the butt of his rifle resting against his thigh and his left hand clasping the barrel. He changed his hold on the rifle when his companion looked the other way.

Victor praised the Krag's magazine construction, and they showed each other their respective cartridges. The Krag used a 6.5 × 55 and the Rigby a .256 Mannlicher, the difference was minute, but the rifles would explode if they swapped.

"I see you've bought yourself a fishing rod too?" Victor said.

"Hmm?"

"Your fishing rod," he said, pointing at Jehans' case. "Isn't that a fishing rod in there?"

"Oh, that. Aye, 'tis my fishing-gad. It belonged to my father."

"May I look?" Victor said, and getting a little nod in reply, he proceeded to open the leather tube and pull out the canvas case that held the six-piece fishing rod. Then he spotted the slanted, white lettering over the cork handle and exclaimed, "This was made by the Hardy brothers! In Alnwick!"

"Oh?"

"They're not far from us in Northumberland! Father and I have shopped with them a few times. Let me see now . . . a Smuggler? I'm not familiar. A prototype perhaps. It must be one of the first rods they produced, because I can see from the rod rings that it pre-dates 1885. A brave choice at the time."

"Why?"

"They're a major manufacturer now, but they were just one of many rod makers in England back then. So you'd have to be a bit of an expert to distinguish a good rod from a bad one. He knew his fly-fishing, your father. May I assemble it?"

Jehans wanted to say no, but said nothing.

The stranger handed the rod back. "I'm awfully sorry," he said. "Forgive me. I was too eager. Fishing rods are a very personal thing. I inherited my grandfather's. He was a dry-fly fisherman. Father generally goes for the salmon. But that's not the point. The point is that old fishing rods are very personal. And I do apologise."

He was about to roll up the inner cloth case when Jehans said, "Nay. Go ahead. Set it together and try it."

Picking up their guns and rods they walked to Inner Breitjønnet. The line on Jehans' reel had dried out when he was a boy and he had replaced it with an ordinary line with a hook for live bait.

Victor had two reels of fresh lines and tried not to feel some disgust – leastways not so it was obvious to Jehans – at the idea that he had used worms on a fly-fishing rod. Victor was not the type of man to revel in the plight of others. Any well-heeled Butangenite would have said that it was *surely just a matter of buying a new line?* and then waited for Jehans' humiliation when he was stumped for an answer.

Jehans watched Victor make loose casts in the air with the Smuggler, like drawings in the sky, which melted away in an instant.

A sense of joy entered him, but also of unease. And a feeling that was utterly unfamiliar. A spark, a force, and soon a sense of surrender.

He felt a deep affection.

Something between his feelings for Kristine Messelt and for Adolf.

He had heard of it, men who liked men, but surely that wasn't the kind of affection he felt now. If so, he should leave right away.

But he didn't move. He wanted this moment to last.

Nobody else had ever been allowed to touch his father's fishing rod. Now he watched in admiration as Victor swung it and then let it come into its own, he had a strength and a suppleness that suited this method of fishing, an ease and control. The pale-yellow line flew out of the rod rings and drew letters against the sky, a U that turned into a J before it moved forward again.

Victor handed the Smuggler back to him and suggested he try it, but the line just fell in a tangle of rings on the water or tumbled to the ground behind him.

"You don't stop sharply enough," Victor said. "Imagine the rod is a stick with an apple at the top. You want to throw it as far as possible. So, you have to stop sharply, at precisely the right moment as you swing forward, so that the apple is flung off. Yes, that's it!"

Jehans sensed that the Englishman was wondering why his father hadn't taught him how to cast, since he'd obviously given him the rod, and he explained that he had died of pneumonia before he was born.

"My father came from Germany," Jehans said. "An architecture student."

Victor went quiet. He offered his condolences, took his own rod and showed Jehans the stages of a good fly-fishing cast. Jehans tried to copy him, oscillating between the desire to master this new technique and going off to fish with live bait.

The fish stopped biting before Jehans even managed to cast his line. But Victor caught two handsome trout with Gerhard Schönauer's Hardy Smuggler, and surprised Jehans still further by releasing the smaller of the two back into the lake.

They returned to the camp, lit a fire and grilled the fish, and as they ate in silence Jehans noted that they had shared out the work without exchanging one word.

Eventually Victor cleared his throat and asked if Jehans might consider being their mountain guide for a week. Lead them to the reindeer. The money would be good.

"Thanking ye. But 'tis impossible. I mun get back to the village tonight. To fulfil a contract."

He said nothing more and certainly made no mention of the fact it was a swingeing contract signed by his own uncle.

There was some movement a way off. A horse and three men were walking towards them. Jehans got up and said he would be on his way.

"You're welcome to stay."

"Nay, I shall be gone afore they get here."

Victor handed him back the Smuggler and they shook hands.

"Damn shame you can't take the job. I could offer you – a great deal of work."

"Aye, but I canna' do otherwise. What have ye thought t' do now?"

"I think we'll each spend the evening scouting a different area, then meet up again, and if one of us has seen any reindeer, we'll hunt them together."

"Nay. Ye mun move in right away. Reindeer are ne'er where ye last saw them."

"Then I think I'll go alone and look for them. I'd prefer that anyway. Which direction would you walk in?"

Jehans checked the wind and pointed up towards Øverlihøgda. He would, he said, perch up there and keep a lookout until there was too little light to shoot, and then go back early next morning.

"Excellent. Goodbye, then, Hekne. And, once again, I can put some work your way."

"Thanking thee, Mr Harrison. In another life perhaps."

*

Jehans had been walking for an hour when he came across the female reindeer. She was standing there, calm, motionless, boulder-like, alone. He knelt down, took the Krag in his hands and released the safety catch.

The reindeer had seen him, but remained impassive.

No calf in the vicinity. Might she be the herd-mother of a larger group that was resting somewhere?

She did not turn away. An extraordinary beast, with flame-coloured streaks that burst through the areas of grey.

Something forced him up. Something bigger than himself. He stood up straight and looked her in the eye. There were no other reindeer nearby. He put the safety lock back on and held the Krag out towards her. As though he was inviting her to take it. So she could hunt him.

They stood like that for a long time before she took a sideways step. And was gone.

He could make no sense of what he had seen.

The sunlight had faded around him, it had happened suddenly. He turned his face to the wind and studied the colour of the clouds as they approached. They were dark and coming fast. He flared his nostrils, sensed the north wind on the air. There was a storm on its way, possibly a bad one. No doubt the fog would soon be rolling in. He must hurry down to the village to be ready to fulfil his cottar's duties at Hekne early next morning.

If the Englishman was walking up towards Øvelihøgda now, he would never find his way back to the camp. And snow could settle up there even in late August.

Jehans hesitated. He knew there was little time to waste. But as he stood there, he realised that he had to face this storm together with the stranger.

Jehans found him surprisingly fast and thought what he had often thought, that if the reindeer were the hunter and the hunter the prey, the hunter would be dead within an hour. And Victor would have been dead in fifteen minutes, walking as he did along the peaks, so as to be silhouetted against the sky.

"The weather be changing, Mr Harrison!" Jehans shouted.

Victor looked round and and called back that it was surely nothing more than a few little clouds.

"Small now," Jehans said, walking towards him. "The other men. And their guide? Be they back in the camp?"

"My compatriots yes. Our guide, I'm not too sure."

"And they have nae mountain knowledge?"

Victor said they were lawyers who had never been outside England before.

The two men hastened back towards the camp, neither finding anything strange about being together again. The fog was starting to seep in towards them as they walked on, a thin haze near the ground at first, but soon thicker and whiter, more woolly. From a perch they spotted a stretch of water below and heard tent canvas flapping in the wind, and set off in the direction of the sound while a visibility of two hundred metres dropped to one hundred.

The camp was deserted. The fire nearly burned out. Victor had no idea where the others might be. Perhaps they had gone out looking for reindeer after all. Perhaps they were out looking for him.

They yelled into the fog, hands cupped in front of their mouths. Victor took off his knapsack and grabbed his rifle. He took off the safety catch and stuck a finger in his ear, which was, Jehans realised, to prevent his being deafened by the shot, and to catch any response quickly. Gripping the rifle in one hand and aiming it at a patch of damp earth to avoid the ricochet, he fired.

They both stood and listened for any return shouts or gunshots.

The mountain was silent for a long time, before a shot rang out, far behind them.

They reeled round, and Victor cupped his hands over his mouth again and yelled, *Over here!* three times.

There was no answer. He climbed onto a big rock, the slight change of position being enough to make his shape blurrier.

"They canna' be *there*. Surely the shout came from *over there*?" Jehans said, nodding eastwards.

"The wind carries sound. They're more likely to be *there*," Victor said, pointing in the opposite direction. "They can't have got far."

He fired another shot.

This time there was no answer.

"Perhaps they're behind a mountain or something now," Victor said.

Jehans relit the campfire, then cut some juniper twigs and flung them on the flames.

Victor nodded approval. "Yes, with luck they'll smell the smoke."

"The guide," Jehans said. "D'ye reckon he were mostly a mountain-man or a horse-man?"

"I'd say the horse knows that better than us. How so?"

"Happen the horse may find its way here in the fog."

Victor fired two more shots and yelled until he had no more breath, then sat on a rock with his gun laid across his knees and flung a few more logs on the fire.

"They in't coming," Jehans said.

"No."

"With the camp so close by the lake they should try to find their way back to it. Then walk along the shore till they meet us. But sommat has happened."

"Hmm."

"This place, 'tis baffling in the fog," Jehans said. "Even-sized dips everywhere. Looks much the same in every direction."

They decided to go up the nearest slope and shout out again.

Jehans observed how much at home this Englishman seemed in the mountains, always taking long, steady strides between boulders, always maintaining an elevated position in the terrain, even when it might be easier to take a detour down. But they had both neglected to drink, so that Jehans now had a splitting headache and assumed Victor did too. Suddenly Jehans heard wild curses in English, the rattle of rocks and a fall. Victor had taken a tumble and was gasping for breath as he writhed in pain. But the first thing he checked was the sight on his rifle, and only afterwards his foot.

They sat down for a while. Victor tugged up some moss, put it to his mouth and squeezed out the juice. Jehans followed suit.

Suddenly they realised they no longer smelled smoke. They walked about carefully, staying close to one another as they sniffed the air, searching for the fire. Victor began to lose pace. At first he dragged his foot, then began to limp.

"Does it hurt?" Jehans said.

"Yes, it hurts."

"So it be worsening?"

"Oh, hell. I'm sorry."

After a while, Jehans said: "We mun get down to the village fast. Whilst it be light. Follow the slopes down. Happen I can find the path."

"Shouldn't we stay here?"

"Nay. Their horse may go back down alone."

"Why would it?"

"If they be parted from the horse. And then it be *us* who mun call a search."

Victor cursed himself. "They were probably right there. Damn it. Three hundred yards away perhaps. Yet we didn't find them."

"'Tis often the way."

"What if the fog lifts and they find the tent empty? Then they'll go for a good two days thinking I've frozen to death."

"Aye. Every man and woman in our village has gone some days and thought somebody were frozen to death in the mountains."

"Problem being, of course, that they were sometimes right," Victor said.

They agreed to head down to the birch forest, and wait out the night there to see if the fog lifted. If it did, Jehans reckoned they could return to the camp. Depending on Victor's foot.

"What about the work you had to get back for?"

"Nowt I can do about that."

Evening fell, though their only clue was the darkening of the fog. The rain whipped their faces, the wood on their rifles grew shiny with moisture and their clothes clung tight to their bodies.

They sat under an overhanging rock, and it was soon revealed that Victor's injury was worse than he had either realised or wanted to admit. His foot was swollen, he loosened the laces on his boot, and only just escaped having to cut it open to get it off. He had to lean on Jehans as they set off again, and the fog was still as thick. When they eventually reached the birch forest, the branches lashed their faces without them even seeing the trees, but they broke off some dry twigs, and took strips of bark, and, with moss and dirt sticking to their numb fingers, they finally managed to light a fire. In the glow of the flames Jehans saw that Victor had turned ashen grey. Their clothes were impossible to dry, and they were indifferent to their rifles.

The flames danced slowly, and the darkness felt denser than it was. Jehans went out and cut some juniper by the light of the fire. They chewed the berries and threw the branches on the fire. And as the juniper dried out in the heat, it exploded into crackling flames, which flung far and wide and illuminated strange shapes in the surrounding thicket, but when the flames died out, whatever they had seen in the thicket was still there. Victor took out a small metal flask filled with whisky, White Horse whisky he said. They passed it between them three times before it was empty. The fire flared up during the night like a blaze of midwinter sunlight, and while one of them kept watch and tended the fire, the other slept, and thus the night passed as they took turns sleeping in a rhythm that was never discussed, but was nonetheless fixed, as though an anxious mother was watching over them, nudging them each in turn not to let the fire go out.

The fog was equally thick the next morning. Victor had a silver pocket watch, without which they would not have known that it was six in the morning when they started out towards the village. They barely spoke, since Victor's foot was getting worse and talking about it would not make it hurt less. What Jehans failed to mention was that they lost their way in the birch-belt and wasted at least six hours before they were back on course.

Initially Victor tried to walk on his own, leaning on his rifle, leaving ugly scratches on the butt and blued steel. Eventually he found a Y-shaped branch and carved it into a crutch with his knife. But he had no more strength, and Jehans had to support him. Soon it became so difficult for him to walk that Jehans hacked down some young birches and lashed them together with the rope he would normally use to tie up a kill.

A stretcher. Victor tipped himself flat out onto it, saying he felt like the biggest fool ever to have set foot in these mountains. Jehans lashed a rope to the front and hooked the other end over his shoulder and started to drag Victor after him. Progress was slow as the stretcher bumped along the muddy path through the birch forest, with Victor only just managing to cling on.

The pocket watch showed three when they reached a stream, where they filled the old coffee pot with water and drank it dry, then did so again. As Jehans took the pot, Victor reached out for his hand and held it. "Thank you," he said. "Thank you. We got lost, right? Before you made this stretcher?"

"Aye, we did."

"Thank you, Jehans Hekne. You won't regret helping me."

It was evening when they finally approached the village, and they had given up all hope of seeing the others long ago. The stretcher was increasingly rickety, and eventually fell apart, leaving Victor flat out on the ground.

It was a long time before they could talk.

There remained one problem without shape or name in the mountains. Jehans had no desire to drag this man down to Halvfarelia where the old folk would be powerless to help and his abject poverty would be all too obvious. He wanted to be the man he had been up there in the mountains. The free man who was Victor's equal. His value measured by the Krag he carried, by the reindeer he hunted and the fires he lit.

Suddenly he remembered a promise from many years ago, a heavy hand on his shoulder, a man who had offered him unconditional help whenever he needed it, in whatever plight he might find himself. Yes. There was one man who could help.

"'Tis just one quarter mile till we reach folk," Jehans said.

"An English mile or Norwegian?"

"Norwegian, sorry to say."

Victor was unable to put any weight on his leg, so they took the leather straps from their rifles, hitched them together and lashed them round their chests and under their arms, so they were firmly bound to one another. Then, with their arms on each other's shoulders and each carrying a rifle in their free hand, they lumbered on.

Visibility came and went with the changing density of cloud over the moon. At times they could see the cart road as a dark undulating ribbon through the blue-grey light, at other times they had to look up at the strip of night sky between the tree-tops and hope that the road ran at the centre of this gap. Such darkness made progress exhausting and they had barely any strength left when the clouds finally lifted and parted before the moon. In front of them was a clearing, and Jehans recognised Widow Framstad's log cabin. He had been told that nobody lived there now, but he saw someone sitting there on a wooden stool by the grindstone, and for a moment he broke the rhythm of the walk.

No. There was nobody there. Just long grass swaying around the grindstone and stool. They found their rhythm again and limped on, as though in a waltz or carrying something between them.

Gerhard Schönauer Comes Back

Kai Schweigaard tapped his pipe out and went out into the kitchen garden. The apple trees were heavy with ripe fruit. It was usually a pleasure to be here in the evening when the branches were dripping with rain, but there had been uninterrupted rainfall for a long time now. For far too long.

Rain was a blessing, both in moderation and in abundance, but when the earth was waterlogged and the fields of wheat and barley bowed their heads, despair ran through his congregation. They feared a winter of hunger, malnutrition and slow death.

Then they turned to the church.

Which was why, at every service, come spring, summer and autumn, he would sum up the week's weather and its impact on the crops. Such things were incumbent on a wise village pastor. His congregation had no doubt noticed that, after Astrid's death, the religious content of Schweigaard's sermons could be rather half-hearted and vague, but when from the pulpit he shared their joy over its being good sprouting-weather, or that the potatoes were safely in the ground and prayed alongside them for them to grow, they lifted their heads and nodded in heartfelt agreement.

From an open window in the other wing, the cries of an infant could be heard, and all his worries melted away. What a wonderful sound! Fru Røhme had given birth to a strong and healthy boy that summer, a boy who screamed so hard that even his anxious father had to accept that he showed no signs of being a stammerer. Schweigaard had not expected that the arrival of little Simen, whom he was soon to baptise, would have such a strong effect on him too, but the birth had blown the dust out of the old parsonage.

He was wearing a red-brown woollen sweater with a grey acanthus border across the chest. Nobody asked, or would ever ask, where he had got it from, but he had wrestled with his feelings many times before he wore it, particularly since the colours reminded him of those in the pillows. It had come from Dovre by post, and they had not met again, yet she had a terribly sharp eye for his anatomy. The sweater was loose enough to be comfortable, but tight enough to show that he kept his torso and stomach trim. When he eventually tried it on, he felt the old nagging unease, but shook himself and reminded himself of how many years had passed, and that Astrid's grave was, like all the others, under the deep snow, and that the winter was, through its white snowy covering, the time when forgetfulness might be confused with purity.

What she said must surely apply to me too. She said it straight out. As directly as any dead woman could: that there was room for two on a man's ring finger.

He wrote a thank you letter in which, quite unlike himself,

he told her in the first sentence that he was sitting in the sweater she had knitted. She wrote back and reported that she had met with loutish opposition to her theory that the pattern had originated in Scotland. They had exchanged two more letters, but then spring came, and the snow melted from the grave, and he could not continue. It was as if she wasn't dead after all. As if she was waiting for him somewhere.

Schweigaard walked around the corner of the house and looked out over Lake Løsnes. It was ashimmer with silver moonlight now, but all through the day heavy, grey clouds had covered the valley sides.

There were words he rarely used. *Merciless. For God's sake.* But he hoped now, *for God's sake*, that nobody was in the mountains tonight for they would certainly meet a *merciless* fate.

Schweigaard slowed down. Stopped and listened. He heard voices. They were coming down the hillside, and making a peculiar scraping sound as they walked. He went around to the courtyard. In the semi-darkness he saw the old iron gate glide open. Two men staggered in, exhausted, wet and unshaven, clinging to each other.

They limped forward. Two men. Side by side. As though they were somehow welded together. As though they had one foot in common.

And they were coming here. Towards him.

He remembered Astrid Hekne's description of the vision she had seen at Widow Framstad's cottage. That she had seen two men limping, side by side, in rhythm with each other, and then collapsing.

Now he was seeing precisely that.

Shivers went all the way up his spine to the nape of his neck, he stepped back from the vision, bumped into the house wall and pressed himself against it.

The men limped in perfect time, still clinging to each other,

177

over to the large rock by the flagpole. One was Jehans, he could see that now. They leaned against the rock, loosened the straps and glided away from each other in a tangle of legs and arms and weapons, and out of this tangle the second man emerged, and so they were two and not two in one.

But—?

Gerhard Schönauer?

"You?" Schweigaard said, barely daring to go towards them. "Are you alive?"

"Has someone reported him dead?" asked Jehans. "We were—"

Schweigaard did not absorb the rest of what Jehans said. The stranger lacked only a fox-brown coat and an easel; apart from that he was the same architecture student who had stood here in the courtyard early one spring morning in 1880. He was as limp and exhausted as Schönauer had been when he was found along the shores of Lake Løsnes after trying to conceal the Sister Bells.

"Schweigaard?" Jehans said. "Have you met this man before?"

Kai Schweigaard crouched down to look in the man's eyes. His face was wet with warm rain, his body was limp with exhaustion as if he had just been born.

He had Astrid Hekne's eyes.

Jehans and the stranger were not alike. Yet their facial features would strike anyone who had known Astrid Hekne and Gerhard Schönauer. As though noses, chins, eyebrows, mouths, eyes and hair had been shuffled about and randomly bequeathed to each.

Dead! He was dead!

The stranger stared blankly before him. He had difficulty swallowing, and only now did Schweigaard realise how much pain he must be in.

"Do you know him?" repeated Jehans.

"No," Kai Schweigaard said, shaking his head. "I was mistaken. I thought it was someone I knew, but it isn't. What's his name?"

"Victor Harrison. An Englishman. A reindeer hunter."

"A reindeer hunter—"

"Schweigaard!" Jehans said. "Schweigaard, we mun—!" He shook him by the shoulder. "His foot. Look at his foot. He needs a doctor."

Minutes later the parsonage was buzzing with life. Candles were lit in one window after another. The workroom near the kitchen was made into a temporary sickroom. Røhme lit an extra-bright lamp, powered by pressurised paraffin, and Victor's foot was examined. At the other end of the house baby Simen screamed for his milk. Even Oldfrue Bressum was woken up by all the noise and came downstairs in a voluminous, threadbare nightgown that had once been white.

"Bressum," Schweigaard said. "We have two guests who are injured and hungry. Could you put on your apron and bring us a good portion of pork, potatoes and sauerkraut as fast as possible. And fetch some bottles of beer."

"What were that the new pastor said?"

"I said, CAN YOU SEE TO SOME SUPPER? And quickly! A hearty supper! Yes, now! No! Fru Røhme must look after her baby! Yes, I do know what time it is. No, it's not exactly 'the dead of night' yet. It's only eleven o'clock! These young men need some hot food. Yes, now! It's serious!"

Schweigaard returned to the sickbed. The foot was badly swollen. They had wrapped rags around his leg from the ankle to the knee and tied birch bark around the blade of his foot with twine.

"We mun send out a search party," Jehans said. "There were others with him. Two more Englishmen we couldna find.

179

Happen they walked down to a *seter*, for they had a guide and horse with them."

Schweigaard had seen it all before, and knew the drill. A farmhand had to be sent to Fåvang to telephone the sheriff and explain who had last been seen and where, and who might or might not be alive. The next call had to go to the doctor, and then the farmhand would wait down by Fåvang church to give him a lift back to the parsonage in the carriage.

A horse was saddled. A knapsack was filled with food. The parsonage's brightest young farmhand pulled on his best boots and warmest jacket. Schweigaard put some money in an envelope and wrote a list of errands, while Jehans dictated the names of the missing men and the exact location of their camp. Schweigaard himself accompanied the farmhand out to the stable, where a huge Døla horse stood waiting, snorting and whinnying.

The farmer climbed into the saddle and disappeared through the gate into the darkness. The clatter of its hooves died away. Schweigaard shut the gate and stood holding the wrought iron.

His confusion, however, was not so easily shut out. It was as though Jehans had carried his own father down from the mountains. He had returned, without having grown a year older.

Schweigaard went back inside. Jehans' boots were standing in the hallway, soaked through, caked with mud and willow leaves. Wet footprints led from here upstairs to the bedroom that Jehans had used in the old days. Schweigaard knocked on the door, but got no answer. He listened out for voices and found Jehans down in the scullery, trembling before the stove with bare feet and naked shoulders, wrapped in the tartan travel blanket.

"Is't Wednesday today?"

"It was. It's Thursday now."

"I mun get back to Hekne early tomorrow for work."

"Sleep here," Schweigaard said. "My farmer will lend you some dry clothes tomorrow."

"But Ingeborg and Adolf mun—"

"I've seen to that. I sent a message to them earlier."

Oldfrue Bressum was bustling about. She had put on two kettles so the water would boil faster and cut the potatoes into tiny cubes, and now she was waving a chunk of meat and a carving knife about.

Schweigaard quietly beckoned to Jehans to follow. Røhme had decided that the Englishman would be more comfortable upstairs, and the two went up to see him, and found Victor sitting up in bed. A fire was crackling in the stove and Røhme had managed to get a drop of broth into him. He reported how he'd got his clothes off, rubbed him dry and lent him some fresh long johns, but the patient was still sweating, very pale and trembling with the pain.

All three of them knew, but did not say, that the earliest they could hope for the doctor to arrive was midday. But Victor was in pain *now*. His foot was just a swollen lump, topped with little nobs for toes. He screamed out for something that might soothe the pain, and such a drug was now unlocked from the cupboard.

"I bought this last year," Schweigaard said, holding out a medicine bottle. Jehans took it and studied the label with the same eager attention as he had felt in the old days when Schweigaard showed him an interesting object or something in a book. "It's called aspirin," Schweigaard said. "They say it does for the body what prayer does for the soul. But it works for nonbelievers too. I've never used it, but the pedlar said it helps with pain."

"All kinds?"

"Headache, gout, toothache – yes. All the usual."

"'Tis hard to believe. That folk can just take sommat – a powder?"

"Yes, Oldfrue Bressum helps herself to it quite regularly. The greater the pain, the more powder, I think the pedlar said. It came on the market just recently."

181

"What a discovery," Jehans said. "Sommat to carry in yer pocket. Ingeborg should have this for her headaches."

Schweigaard was taken aback. Here was the grown-up version of the Jehans he had known before his confirmation. Quick, talkative, someone who thought about what he said. Without a trace of the silent and morose youth with sweaty shirts and fluffy facial hair.

Jehans went over to the water-bucket in the sickroom. Using the tin scoop he filled a glass and took it to Victor, who was breathing heavily with wide-open eyes. Schweigaard observed the almost surprising confidence with which he took the stranger by the arm, shook him and said something in a mix of English and Norwegian. The glass exchanged hands, rather quickly considering the stranger was so ill, so quickly it was hard to see which hand belonged to whom.

When Jehans handed the medicine bottle back, it was empty.

"What happened to the rest?" Schweigaard asked. "Of the powder?"

"Was he nay meant to have it all?"

"I don't think so," Schweigaard said, trying to decipher the writing on the back. "Oh, well. I've got more in my study."

Røhme tapped Jehans on the shoulder and whispered something. Jehans followed him out and came back wearing Røhme's best clothes: long trousers, a light-coloured shirt and a black-and-white waistcoat that Fru Røhme had knitted before their wedding.

Oldfrue Bressum hobbled in with the supper. The meat and potatoes were very finely chopped so the invalid could be fork-fed. Grumpy and uninterested she set down two plates, but then something stopped her in her tracks, and she stood gawping at the stranger.

She shook her head. Said she must be tired. Very tired.

She sees it too, thought Schweigaard. The similarity. Even she can see it, after twenty years.

Jehans grabbed a plate and tried desperately to get the stranger to eat. Still in the same strange blend of Norwegian and English.

He learned those words here, Schweigaard thought. From me. But there's something different about him. Schweigaard had never observed the capacity in Jehans to be so caring. But some change or other, a huge change at that, must have come over him up in the mountains.

Victor managed to eat a bit, but suddenly closed his eyes and sighed.

Then, falling back with an open mouth, he went into a deep sleep.

Jehans ate his own food and set his plate aside.

"Forgive me, Pastor. For storming in upon you."

"Please, don't call me Pastor," Schweigaard said. "You're always welcome here, no matter for what reason, at any time of the day, you know that. I'm glad you're here. Very glad. But now tell me what you know about this man. Who is he? Why is he here?"

Jehans told him about the hunt last year and about the reindeer they had shot and the money he had spent on a Krag.

Schweigaard leaned forward in his chair. "He's English, you say, but speaks Norwegian?"

"He understands Norwegian well enough. But he'd ginner speak English. Said he once had a nursemaid or sommat from Norway."

Suddenly Jehans' voice trailed off. He lowered his head before shaking himself and straightening back up. Their eyes met and Jehans said:

"I were too impulsive back then. Much too rough with thee."

"You were only fifteen," Schweigaard said. He got up and accompanied Jehans to his old bedroom.

*

The grandfather clock struck two.

Schweigaard had been sitting in the same position since it struck last. The hearth had gone cold and the sitting room was lit by one lonely tallow candle.

This was going to be a difficult night. If this was the brother he thought had died in Kristiania – had the two of them been separated at Astrid's wishes? Or did they just take him?

Up in his study he unlocked the bottom drawer. It was empty apart from a wedding ring case and the letter he had been given at the Birthing Foundation all those years ago. The last thing Astrid Hekne had ever written. The letter paper was lined, and she had started writing in the top left-hand corner, so she undoubtedly had a lot to get off her chest. But all she had managed to write was: *Dearest Kai, Jehans—*

She had taken the time to write *Dearest*. Because she wanted to confide something in him. But the most pressing matter, it seemed, related to Jehans.

He had always thought the words had come out like this because Edgar was dead, but could it be that it was already decided that *he* would take care of Jehans, because Edgar had been chosen to grow up elsewhere? The writing was faint, and he couldn't bring himself to look at the page too closely, but it seemed the next word she had started on began with an *s*. And was it an *h* that came next, before her hand weakened and let go of the pencil? Had she started to write the word *shall*?

". . . shall grow up under your watchful eye," for example?

There was no *and* at least. An *and* that would have been there if he was supposed to look after both children.

Could she really have intended that they follow such different destinies? That they might each reach a greater goal individually than they could together, here at home? Or that they both had to accomplish something first in their respective places to achieve this goal?

Kai Schweigaard had not been so uneasy for years. He sent Røhme off to bed, and paced back and forth in his stockinged feet. He looked in on Jehans and then on the Englishman again. Noted that this man who called himself Victor was lying in the same room as Gerhard Schönauer had lain in when he was ill.

The room in which Astrid Hekne and Gerhard Schönauer had spent their wedding night.

It was impossible to take his eyes off him. He was about the same age as Schönauer had been in 1880, and it was as if he had come here, oblivious that he had torn down Butangen's old church, made Astrid Hekne pregnant, sketched most of Norway's remaining stave churches, sunk the Sister Bells in Lake Løsnes and travelled back to Dresden to die of pneumonia.

Kai Schweigaard's mind continued to whirr. He sat in his study before a tallow candle. Opened the *kirkebok* once more and stared at the page where he had entered the birth of Jehans Hekne. March 23, 1881. On the next line: *Edgar Hekne. Stillborn. Buried in Kristiania*.

He had held an emergency baptism for Jehans on his return home, and a little ceremony in the church for Edgar. But he never quite managed to bury the nagging doubt about what had really happened to him.

He felt tempted at times to take the *kirkebok* to a spiritual medium and summon up Astrid Hekne. To place a pen in the medium's hand and through telepathic writing get an answer as to whether or not he should strike this from the register.

He opened the window, looked out into the night, and caught himself listening for the old church bells.

Perhaps there was only one way to prove who this man was. Through something that lay in the depths of Lake Løsnes.

Or – was there another way to get a sign? With something that had been rediscovered just in time?

He vacillated for a while before suddenly getting up to fetch the two pillows. First Schweigaard went in to the stranger, and laid the goat's hair pillow gently under his head. The Englishman mumbled something incomprehensible before turning his head and falling asleep again. Then he went in to Jehans and placed the other pillow under his head.

Schweigaard sat on a stool in the hallway, midway between the two rooms, in the glow of a tallow candle, and kept watch.

Your Mother Wanted You to Have This

Somebody had come in to the room. Between sticky eyelids Victor could just make out a tall, dark figure adjusting his pillow. The figure stood there and watched him. Footsteps disappeared, a door closed and he noticed before he fell back to sleep that his cheeks were slightly itchy.

When he opened his eyes, the sun was shining through the window. The room was large and bare. A bed and chamber pot. A stool by a desk. A wardrobe. A small stove and log basket. His knapsack and rifle next to a chest of drawers.

They had lent him some pyjamas, blue-striped and worn out. He pulled up one pyjama leg. Dear God. Was that his foot? His leg was covered with burst blood vessels and so bloated it was cylinder-shaped.

But he was alive.

He yanked himself round and put his feet on the floor. The pain came like a shower of electric sparks. Deep stabbing in the sole of his foot, a hammering, toothache-like pain travelling up his thigh.

Faint and in a sweat he hobbled over to the chest of drawers where his Rigby was. Someone, probably Jehans, had laid the hunting rifle across an open drawer, to let the water drip from it freely. He had removed the bolt and oiled the barrel.

It was badly scuffed. Oh well. He had admired his father's Gibbs precisely because it looked as if it had seen some action.

He hobbled over to the window and looked out over a huge garden. He had no idea where he was. On the slope below was a simple, whitewashed church, and from there the terrain hurtled towards a long, narrow lake. Steep fields ran down towards to the water's edge, while on the opposite side there was nothing but forest, and a cart road that wound over the crest of a hill. He pressed his face against the window and looked to the left. Above some farms was a row of dark rock formations, beyond which was what he took to be the mountain from which they had descended.

Could this be Butangen? The village that Ragna had mentioned?

Footsteps outside his room. He grabbed hold of the window-sill and turned. A slender, black-clad man in his forties came in. In near-perfect English, he told Victor that he had been given some "modern medicine" for the pain, that a doctor was expected later that day, and that he himself would be around in case of any language problems.

Victor apologised for not having caught the man's name or title in all the confusion on the previous night.

"Schweigaard. I'm the pastor here."

Victor sat down and tried to hide the pain he felt in his leg.

"Jehans. Where's Jehans?"

"Back on the farm working. Set off at the crack of dawn."

"Will he be back tonight?"

"Not for some days. Jehans is . . . busy. Bound to his work. A lot of work. On a big farm and on a smaller one too, which he runs himself. It's complicated. He said he'd go back up into the mountains at the first opportunity to see if your tents were still standing. Leave some messages there, bring the equipment back and generally sort things out as he thinks best."

"He saved my life," Victor said. "Do you know him well?"

"Both very well and not at all. As so often with people."

"It's all rather embarrassing. But I've never seen fog come in so fast."

The pastor kept staring at him oddly. He didn't appear to be quite listening, and as he moved about, it seemed to be with the aim of viewing him from different angles.

"The others in my group?" Victor continued. "Is there any news of them?"

"Not yet. We've telephoned the sheriff. Fortunately, there are telephone lines to some of the villages in Østerdalen, and with luck the farmhand will bring us news when he gets here with the doctor. Though it usually takes two or three days before anything's clear."

"It's an awful situation."

"Sadly, human beings aren't in control of everything that happens," Schweigaard said. "And in the mountains we're entirely at the mercy of the fates. Let's keep our hopes up, Mr Harrison. Did you get some sleep?"

"Later in the morning, yes. A bit restless up until then. But that's to be expected."

"You were given rather a large dose of medicine. Did you have strange dreams?"

"The fever, no doubt," Victor said.

The pastor said "hmm." He kept dropping out of the conversation – and if he wasn't outright staring, he seemed markedly *inquisitive*. Then, as though suddenly aware of it, he shook himself and asked if he should send word to Victor's family. "If you have an address, I can organise a telegram."

"No, no," Victor said, limping towards the bed. "They're used to me being out on my travels. They're not expecting anything except my return home in three weeks. I've always found it easy to get along in new places."

"Just one thing," Schweigaard said. "The sheriff – as regards your missing travel companions, he needs your full name. And a date of birth."

"Naturally," Victor said. "I was born on March 28, 1881. On a passenger ship, between Norway and England."

The doctor arrived with the farmhand at one o'clock. There was still no news of the rest of the party. His foot was quickly and rather roughly splinted and bandaged. Victor had to resign himself to staying at the parsonage for some time, but he would probably be able to support himself on crutches in a few days. The doctor left some tablets and rushed off.

Silence.

A light wind blew in through the window. A while later he heard heavy footsteps outside. The door was opened without a knock, and a very old woman with bushy hair and a shapeless body stomped over to his bed. She pulled back the duvet and poked at his splinted foot with her index finger and muttered something he didn't quite understand, something about *escaping the saw*. She stuck her face right into his and uttered more nonsensical prattle through a haze of bad breath, it sounded something like *So the painter weren't dead after all*. Then, without replacing the duvet, she went over to the drawers and started poking about in his knapsack. Moments later a young woman entered with a plate of food and there began a terrible commotion that continued until the pastor came, seized the old woman's arm and ushered her out.

Victor was soon sitting up with a pillow at his back, drinking strong coffee and eating slices of bread with hard-boiled egg, anchovies and parsley. The pastor sat down on a stool, apologising for the intrusion.

"It was a diversion, of sorts," Victor said.

"She's getting so old. Loses track of time completely for long periods. Confuses past and present. She mistook you for a guest we had here once. But anyway. Did you understand everything the doctor said?"

"Some of it."

"He asked me to thank you for the envelope with your payment. Most generous."

"The least I could do. But the man I'm truly indebted to is Jehans. I want to thank him properly."

The pastor drank his coffee in little sips, as though trying to spin out time. They had been speaking English, but Schweigaard asked if it was true that he knew some Norwegian. On account of a nursemaid or something?

Victor nodded. "Yes, and there's more. My mother is Norwegian too. Born in Ålesund. We spoke a lot of Norwegian until I was seven or eight. I had a Norwegian nanny. And my father occasionally took me to Lærdal to go salmon-fishing."

"Forgive me if I seem overly curious," Schweigaard said. "But it's not often we get visitors from abroad, and I've been the pastor here since 1879. It would be wonderful to hear a little about your life in England."

They finished their coffee and lit their pipes and Victor told him about Finlaggan and the plantation in Ceylon but very little about his mother or Joseph, and not wanting to appear skewed he hardly mentioned his father or grandparents either, so the person he talked about most was Kumara. It sounded almost as though the two of them lived alone at Finlaggan.

"It's the same here," the pastor said. "A big house can feel dreadfully empty."

Victor noticed how openly Schweigaard spoke, and

immediately his British reticence gave way to his desire to talk about his family and Ragna, revealing rather more than would have been fitting for *Burke's Landed Gentry*.

The pastor needed to be going. He told Victor the church-warden had begun making him a pair of crutches. Victor thanked him and said: "No doubt I've a few long days ahead of me here. Is there anywhere I can go fishing?"

The pastor bit his lip. Glanced quickly at the bandaged foot, then out of the window and said:

"Only from a boat."

The two men scraped out their pipes and the pastor went off to his duties.

Victor was left feeling rather impatient and curious. The pastor's questions had been strangely personal, yet conspicuously general. Supporting himself against the wall, he limped out into the corridor. On either side of the generous hallway there were three pale-blue doors with grey doorframes. It looked like the bedroom wing for a large family, but as far as he knew the pastor was unmarried, and all that could be heard was the occasional little noise from downstairs.

He pushed one of the doors ajar and found a room as empty and bare as his own. The next was the same. But behind the third door he felt a warmth. The scent of human habitation and the remains of a fire in the stove.

The room appeared to belong to a young boy. The furnish-ings, the time at which everything had stopped, the adventure books, the toys; they all reminded him of his own boyhood room.

Extraordinary. This must have been where Jehans had slept.

The shelves were filled with carved wooden toys, arranged much as he had arranged his own toys as a child, in neat rows, both for the look of it and to heighten his excitement for the next morning's play. Books on another shelf, a desk with pencils in a cup and a world map pinned above it, and more books about mechanics and electricity. He glanced through them. The language was largely incomprehensible to him. He and Ragna had only spoken Norwegian; he had no memory of trying to read or write it.

Pulling out a drawer he found a pile of drawings. A boy's dreams of heroic feats of engineering. Intricate plans for dams, cranes, hoists and steam engines. A wooden box filled with old paintbrushes.

He opened another drawer. Was astonished not to feel any guilt about going through another man's things. Found a little book with a brown cardboard cover. *Meyers Sprachführer für Reise und Haus*. Some sort of travellers' phrase book. He opened it carefully and on the title page, in the top right-hand corner, was the name *Gerhard Schönauer* in an elegant hand. Presumably the architect. Jehans' dead father.

Underneath it lay an oblong sketchbook. Shifting things made something lower down in the drawer rattle. A round tobacco tin. *Grousemoor*. An English classic. Victor twisted off the lid and found pencil shavings and dried-out erasers.

The sketchbook was bound in blue-grey canvas, its covers held in place by two tie-up laces. He opened it and found a travel itinerary from 1877. The young Schönauer had, it seemed, visited London to study the buildings of Christopher Wren. There they all were, St Paul's Cathedral, St Bride's Church, the Church of St Anne and St Agnes, and others, all exquisitely drawn, often with details of structures both inside and out. It was clear that this German had a real love of classical English architecture. And here was Cambridge – with surprisingly lively sketches of street scenes along with more architectural studies of the Wren Library and Pembroke College Chapel.

But what was this? Towards the end of the sketchbook were

drawings of a country house, and then another, all in the classical English style Victor loved so much himself. Victor almost expected to find one of Finlaggan on the next page. The final pages were filled with sums. This man, whom he now knew for sure to be Jehans' father, had spent the last of his travel grant in London on May 29, 1877 on a Hardy Smuggler for three and a half guineas!

Victor turned. And there it was. Lying on the chest of drawers was the leather case that contained the very same fly-fishing rod. Limping over he saw that the Krag had been laid across an open drawer to dry, just as he had found his Rigby.

He lifted the rifle. There was something of the Norwegian spirit in it. An idiosyncratic, clever construction, common sense paired with unusual solutions, made in a determined effort to ensure it resembled nothing else. The side magazine, in particular, was ingenious, reloadable even when the weapon was ready to fire.

Then something made him stop.

In the open drawer lay a tiny knitted jacket. So small it had to be for a newborn baby. Exquisitely made, knitted in the softest wool, deep red, with a patterned border the colour of autumn birch trees. And beneath it a row of black crosses.

The colour combination was unknown to him. But he remembered the pattern clearly.

It was precisely the same as his little jacket at home at Finlaggan. The one Ragna had given him when she left, saying: *Your mother wanted you to have this.*

I Have Buried You Once Already

Fru Røhme surpassed herself that evening. Herr Røhme looked after Simen, giving her plenty of time to prepare a magnificent platter of roast veal. The potatoes were fresh in from the field that day, and so carefully chosen they looked like goose eggs of identical size and shape. She had peeled and boiled them, and then roasted them in the oven, making them crisp and golden. Schweigaard asked her to prepare a plate for Oldfrue Bressum and take it up to her room with a bottle of apple wine. And, if possible, she should lock the door behind her. As he came to table with Victor his only regret was that Jehans could not be there. They had sent word to say he was welcome, but received a reply to say he was too busy working at Hekne.

Schweigaard had been dithering all day over what he should or should not say to Victor. He was meant to write a sermon, but caught himself staring out at Lake Løsnes, and each time he had thoughts of salvation, he felt that the words applied to *him*. If this man, this Victor Harrison, really was the chosen one, one of two chain-brothers needed to raise the bell, well then, he had the capacity to release Schweigaard from his torment.

But he had said he was born on March 28. Five days after Jehans. If he had wanted to hide something, wouldn't he have given a date long into the summer? Made a proper job of it – August 2 or October 18 or whatever!

Yes. This Harrison fellow must know something. And yet: there was clearly something he didn't know.

Just as Kai Schweigaard both knew and did not know what he was about to get involved with. He was sure of only one thing: that to meddle with a person's identity was hazardous. Victor seemed to have a harmonious and busy life, he was a little pent up as regards his mother perhaps, or women in general, but he exuded joy when he spoke of his father and grandparents – and the dog – and not least their place in Ceylon.

Yes. He already had a father. And that father had a son.

Suddenly the swing doors opened, and Oldfrue Bressum staggered in. She was wearing a gaudy red headscarf and a stained apron that was on back to front, and Schweigaard realised that she must have seen her chance to grab the serving dish. She plonked it down on the table and nodded with satisfaction, as though she had made the food herself, and said she was sure there'd be no end of good meat now that the German was visiting. Then, grabbing Schweigaard by the shoulder, she pointed at Victor and whispered that he was far too kind *t' that man there*, at which point Fru and Herr Røhme dashed in to avert further disaster.

Schweigaard fiddled with his fork, uncertain what to say. Noticing his discomfort, Victor praised the potatoes and meat and moved the conversation elegantly onto fishing, and it became a harmless little interruption in an otherwise flawless conversation. Schweigaard suggested that after dessert they might defy doctor's orders and go trolling on Lake Løsnes. Victor considered the pulling of heavy trolling spoons after a boat both primitive and unsportsmanlike, but he refrained from criticism, saying simply that he was a fly-fishing man himself.

"Some of the foremost fly-fishers in Britain are priests," he said. "They're behind many of the finest flies too, Greenwell's Glory, for one. I imagine their interest comes from all the free time they have in the middle of the day?"

Schweigaard gave him a slightly glorified view of his week. His work with the school and the poor, and the issuing of bounty payments to the local trappers for birds of prey and other predators. He worked long days and nothing – services, weddings, confirmations and funerals – could ever be deferred if he was sick.

"Lucky then that you didn't have the burden of *my* funeral," Victor quipped.

Don't say that, thought Schweigaard. I have buried you once already.

Men talk best in a boat. And there are certain things men will only say in a boat.

Evening was drawing in around them on Lake Løsnes. The trolling spoons were in the water and Schweigaard rowed with steady strokes. It was good weather, very few mosquitoes for the season, and the tops of the spruce trees shifted gently in the wind.

"I've been thinking about Jehans," Victor said. "What plans does he have for his life?"

"Truth is, he has the talent to be an engineer. But as things stand? Well, poverty and a responsibility for his foster parents are one thing, but his greatest weakness is that he refuses help from anyone else. He has to struggle for everything himself. What he wants most of all, it seems, is a farm. A place of his own."

"How much would that cost?"

"Anything between four hundred and four thousand kroner. A thousand perhaps to buy the freehold for a farm like the one he lives on."

Victor cleared his throat. Said there was something he had to confess.

"It was wrong of me, perhaps, but I was in Jehans' room because I wanted to look at his rifle, the Krag-Jørgensen. I caught sight of a little knitted jacket in a drawer. I was just wondering – is that a common Norwegian pattern?"

Kai Schweigaard stopped rowing. Behind them the fishing lines slackened. Victor was about to apologise when Schweigaard said:

"A common pattern? I'm not really sure. Why do you—"

"Oh, I just thought it was rather nice."

There was silence between them. Schweigaard began rowing again.

"They're called *koftes*. The pattern is called the eight-petal rose, so I'm told. The little crosses are common on infants' knitwear here. They're meant to protect the child from evil forces. That's why they run all the way round the chest and back. Jehans' mother knitted it before he was born, and he was wearing it when I fetched him home. I kept it as a memento when he moved out."

"A memento of him as he was – as a child?"

"Of her, to be honest. Of Astrid Hekne. But it's only right it should stay in Jehans' room."

"That name – Astrid. Wasn't it her grave we passed on the way?"

"Yes."

"The grave is well kept."

"It is indeed."

They had seen no signs of fish. The air had turned icy. Fearing impatience might oust his companion's politeness, Kai Schweigaard upped the strength of his oar strokes and hoped that they were on the right course.

"Tell me – what's that over there?" Victor said, pointing towards a flat mass in the water under the spruce trees.

"Oh, that's a raft Jehans made as a boy."

"With dreams of sailing away?"

"It's a very long story," Schweigaard said.

"Well, we're two men in a boat, one with a leg stuck in a splint."

At last Kai Schweigaard had an excuse to tell the story of the Sister Bells. When he came to the events of 1880, it was late and the light was fading, so he could not see Victor's reactions to his story, and from that, he also knew that Victor could not see the deep effect the story had on him. The darkness grew deeper and deeper, and by the time he reached the Silver Winter and the sinking of the church bells, it felt as though Lake Løsnes itself laid out the final part of the story.

"And who are these chosen men?" Victor asked. "Who will raise the bell?"

"I have heard tell," Schweigaard said, "that only brothers born without sisters between may raise it." He pulled on the oars again, and wondered if he ought to say it.

Yes. It was essential.

"Jehans had a twin brother. But he died shortly after he was born."

He lifted the oars and tried to see a reaction in Victor, but it was too dark. They were just two hazy figures to each other, gently shifting form.

After a while, Victor said: "And Jehans tried to find the bell and bring it up. Without success."

"Without success," Schweigaard repeated. "Though we're pretty sure we know where it might be."

"Has anybody else tried to bring it up?"

"Attempts have been made. I believe some German engineering students came here soon afterwards and tried."

"So why hasn't anyone managed it? Legends aside?"

Schweigaard cleared his throat. "One can only assume that the bell has sunk into the mud. The only thing a dredging hook could attach itself to would be the cannons at the top of the bell. If those are pointing downwards, there'll be nothing for it to catch onto. But according to local folklore the bell rope might offer another solution. This may seem rather ... occultish, but when Eirik, the father of the Hekne twins, had the bells cast, he also ordered two bell ropes. He had taken some locks of their mother's hair when she died and he had them woven into the bell rope. Gerhard Schönauer knew this story, and I suspect that, given his state of mind, he might have attached the ropes to the bells before they were transported. So that one of them now lies coiled on the bottom of the lake somewhere below us. And if one were to believe such things, the rope may possess a will of its own, and have the power to decide over exactly whose dredging hook will catch onto it."

"D'you really believe such things, Herr Schweigaard?"

"I . . . I try to let reason be my guide. But the older I get the more I doubt everything. When I first arrived here, folklore was omnipresent. Now we have a railway, regular post deliveries, more insightful newspapers, a school system and machines that could eventually eliminate the more gruelling elements of farm labour. And with each progressive step, I see the old beliefs disappear."

"That's a good thing, surely?" said Victor.

"Hmm, I always thought so. I wanted to be rid of all the old ways, preferably overnight. But I'm not as bombastic now. We've lost our sense of wonder. I don't think I reach into the depths of people in the same way as I did. They're so quick to settle for any explanations they're given. They accept change too eagerly, they're not as wary of consequences as those before them."

Victor adjusted his grip on his fishing rod.

"So – you miss the things that *you* yourself sought to banish?"

"Not altogether. Not the sudden deaths, the malnutrition, the phlegm. Yet – there were so many kinds of – what I describe as *shadowy corners*, or dark *mine shafts* in faith and superstition. I've sometimes compared it to being lowered into a mine with a lantern. When I climbed down into it, there were so many extraordinary things to be found. Memories, thoughts, quirky impulses that had taken strange shapes and influenced the way people lived. Veins of silver and slag intersected with each other. And continuing the metaphor, I found that the deeper I went into this mine shaft, the stranger the creatures I encountered, and I could never reach the bottom. But nowadays the light seems to burn too brightly, so that it's merely shiny and clean down there. And yet it is not. The slag and strange rarities are now just concealed behind an apparent logic and rationality. But man is not a rational being, and to truly understand a human being, one must seek the irrational explanation."

They were out on the lake again the next evening. The sun had long since set, and the boat slipped through the semi-darkness and autumn cool. Victor had caught a medium-sized trout this time.

"He's over there!" Victor shouted suddenly, pointing towards land. A thin figure stood on the shore. He had climbed onto a tree stump, making his silhouette visible against the sky, and when he saw them turn the boat and come in his direction, he raised a hand in greeting.

Kai Schweigaard guided the boat into land, and Victor reeled in the line.

Jehans was quite near the barn where they had stored the materials from the stave church: the timbers and beams that had been carved in the time of the saga kings that were gone from the village forever now, but had left faint memories and smells here.

Another figure appeared behind Jehans. The farmhand.

"We've had word from Fåvang," Jehans said.

"Really?" said Schweigaard. "Good or bad?"

"Tell them," Jehans said, looking at the farmhand.

"Alive! They be alive. Takin' a trip further north now. Thanked thee for your company."

It was as though the boat itself floated higher in the water. Talking to himself in his mother tongue, Victor thanked the powers he believed in.

The farmhand gave a bow and went back up.

Jehans said he had been in the mountains to fetch Victor's tent and equipment, and that the others had already collected their things, leaving his tent standing alone.

"And ye?" asked Jehans. "Have ye caught any fish?"

"Just the one," Victor said, lifting the wooden pail containing the trout. "It bit the instant we came out here. It's been very quiet since."

"Nay wind enough?"

"Perhaps," Victor said.

Schweigaard said nothing. The silence was getting awkward when Jehans surprised them by holding out a large basket with a lid. "From Oldfrue Bressum," he said.

Jehans leaped into the boat, and shifted his balance to stop it rocking. "Shall I row?"

Schweigaard shook his head. An alliance had instantly formed between the two young men, an alliance that excluded him, and as they went back out onto the lake to carry on fishing, it was as though he was rowing back to the past with two unknown souls aboard.

Jehans opened the basket and took out a large speke ham and flatbread. The spell broke, and they were suddenly just two young men in a boat again. The basket also contained a wooden cup of sour cream and six large bottles of *godtøl* from the Lillehammer brewery. Jehans snapped off the corks and handed a bottle to each of his companions, then put the *speke* on the thwart and sliced it carefully with his hunting knife. He handed a paper-thin slice to Victor, who hesitated a moment before tasting it, swallowed it and immediately asked for more. Victor was soon using his own knife to slice the meat as he had seen Jehans do.

"Oldfrue Bressum sent all this with you?" Schweigaard said. "Of her own accord?"

"I came up for my Krag and fishing-gad, but she bid me stay a moment and began to rowk about in the larder. Then she gave me this basket and I understood it to mean she would have me go wi' thee fishing."

Jehans took a couple of swigs of his beer before wedging the bottle between his knees and casting his line.

They're different now, thought Schweigaard. So strong and decisive. As though liberated from something. Or perhaps exalted *to* something.

"I've noticed," Victor said, suddenly speaking Norwegian, "that the old lady is very fond of her food. Perhaps she's hoping for some trout."

"Harrison, you've nailed it!" Kai Schweigaard said.

"Ye have indeed!" said Jehans.

"Cheers, to Oldfrue Bressum!" Victor said. Soon three long-necked bottles were clinking against each other.

Schweigaard rowed as hard as he could towards the place where the bells had sunk that winter, and where he assumed Gunhild still lay. He navigated by the subtlest details, by the smell of the forest as they approached it, by the vague shadows on the shoreline and the burbling of the stream as it met the lake further up. They would soon row over Gunhild's resting place, where his inner life was deepest and darkest. He slowed down.

"Do you hear that?" whispered Schweigaard.

"Hear what?" Jehans said.

All Jehans could hear was the dripping of the oars and a slight creaking as he and Victor shifted in the boat.

"The stream," he said quietly. "Further down. There, in the distance."

"What about it?" Victor said.

"There are usually small fish over there. And bigger fish come there to hunt them sometimes. We should put out a trolling spoon when we get closer. If you throw it out, Harrison, and drag it along the bottom, you might just get a bite."

"But surely it'll get stuck?" Victor said. "These trolling spoons are heavy."

"There are stones at the bottom. It's not a problem if it catches."

Jehans took Schweigaard's rod, and soon the shoemaker's cord whistled out from both big reels. All three men were silent. The dusk lay deep and blue, and the tips of their rods stood out against the sky. Schweigaard rowed them gently towards the mouth of the stream, still navigating by a compass of murmuring water, shadows and forest fragrance. His eyes had grown accustomed to the dark, but the moment was approaching when the night grows so dense that the human eye cannot keep pace.

They passed the mouth of the stream and came out where a sudden drop made the lake very deep. The two men let out their lines further and further, until the trolling spoons scraped the bottom. And now he suddenly became aware of another smell, the warm fragrance of tar from the boat, and he heard how the wood creaked, and sensed a night sky that arched into infinity. And it was as though he were back inside the ancient stave church, staring up at the ceiling, which was so dark that it too touched a kind of infinity.

The moment was shattered, just as a moment is shattered when someone talks during Mass. The evening chill was fast being ousted by the night cold.

"Oh!" Victor whispered. "I think I—"

"What is it?" Kai Schweigaard said, lifting the oars.

"It just won't – what was it you said?"

"Be sommat moving? Tugging at the line?" Jehans said.

"No, it's ... No. It's completely calm down there."

Schweigaard tried to work out precisely where they were, but all he could say for sure was that they must be close to the steep slope which the bells had rolled down.

"Really big trout can stay very still," Schweigaard said.

Victor tugged down his jacket sleeve so as to wrap the hard shoemaker's cord round his fist without cutting himself.

"No. Yes – I can feel something. *Something*."

"But what?" whispered Jehans.

"He's saying he thinks he's got a fish," Kai Schweigaard said.

"I shall bring it in," said Jehans. He crawled back to his rod and started to wind his line back in. The reel whistled in the dark. Then he let out a shout.

There was a rasping of heavy woollen outdoor wear and the boat rocked. It was soon clear that both Jehans and Victor had landed something big. The boat and their lines jerked in tandem and for a moment Schweigaard assumed they had hooked the same fish.

The brothers talked rapidly and in hushed voices.

All of a sudden Victor's line switched direction. It sliced through the water, threatening to cross under the boat, and they quickly swapped rods to avoid them getting tangled.

It was in that moment, as the two men exchanged rods, their lines skimming through the water like threads in a weave, a weave with length, depth and breadth, that Schweigaard heard that they had made their own language, a mix of English and the Butangen dialect, and in the darkness the differences in their dress were invisible, the two were equal, he even found it hard to know whose voice was whose. Their exchanges were short and instinctive, as if they'd already understood each other's thoughts a second before, and when whatever they had hooked changed direction, they switched rods as in a four-handed game. The lines must have taken a colossal weight and been stretched to their limit, because all at once they both snapped. The boat lurched and there was a groan in the water, it seemed alien and from another time. The rods sprang back, weightless, and the vast lengths of line that they had guided in a pattern nobody could see sank into the depths of the lake.

Love's Braid

As he hurried over to the *seter*, Jehans reflected on what the Englishman had said. That he had saved his life.

Well, yes.

That he wanted what was best for him.

Thanks be.

That he would therefore make him an offer that he was free to think about. But only until Thursday. Then he would probably be fit enough to take a horse and carriage to the railway station and the boat to England from Kristiania.

Well. It had been an eventful few days. And what was this offer exactly?

He was asking Jehans to go with him.

To England?

To England. To take two years' work on a good salary. Initially on the estate he ran with his father. The work would include forest management and hunting. Board and lodging included. Jehans would, of course, need new clothes and new boots, for which he would pay. At quiet times the farm labour would be delegated to the tenant farmer. This would last a few months. Then they would leave for Ceylon.

Ceylon?

Ceylon. South of India. To oversee a plantation and hunt. He had wanted to shoot a leopard all his life, but it was difficult and occasionally dangerous and you needed to be two. Two good team players who weren't intimidated by fierce animals or monsoon rains. And Jehans would, of course, bring the Krag along. He'd have to change the rear sight, rifle sights that went beyond two hundred yards were banned in the colonies, the British were afraid of snipers attacking the administration, a stupid rule admittedly, but it was just a rifle sight, wasn't it?

But twenty-four months?

Yes. Six months in Ceylon. Back to Finlaggan for the autumn, then hunting and game management, and later perhaps another trip to Ceylon. And when the two years were up, he'd pay for his home trip.

And this was salaried work?

Victor quoted a sum in Norwegian kroner. Jehans fell silent. Victor said that this would be his *monthly* payment. Jehans totted it up in his head. Enough to buy Halvfarelia.

Were such wages common over there?

No. They were the wages of those who saved lives in the mountains.

"Two years!" Kristine said.

Yes, it was indeed a long time. But he would write to her. She understood, but was it really what he wanted? Did he truly want to go? No, he didn't have to answer. There was no point in asking a man if he wanted to go hunting and fishing for two years and get paid for the pleasure. But who exactly was this Englishman? Could he be trusted? It seemed so. Jehans had saved his life, after all. But would this Englishman save *his* life if it came to it? He believed so. That he was made of such stuff. Yes. Even if that tiger attacked him? Leopard. Right, leopard. They could bite too. Well, folk went to sea and to America to earn money. That wasn't without its risks. And it was a very large sum of money. A suspiciously large sum. What did he really know about this man?

Had he told him everything about himself? Not much, no. But he ... He what? No, nothing. What is it you don't want to say, Jehans? No, nothing. Just that he has a lot of money. Enough to travel a great deal. That's probably how they live in England. Yes. But if they lived like that over there, Jehans would probably meet another girl, and rather have her. No, because he wouldn't want a girl who lived like that. He'd only be going to see what it was like there and to earn some money. And then they wouldn't be serfs anymore. Not to anyone. Because there'd be enough money to buy Halvfarelia. Yes, he might change a little. But that was why he was here now; to promise himself to her. So he'd be hers even if he changed.

"To promise yourself to me?" Kristine said.

"Aye. And thee to me."

"And how's that to happen?"

"By my going down upon one knee before thee. Just so. And asking thee to marry me upon my return. I be asking thee now. Like this."

"Jehans Hekne. Ye be asking for real. Asking me for real."

"Aye, I be asking. Asking thee in proper fashion. Asking thee if ye will be my betrothed."

Kristine got up, took his hands in hers and made him get up, then said:

"I would wed thee straight, Jehans Hekne. Here and now, in this common everyday skirt. With the Brekkom Mountain as our priest and the Krag as the church bell. If we only had a ring."

He took something from his pocket. He had spent the whole night making it. At home in his little hut in Halvfarelia, he had taken the reel of electric wire that Schweigaard had given him, and pulled out metre upon metre of wrap wire. Shiny and as thin as sewing thread. And in the glimmer of a tallow candle he had made a braid and plaited the braid into ever thicker braids. Then he had shaped it around the muzzle on the Krag and linked the ends on the outside so they wouldn't prick her skin. But the ring had proved too soft, it would be useless when she worked. So he had gone outside and crawled under the *stabbur* to fetch some of the thicker, galvanised wire they used on the hay-drying racks. What he held out to her now was his fifth attempt.

The flame-orange wires twisted themselves round the thick, dull wire, like a sparkling serpent moving across something solid and grey, and new colours revealed themselves each time she turned it in the light and they continued on and on, deeper and wider, in an endless, enchanted circle.

Osvald said he had never heard such nonsense.

"October be the earliest ye may travel. On *faredagen*. With any other folk who be after changing employment. 'Tis written there in yer contract. And how d'ye think it'll go for Halvfarelia when naebody comes from there t' work for me on Hekne? Have ye warned them?"

"Nay," Jehans said. "Not yet. But many a landowner lets widows or old folk live in their cottages till they die. Surely ye can show some charity. I shall be back in two year, and then I shall take full responsibility for them."

"Aye, ye shall take full responsibility for them alright!"

"I shall make money enough to buy Halvfarelia. I can get a good lump sum right now as down payment from a job I am offered. If ye let them live in Halvfarelia I shall pay thee in instalments."

Osvald rose from his high-backed chair and stared out of the window.

"Ye would have me go wi'out labour or contributions from a holding for two year. And then sell it to thee for loose change. Ye can hear for yerseln 'tis laughable. Yet ye are fool enough t' ask."

"I beg o' thee, Osvald. Adolf's family have tended that land on Halvfarelia for nigh on eighty year. Your father were lenient. And he were my grandfather."

"Father were much too kind. He were clever alright, and exact in his work. But too soft. A farmer canna' let himself be driven by womanish feelings. His duty is to the land and to his heirs and nowt else."

"Sommat mun be done for the old folk, Osvald."

"They in't that old. 'Tis that back pain they lay all the blame upon. Well, I shall try to go easy on them. But remember, Jehans. 'Tis all yer doing. 'Twas ye who walked away from a lawful contract. And I canna' let folks gad about as they please. I have Hekne to look after."

Osvald was still standing by the window. He was wearing a black waistcoat with silver buttons and a dazzling white shirt. A shudder went across his shoulder blades, making the glossy fabric on the back of his waistcoat quiver slightly. When he turned around, there was a faint sneer on his face.

"Ye have turned the heads o' my other cottars. Made them restless wi' yer giddy ways. Which ye inherited from your mother. My mind is made up, Jehans. Leave. Just go! Ye can never go back to Halvfarelia. Happen the old folks mun get out o' there too. We shall see. Get out now, Jehans Half-Way."

Jehans left. Behind him the scarred old farm buildings stared at him. He had left the farm in anger so many times before, but this time his anger had changed into the need for revenge.

Two years, Osvald. Then ye shall see.

Back at Halvfarelia he stood by the sawbuck in the yard. There were wood shavings on the ground and the bow-saw hung on a wall. Adolf must have chopped a little wood. His back was bad these days, and they liked nothing better than to sit inside making a fire. They probably had another ten years left to live. Sitting there together, close to the stove so as not to waste heat.

Going out to tend the vegetable patch and milk Sunbeam. They had cultivated this patch of land all their lives, but it would never be theirs. No letters had come from their children in America for two years. They would leave no mark on the world other than the things Jehans might tell.

He owned as little as they. Had nothing to offer Kristine. He went in to see them, and they knew at once he was going away.

"It were clear to see," Adolf said. "I have seen it afore. I saw it in yer mother."

He prepared them for the worst. It was impossible to know exactly what Osvald might do. But he would send them his first month's pay and ask them to share the money with Kristine. They would not starve. Not for his sake. And in two years he would come back and turn the world on its head.

Ingeborg cried and Adolf cried and they got up and embraced him one at a time.

"Do it, lad. Do what ye mun. If we pass away, get Osvald. Make him pay."

Jehans went over to the fence and tore up a fistful of grass for Sunbeam. She munched it and bellowed when he bid her good-bye. In the cabin he packed the little he owned. It was no more than he could carry in one go. A blackened coffee pot, a hunting knife, his binoculars, some cartridges. He took an oiled rag and rubbed the steel on the old chamber charger before hanging it on the wall. He could not bear to go to Adolf and put it in his hands. That would make his goodbye into a final farewell, the final farewell that it might well be.

He changed into his best clothes and bundled up his work clothes before putting them in his bag. Then sat for one last moment with the door open and looked out towards the sheep byre and little potato field. Swept the floor with the besom and straightened the sheepskin that lay on the plank bed. They would accompany him to the door when he left, then Ingeborg would come back here and stand and gaze at the room and the emptiness and Adolf would follow her in and take the chamber charger down from the peg.

He shook off the thought. It was time to go. He put on his knapsack and went outside. They were already standing in the doorway, and then he could no longer control it. He ran over and squeezed them both and his tears flowed onto Ingeborg's soft, wrinkled skin.

He struggled again with the feeling that he was on the run. He also felt a growing sense of envy. As he had throughout his life towards those grander folk born in rich men's beds. A kind of suspicion of Victor Harrison, of his money, of the opportunities life offered him. If the two of them were to step aboard the English ship and change tickets and clothes, what would he be then? Would he become Victor Harrison if he put on his elegant jacket and slung the Rigby over his shoulder? Would Victor Harrison become Jehans Hekne if he pulled on his homespun trousers and picked up the Krag on his way out?

What was it? What was it that continually made him want to compare himself to this man?

He passed the sheep byre and looked at the timber wall that Adolf had built around its entrance. The magnificent stave church portal had once stood here. Jehans' great-grandfather had moved it here to prevent its being burned, and his mother had given it to his father in exchange for the church bells remaining in the village.

None of their plans had turned out as they hoped. He felt closer to his parents in this moment than ever before. Perhaps there was a similarity between what he was feeling now and what his mother had felt when she agreed to go away with a foreign architect?

Was it just a simple matter of leaving? Was that how his mother had thought? That it was just a matter of going? Or did she also have doubts, growing doubts, as to whether she could ever be truly comfortable in a new country? Doubts that muddied her desire to travel, made worse by a niggling suspicion about the man she was going with? A foreigner with other customs, customs that might not surface until they arrived in his home country? When they met other people, for example, was she also frightened that she might not be good enough? Refined enough? That she'd seem to them like something he'd found under a juniper bush in Norway?

In that moment Jehans was with the mother whom he had never known. A split second later Victor stepped into his thoughts to join them, and there was an instant connection between the three of them, a harmony, an empathy, but then it felt as though *he* was being pushed out, as though there was something he should not know.

He had felt something similar on the odd occasion before. That a choice had been made long ago. That there had been a momentous event for which nobody had held a ceremony. And right now it felt as though he was very close to this event, but that his mother didn't want him to get close enough to see it. He felt an anger rising in him and a kind of grief, like the grief he often felt for a brother who had died at birth. A dead brother he thought of when he was out hunting reindeer, and almost only then.

Victor's face again.

His absolute confidence in handling his father's fly rod.

The feeling of having seen him before. In some drawing perhaps.

The way Schweigaard had looked at them as he rowed the boat right over the church bell, despite there being more reliable fishing spots.

And he thought: This possibility lies in waters that are way too deep.

And he let his doubts grow, and when they were full-sized they reached all the way back to the moment of his birth.

There was something that had to be done before they could leave Norway. Something that would tell Jehans everything he needed to know about Victor Harrison without Victor Harrison needing to know anything.

A Waterlogged Bell Rope

Breakfast passed rather too quietly. The melancholy of parting and the thrill of a forthcoming journey should have filled the moment, Victor was leaving tomorrow, with or without Jehans, and this last day ought to start with thanks for the pastor's hospitality and promises of a reunion. But a tension in the air hampered conversation between the two men.

Victor reached across for the butter and cheese, and shot a discreet glance at Schweigaard. His host had seemed more reserved ever since the night they had gone trout-fishing. As though he was in two minds about something, or had a suggestion he did not dare put forward. Being a polite guest, Victor had no wish to appear mistrustful, and he tried to be cheerful, saying that he planned to take full advantage of the beautiful autumn weather by borrowing Jehans' fishing rod and taking a fishing trip on his crutches.

But meanwhile, behind all the good cheer, his own uncomfortable thoughts began to pile up.

Initially he had felt a straightforward desire to help and reward Jehans. He had seen him as a Norwegian Kumara. But down in the boat he had felt an almost palpable urge just to have him close. That that would be enough.

213

Enough for what?

He had invited him to come to England. And Jehans would give him an answer that evening.

Now, as Victor negotiated his way up a stream high above the farms, hoping to find a good fishing spot, he regretted his offer.

Little suspicions had grown in him over the past few days, suspicions that he had pushed aside only for them to return. Unknown possibilities that tried to form a pattern. An impossible pattern of impossible events, informed by the pastor's account of the events of 1880 and Ragna's strange hint about Butangen.

Every year he had looked forward to opening his presents on March 28. Ragna had always told him he was born a few weeks early, and that the ship's doctor had saved his life.

But was it possible? Might this Gerhard Schönauer, the man who had owned this fishing rod, have had an affair with his mother? Victor counted backwards from his birthday. Concluded that he must have been conceived in late June. At the height of the salmon season. The pastor had mentioned that Schönauer had sketched many stave churches in Vestlandet. There were several near Lærdal, where his father liked to fish. They had even visited Borgund and Urnes together!

What if his mother had met Gerhard Schönauer in Lærdal?

Was *that* why he felt such an urge to use his fishing rod? To know if there actually *was* some connection? Stuff and nonsense! It had been made virtually in his own backyard! In Alnwick! By the Hardy Brothers, whom he had met in person!

As he walked on, the possibilities seemed to whirr about him. An abyss opened up before him, an abyss he felt a reckless urge to leap into, just to see what sort of landscape he might land in.

Did he really have – a half-brother here in Norway?

His foot was very painful, and when he finally found a tarn, he lay down on a flat rock warmed by the sun. All of a sudden he felt enormously heavy, as though he had become part of the rock, and when he woke up, he felt he had to shake the rock's essence out of his body before he could move.

The trout were difficult to outwit, yet he still found it difficult to leave the place. Eventually he hobbled back down the slope, and an hour later he left his crutches in the parsonage hallway and hung up his jacket.

When he turned round, he looked straight at Jehans.

"I borrowed this," he said apologetically, holding out the fishing rod. "Apologies. I should have asked."

Jehans left him holding out the leather case. Made no move to take it. Just nodded.

Victor had no idea what the nod meant – that borrowing it was no problem, or that he should have asked? Either way it seemed a discourteous gesture. Was it some sort of *mannjevning* – the Viking version of arm wrestling to establish the hierarchy between males – before he accepted the job offer?

Or perhaps this wasn't discourteous behaviour, between half-brothers?

Jehans stared at him for a long time, then said, "I shall travel with thee to England."

"Excellent," Victor said. "Excellent."

"But it were best if an advance on my wages were left with the pastor here. There be folk I mun take care of. But there be one condition besides."

"And that is?"

"That we go out on Lake Løsnes tonight."

Two men in a rowing boat in the twilight. A glistening stretch of dark water and the shadow of the boat that moved still darker across its surface.

He noticed that Jehans was watching how he fished. At first he cast the line and locked the reel so it would lie high in the water, but Jehans refused to start rowing until the spoon reached the bottom. Only then would he lock the reel.

As though he was the one to decide.

Up in the hallway, Victor had tried to refuse. Saying he wouldn't be much help with a splinted leg. Might it not be better to try to raise the bell when they got back?

No, Jehans had said. It had to be done now. He wanted to make a final attempt before leaving the village.

But why *now*? Going by what the pastor had said, hadn't he grown bored of looking for the bell as a youngster?

Just one last attempt, Jehans had replied. He had felt something when they were trolling. When his hook had got stuck. And he had taken careful note of the place.

So – he thought it was the church bell that he'd felt?

Yes. The trolling spoon had hooked onto the bell rope.

Hmm. Why hadn't he said anything?

It's not much to ask, Mr Harrison. I just need help with keeping the raft steady. I've prepared it. Set up a pulley, secured the logs and replaced some of the ropes.

This was not the man Victor had come to know. He was like a man bewitched or possessed. Speaking in a tone that seemed oddly uncharacteristic, he pronounced that he had taken his leave of folk, but not of Lake Løsnes. That the bell must rise before he could travel.

But he made no mention of what Schweigaard had said. That only brothers from the Hekne family could raise the bell. It seemed he was entirely alone in this task, and that he just needed help from any random person, making Victor even warier.

"We can't carry on all night," Victor said. "What if we don't find it?"

"We shall leave together whether or not we find it."

"That's good to hear. I think raising a church bell might be easier said than done."

"So we shall do it in silence," said Jehans.

They rowed on. There was something unnatural and strangely corrupt about all this. About searching beneath the water for something that had once been part of a church. Something that called souls to God.

He wanted to get away. As fast as possible.

The minute he got back to Finlaggan, everything would return to the way it was before.

Ragna's thoughtless hint. Revenge on his mother. Yet, Ragna couldn't possibly have known Gerhard Schönauer!

Nonetheless, it had been thoughtless. Typical of a nanny. Believing that blood was always thicker than water. He refused to believe it. *Couldn't* believe it.

That he had a half-brother here in Norway.

What was the meaning of all this? Was he supposed to look into the faces of utter and complete strangers, and then, in addition, take *pleasure* in their resemblance to him? How could he ever look his father in the eye if this were true?

No, he wanted to get away from here. Reclaim his own sense of honour, and now.

On the way here, Jehans had, without meeting his eye, told him what was going to happen. First they would put out the trolling spoon and shoemaker's cord. When the fishhook caught in the bell rope, they would tie the line to a buoy and guide the raft over it. The raft had a hole in the centre, and through it they would lower a dredging hook and try to fix it in the bell's cannon or the travel chest in which it might still be contained. The bell was probably buried in mud, but he thought this would work. If it got stuck, they'd have to rock it. Back and forth. The raw planks of pine they had with them in the boat would be placed over the hole in the raft when the bell was lifted clear of the water, and there it would rest while they got back into the boat and pulled the raft ashore.

Jehans was watching him closely now, but Victor gave no indication of what was in his mind. Meanwhile Jehans held his trolling rod between his knees as he rowed on.

There was something unnatural about this. Terribly unnatural.

As abruptly as when a fish is hooked, Victor felt a tug on his line. Jehans stopped rowing. Victor felt his rod grow heavier in his hands. Something was opposing him from below. Something that sided with Jehans and not with him.

When he let out more line, it seemed to sink gently back down, and when he pulled at it again, the same strength was required to lift it.

Like a waterlogged bell rope.

Soon they were on the raft, pulling the priest-boat behind them. From then on Jehans did everything, and still not a word was spoken. They were on their knees, the water running over their legs. Jehans lowered the dredging hook through the hole in the middle and released the rope from the pulley until it was slack between his hands. Then, lifting the hook a little from the bottom, he began to guide the rope back and forth behaving almost as though Victor was not there.

The raft was reacting more and more strongly to the pendulum movement of the dredging hook.

Victor felt an urge to escape, and a shudder went through his body. But just then the rope tightened between Jehans' hands. The dredging hook seemed to be stuck in something. Jehans hooked the rope to the pulley and a loud ticking scudded across the water, like a clock without dials, a clock without contact with time.

The rope trembled, the water splashed and there began a tug

of war. The raft lay deeper and deeper in the water as the pulley took on more and more weight. All at once they tipped and had to grab each other so as not to fall off. Something very heavy had come loose under them and now the raft became the outermost point of a large and slow movement in which they swayed from side to side. Jehans still barely looked at him, they were just two wet men holding on to wet ropes. But then Jehans turned and lit an oil lamp and they could see a dense patch in the water.

A crack was opening up in Victor.

He could not stop thinking of the knitted jacket Ragna had shown him.

Your mother wanted you to have this.

He realised now that there was only one possible explanation for this. The pastor had told him that Astrid Hekne had known she was going to give birth to twins. She had prepared herself diligently. Knitted clothes.

But. A woman who knows she's going to have two children would surely make two jackets?

Wouldn't she?

Jehans turned his back on him and leaned over to the priest-boat, and began lifting the wooden planks on which the bell would rest when it was freed from the water. He did not ask for help.

Down in the water, directly beneath the taut rope, Victor could see something massive and dark. It could be a tree root, it could be a church bell, but it was constantly changing shape, perhaps because the mud was loosening and coming away.

Over this amorphous form, he saw his own face reflected in the water's surface, and it was not as before.

If I am not who I am, I must relinquish Finlaggan. Hand the estate over to Joseph. And the plantation. Leave my father. On account of this Norwegian. Yesterday, there was nothing I wanted more than to have this man at my side for two years.

Now there is nothing I want less. Two years together, he and I, pretending that we're still the same two men we were?

He was about to break the silence they had agreed upon. Break it to ask Jehans straight out what he knew. Who had chosen between them, and why?

But it was better not to know.

He told himself that whatever it was that they were pulling up could not possibly be a church bell. It was just a huge root of a pine tree. Or the top of a giant wooden column, a remainder of the stave church that they had built here once.

He wiped his palm on his sleeve. From his belt he slipped out a knife.

The first incision made a gash in the rope, which was so taut and so wet that the severed threads spiralled outwards, releasing droplets that splashed against his face and hands as he cut himself free. Without rocking or any other warning, the rope snapped, the raft keeled over. Victor was thrown headlong and groped for a hold and thought he heard a sigh in the lake as something settled on the bottom.

Farewell Butangen

Far across the lake, Kai Schweigaard saw the rope break and the lamp go out.

Moments later, he spotted two figures on the raft, one of them got up onto his knees and made a grab for the other. Shouts and abrupt movements. What were they doing out there? If something was wrong, surely they would send out a distress signal?

Now one of them tumbled into the rowing boat. An oar

splashed into the water, the boat went in circles, he heard angry voices, words and half-sentences. Were they fighting over an oar? The boat freed itself from the raft, then headed in erratic semicircles for land. The raft followed, more slowly, but on a steadier course.

There was forest between where he stood and the bay where they would come ashore. Kai Schweigaard started running in its direction.

They had been out on the lake for over two hours. When he had accompanied them down to the water's edge, Victor had seemed morose, but Schweigaard had assumed he was just tired and grumpy and that his foot was causing him pain. Jehans had told him what they were going to do, but had not revealed his true plans. Just asked to borrow the priest-boat and said that they might need some help with lifting when they got back.

Schweigaard was running through the forest now. Below him he thought he heard a keel hitting a rock. Then the splashing of water. Someone had fallen into the shallows. The muffled sound of punching into soaking wet clothes. Snatches of angry accusations. *Rope canna' break like that! Ye surely did sommat. The knife! Where's the knife? Ye had a knife!*

Then Victor's voice: *There was no bell! Just a tree root. Join me in England, Jehans. We can leave tomorrow. For God's sake, man! Let things be as they were!*

Schweigaard was out in the open now and able to see them. They were standing by the boat. Jehans punched Victor hard in the belly. Pulled him back up and slammed his fist into his ribs. "It wouldna' have cost thee a thing! Nowt! Nowt!"

The raft was about to drift away, the priest-boat's oar was floating on the water, and dangling from the pulley was a piece of rope.

"What the hell would you know?" Victor cried. "What would you know about what it might cost me?"

221

Jehans kicked him to the ground and punched him again.

"I wanted to go out there! With thee. With thee!"

At last Schweigaard reached them, and Jehans retreated. Schweigaard helped Victor up from the water, and when he turned, Jehans was gone.

The lamp burned out and the sitting room fell into darkness. But they could hear each other's movements, and Kai Schweigaard noticed that Victor was shifting restlessly in his armchair. And he was sniffing, though Schweigaard did not know the cause. They had not seen Jehans again. His Krag, his fishing rod and the rest of his belongings were still up in his room.

"If he had just come with me," Victor mumbled. "He would have understood."

Schweigaard grunted.

"But he's never had responsibility for something entrusted to him by his parents. So he could never understand the situation. Not before coming over to see us. Then he'd have understood."

"To your estate – to Finlaggan?"

"And to Ceylon. He'd have liked it there. I'm sure he would have liked it. But it's irrelevant now. It's got nothing to do with either of you now. Nor has anything else."

They sat in the dark for a long time.

"You should know that I betrayed someone once," Schweigaard said. "I was as close to the very same church bell as you were last night. Time has passed now and I'm a different man. Time will pass for you too, and you'll be a different man."

Victor got up from his chair. "You should have been honest. Both of you. Laid out the facts. Then I could have just gone away. Out there on the raft I offered him two years' wages for saving my life. I said I would send it to him as soon as I got back. Can you guess his reply? He said he didn't want my money. That since I was his brother, the money wasn't mine to give."

"Jehans can be very blinkered," Schweigaard said. "There's a kind of ingratitude. And he can't see to the left or right of his goal."

Schweigaard listened for noises out in the hallway. There was nothing.

"Do you know if they'd chosen a name?" said Victor. "For the other boy?"

"Edgar. They wanted to call him Edgar."

They were silent again.

"Is it true?" Victor said. "Am I really his brother?"

Schweigaard thought about it and said: "Only the church bell knows."

Schweigaard woke up in the small hours, still in his sweat-drenched clothes, stiff from having fallen asleep in his armchair. Victor's chair was empty. He went upstairs to his bedroom and found it deserted. Deserted in the same way as when Gerhard Schönauer had deserted Butangen, empty with the same vacant emptiness. No clothes in the cupboard, no rifle in the corner. Only the odour of boot polish, the vapours from gun grease. But nothing of *him*. Not the faintest trace.

Schweigaard looked out of the window.

There was a difference in the way each man rowed a boat. And each had his own way of leaving. His own way of coming back home. His own way of fishing. His own way of brooding.

But they all fled in precisely the same way. With hurried, unsteady stokes of the oars. Repeatedly turning their heads to make sure they were on the right course. And never lifting their gaze to the place they were leaving.

This was how Victor Harrison rowed now.

Schweigaard dashed into Jehans' room. Opened a drawer, seized something and hurried down to the mooring.

A mallard with blue-black wings among the cattail grasses.

A thin, grey haze over the water. A call between the only two people awake in the village. A pastor who stretched up his arms to make himself visible.

Victor had gone a long way out. He stopped rowing. Then began to row again.

Schweigaard just stood there. He did not yell out. Nor move.

He just stood there calmly, and was Kai Schweigaard.

Victor rested his oars in the water. Then turned and rowed back into the shore. All he had in the boat were his crutches, a scuffed Rigby rifle and his knapsack.

Schweigaard leaned forward, grabbed the bow of the boat and passed Victor a little book in a brown cardboard cover.

Meyers Sprachführer für Reisen und Haus.

Victor took it without asking what its purpose might be.

"Come back here, Victor. Come when you can."

"No. He'll never call upon me, and I'll never call upon him."

Kai Schweigaard stood at the water's edge as the day approached. He alternated between looking back up the slopes to the parsonage and out over Lake Løsnes. Victor lowered the oars into the water and nodded briefly. Schweigaard said:

"There's one thing you should know, Victor. When an ox loses its foothold, it stumbles then rises again. But when a bird loses its footing, it takes off and flies."

Second Story

The Crack in the Mirror

Mystische Clara

IT WAS TIME FOR MASS IN THE CITY OF DRESDEN, AND in the Königlicher Großer Garten Halfrid rang out from the belfry of the Butangen stave church. She still rang with the same sonorous tone she had always had in Butangen, but it was impossible to get anything but a lonesome, doleful sound from her now, a mournful call that spread in circles around the city. The sound ruffled the surface of Lake Carola, then continued across the Zoological Gardens, through the open windows of the royal villa near Strehlener Straße, before it turned into the promenade and floated into the Matthäusfriedhof cemetery where it caressed the grave of Gerhard Schönauer.

Nearly twenty-five years had passed since he had been admitted to Dresden's city hospital with incurable pneumonia. The graveyard was so close that, without knowing it, he'd had a view of it from the bed where he died. His little tombstone was now covered with moss, the umlaut in Schönauer was long gone, and the carved numerals of his dates had started to merge into the surface. The gardeners saw all the signs that this was a tombstone that would be torn up and crushed into gravel as soon as its contract expired.

The sound of the bell continued to ring out. It slid over the rooftops of the grand buildings in the Altstadt and past the Baroque palaces around the Frauenkirche before it passed the steamships on the River Elbe and skimmed over the roofs of the synagogues and along the Brülsche Terrasse. While,

227

in the other direction, the sound waves struck the high, brick facade of the Sächsische Polytechnikum, Europe's best engineering college. From there it continued beyond the city, but in an unfortunately shaped backyard part of the sound was transformed into an echo, and echoes have a tendency to look for their origins, so it turned tail and ran downstream across the Elbe, where it met some newborn sounds, but found some even stronger sounds behind the treetops in the Großer Garten, where it finally found its birthplace in the belfry of a tar-black wooden church with multiple pointed spires, beautifully located in a clearing beside a lake, and like a bird that folds its wings when it lands in its nest, the echo came to rest.

The church was a sunburned relic of the age of the Norse kings, incongruous in both time and place. It was so different visually from anything else in the city, it took time for the eye to accept it. Its reconstruction had taken more than two years, all paid for by Queen Carola von Wasa. From the very first day the Königliche Butangen Stabkirche became a popular destination. Its acquisition helped confirm Dresden's place as Europe's art capital, attracting far more visitors than the Wang Kirche, which had been rebuilt in East Prussia forty years earlier in a remote spot at the end of steep, inaccessible cart roads, and reconstructed with little attention to historical accuracy. Butangen church, by contrast, had its original exterior and seven-hundred-year-old patina.

The church was consecrated and in regular use. The quality of its priests varied, they were often young chaplains affiliated to the Christuskirche, sent to cut their teeth. It was open to the public from eleven until six most days in the spring and summer, in groups of no more than twenty and always with a guide. Cigars had to be cut and pipes knocked out at a radius of fifty metres around the church, where an artificial stream also acted as a precaution against grass fires. At this juncture, public notices also urged visitors to end their conversations in the queue to encourage an attitude of pious devotion.

The notices were soon taken down. The public had no problem knowing how to behave before such a work. After studying the roof with its fantastical carvings of dragons, people often stood for an age in front of the portal, a tiny entrance door surrounded by a massive carved border filled with mysterious patterns and mythical creatures, the most powerful being a serpent that curled itself around the door with snapping jaws. These creatures guarded the church from evil, a fortress from Norse times that defended the old faith. Not that the visitors really understood the nature of this faith, though perhaps they got some sense of it when confronted with the portal. Everyone had to bow down to enter, be they nobles or ordinary citizens, which was as it should be, for this intermediate state, this gesture of humility and worship, made them more receptive as they left the present behind and stepped into the church. Guided only by reason, they might appreciate the carvings as folk art, but as they passed through the portal they had to acknowledge that this art imparted a deep sense of calm, and when they straightened up in the silent scent of tar and time, they saw that this perishable wood could be as sacred as cathedral stone, just as common words can make a prayer.

Some visitors to the church also came looking for answers to a pressing question of the time: what it meant to be German. The nation had been formed relatively recently, and they were a people in search of an identity, a people who longed to find their common roots. Many believed that their true origin was in the ancient Germanic culture, which had so much in common with the Norse culture that it might have been tapped from the same barrel of mead. Richard Wagner's name had not always been popular in Dresden, but his magnificent *Der Ring des Nibelungen* fed on these myths, and some thought they recognised the

229

opera's heroic figures in the carvings on the portal. It became a kind of Rosetta Stone for anyone who wanted to draw parallels, who saw in this magnificent Norse monument the forces that made Brünnhilde ride into the flaming funeral pyre in *Götterdämmerung*, or who saw the writhing serpent in the trombones' menacing attack in the prelude to *Die Walküre*.

This idea – that the church contained something of themselves, something that had almost been lost – was exploited to the full in the brochure. Whole pages were devoted to explaining the carvings and the shared Germanic-Nordic roots of the portal. The text was written by Professor Ulbricht from the Academy of Arts, the man who was largely credited with having brought the church from Norway to Dresden. Gerhard Schönauer's name was mentioned only in passing, and the chapter describing the actual transfer and reconstruction seemed hurried.

As a place of worship the church itself attracted the more religiously inclined, but it appealed to an even greater congregation after Halfrid was raised in 1882. The original bell rope had come with her from Norway. Dark, smoothed by the sweat of hands over the centuries. The churchwarden knew much of Halfrid's story, but not that lengths of Astrid Hekne the Elder's hair had been woven into the rope. If he had, he might have thought this was the reason for the strange feelings he got when he pulled it and Halfrid rang across the city for the first time. She sounded so very lonely and sad.

Until then the church had been admired. From then on it was *loved*. Rumour spread: the bell sounded sad because she had lost her sister bell in Norway, and was calling out to her in vain. And those of a more romantic bent claimed that the bell in Norway rang out in reply. Teams of engineering students had been sent to Norway in 1883 and 1885, in the hope of finding and raising the second bell. But they had returned crestfallen and devoured by mosquitos, with tales of an irascible pastor and hostile natives. Many people concluded that it was best that the bell ring out alone, that longing was sometimes sweetest.

There was one man who had lived with the stave church's ancient smells and creaking sounds for so long that he knew its every quirk. He tended to the cold smell of old tar and pine every day, as a fearless but respectful beekeeper tends to his hive. This man was the churchwarden, Karl Gustav Emmerich. As a young carpenter's apprentice, he had been present for the entire rebuilding of the church. He was among the few men who had got to know Schönauer, and among the even fewer mourners at his funeral.

The nearer the church came to completion, the more it seemed to close about him like a home. And when the other carpenters packed up to go, he stayed behind to work on the final, niggly details for which nobody else had the patience. He spun out time, and when the stave church was consecrated, he was still busy, changing window putty for something more neutral in colour, putting wooden pins where a poor craftsman had used iron nails, and he slipped almost invisibly into being the churchwarden.

In many ways he was like Herr Røhme in Butangen. A man of few words, underpaid, diligent and multiskilled, a man in overalls who ate lunch alone and who put all his love into this crooked and fickle building. When the day was over, he liked to sit on the bench outside as the church mirrored itself in the surface of Lake Carola, and watch it change shape with the ruffling of the wind on the water. Once he thought he saw a figure staring out of an open hatch in the bell tower, but when he turned and looked up, there was no figure and the hatch was, of course, closed.

He had never actually seen Halfrid. She had been hung according to Schönauer's wishes, in line, he assumed, with old Norwegian lore. When they hoisted her up into the tower she was wrapped in canvas, and Emmerich had to go up into the berry alone, pull off the canvas with closed eyes, then hurry back down. Years ago Emmerich had needed to go up there to chase away a kestrel that had nested there, and again he had draped the canvas over the bell, while looking the other way.

As time passed, Emmerich got the feeling that *more* had come with the shipment from Norway. This feeling came to a head at New Year's Day Mass, 1883. The church was full, and the sermon was well received, even if the priest's delivery was a little faltering, and in recognition of the church's origin they tried to sing three verses of "Stille Nacht" in Norwegian.

As Emmerich bid farewell to the congregation at the door, he heard something that gave him pause to think. A well-dressed couple, both wearing very heavy woollen coats, complained that it had been terribly cold where they had sat. Still shivering, they pointed to the spot, on the furthest end of a pew closest to the wall. He promised to investigate, but had no idea what could have caused it. The weather was mild for the time of year, and nobody else had complained. He concluded that one of the timbers might have warped to create a gap in the outside wall.

The priest and organist never paid him much attention, so he locked up and ate his lunch in solitude, slices of rye bread with cheese and a drop of coffee. Then he stretched out on a pew and took forty winks, a practice adopted by many a canny church-warden, since by the time he wakes up the water or snow that the congregation have brought in on their shoes will have dried.

Later, as he pushed the broom down the aisle, illuminated by the dappled light from the tiny glassless windows high above, he became aware of a forgotten hymn book. It was lying exactly where the couple had said there was a draught.

He put down his broom, sidled to the wall end of the pew and noticed that there was indeed a cold draught there. As he sat down he seemed to hear a whisper. Or was it a soft croon?

Whatever the case, it was in another language. Not hostile, not frightening, although the voice appeared to come from inside the wall. Then it died away, and with it the icy draught, and he picked up the hymn book. Written in gold letters on the black cover were the words *Landstads Kirkesalmebog*. It seemed to be in Norwegian or Danish.

But the couple who had sat here – surely they were German?

He put the hymn book on a shelf in the porch, in case someone came back for it, and swept the event from his mind just as he swept the floor clean.

At the next New Year's Mass in 1884, the hymn book turned up again in the exact same place, the place Emmerich would eventually name *die Fröstelstelle*, and which the organist called *die Gruselbank*. This time it lay open at Psalm 130. Emmerich said nothing, assuming that the organist had given way to some bizarre urge to make fun of him.

Some months later, old Professor Ulbricht came to give his annual tour of the stave church for architecture students. Emmerich rarely listened to these talks, he'd heard it all before. But he pricked up his ears when, in answer to a question from a particularly inquisitive student, Ulbricht told a story which Emmerich had never heard before. A story so grotesque, Ulbricht warned his audience, it could hardly bear the telling. The church had been viciously cold during the Norwegian winters, with temperatures often dropping below thirty degrees on Herr Celsius' scale. One morning, during a New Year's Mass, just before the church's transfer to Dresden, an old woman was said to have *frozen to death*. He went on to describe how the men always sat on one side of the aisle and the women on the other, and raising his arm he pointed to the spot in which she had probably died.

He was pointing straight at *die Fröstelstelle*.

*

It was during Christmas Mass one year that the problems began in earnest. It was Emmerich's responsibility to hang the hymn numbers up on the board. But when the service was underway, it turned out that he had inadvertently swapped the numbers about, so that the congregation began singing hymn number 130, "Aus tiefer Noth ruf' ich zu dir", while the organist played hymn number 140, "Lobt Gott, ihr Christen allzugleich".

He shuddered at his mistake. But there it was, number 130, in white numerals against a black background! Before the next Mass, Emmerich checked twice over that he had the correct numbers, but still there was confusion. Again the numbers had been changed, and the congregation tried to sing hymn 130 to the wrong melody on the organ. And worse still – this time another hymn number had been altered, forcing the organist to stop a second time and come down from his stool to tell everyone what they were actually meant to sing. Emmerich wished the floor would swallow him up.

When the church was empty again, he took the numbers down from the board. He sorted them, put them back in their case, and closed the lid. The he walked back along the rows of benches. And there it was. Again. In the same place. *Die Fröstelstelle*. The old Norwegian hymn book. *Landstads Kirkesalmebog*. Open at hymn number 130. He spelled out the title of the hymn, "Her kommer dine arme smaa" written by a certain A. H. Brorson.

This time he left it lying there. Went home to his lodgings. And slept badly.

On his return the next day, he spelled his way through the words. There were no melodies in the hymn book, and he spent the next few days leafing through books of church music and a three-volume work on German songs, hoping to find a version in German. Without success. Reluctantly he had to involve the organist, who on the evening of the sixth day of Christmas finally found it in a Danish hymn book from 1853, and thought, or hoped, that it might go to the same melody as the German hymn "Den süssen Schlaf erbitten wir" by Schulz, known to the organist from a pamphlet of family devotions for the evangelical Lutheran colonies along the Volga.

The New Year's Mass was about to begin. The melody was not approved for church use. But without the priest's knowledge, and as the congregation stooped through the portal and Halfrid rang above their heads, the organist played the melody he hoped belonged to "Her kommer dine arme smaa".

Now, at last, the hymn board was left in peace.

From then on, the organist played the melody before every New Year's Day Mass, and sometimes on an ordinary Sunday too. Emmerich thought the matter was resolved, and was relieved not to have to tell the priest what he had thought was happening. But then the usual organist tittle-tattle began to take hold, and what Emmerich had feared now happened. Rumour spread that there was a Lutheran ghost in the church, a story that was shared with glee, since spiritualism was now an important talking point in every drawing room across Europe. And soon after Ulbricht's tour the name of the woman who had frozen to death also surfaced. Her name was Klara, he was unsure of her surname, it was impossible to pronounce, but he thought it began with "Myt", and that was enough for her to be nicknamed Mystische Clara, or sometimes Mytische Clara. Klara was commonly spelt with a K in Germany, but Clara stuck, because the C seemed more refined, and hinted at a younger woman with a certain physical allure. Klara Mytting was soon resurrected, but she was now quite different from the woman who had trudged hunchbacked through Butangen year after year, with the water-yoke weighing her down. Instead, the Dresden residents transformed her into a graceful Madonna in flowing robes. Emmerich suspected that Klara had nothing against this herself, after all, even she must have been young once, and the dead are free to choose their age when they return as ghosts.

A day in September 1904. The sun shone over the Großer Garten, and Emmerich had worked himself into a healthy sweat weeding the church grounds. It was half past four, and he could have gone home long ago, but something made him wander back into the church, lock the door and take a nap on the Norddølum family pew, with one arm under his head and a newspaper under his shoes.

Suddenly he sat up.

The bell. A faint ring of the bell.

It happened now and then that sounds issued from the belfry whose source he could not identify, rather like the shots that used to ring out from the forest where he grew up. But he was particularly on the alert now, it being just twelve days since he had last thought he heard it. That day Halfrid had given a very powerful ring, and he had rushed to the bell ringer's platform. Where the rope hung as taut as usual.

And now it was happening again.

The bell was ringing by itself.

Halfrid struck three times.

She usually sent out a melancholy, trembling sound. But that was not the sound she had made twelve days ago, nor the sound he heard now. Just three short chimes. A warning that was not supposed to travel very far.

Emmerich heard footsteps out in the weapons porch. He walked over, seized the wrought-iron handle of the portal door and opened it. Outside, in a halo of late sunlight, he saw a young man who wanted to come in. He filled the doorway and, dazzled by the light, Emmerich and could not see who he was, and he drew nearer without a word and stooped to pass through the portal, and the impossible became possible before Emmerich's very eyes, and a young architect was resurrected there in the church, a young architect whose coffin he had walked behind many years ago, was now standing inside the portal. Emmerich closed the church door and stared at Gerhard Schönauer, who was not a day older.

Harum-Scarum in All Ye Do

A young man and a very young woman held their new life in their hands and found it heavy.

Too heavy.

It had been a longer and steeper walk than he had expected, and when they finally reached the top of the last slope, thirsty and dripping with sweat, and saw Hellorn for the first time, she wondered why they had stopped, and when she realised that they had arrived, that this was it, she was furious.

And then her fury was replaced by something far worse, which would in the future cause Jehans Hekne more knots in his stomach than anything else.

Kristine Messelt was *silent*.

She stood there for a long time, expressionless, before she bent down to pull up a slab of rock. She had to change her grip several times to get it loose, and most of the rocks round here were even bigger.

"Feel this."

"Aye," Jehans said. "I know."

"Nay, come right here! And feel it!"

Jehans let her ease the rock into his hands, shifting his feet to avoid falling over. The edges cut into his palms, and it was so heavy that it could have served as a suitable measuring weight for her anger.

"Ye knew? And yet?"

"I meant I knew how heavy the rock were. But happen it in't so bad here as it looks. We can—"

"*In't so bad?* There are rocks all around us, Jehans Hekne! There in't room for more rocks! In't space to build a house! No open ground to plant one single potato! Scarce twigs for a goat, afore she dies a death in the winter! Have ye ever been here afore? Answer me, Jehans. Have ye? Do nay twist and turn. Answer me!"

"Long ago. I canna' recall its being so bad."

"Then it were surely midwinter. Naebody who has been here can forget how bad it be. Look! Just a cruked overnight hut! And what be it built of? *Rocks!*"

The plateau was sunny and flat, about thirty square metres in all, but looming over them was a dark mountain wall, bare rock all the way up, except where the occasional little pine tree had taken hold. He was about to follow her, but she threw a punch at him in the air.

"'Tis ye all over, Jehans. Harum-scarum in all ye do."

The rocks clattered wherever she walked, telling him, and doubtless her too, that they lay in layer upon layer. Had it not been for its position in the landscape, it might have seemed like a dry river bed or tarn, and he had had a strange thought as they came here that they were coming to a place where there were fish, lots of fish, big fish, only to find that the tarn had gone dry, so recently that the fish were still lying there rotting. The difference here was that they could not go to another tarn, because he had used up all their money to buy this place, and there was nowhere else to go.

Hellorn had once been one of the smallholdings owned by the Hekne family. It had been settled so long ago that nobody could even remember when the landslide had hit. Kristine agreed that its early settlement must at least indicate good farmland, and since it faced south-west it must catch a fair amount of sun. The inhabitants must have decided against clearing the ground again, for fear of more landslides, and carved out another little farm further down in Butangen instead. Later the Heknes had only gone there in times of fodder shortage, to gather leaves from the crooked willows and birches that grew between the rocks.

He had told her all this on the walk up here, including that there had been a landslide, but that there'd be rich soil under the rocks, so it was actually just a case of *unpacking* it. And the River Breia ran through it, bringing fresh water all year.

She walked over to the small stone hut, the only building around. Shoved the plank door open and peered inside. She shook her head, and wandered over to a slightly gentler slope, where a pine tree had managed to put down some roots. Followed the slope to the very edge. As though taking measure of his idiocy.

He rocked a stone slab with his foot.

"Happen we can crack them in half with a sledgehammer."

"If we owned a sledgehammer," she said.

"We can borrow a sledgehammer. Can borrow two sledgehammers."

"Do na' give me a sledgehammer, Jehans. I shall split your head open with it."

This was not how this day was meant to end. Nor this marriage.

After punching his brother, Jehans had marched straight up to the *seter* and told his betrothed that his travel plans had come to nothing, but that on his way over the mountain he had come up with something new. His brother had left a monthly allowance meant for Adolf and Ingeborg, but he must now swallow his pride and pawn the Krag, then swallow yet more pride and go to Osvald and try to buy Halvfarelia in instalments. Kristine was, he said, free to wait with the wedding if she wanted. But her stint as a dairymaid was over for the year and she went back down to Imsdalen and fetched her Sunday-best skirt and took a bar of green soap for her hair and planned a bouquet of wild autumn flowers. Next day they walked for eight hours from the *seter* to Butangen, and two days later they were married by Kai Schweigaard with Adolf and Ingeborg as witnesses, and Jehans transferred the ring of galvanised wire and wrap wire to her right hand. Her parents came from Imsdalen, and her father walked her up the aisle, but they went back before evenfall and Jehans saw her shed a tear because the wedding had been so small.

They spent their wedding night in a little log cabin in the parsonage grounds, but Jehans felt the presence of other people in the room and was incapable when they were finally naked. They went to Halvfarelia, she liked it and said his little hut was rather small for the two of them, but it would suffice. She had earned twenty-four kroner over six years as a dairymaid, and she gave this to Jehans so the deal could be sealed. Adolf said his back wasn't so bad as to prevent him from helping them to build a cabin over the winter, and from the spring they could start working the land. *If* Osvald is willing to sell, he added.

"Back again, Jehans Half-Way? When I were thinking ye were on yer way t' England no less. As folk be saying."

There was another landowner in Osvald's office, his name was Ulrik Stulen and he was known in the village for his vast knowledge of horses, though the locals called him Stulsmyggen because he had such a pointed nose. He made signs to leave, but was stopped in his path when Osvald rushed to say: "That wedding o' yorn weren't up to much neither. This girl ye have wed.

I meant, bairn. That pastor o' yorn will wed anyone. She canna' be more than sixteen summers old."

"She is indeed. Though it be nowt o' yer business."

"So skinny and frail, poor thing," Osvald said, leaning back in his chair and looking at Stulen. "Pretty though. I'll give her that. Don't ye agree, Ulrik? Happen that was why ye didna' invite yer uncle to the wedding, Jehans. So she wouldna' see what a real farmer looks like. Take one look at me and be filled with regret and swing those hips right over here."

Stulen did not find this amusing, and quietly cleared his throat.

"Ye have ne'er called yerseln my uncle afore," Jehans said.

Osvald shrugged. Behind him were two handsomely framed maps of his vast estate, including fields and forestlands, and lying on the table before him were the plans for a new barn. Jehans noted that Osvald had expanded Hekne in the last few years, buying back the fishing rights and an old *seter* which the family had lost more than a century previously. Near him hung an old, dry birch rod. The sun shone through the window and glinted on his balding head. Resting his coarse hands on the arms of his chair, he stretched back.

"Look here, at the calendar," Osvald said. "'Tis but a few days ago this Jehans fellow were here and broke his cottar's contract. Being a kindly man, I let him off. Meantimes he gets wed and now he walks back in. But despite all. I shall hear thee out, Jehans. We shall try to reach sommat."

"I want to buy Halvfarelia," Jehans said. "The place where I grew up. Pay for it over ten years. But be free of doing any work in kind. So we can all live and work there. Kristine and Adolf and Ingeborg and me."

"Return to Halvfarelia? Impossible."

"Oh?"

"I told thee last time we spoke. I canna' sell my houses to my farmworkers. There are some *want* t' work and not dream. Do ye not comprehend that Hekne needs work? That it takes folk?"

"I have made my inquiries. A smallholding o' that size were sold in Brekkom this summer. It cost seven hundred kroner, and they got a strip of pine forest and wood for cutting wi' that."

"So ye reckon Halvfarelia is worth seven hundred kroner?"

"Seventy kroner a year for ten years."

"Reckon ye havna' heard of interest rates. But nay. Hekne shall ne'er be broken up."

"Half the cottars' smallholdings in Ringebu and Fåvang have been sold now," Jehans said. "Released as freehold."

Stulen butted in, saying he was expecting the farrier and had to leave. Osvald ignored him and went on:

"Jehans, my lad, do ye think I do nay read the papers? I know very well what folk do elsewhere. Good Lord. They be selling off smallholdings. And buying machines. Mowers and harvesters to replace manpower. And that's all well 'n' good on flat land. But folk who believe in machines have nay seen how steep it is in Butangen. And how big our crops be, cos the sun gets such a good hold here and the snow burns away so fast. Aye. Cottars may live frugally, but 'tis even more frugal in town. There will always be men, good, strong men, who want to be cottars. Happen I have been a little too hard on my workers this past year. But that'll be set right now. For the cottars too. They shall have more time now to tend their own land and go in the forest for wood. So my answer is nay, Jehans. I have already gotten new cottars for Halvfarelia. The old folk mun find another place to live."

Jehans staggered as though he'd been shot. It was impossible to see whether Osvald actually meant what he said. He was acting as though it had been a very hard but necessary decision to make.

"I shall leave thee t' tell them, Jehans. 'Twas ye who chose for them."

"Ye have nay got new folk in! Ye said it yerseln. That it were just a few days since I were here."

"And I suppose ye have knowledge of who did or did not come here and enquire? New folks are moving into Halvfarelia, Jehans. Decent workers who honour their contracts. Not agitators like thee. Hekne is not a poor box with an open lid."

Jehans was about to say that he could pay the same sum over fifteen years. Taking into account the value of the krone, if necessary.

Osvald looked at the map on the wall behind him. "But ye can buy Hellorn, Jehans."

Stulen burst out laughing, and declared he was *definitely* going now!

"But Hellorn has na' been lived in for an eternity," Jehans said.

Osvald's son Martin came in. Hekne's *odelsgut*, the oldest son and heir. He was thirteen or fourteen, and had grown hugely in the past year. The door was wide open, but Stulen did not leave, and Jehans knew that whatever he said now would spread through the whole village, because Stulen was expecting the farrier and when a farrier got wind of something, it was as good as making a public announcement.

"Jehans wants to buy Hellorn, Martin," Osvald said. His son closed the door behind him, and seemed to be sniffing out the most advantageous thing to say. Ulrik Stulen stood quietly by.

"Some say that the Heknes started out at Hellorn," Osvald said. "For Hekne means rocky ground. Aye! Do nay come here 'n' say I lack interest in history."

"Happen it were a fine place afore the landslide," Martin said. "One o' the first smallholdings. 'Tis just t' heave the rocks t' one side, Jehans. Ye took those slates down from the barn roof, so ye can surely clear Hellorn?"

Osvald began to tell, in his usual mean way, how his sister

Astrid had gone up to Hellorn once to gather young birch twigs as fodder for the cows. It had been a lean spring and her action had saved the whole family from starvation. But Osvald managed to twist the story so as to mock anyone "goose-headed enough" to let supplies run so low they had to go out and scavenge.

Perhaps even Osvald realised he had gone too far. It was as though a draught swept through the room, a cold reminder of what everyone ought to know:

When the dead are offended, they come back to life.

Jehans thought of his mother. What would she have done if she were here? Tear down the birch rod perhaps and whack Osvald across the cheek, tear the maps from the wall and force Osvald to eat them, then slap him again with the birch.

Or something more cunning?

It was as though Jehans followed his mother's gaze to the map. A thick line marked the Breia. The river flowed right through Hellorn's property boundaries. All at once he felt the old determination of his youth and the excitement he had felt when he drew mechanical devices and installations. He could feel that something had been aroused in him. Hot metal bubbling in a cauldron. But as he stood there he was careful not to show the heat that rose.

"It may just be possible," Jehans said calmly, looking at the map, "that we could clear Hellorn."

Out of the corner of his eye he saw Osvald and his son exchange glances. As though their little joke had backfired. Jehans said, "How much do you want for Hellorn, then? As marked out on this map."

"Well. That Krag ye bought. Folks say it cost thee fifty kroner or more. So, three hundred kroner. Fifty a year over six years."

"I canna' pay three hundred for a place that in't liveable for a year."

"Bah! 'Tis cheap. Three hundred kroner over six years! With no adjustment for inflation."

Jehans shrugged. "I mun talk wi' Kristine."

Osvald laughed. "Ha! I knew it! That ye be the sort who mun ask his wife's permission."

Martin laughed. Ulrik Stulen was silent.

Jehans was untouched.

Then Osvald's expression shifted as though he'd discovered a leak in his boat, and he said swiftly: "But the first payment mun be today. And 'tis customary for the first to be double the annual rent. That be one hundred kroner. So I have less paperwork when ye fail to pay rent next year."

"Deal," Jehans said. "Hellorn as marked there on the map."

"Deal? Ye do na' have a hundred kroner."

"Indeed, I do. I have it right here," Jehans said, taking an envelope from his jacket pocket. Forty for a pawned Krag, forty from Victor Harrison and twenty saved up by Kristine Messelt.

"Jehans, stop," Ulrik Stulen exclaimed. "Steady up now. Ye surely canna' mean to pay good money for Hellorn?"

"Hellorn shall be mine," Jehans said. "Write out a deed of purchase now, Osvald. Ulrik Stulen stands there as a witness. As does yer son."

He told Kristine everything that had been said in Osvald's office except the bit about asking his wife's advice. He had never asked for anybody's advice, but now he began to see what a big mistake he had made.

"Why did ye not come and ask me? Ask me what I wanted?"

"I knew what ye wanted! Ye wanted yer own land! And Halvfarelia wasna' for sale!"

"That doesna' say ye should buy sommat unfarmable! Why d'ye think Osvald were in such a hurry? Did ye not see that he wishes thee harm? It were *this* he wanted. That we should stand here quarrelling. To wear thee down! And wear me down!"

She turned her back on him. "And what about Adolf and Ingeborg?" she said.

"Nowt can happen afore *faredagen* on April fourteenth. He canna' throw them out before then. No new cottars will come this winter."

"'Tis *faredagen* on October fourteenth too," she said. "Depends on the contract."

She still had not turned to him.

"Ye should have gone with yer brother," she said. "Left the bell at the bottom o' the lake. Not even tried. Just gone with him."

"Let me show thee sommat. The thing of worth round here in't what ye can see, but what ye can hear."

"I hear only foolish prate and empty words."

"Ye hear sommat more."

"Aye, I hear the roar o' the Breia."

He told her his plan for the river and waterfall.

"And ye tell me this now?"

"Aye."

"To surprise me? I've had surprises enough for one day, Jehans Hekne."

"It'll work. They have done it in Lillehammer and Tretten and all the villages up in Fron."

"We mun grow sommat to eat before that. And winter in't far now. Well, well."

They were silent. He tapped a rock with his foot. It clattered against the rock underneath.

"I have nowt else to offer thee. Go back to Imsdalen if ye mun. I shall do some logging this winter, and ye shall have all yer money back."

"I shan't go back to Imsdal."

"Oh?"

"Did ye nay hear me say *well, well*? I have done with wailing. I wed Jehans Hekne and I knew there were easier matches. I can work night and day when I be angry. And I shall always be angry so long as I look upon Osvald Hekne. He shall get his comeuppance. So that he knows it. I shall stay with thee, Jehans."

"I thank thee, Kristine." He started walking towards her. "And I be sorry."

She crossed her arms and did not let him in.

"I shall stay. So long as ye promise me one thing. One thing."

"And that be?"

"That ye never do the like o' that again. Decide over my life without asking me. Never."

He promised.

"At least there's a good view from here," Jehans said, looking out.

"Aye. And that means there are views from the village and up to us, too. Come and put yer arms about me now. Let's stand here on the edge so everyone can see us. So everyone sees the two biggest fools in Butangen. The man who bought Hellorn and the maid who wed him."

Galerie Apfelbaum

He was halfway up the bell tower when he stopped.

Through the gaps in the log walls he could see Dresden. He had never seen a city with finer architecture. But he was in too much turmoil to take in the view.

He heard the chatter of jackdaws in the trees just beyond

the walls of the bell tower. The stave church had a heavy, spicy fragrance. Had he not known better, he would have thought it was incense, but it was probably the smell of tar which he had noticed in some of the log houses in Butangen.

Victor had walked in here as visitors to a church generally do, without expecting to be watched by anyone or asked anything, but had been met by a rather confused-looking churchwarden. He greeted him in the little German he knew, sat on the far end of a pew and felt a cold draught from the wall. Gazing about him, he got a strong sense of how the church would have felt in Butangen. As though he could walk out of the door and bump into Jehans and the pastor.

The warden followed him with his eyes as he got up. He opened a narrow side door and then stepped aside, motioning for Victor to enter. Now, halfway up the third ladder, Victor realised where he was going.

Towards a church bell.

No. Nobody had the right to add him to a family picture that was not his. Tar would never be the smell of home. The smell of home was Rangoon oil, peat bogs, the smoke from Eley shotgun shells and Kumara's picnic lunches.

Victor climbed back down, sneezing a little from the dust, and stopped in the church room, a hazy light surrounding him. The warden said he had never let anyone into the bell tower before.

"It must all have been a misunderstanding," Victor said. "I had no wish to see it."

"Apologies," said Emmerich. "It's just that – that you're very like someone I once knew. The young man in charge of moving this church. He had a special connection with the church bell above us, and I – well, I apologise."

Victor wanted to leave. He reached the portal and stooped down to walk out into the daylight, but stopped when he was met by the chill outside air, a wind with the faintest hint of coke fires burning in the city's buildings. Behind him the old stave church lay warm and dark.

He turned and said, "Tell me then. About Herr Gerhard Schönauer."

Emmerich led Victor to the sacristy, where he kept a tin of biscuits and a thermos of coffee, and he told him about the rebuilding of the church and his brief friendship with the gifted Schönauer. The architecture student had been born in Memel in East Prussia, was talented as a painter as well as an architect, but had been the victim of some sort of intrigue in the last year. They had shared a bottle of cheap tokay in his lodgings, Schönauer was coughing badly and had awful breath, but was eager to tell him how he had just finished working on a large oil painting. It was a variation of a motif he had first painted in Norway, and he had completed it partly under the influence of a fever. The painting was rolled up and standing in a corner of the room, but he was reluctant to show it. Between fits of coughing and knocking back the sour tokay, he had told Emmerich that he had got married in Norway and that his new wife was pregnant, but that his pneumonia might well prevent him from ever seeing the children grow up.

"The *children*?" Emmerich had asked.

To which he got no real answer.

The only people present at his funeral had been Professor Ulbricht, two Norwegians, a couple of construction workers and himself. A misunderstanding had meant his parents did not arrive until the coffin was in the earth, and Emmerich suspected that nobody had informed his landlady of his death, since, when he brought her the message, she was angry because Schönauer owed her rent and she had to clear up after him.

"So I did it instead," Emmerich said.

249

"You cleared out his room?"

Emmerich nodded. There had not been much apart from the empty tokay bottle they had shared. The bed was made. He had framed a drawing of a young girl with curly hair. Hanging over the back of a spindle chair was a shabby red-brown coat with figures of eight embroidered around the buttonholes. In one pocket a pipe, and in the other a bottle of cough syrup. There were brushes and tubes of paint scattered around. And in the corner by the wardrobe stood the oil painting. Emmerich unrolled it and saw a rather wild depiction of a woman in red, and wondered if Schönauer had been insane or a genius. It was a disconcerting image, since it was hard to decide if the woman was dead or alive. A small self-portrait in pencil lay pressed inside the rolled canvas, as if Schönauer had wanted to be face to face with her.

Emmerich paid the rent and took everything with him. He gave the coat to a beggar, and used the shoes himself in dry weather. He wrote to Schönauer's parents offering to send them the painting and self-portrait for the cost of the postage, but received no answer.

Victor asked why the warden had wanted to send him up into the bell tower.

"I'm not sure why, but it occurred to me that you wanted to go up there," Emmerich replied. "To put yourself to some kind of test."

"Nobody else has been up there?"

"No."

"I don't need to undergo any tests," Victor said. "I am long finished with those tests that were meant for me. I am who I am."

"I can see that," Emmerich said.

Victor got up to leave.

"How much was the rent?"

"Three marks," Emmerich said.

"It must have been a small room. Even in 1881."

That night Victor stayed at the Hotel Goldener Engel, which was marked with pencil in *Meyers*, and the next morning Emmerich handed him the rolled-up canvas with the painting. No thanks, he didn't want the three marks back with some twenty years of interest. Absolutely not. But thank you. And – farewell, Herr Harrison.

In his hotel room, Victor unrolled the painting, but sat for ages studying the little self-portrait of Gerhard Schönauer. It was like gazing at his own reflection. Although a rather more honest depiction than the painting of him in the ancestors' gallery at Finlaggan.

Victor turned his gaze to the red-clad woman in the painting. She was not, in his eyes, at all sinister. Independent-minded and decisive, perhaps. Although yes, neither living nor dead. He released the edges of the canvas, letting it spring back into a roll, and the red-clad woman and Gerhard Schönauer hid themselves in each other again.

Later that day he stood in the cemetery outside the city hospital in Friedrichstraße holding a bunch of autumnal flowers. He could not find the grave and was reluctant to ask anyone. He walked back to the city centre and bought a pair of binoculars. Back in the cemetery he scanned the tombstones as if he were scouting the Highlands for red deer or the Norwegian mountains for reindeer, and fifteen minutes later the inscription GERHARD SCHÖNAUER loomed through his lens. He put the flowers on the grave and sat next to the headstone, as though they were resting together after a mountain hike and looking at the view, and said:

"I'm here to bid you farewell, Father."

He knew he ought to say something profound at a moment

like this. But it was just him and the headstone and he sat browsing through *Meyers Sprachführer* and looking at Gerhard Schönauer's notes in the margins. Coming across the pages filled with words beginning with K, he found two fingerprints on the paper.

Kuß. Kyss.

What had he wanted from life, this architecture student? Perhaps he wanted only her. Fräulein Astrid. And to bring her to Germany. With the baby.

Jehans growing up in a German city? Victor found it hard to imagine. He ventured to think of himself growing up in Germany. It was a little easier to imagine.

Victor sat and thought about the pastor's strangely meaningless parting words. His thoughts ran back to a Hardy Smuggler that was still somewhere in Norway. He had never held a better fishing rod, though it was really nothing more than an averagely good rod.

If it really is the case that Jehans is my twin brother. That a choice was made. Is there something unique about me? Something that made my mother choose me rather than Jehans?

An hour later Victor got to his feet. When he had first sat down by this headstone, he had had two fathers to choose from; now he had only one. He went to the cemetery gardener and asked how long the tombstones stood before a renewal fee had to be paid. Thirty years was the reply. Victor took a final stroll past the grave and discovered that his flowers had disappeared. He thought they must have been stolen by a young boy to charm his sweetheart and wondered if this was a better use for them.

The Dresden art dealers were clearly tired of looking at the immature works of students from the Art Academy, and merely shook their heads when Victor mentioned the painter's name. The fourth dealer he visited was Galerie Apfelbaum in

Heinrichstraße, run by the Rathenau family. The owner had a pointed beard and large, gold-rimmed spectacles, and he said he would like to look at it. Yes, even the work of an unknown student.

He perused the painting for some time. Picked up his pocket watch, shouted *Elsa* into the backroom, said something in a foreign language and then disappeared.

A girl in a grey-green dress with loosely fitting sleeves, scarcely more than eighteen years old, appeared from behind a curtain. She had large, almond-shaped eyes, so large Victor was unsure whether they made her beautiful or strange. She was slight, with a narrow build, without that making her the least boyish. Her brown hair was set up in a tight bun fixed with a long wooden pin that had a tiny parrot with a red beak carved at the end.

Without asking where he was from, she switched to English. "Is it a copy?"

Victor shook his head. "That's unlikely."

"It's technically brilliant. Brilliant. And inspired."

"I agree."

"Who's the artist – let's see now – Schönauer?"

"He was a student at the Academy until 1881. He was responsible for the rebuilding of the stave church in the Großer Garten here in town."

"Wasn't that Herr Ulbricht? The old professor?"

Victor told her briefly what he knew about Schönauer and the reconstruction.

Elsa Rathenau nodded. "This painting has a truly unique power. Do you know the Norwegian painter Munch?"

"No."

"This female figure – dressed in red – she's sort of ... otherworldly. Without the image seeming unrealistic or pretentious. She looks like someone who might really have lived. Someone the artist actually saw. Or – was allowed to see. I see self-sacrifice and a will in her. As though she's guarding something."

"He started it in Norway. So this woman has something or other to do with the stave church, I think."

"Hmm!"

They stood for a long time. She said, "The colours. Do you see how specific he's been in their selection? Only using pigments known from ancient times. Pigments with mythical associations. These brushstrokes on her cheeks, for example, must be in *Caput mortuum*. And here in the shadows he's used burnt umber. A colour associated with death and ghosts."

Victor cleared his throat, not knowing what to say.

"I presume it'll be easier to sell at auction," he said at last. "Here in Dresden, where the stave church is."

"That sounds sensible," Elsa Rathenau said. "The stave church has its admirers. My father will need to decide on the valuation. If you come back tomorrow?"

It was drizzling when he returned to the gallery, and once again he and Elsa Rathenau stood looking once again at the painting between them. Clearing his throat, he walked round the counter so they stood side by side.

"It's as if the picture invites me to move closer," she said. "And asks me to dare to cross the threshold to get to know this stranger. And there's a certain recklessness too. As if the artist is staring at his own downfall and yet chooses to cross the boundary. It demands you surrender to it."

He alternated his gaze between her and the painting.

"To spend more time with it than you actually dare," she said.

"Exactly."

"It's almost like accepting a stranger's invitation. To share a simple supper, perhaps."

"Hmm."

"Or just have a coffee and talk a little about oneself."

Victor cleared his throat again and did not meet her gaze. When he had finally decided to say yes, yes, please, let's go, the moment had passed and daring to wait no longer she continued in a cooler tone: "We take a lower commission on student works. Only twelve percent. The next auction is in three weeks. Where should the money be sent when it's sold?"

He took out a folded note with a name and address.

"Send it all here."

She looked at it and frowned. "I see," she said. "But we'd like to have a receipt from the artist. There are occasionally police checks."

He hesitated. Then opened the folder and hesitated a moment before showing her Gerhard Schönauer's self-portrait.

"Look at the signature. Schönauer."

She looked back and forth between him and the drawing, and noticed that it was dated 1880, twenty-four years earlier.

"Yes," Victor said. "He drew me *before* he died."

"Well now, you *are* full of riddles! Perhaps you're one of the undead!"

"Keep it," he said. "The self-portrait. As a memory. If you want it."

"That depends on whether you're coming back to Dresden."

He looked down. He wanted to invite her for dinner, but her life was here in Dresden and it was unthinkable that he'd ever return to Dresden. Elsa Rathenau went into the backroom and he heard a drawer being pulled out. On her return, she handed him a small photograph of herself mounted on thick card.

It had been taken in a studio, by a photographer who was as skilled in his art as Gerhard Schönauer was in his. He gazed at it for a long time before he tucked it into his inside pocket and gave a little bow. The shop bell rang over the door of Galerie

Apfelbaum, and he met her gaze through the wet glass as it closed behind him.

When he arrived home at Finlaggan his father threw his arms around him and said that the case containing the Rigby and other equipment had arrived the week before. "Why did you send it on separately?" he asked.

"I spent a few days further south in Norway. Just to look around. Wanted to travel light."

"Rather alarming, Victor. Receiving your rifle like that. With no proper message. I thought to myself, that's how it comes, the property of a man who's disappeared abroad. A trifle ... unnerving."

"Yes, Father. And the dead tend to arrive at a later date. In their own carriage. Smelling decidedly foul. But here I am. Alive and well. Any news from Mother and Jo?"

His father shrugged. He wandered over to a picture frame that contained a scrap of Scottish tartan. All that was left from the ancestor who had grown up many centuries ago near Lake Finlaggan in the Hebrides, and had ended up settling here. His father often went to this unusual relic when he felt lost or undecided. To this portrait without a figure, which ought by rights to hang at the top of the ancestors' gallery.

"I think they should do their own thing there in Florence," he said. "And we can do ours. Good news from Ceylon, by the way. Excellent news. Kumara got the new rotary dryer going. But said he misses Finlaggan. Said it straight out. Oh, and there are some letters for you in your study."

His father indicated a door on the left of the corridor, even though Victor's study had always been the one on the right.

"You need the space," his father said. "I shan't be needing it from now on."

The study had been cleaned and tidied and fitted with

bright new lamps and by the fireplace were two modern sofas so that four people could sit in front of the hearth. Someone had polished and waxed the old deep-red leather desktop, and his father's scratch marks were now gone. His father had taken down his map of the Transvaal and had framed a map of Ceylon that Victor had bought when they had first been there together.

Victor glanced through his letters. One had a Norwegian stamp, sender Kai Schweigaard.

What if they had chosen Jehans back in 1881? Then it would have been *him* standing here now, holding this letter, while I'd have been up in the Norwegian mountains, ragged and penniless.

Or perhaps he wouldn't be standing here at all? Perhaps he'd have stuck it out on that raft with me?

Victor threw the letter unopened into the fire. The envelope turned black, but the paper remained whole, and his name and address were clearly visible. In the flames the pastor's elegant writing turned a sepia brown. He prodded the burning letter with the poker and watched his own name disintegrate into black flakes that fluttered up the chimney.

Settlers

Kristine shifted one slab of rock after another. They banged and clattered against each other, and she said nothing. Eventually she got down to a rock that was wedged in the earth. A thick dust rose into the air as she wrenched it onto its end. She shoved her hand in underneath it, and when she removed it black soil and earthworms ran between her fingers.

Rich arable land.

Yes. Hellorn *had* been inhabited. Long ago.

By the fifth day they understood exactly why nobody had ever been foolhardy enough to attempt to clear the place. Where the ground wasn't covered with rocks, the dwarf birches and willow had sent their roots into the earth beneath and woven them into a dense chain mail. The roots were so firmly entangled that it would take an entire day to free up a patch the size of their bed in the stone hut.

Sleep took them after a backbreaking day, and their growing misery erased their desire, despite their being so lightly clad in the hot autumn weather. They borrowed picks and shovels and a hoist with a chain, and hoped to clear enough land to be able to set a year's supply of potatoes in the spring.

Schweigaard came up to see them, and was more worried than ever. He suggested they spend the winter at the parsonage. Jehans thanked him, and said *maybe*, before turning to heave another rock into place.

And *no*, he did *not* want to write to his brother in England. He had accepted the envelope that Victor had left behind, with a month's wages meant for Adolf and Ingeborg, but that was out of bare necessity and would be repaid in full.

Listening in on their conversation was Kristine, with bloodied hands and a grey, dusty face streaked with sweat, as you'd expect of someone clearing rocks all day.

One week later the stone walls of their hut were fixed, the roof was made tight and Jehans had built them a better bed, which they covered with straw and sheepskins. They went down to Halvfarelia to borrow some tools from Adolf and Ingeborg. Neither of them had heard anything from Osvald.

They carried up a little kitchen stove from the parsonage, section by section, together with some porridge oats and dried meat and a sack of pearl barley, which was a wedding gift from Oldfrue Bressum.

"We need a barn,' Kristine said. "And ye know what that barn mun be built from."

"From what we have."

"And since 'tis easier to carry down than up, it were best we build it there," she said, pointing further down the slope.

They cleared a path down, and with axes and saws built a wheelbarrow sturdy enough to withstand heavy use. They made the axle from a huge cross-slice of pine, and nailed a piece of pigskin inside the hub to provide lubrication, which to their surprise prevented any overheating, however heavy the load. Flat rocks were laid along the path, so the wheelbarrow could roll more smoothly, and six days later Hellorn was no longer just a pile of rocks, but a pile of rocks with the stone foundations of a barn. And from these foundations, a neat flight of stepping stones led to the stone cabin with a stovepipe poking up between the roof tiles, from which rose a ribbon of smoke.

By day twenty the barn's foundations had begun to look like walls, and a gap on one side indicated that a doorway was planned. The autumn cold had set in, and the plot intended for a potato field was now double the size of the sitting room floor at the parsonage.

The following day Jehans went down to Halvfarelia to collect some potatoes. There was a sharp chill in the air and the leaves had fallen, but the nights were still relatively mild, and his foster parents always kept their potatoes in the ground until the first frosts came and the grass lay flat.

Then it struck him that *faredagen* had been and gone.

Halvfarelia felt strangely unfamiliar the instant he went inside the fence. The old cow had always bellowed on his arrival, but she was nowhere to be seen. The door to his hut was open, a goat was grazing in the yard, and near the potato field stood an emaciated woman with three little ones hanging on her skirts. He went over to her and asked after Adolf and Ingeborg.

"Gone away," she said.

Her dialect was from one of the Frons villages. Osvald had managed to get new tenants in from a day's journey away. Cottars who knew nothing about the goings-on at Halvfarelia.

"It were agreed I fetch some potatoes from here," Jehans said.

She disputed this, saying that Osvald Hekne had promised they could take the farm exactly as found, which included anything growing above or below ground and the firewood in the shed. If he didn't leave, she'd send her husband and boys after him, since she'd now realised who he was.

"And who might I be?" asked Jehans.

"A man who ran from his duty."

"Is that you?" Kai Schweigaard said. He was standing in the hallway in his overcoat and walking boots.

"Were ye on yer way out?" said Jehans, even though the pastor's clothes exuded a gust of cold air.

"Me? No. I just got in."

Schweigaard hung up his coat on the hook, and signalled that whatever was said now should be said behind closed doors. Jehans headed up the stairs to the pastor's study, but was waved back down. The door Schweigaard chose to close behind them was the door to the sitting room. There was no fire in the hearth, and the room felt gloomy. Jehans sat on the edge of a rickety Biedermeier sofa while Schweigaard remained standing.

On the morning of October 14, the old folk in Halvfarelia had been sitting by the stove. They had put their coffee pot and porridge pan on the heat earlier than usual, because it was such a cold morning, the autumn gloom descending upon them from the mountains. They had not even made their bed when a group of strangers opened the gate, led by a hired farmhand from Hekne. He was there, he said, to show the place to the new cottars. He seemed just as surprised that Halvfarelia had not been vacated as Adolf and Ingeborg were to be told they should have been out on the previous day.

Adolf stood up and protested, saying that Osvald had not given them proper notice, that there were fixed deadlines which should be observed, because farms needed a proper handover period of several days, and what about the potatoes and vegetables they still had in the ground?

But the farmhand read out a statement that was clearly dictated by Osvald, since the name *Jehans* came up in every sentence. *Jehans* had reneged on their cottars' contract, and *Jehans* had been informed at the time that Adolf and Ingeborg would have to leave Halvfarelia. Osvald assumed therefore that *Jehans* had conveyed this fact to his foster parents. But the contract was signed by *me*, said Adolf. No, that was irrelevant. For the contract had to be honoured. Meaning that *Jehans* ought to have turned up for work. When *Jehans* failed to appear, the contract could be terminated.

But we ought to have got notice long beforehand, said Adolf.

They had been given notice. *Jehans* had been assigned that task.

That was when Ingeborg snapped. She got up and snarled:

"How did he get to be so evil? That man Osvald. I should like to know! And I shall ask him! I shall go straight down to Hekne this minute! I shall be happy to move out o' Halvfarelia just to be a free citizen at last and go down there and say it to his face. I have wanted to say it for thirty year, and if I die on my way out, it shall have been worth it!"

Adolf hushed her. The new cottars muttered. They were a husband and wife with six bairns, from four to fourteen, and they said this wasn't what they'd been told to expect. They didn't want to throw out any old folks with winter approaching. The agreement was that they would come to a vacant smallholding, and that was it. Perhaps they could stay at Hekne until after the winter, there must be room in the workers' accommodation? But then the little ones started to scream and the autumn wind blew, and they weighed their own needs against those of the old folk. They had left their home behind, travelled far, come all the way here with all they owned, the horse first and the cow last, with tools and bedding and kitchen utensils piled onto a cart and a barrow.

It went the only way it could.

The old and new tenants, both, tasted the punishment and anxiety that the little folk exerted upon each other in the scramble for food and housing, and which made it so hard for them to stand together against their superiors.

The old folk were granted an extra two days to leave the smallholding that Adolf had inherited from his father and grandfather and which Ingeborg had tended since they were married. And when the new tenants moved in, they felt the warmth of their last fire.

Jehans could not bear to stay sitting, and listened to the rest as they stood around the fireplace.

"They should ha' sent for me," Jehans said. "I would ha' talked him round. Tried to make sure – I could have helped them move out at least. Where be they now?"

"They went to Hilstad to ask if they'd take them in as paupers."

"What a foul muddle I have made," said Jehans. "Folks mun come and clear up after me. The money in that envelope should have been theirs."

"I've my own share in this foul muddle," Schweigaard said. "Which is why—"

Jehans interrupted. "But were the Hilstads able to take them in?"

"Yes, of course, they were more than happy to. They're good people at Hilstad. But nothing that monstrous can happen in

a village without the pastor hearing about it. Adolf and Ingeborg are doing well now. They're living in Widow Framstad's
old cabin."

"What? The little cabin on the road up to the *seters*?"

"Yes. She left it to the church when she died."

"But that were a long time ago."

"We've kept it in good order and let the occasional lost
soul live there when needed. Every year my tenant farmer has
tended the vegetable fields, set the potatoes and topped up the
woodshed and barn. But then this autumn, I had the feeling
something was going to happen, so I kept it empty."

"Ye had the feeling sommat were to happen?"

"Yes. More and more I get the feeling that I know what's
about to happen. It isn't often I'm pleased with myself, Jehans.
But that day, when I showed them the old midwife's hut, I
certainly was."

Jehans breathed out.

"Something else happened that week," Schweigaard said. "A
letter came here from Dresden. With a money order. From an
art gallery. They've sold a painting by your father. Maybe he left
it with them to sell some time. It's all rather unclear. The letter's
addressed to me, but the money is yours."

"Mine? But how did these folks know about me?"

"It doesn't say. It just says they've sold a picture. But I have a
feeling Victor Harrison might be behind this."

"Victor? And how could he be sure *I* would na' want the picture? If it were fine? I'll wager it were worth a good deal more.
He has sold it and taken half. At least."

"You really must find a way to forgive your brother," Kai
Schweigaard said. "I'm certain he'll come back. He must. You
know that. Sometime or other. And then you'll have to forgive him. Use your imagination. We tried to pull him up by his
roots."

Jehans shook his head, whether at the idea of forgiveness or a homecoming was unclear, perhaps it was at both.

"The money. Be it much?"

"Yes. Ninety kroner in fact."

Jehans crossed his arms. Then uncrossed them.

"'Tis a trick o' some kind. A kinda pay-off. Happen there were no picture at all. Send the money back to Victor. It were better he had chosen not to believe the bell had any meaning. That it were just metal."

"But it isn't. I said that once. That it was just metal. And I was very mistaken. But you need to concentrate on yourself now, and your own life. You aren't your brother. You shan't ever be your brother."

Jehans slumped down onto the sofa and put his head in his hands.

"'Tis all so wretched. So mean. We toil away up there, but I know deep down it'll come t' nowt. Hellorn can ne'er be made liveable. I had some notion about sommat I might build up there, but now – nay, 'tis pitiful."

"Jehans," Kai Schweigaard said, "you must begin to *believe*. Believe in God by all means, but you'll get more out of believing in yourself. I know that something is going to happen soon. For you and Kristine. *Something big*."

Jehans got up. He'd grown thin and had to tug his trousers into place. Back in the hallway he laced up his dusty old boots, and when he got up again his neck was bowed. It was not, however, the bowed neck of a defeated man, but of a bull going into attack.

"I shall get Osvald," he said. "In some way or other I shall get him."

"No doubt you will," said Schweigaard. "But you won't do it as a cottar."

"Happen not. I shall call on the river for help."

*

Jehans and Kristine were forced to part ways that winter. They did not have enough supplies to get through the cold months in Hellorn, and there was no work for them on any of the farms. Kristine went back to Imsdal to find work, and Jehans did some logging in Ringebu for a farmer to whom he had sold reindeer meat. They had talked about celebrating Christmas together, but the weather conditions over the mountains were so harsh it became impossible to arrange it. So Kristine spent Christmas in a loft in Imsdal while Jehans stayed in a cabin with a lumberjack. They were paid by the trip, and nobody protested as their axes rang out through the forest, even on the first day of Christmas.

Jehans was unsure what she was thinking. All he knew was that she had no great desire to return to Hellorn. Sometime before Easter he skied across the mountains to fetch her, and the first thing he did was to look at her belly. She shook her head and said, "Thank heavens," filling him with a sense of gloom that was to last long into the future. Come April, the snow had melted on Hellorn, and she remarked that Hellorn was the first farm to be snow-free in the spring, and he said at least that was something.

In the black patch of earth amid the sea of rocks they set potatoes they brought with them from Imsdal. Kristine washed them one by one and put them out in the spring light to sprout. They looked as soft and wrinkled as the faces of old folk, but Jehans and Kristine were so weak and hungry they almost felt tempted to eat them. But into the earth the potatoes went, and there in the earth they used their last strength to send forth shoots that reached for the light, and immediately they poked above the ground, they shot forth leaves and drank in the sunlight which they sent to the tiny dried buds of new life deep in the soil. But whether something grew there or not was the earth's secret, like the secret in Kristine's belly.

The potato setting was the first thing they did together that might yield something. They planted two hundred potatoes and immediately began guessing at how big the crop might be, multiplying two hundred by all the things that had influence, the sun, the rain, the earth, the warmth. And they hoped they would lift the first new potatoes by late spring.

The landslide had swept away the path that had once been used. They acquired a thirty-metre-long hemp rope, knotted it at forearm-length intervals and fixed it on rocks and crooked pines, so they now had a fully functional handrail, allowing them to carry heavier loads without the worry of falling over. They continued to break rocks and build and clear land, and the invisible life of the seedlings under the earth gave them hope, and they were aroused and went inside the stone hut and lay with each other without washing the dirt from their hands. And they fell into a slumber and were glad when the rain set in, and they went outside and let it wet their faces and hands, and told each other that this was exactly what the potatoes needed. And back in the stone hut they lit the stove, closed the door and paused for a moment to listen to the rain, but soon their hands reached out to each other and then to something practical, as they made a new handle for a shovel or ladles for the kitchen, or measured for the timbers that would have to replace the mud floor if they were to survive there until winter.

In the afternoon the rain grew heavier and towards the evening a strange creaking could be heard from below. They dashed out and saw that one of the walls of the barn was leaning at an angle, then one corner came crashing down before their eyes.

"Happen I laid the rock askew," Kristine said. "It mun all come down and be built again."

The rain ran down her cheeks, but by the way she trembled he could see she was crying. "My fault," she said. "'Twas my fault."

"Ye canna' be blamed. Ye have never built a barn afore. And nowther have I. Likely the ground were frozen and has thawed."

"Aye. And 'tis better the barn fall now," Kristine said. "Think if it fell after it were full-fettled."

That night he thought he heard a rumbling in the mountain wall. But he said himself that the world must surely have emptied itself of misfortune that day, and if it had more, it was welcome to empty it out upon their heads now, so that nobody need trouble themselves over making a grave.

Next morning it was winter again.

The snow drifted down, the wind was bitter, and Kristine was nowhere to be seen. He ran out in his shirtsleeves and found her by the potato field. The stubby potato shoots, the tiny, regularly spaced bouquets that had been such a fresh, dazzling green the day before, were now frozen through and dark against the snow.

"We mun melt the frost with water," Kristine said. She grabbed buckets and they rushed down to the River Breia, and ran back and forth, pouring water on the potato shoots. For no matter how cold running water may be, it will always be above freezing.

But soon both they and the potato shoots were cold and limp.

She said nothing, and they turned to look out over Butangen. There was some snow down there, though very little, but the folk there had waited with potato setting because they knew the lore of the weather.

Far away, beyond the Løsnes Marshes, he thought he saw a cloud of smoke coming from the railway near Losna. It's hopeless, he thought. I thought I knew how hard it would be. I was wrong. It's impossible. Nobody breaks new farmland nowadays. Not by hand.

He got up, and leaving the water buckets behind he walked back down to the Breia. The river was crashing over the white slopes, fresh, powerful. Swollen with meltwater, it roared with huge force.

When he got back, Kristine had wrapped her hands in leather strips and had started to turn the pile of rocks back into a barn.

The snow melted again, and they had a week of warm weather. They got some more seed potatoes, but they planted them in silence, with no burning expectations of how well the autumn and winter's food might be growing beneath the ground.

He often went to the edge and looked down over Hekne. The planting season had been going for a while now, and the villagers were getting impatient for the *onnemellom* – the in-between season – the calmest time of year, a time of sunshine for the people and fresh grass for the cows, and with that, milk and butter and some rest.

Then the rain set in. It was unusual to get such torrential rain at this time of year, but it came. Wet and gloom for days on end.

They continued working, but he thought: Even my stubborn grit has its limit. Kristine's has too. She may reach that limit later than me, but she *will* reach it.

It was then that Jehans saw a tugging movement in the top of the pines to which the hemp rope was tied. They heard muttering and chatter, and far down the slope one voice said this couldn't be the right way, and another grunted and said that there was a rope there, so it had to lead somewhere.

Then they appeared.

One after the other.

All the farm labourers who had been ploughing and planting at Hekne for Osvald. All the cottars from Hekne's eight tied smallholdings. There were folk from Heknemoen and Gardbogen and Arnestua, and even the new folk from Halvfarelia were there, as well as the widow from Solfritt with her children, and others from Hekneøygarden and Bjørnstad.

Kristine and Jehans dropped the rocks they had in their hands and stared on in disbelief.

One by one they came up, and stood at the edge, chattering away, looking around, and helping each other up onto the plateau. And their number kept growing, from being ten they soon became twenty, and then from twenty they became thirty, and at the very back, helped by folk both behind and before them, came Adolf and Ingeborg. Jehans rushed over to them, and still nothing was said about why they were all here, until Torger, the cottar from Hekneøygarden, stepped forward.

He was one of the scythemen who had stepped aside for Jehans when he had scythe-chased Osvald.

"There be a goodly bit o' the day left," he said. "We have worked long days down at Hekne cos Osvald got it into his head that new ground could be broken in the south field. But then came the rain and the earth were unworkable and progress slow. We did nae even have our lunch afore we mun leave. He did nae consider that the work would go down well on *our* farms. So we stopped on the road and talked. About the way Adolf and Ingeborg were slung out last year. About how Hekne were before. We agreed that if we would work for Hekne folk, it would be Kristine and Jehans Hekne. There are more folk t' come behind us, and they have food wi' 'em and tools."

One-Room Palace

In eight days, more than two hundred man-days were worked at Hellorn. On reflection some said it was closer to three hundred man-days if you took into account how late they continued into the evening, and how efficient it was when they made a human chain and passed rocks directly to the folk building the barn. Everyone kept ratcheting up the tempo and clamped down on any slacking. They were from twelve years old to eighty-eight, so work was divided between the quick and wise, the strong and pedantic, the dogged and daring, and when Kristine totted up their ages for fun they came to twelve hundred years of experience in breaking land, timber construction, masonry and carpentry. The ancient holding was completely cleared of rocks, and the walls rose by the hour, some joking how easy it was to build when the materials were so close at hand. It was as if this unruly mass of fallen rocks had surrendered to a superior force, and decided to behave and turn itself into a farm, so that after much lifting with long iron bars and fingers, the rich, black soil lay open and the rocks now formed stone barns, a pigsty and neat stone walls.

Jehans took a few minutes' break. Leaned against his crowbar and looked beneath the crags, where a small cabin rose from the ground up, log by log.

And for the first time ever, he felt he *belonged*. That he was one of the Butangen folk.

And realised that folk had probably always counted him as one of them.

The son of the Silver Winter.

It was as though Butangen itself, with all its hundreds of years of quiet, accumulated wisdom, came into blossom. Rarely did the old folk need to ask him or Kristine what they wanted, the design of a structure or its location, they knew they knew all the right ways to do things, for their parents and grandparents and forebears had long since discovered the wrong ways at terrible cost, and these were warned against and never repeated.

They fetched timber from a plateau above the crags. The pines were stunted and seldom really straight, but that was all that was available. A team of eight with axes chopped the wood into logs and floated it to the waterfall and sent it over, then the logs were pulled out at the bottom and stripped, so they glistened pale yellow and smelled of new house.

Borgedal the Younger directed the construction work. As the son of Borgedal the Elder, he was the village's second best master builder. The plan was to build a cabin with two separate rooms, but after a hurried exchange about limited timber lengths, location and available time, they concluded that this was not immediately viable, and the house was affectionately named Ettromsplasset – the One-Room Palace – even before the first row of logs was laid in place.

Concerns were raised about how to obtain the necessary birch bark to lay under the stone roof tiles, since the birch sap had dried up long ago, making it impossible to peel the bark off. It was then that perhaps the biggest and most generous gift came from the poorest villager. Widow Fløter, who wove baskets for a living, brought up all the birch bark she could carry, saying that they could go back for more as there was plenty where it came from. She said Kristine and Jehans were welcome to help her sometime when they had things in order, not next year or the year after, but sometime, sometime, if they could.

Other gifts were small, but everything helped. A lump of sourdough that had been fed for nearly eighteen years. Newly forged axes and a saw blade. Four hens. And the farmer's wife from Nyfløt brought a bunch of long twigs wrapped in grey cloth. They were black- and redcurrants, cuttings from her strongest bushes, which were not planted until she had prowled around like a cat looking for the sunniest, most sheltered spot. Finally, some animals arrived that few saw much worth in, but which a quick calculation showed could provide them with meat in a matter of months: three hardy farm rabbits.

On the eighth day, as suddenly as they had begun, the

villagers declared they were finished, and as they stood at the top of the path waiting to go down, a new seriousness was in the handshakes. Part pact, part thanks. An expectation.

The rope jerked hard at every metre as the helpers made their way back down.

Then they were two.

They moved into their one-room palace and could finally sleep in a dry bed, walk upright without banging their heads, sit on chairs and eat at a table, cook on a stove that wasn't so crooked that the fat went to one side of the frying pan. And they lay with each other as they farmed the land, fiercely and with steadfast vigour, followed by a quiet moment in which they admired all they surveyed, and registered their anticipation of what the next year would bring.

But despite their being rescued, Kristine's restlessness grew. It was as though she could only draw strength from injustice, that she was not content unless she had something to conquer, whether it be rocks or a blizzard or sour cream that refused to turn. And what they could both see, but neither said, was that no matter how much help they received, they could never turn Hellorn into a decent farm. The rabbits had multiplied and hopped about freely in the stone barn, and since they were ready for slaughter after a couple of months, each doe could provide them with fifty to sixty kilos of meat in a year. Doubtless they could get a couple of goats up here too, but the harsh truth was that it would be impossible to bring any larger livestock up the steep slope.

A farm without cows was not a farm, and Kristine Messelt without cows was not Kristine Messelt.

Presumably cows had once grazed on the stretch of flat ground at the edge of the holding closest to the River Breia. But this was now a wilderness of rowan, pussy willow, ferns and spindly birches, such an unmanageable tangle of roots and stumps and branches that the villagers had named it Vrangjordet – the Obstinate Field – and left it untouched.

"I shall get a calf," she said. "Bind its hooves and carry it over my shoulders. If we bring her up here when she be small, she will grow up here. It'll work. All we need is a place she can graze."

She always had some sort of secret plan brewing. One night, just as he was dropping off, she said to him, "Jehans. Tomorrow ye mun go down to Vrangjordet and cut away the bushes and make an enclosure. No, not all Vrangjordet. About an eighth part. I shall leave early and do na' frustrate my plans by stroking me when I wake up. I shall be back in the evening."

He made the enclosure of rowan twigs which he wove between posts, and with each metre he made he wondered what she had planned, and he took a moment to sit down and gaze about him and think that maybe this was something to be proud of.

Late into the evening the rope tugged. Kristine came up, scratched, bloody and dishevelled. On her back she had a pack-frame and over her chest a harness, on which she carried two six-month-old piglets.

Despite the fact she had tied them securely and bound their trotters, they had gnawed through the ropes, wriggled free and bit and kicked her till she bled, nonetheless she was in good spirits, saying it was a sure sign they were a match for the task ahead.

She had borrowed the piglets from someone down in the village, there were another four below, tied to a tree, which must be fetched before they bit through their ropes, they would be returned when it was time for them to be slaughtered, she had driven them up here alone, but there was no time for further explanation. An hour later, she and Jehans had carried all the pigs up and released them into the enclosure.

Six pigs, Jehans thought. They will have eaten the shrubs and leaves in the enclosure in just a couple of days.

Still Kristine did not reveal her true plans to Jehans. The next day the pigs rooted about, eating the ferns and foliage on the small bushes, and after that chewing on the remaining twigs. Then they started to squeal for more food. They overturned the water troughs and grew extremely ill-tempered.

She stepped over the fence with a potato hoe and hacked at the ground. "Ye mun start now! Go to it!" she said. "We do na' have much to eat either."

After a day of loud squealing and fretting and battering at the fence to get out, one of the piglets began digging with its front trotters around the roots of a pussy willow. It burrowed its snout into the ground, shoving the earth aside and digging deeper and deeper, until it found something to grab. It was then that the power of its big, strong neck came into its own, and it bit and dug and tugged and soon it freed a tiny root from the soil. The others rushed in wanting to steal it from him, but the piglet defended itself and chewed the root to shreds, saliva and soil running from its mouth. The sun had nearly gone down as the other piglets set about doing the same, digging and grunting and gobbling.

"The old dairymaid told me once that t' understand an animal I mun understand what that animal were created for. How it lives wi'out folk. Why is the pig's snout as 'tis? 'Tis not a neb wi' big nostrils. 'Tis a tool for digging. The pig's neck is not so broad and strong to give us fine meat. 'Tis so cos the pig is created to rowk in the dirt."

The piglets grunted and rooted about late into the evening, and come sunrise they were already in full swing, digging and eating and clearing the land. They had even begun to overturn the rocks.

"That be a big rock for such a small piglet," Jehans said.

"A great-foul rock indeed."

"Did ye know? That a pig could turn over such a rock?"

Kristine shook her head. "Nay. Happen even we may strike lucky once in a while."

"'Tis me who has struck lucky," Jehans said, hugging her.

The pigs wrenched the rocks loose, threw themselves over the pale earthworms that surfaced and gobbled them up, and only when the whole field had been churned up were they moved on to another spot. Kristine and Jehans took iron bars and broke up the rocks and stumps that remained, while the pigs continued elsewhere so that bushes, twigs and weeds vanished, and after wandering through their stomachs and intestines for a few hours, the vegetation turned to manure, which the pigs trod into the soil with no thought of the service they were providing, and all the time the pigs grew bigger and turned into meat and lard and offal.

They could finally relax and stretch their bodies in the warm sunshine. They slaughtered two rabbits, lifted some new potatoes and carrots, and ate and drank water from the Breia. And they lay with their stomachs full, in the evening sun outside their one-room palace.

"Think on't," she said. "We canna' eat twigs or leaves. But the rabbits can. And just now we ate the rabbits. And aside from that they have given us fur and manure."

"'Tis good," he said. "'Tis as it should be."

"But ye would rather be in the mountains with your Krag," she said. "I see it in thee."

"Aye. But ye see it less in me this year than last."

"But ye mun not lose the feeling entirely. For then ye will lose yourseln. We mun get money so ye can release the Krag from the pawnbrokers."

He turned away from her then.

For there had been money. A brother's money for a father's painting. But it had been returned.

Jehans looked at her and felt the breeze coming in from the

Løsnes Marshes and the winter that would soon be upon them. He looked at her belly and wondered what kept her from having children with him. For while everything about them ate and jostled and gave birth and sprouted and grew, they still remained fallow.

How the Pastor Will Die

Kai Schweigaard stood at the altar and felt the chasuble's comforting weight across his shoulders.

It had been made for use in the freezing cold stave church, and was so warm he could only wear a thin tunic under it. Loud hymn-singing had begun and the deep sounds of the organ reverberated along the floorboards. Herr Røhme was standing at the back of the church, dressed in his smart suit, ready to come to the rescue should any problems arise.

It was Whitsunday. The year was 1905. It had been an eventful and momentous week. That Wednesday Norway's union with Sweden had finally been dissolved, and Schweigaard had raised the new national flag, as had almost all the local farms. The celebrations had been marked in big and small ways during the days that followed, and moments ago, as he sat in the sacristy with the window ajar, before the start of Mass, he caught snatches of conversation: *Shame! It in't at all seemly!* Up in the pulpit he understood what all the fuss was about. Four women were sitting together in the middle of the church, tight-lipped and eyes staring straight ahead, while the other women stared at them uneasily.

In contrast to the more sombrely dressed women, the little

group were wearing traditional *bunads*. Two wore bodices of red and dark-green tartan. The other two costumes were dark, but embroidered with bright yellow and red flowers, and resembled something Widow Stueflaaten had shown him.

Schweigaard waited until there was silence in the church and then began Mass with a few carefully chosen words, suggesting that while folk wore their best clothes to church, clothes might also represent a flag, *the flag we have finally claimed for ourselves*. And with that he won some acceptance for the four rebellious women.

The organ set to, but as the service went on a minor melody resonated in Schweigaard, a deeper connection with the human condition. Strangely enough it was on this and other important festivals, when he presided over the loftiest rituals and most formal liturgy, that Schweigaard felt most open to religion again. A paradox, he knew, since it was at such times he focused on the most abstract teachings. The seas that parted for Moses' staff. The word that was made flesh. Jesus who rose from the dead. The Saviour's cry. *Effata!*

He still liked to imagine the real events that might lie behind these stories. It was as if faith itself took a risk when it made such extraordinary claims, as if it was throwing down a gauntlet, demanding that wonder ought not to be removed from religion. It was as though God laid himself open, invited him to a man-to-man discussion about rationality and faith, and when he spoke of miracles in his sermons, Schweigaard was remarkably steady, seeing that it was one of the most difficult aspects of the Bible: to speak of the widow of Nain when the family in the front pew had lost their children. When a blind man sat in the church, and he contended that Christ could mix saliva and earth, smear it onto his eyelids and give a poor man his sight back. It was not easy to turn these miracle-stories into parables, the villagers of Butangen heard what they heard, and these sermons demanded he muster every bit of humanity and liturgical gravity he possessed, and having a chasuble helped. Dressed in the Church's holiest garb, he felt the huge embroidered cross upon his back like a powerful father's hand, irrespective of his doubts and sense of impotence.

Up in the pulpit he began telling the story of the Pentecost: *And suddenly there came a sound from heaven as of a rushing mighty wind, and it filled all the house where they were sitting. And there appeared unto them cloven tongues like as of fire, and it sat upon each of them. And they were all filled with the Holy Ghost, and began to speak with other tongues, as the Spirit gave them utterance.*

He could go no further.

He pretended to cough, but came no further. He was suddenly reminded of the Hekne Weave. It was said to depict birds spitting tongues of fire towards the earth. He had always assumed they were bringing destruction.

But were they perhaps bringing wisdom?

He had always been irritated by the new Norwegian Bible translations, where the tongues of fire were divided *after* the fire had entered the house, rather than as the older texts and the English Bible presented it, outside the house.

As the weave, presumably, presented it.

He cleared his throat.

"There lived in Jerusalem . . ."

The service was over. He walked out into the fresh air and round the church to the entrance steps. The bells rang and the doors opened. He nodded, smiled and shook hands. The order of precedence was unshakable. Farm owners sat at the front of the church and came out first. Thus the firm handshakes at the beginning: You're one of us, Herr Pastor, through your office if not your wealth. Then the cottars: rough, working hands, old hands with wrinkled skin, the occasional slender widow's hand, the small, firm hands of children who reached up. And lastly the paupers. The more clingy. Help us. Come and visit us. Thanking ye, Herr Pastor.

No handshake from the Hekne farm.

And none from Jehans and Kristine.

But Adolf and Ingeborg were there, among the last as always, he bent-backed, in neatly patched *wadmal*, and she in her Sunday-best skirt, with a shawl over her shoulders. He could tell from their handshakes that there was something they wanted to say, but that this was not the place, and he gave them an understanding nod.

Back in the sacristy Schweigaard hung up his chasuble. He was a bit sweaty, so flung off his tunic too and put on something nice and dry, and when he re-emerged he was a very ordinary priest.

But then, as he passed Astrid's grave, he stopped. There she lay, with her face to the east, waiting for Judgement Day. After his blasphemy at the Birthing Foundation all those years ago, he sometimes felt like the Flying Dutchman, a lost man who could only be redeemed by the kiss of a woman who truly loved him. But the only one he wanted a kiss from was dead.

As he strolled back up to the parsonage, two old friends followed him close on his heals. Longing and bitterness. Was his self-sacrifice perhaps a protracted suicide? Not even Fru Røhme's picnic lunches could distract him from the impotence he had felt in the last few days as he sat in the priest-boat, looking towards the village, dressed in a sweater from Dovre. Was there anybody here who actually needed him? *Him* as a person? They needed a pastor, of course, and he could perfectly well go by the name of Kai Schweigaard and be Kai Schweigaard, but was there anybody who actually thought about Kai Schweigaard and *needed* him? Widow Stueflaaten had doubtless found a new husband by now. He was nearly fifty and a bachelor. The bell was stuck in the mud at the bottom of Lake Løsnes. Victor never replied to any letters. Jehans was doing something completely at odds with what he was destined for. The Hekne Weave was lost forever. Astrid had sent one of her sons to a new life in England, but it was not for him to understand why. The Hekne wheel rolled slowly but remorselessly on without him, and if he stood in its way he would only be noticed as a little bump in the path of fate, as he was mowed down.

But still. Pain and remorse were life too.

He ended up in the priest-boat again that evening. He attached a new trolling spoon, recommended to him by Herr Paper Cone at the colonial store. Made in Romsdalen, it was hammered out of old dinner spoons and named after the River Rauma. He cast his line and let it sink to the bottom.

Always the hope. The fisherman's prayer. Lord, give me a trout so big that I won't have to lie about its size.

But as always out here on the lake, rationality sank to the bottom. Thoughts that had only ever been fleeting glimpses, like bitter experiments, now loomed large and demanding. He realised that the episode with the brothers that night had forced him closer to a long-postponed confrontation with his own reason. He thought of Klara Mytting who had frozen to death in the stave church. She had believed in all kinds of strange things, even that the Holyblight – the verdigris that formed inside the Sister Bells – could cure diseases. Her whole generation were like that, no phenomenon ever seemed beyond belief. They were often outright naive, they saw a sequence of events and automatically deduced a cause. Somebody walked under a ladder or spilled salt and their cow was killed by a bear, and the ladder or salt were to blame. He accepted that the Hekne Weave had existed, but not that it had any capacity to tell the future. If it had, folk would just have stared at it endlessly and believed its predictions to be absolute fact. They would just have frittered their time, since it would make no difference what they did with their lives. Everything would be fated.

Instead, it probably showed something indistinct, multifaceted. Perhaps it had an ability to make people think, to grow more aware? Thus it might help people towards what he liked to call *deflected fate*; showing them things that *might* happen but could be avoided with forethought? Perhaps it taught them to identify the evil one's footsteps in the hallway, so they could bring out the silver crucifix in time?

And why, he wondered, was it said that the sisters had been buried under the church floor, when only their pillows were there?

He felt a tug on the rod. But it seemed to be the sedge grass, since the tip of the rod just bent under a slight weight and stopped vibrating. He reeled it in and rinsed the hooks. Cast out the trolling spoon and let it sink.

What if the Hekne Weave *did* have powers? What if he allowed himself to think it? If he turned the tables, this priest, who defended miracles? What exactly *was* impossible? The place of spiritualism in religion was fiercely debated among priests, and he saw advertisements every day in the papers for clairvoyants who offered their services. In England it was permitted to bury the dead in lead-lined coffins, in the hope that they might be brought back to life some day. He rejected such nonsense out of hand, but premonition? He had experienced that for himself several times. Particularly with Røhme. Schweigaard would hear his warden enter the hallway downstairs, and then minutes later see him outside in the courtyard before coming in and making the exact same sounds that he had just heard. Schweigaard just shrugged these things off, they were as they were, and he had recently developed an interest in Augustine's defence of miracles – the idea that inexplicable events are not contrary to the laws of nature, but merely contrary to the laws of nature as we presently know them.

He himself had seen a wire fitted to a glass dome followed by a blinding light that shone into every corner. He had held a telephone receiver in his hand and talked to someone far away in Kristiania. If someone had told him fifty years ago that these things would happen, that there was an invisible force called electricity that could drive motors, produce light and transmit sounds, he would have dismissed it as impossible.

These paradoxical thoughts floated in and out of his head, but as darkness fell, it was as though Gunhild was gently rocking the boat.

He suddenly remembered Adolf's handshake earlier that day, and the look in the old couple's faces.

What might they want?

The stave church's portal had been found at Halvfarelia. Hidden there, serving as the back wall of the sheep byre. He had spoken to them about the Hekne Weave when Jehans was small, but many years had passed since. What if the weave had been similarly hidden, and they had found it at Widow Framstad's cottage? Even if only part of it? Cleverly hidden perhaps. Rolled up under a roof, or within a wall. In a lowly and inconspicuous place, like a birth in a stable.

They had made themselves comfortable. The cow was grazing outside the cabin. The stove was humming inside. The coffee grinder hung on the wall, and they had eaten their fill.

Schweigaard said he hoped he wasn't intruding, he just wanted to see how they were getting on. They talked about Jehans and the huge team effort that had been made up at Hellorn. Eventually Schweigaard realised that the handshake on the church steps must have signalled gratitude rather than any secret.

"And Osvald?" Schweigaard said.

"We have heard nowt from him," said Ingeborg. "But I hear that the cottars be amutterin'. Some of them mutter pretty loud too."

"That's hardly surprising."

"Aye," she said. "I hear they be planning sommat big, but 'tis best that the pastor stay well out of it."

Kai Schweigaard gazed about him. It was here, in this very room, that Astrid and Widow Framstad must have performed some sort of ritual that told her she would give birth to twins. Old Ingeborg could see his mind was wandering, and cleared her throat. "Looks to me like the pastor has sommat to ask us?"

Kai Schweigaard gathered himself and asked straight out about the Hekne Weave. They seemed unsurprised by his question. But shook their heads.

"Nay," said Adolf. "'Tis not here. We would have known."

"So you knew about the portal?" Schweigaard said.

"Aye. We knew all right. But my father were told by the Heknes as was that we mun say nowt about it. Not unless a priest or one of the Heknes came and asked us straight out. And then young Astrid came and she asked. But the Hekne Weave , it were ne'er here in Halvfarelia. We would ha' told thee."

"I keep wondering whether they hid the weave in the village somewhere," Schweigaard said. "As they did with the portal."

"Hmm," said Adolf. "In't so sure their first concern with the portal were to hide it. That that were their thinking. I reckon it were more that folk here were so clever at putting things t' good use. Everything were so precious back then. Happen they thought it were too good to cast aside. That it could be put to use."

"Ha!" said Ingeborg. "That brings sommat to mind. I remember when Jehans said the word *rubbish* the first time. D'ye remember, Adolf?"

Kai Schweigaard frowned and looked at them questioningly. Adolf said: "Rubbish. Aye. It sounded so queer t'us. It were sommat quite new t'us. That word. There were no such thing for us. We mended and sewed and forged things till there were nowt left to mend. I got my potato hoe from the wife's mother. 'Tis on its sixth shaft and second blade. Different iron. But 'tis still her mother's hoe."

Schweigaard said he was almost certain the weave had been taken down in 1813. Apparently because the birds frightened the soldiers from going into battle. Could folk really have believed in such things?

"They believed in signs, at least," said Adolf. "Sat, studied, mused. It were an art, in the olden days, to know how to read signs. All kinds o' signs. In the behaviour of animals and shifts in the weather, the dorsal fin of a perch and how the rowan blossomed. It were important. How else could they get by?"

"But would they have been scared at the sight of a bird in a weave?"

"Who knows," Ingeborg said. "But they weren't afeared by what they *saw*, only by what they *thought* they saw. And then they egged each other on. Remember folk were starving in 1813. Naturally they was afeared. Worst harvest ever. And then folks believe all the easier. For 'tis said the birds spat fire upon them that stood on the ground with swords. Soldiers, that is. But I heard sommat quite different about why it were removed."

"Nay, Ingeborg," said Adolf, "d' nay talk about this now."

"Oh, come now. It were only a superstition."

"But such a terrible thing," Adolf said.

"Nonsense, this be our pastor."

"Aye, precisely."

"What is this?" Schweigaard said.

"I heard say," said Ingeborg, "that the Hekne Weave were taken down for it told of how Butangen's last pastor would die."

"But how can there ever be such a thing as the *last* pastor? Surely there'll always be a new one?"

"Nay. The last shall be the pastor when Skråpånatta comes. At the end."

And the Hay-Rack Wire Sparkled

The water crashed over the rocks, losing all form as it shattered into a white froth that glinted in the light. The river's entire weight and tumultuous energy were transformed into a rush of droplets, a weightless blur that smashed against the rocks below and gathered in a foam that roared down towards the village. Jehans went in closer to the churning waterfall, so close that the water droplets fixed themselves to the hairs on his bare forearms, for a brief moment like shiny fleas' eggs, before turning into rivulets that ran across his skin.

A hand also covered with water droplets stretched to take his, wet skin touching wet skin, and the droplets found a common path and trickled between their fingers.

"Will it work?" Kristine said.

"If not, we shall turn it into an irrigation system."

The waterfall had doubtless looked the same for a thousand or two thousand years, but now a curious and rather rickety construction had appeared alongside it, a long path of wooden posts and planks that stretched forty metres up.

A year had passed since they had been rescued by the villagers. What they stood before was the River Breia, what they looked at was a water channel. Rather makeshift perhaps, but a water channel nonetheless. Which, according to their calculations, could carry six hundred litres of water per minute. A mere splash, however, compared to the entire contents of the river.

They had cut down some large trees that winter, he and Kristine, up on the plateau above Hellorn. One by one, they had dragged the logs on a sledge to the banks of the frozen river, and when the ice melted in the spring, they had rolled them out into the water, floated them down to the village's only sawmill, and then hauled the sawn planks back up to Hellorn. This made the villagers think they were busy making roofs or floors, and Osvald that things were going too well for them. He demanded they buy shares in the sawmill to use it, but the other farmers objected, no, they said, it went against custom, and would hinder folk of humbler means from getting construction timber.

The building of the water channel was the coldest and wettest work Kristine and Jehans had ever undertaken, and they could only manage two hours before they had to go back to the cabin to warm up by the stove, pale, shivering, emaciated. They had completed less than ten metres before the beginning of May, and then they had to sow seeds, set potatoes and prepare the newly cleared ground.

There was still not enough grass to graze a calf, so they bought two young goats which they carried up over their shoulders before releasing them into the wilderness on the outskirts of the farm. Not until June had they been able to start work on the river again, and now they had worked for six weeks nonstop, wet through and chilled to the bone.

At first he had pictured a turbine powered by water running from a channel, but it was too complicated, and impossible to make out of wood. The waterfall was surrounded by swathes of rocks and crooked birches, and he would have to construct it while standing mid-stream.

Kristine persuaded him to use something that they knew to be reliable. Something that had always been made of wood. A waterwheel like those found on flour mills and sawmills every-where. He remembered from all his old books that a wheel that took water from above retained two-thirds of its power, while one that turned with its bottom below the surface of the water retained only one third. This made the choice very easy, but it would still lack the necessary speed. So they built a small shed next to the waterwheel and on the most solid wall he planned a wall-mounted gearbox of pulleys and drive belts – pulleys and drive belts he did not yet possess.

It proved a watery ordeal, working in the icy chill and constant roar of the river, with connections breaking and fittings sliding out of place, they had to erect a supporting wall out of stone and timber, but with that done the waterwheel was finally complete. Four metres high, black and wet, there was something medieval about it, rough-hewn and crude, as though built out of a dismantled stave church.

She let go his hand and said, "Off wi' thee now. And 'tis vital ye succeed. For I want sommat in return for this ordeal. Sommat that shall be mine alone."

So Jehans left for Vålebrua and went into the train station, where he asked if the telegraph operator might be interrupted in his work for a moment. Fløtersønnen came out. He was wearing dress trousers and a waistcoat, with a pencil tucked behind his ear, but had not changed a jot. It was six years since they had last seen each other, and they shook hands. Jehans asked if they could meet after work.

"'Tis concerning electrics. I wondered if ye might lend me some wrap wire and a magnet from the workshop here."

Fløtersønnen turned out to be married and renting two rooms above a grocery store. There was pea soup and flatbread for supper and Fløtersønnen took his little girl on his lap and fed her with a spoon before eating his own.

"'Tis a mighty queer thing living here," Fløtersønnen said, his eyes roving about the kitchen in which they sat. "We mun buy everything here. Even spuds and milk."

Jehans looked around. There were no heavy tools for digging or carpentry, nothing but pots and pans.

"Happen 'tis better t' buy things than have t' make them yersen?" Jehans said.

"Indeed. A little accident back at home has the power to turn life on its head. I were thinking of my mother t'other day. Once, when I were a bairn, she spilled a pail of milk. That pail were meant to last us all the week and I were little and hungry. Without the pastor I'd still be up there working myself to the bone."

Jehans cleared his throat and took out a little book he had fetched from Schweigaard. "I were asked to send thee greetings," he said, placing Dietrichson's *Physics Textbook* on the kitchen table.

Jehans planned to make a dynamo. It didn't have to be big, just enough for three or preferably four light bulbs. And he would need to borrow those from somewhere too. No. He had no money at all. Not a single krone. Not now. But it would come. And soon.

As a boy Fløtersønnen had had a habit of tipping his head right back when he was thinking, and he did so now.

For a long time.

"Problem be," he said, eventually, "the anchor in a dynamo mun be magnetic. To make electricity, we need a magnet. And to make a magnet, we need electricity. But we share a workshop here with the railway. They have some big batteries. And we need lots of copper wire. I know of a broken electric motor."

They went to the stationmaster who lent them a key to the workshop, with the warning that if Fløtersønnen did anything to delay any of Norges Statsbaner's trains by just one minute, then he could expect instant dismal. They found the twisted remains of a railway track in the workshop, and various other scrap metal which they collected in a box. The electric motor proved to be completely burned out, so Fløtersønnen let himself into the telegraph office and took a coil of lacquered copper wire, intended to repair the coils that converted the current in the telegraph wire into mechanical movement and then into Morse code.

"Ye be risking your job now," Jehans said. "Ye canna' do that."

"There be only one telegraph operator in the village, so the stationmaster canna' throw me out just like that. Follow me, Jehans. We mun visit a blacksmith I know."

Torgersen was also the son of a cottar who had taken up an independent trade. He ran his blacksmith shop from his home opposite the cluster of shops in Vålebrua. He immediately rejected the section of track, as it would not be sturdy enough when it was spinning fast, but since it was in a good cause, he dug out a large steel cylinder.

Thus began a long evening and night of heating iron, hammering, of trials and errors. They noted that all the knowledge they were drawing upon here had been passed on to them as children in Pastor Schweigaard's Sunday school. Shoulder to shoulder now, they continued to work in the orderly, slightly chilly workshop, surrounded by the glow of paraffin lamps and the smell of burnt coal and hammered iron.

"What o' the church bell?"

"It lies where it mun lie."

Fløtersønnen stretched his neck.

"Lake Løsnes is filled with water from the Breia. Dam the river, and ye shall find the bell. Is that what ye be planning? In truth?"

"We would need a dam the size of Lake Løsnes."

Jehans glanced sidelong at Fløtersønnen and wondered if the

brotherly feelings he had for this childhood friend were simpler and perhaps superior to those he had felt for his real brother during their time in the mountains.

They lined the steel cylinder with baking paper before wrapping it with lacquered copper wire. Back in the railway workshop, they connected it to an electricity current from an accumulator, and knocked the cylinder gently against the table for two minutes.

"Here goes," Fløtersønnen said. He put an iron nail on the workbench and guided it towards the steel cylinder, and then, when it was a few inches away, he let it go. It skidded across the table and latched onto the cylinder with a click.

"Praise be," he said. "We have a magnet!"

From then on, the steel cylinder was called the anchor. They handled it with great care as though it were made of glass, since it would lose its magnetic force if it knocked into anything.

Back at the blacksmith's workshop, Torgersen had already made some sturdy pillow block bearings, partly out of bits taken from an old harvester. And now, as the hours ticked by, the scrap metal and the anchor and electromagnet came together to form a dynamo, a fairly substantial one.

"'Tis mighty heavy," the blacksmith said when they were done, and Jehans knew what it meant when a blacksmith said something heavy.

"Aye," said Fløtersønnen. "But 'tis not too great a challenge to lift." The two cottars' sons knew what he was saying. Those forty kilos of dynamo were infinitely easier to carry than forty kilos of granite rock on another man's land. They connected the light bulb and put a crank on the axle.

"Wind it up now, Jehans!" Fløtersønnen said.

Jehans turned the crank. But nothing happened. He adjusted his position and tugged at the crank as hard as he could.

"Hmm," Fløtersønnen said.

They discovered that the distance between the magnet and anchor was too great, and they carried on through the night, improving the suspension, adjusting various connections and hammering out protective plates, and as the sun rose and they turned the crank again, the light bulb filled with a yellow glow, and they thought they had before them the machine that could replace the sun.

Kristine Messelt was standing next to the pigsty with mud on her boots and blood on her hands. Two young sows had grown quarrelsome and had bitten each other. Kristine grabbed one, straddled it and gripped it between her knees before emptying a pail of water over its wound to see how bad it was. Their iron cooking pot had been left by the front door with the remains of their morning porridge. She had been cleaning it with a birch brush and soap, but now a greyish layer floated on the top, and he understood that she had been interrupted in her task by the rumpus in the pigsty.

"I need help carrying, Kristine."

Together, they towed the forty-kilo dynamo down to the river. But it proved harder than expected to transfer the energy from the waterwheel to the alternator. It lacked the necessary momentum. He had to go back to Vålebrua and ask the blacksmith to lend him some steel pulleys and drive belts, and it took a few more evenings before Jehans stood with two pieces of galvanised hay-rack wire in his hands and thought he saw them vibrate on demand.

The power line up to the cabin was the most makeshift thing of all, a row of poles leading up the slope from the River Breia with cables made of old hay-rack wire.

Several weeks later, after Kristine had been left on her own all summer to tend the crops and livestock on Butangen's toughest farm, he finally clambered up into the waterfall and opened the intake to the channel. A rock came loose from one of the pipe's supports and bounced down, nearly hitting the waterwheel. The wheel shuddered, then gradually started to turn, faster and faster.

In the shed, he saw the power travel through the drive belts and increase in speed for each pulley they shifted gears through. The hum of the dynamo grew stronger and deeper. There was a faint smell of burning and he could feel it was already heating up, although there were no visible flames or sparks.

He ran alongside the poles and thought he heard a whistling from the hay-rack wire.

"Kristine!"

"Now?"

"Aye. Now."

"Come on, nay, leave yer shoes on."

Hanging from a plank in the middle of the room was a glass light bulb.

Kristine blew out the candle and the cabin grew dark, and all that could be heard was the squeaking of metal against metal as he screwed the bulb into the socket. Suddenly a screaming yellow-white light flooded over them, spilling into every corner of the room, over the ceiling and over the floor, and they blinked and turned their eyes away from the light, and realised they had never seen every corner of their cabin before, not even when the door was open in the summer. The log walls were a paler yellow and smoother than they had thought, and as they gazed about them, the glow of the spiral inside the bulb danced across their retinas, following them wherever they looked, and refusing to be blinked away.

Their excitement lasted a good five minutes. They hugged each other, then pushed the other away and held each other at a distance, before hugging again and holding each other at a distance again, though neither really understood why, until they realised that they could see each other clearly, despite the dark, and that they liked what they saw.

"Ye be soaked right through, Jehans. I hadna' noticed."

They both thought the light would soon fade, flutter or disappear, but it kept going, on and on, maintaining its strength, minute by minute, it did not flicker or flutter, the lamp emitted no smell, soot or smoke, and the miraculous possibilities multiplied before their very eyes: it wouldn't blow out in the wind, it didn't need to be refilled with paraffin, it wasn't a fire risk and it could even be lit in a barn near the hayloft. It could be turned on and off without hitch, yes, when it shone, it did just that, it shone! They stood there in complete awe, their eyes drawn to the bulb again and again, although its brightness stopped them looking straight at it, as if some ancient sun god had chosen to make an appearance here in their humble one-room palace.

"Let's go outside," Kristine said.

There was one window in the main wall of the cabin and another by the front door, and the light shone equally brightly from both. Suddenly the little house looked bigger, more welcoming, less mean.

They looked down over Butangen, invisible now because none of the windows were lit strongly enough, and Jehans remembered what Schweigaard had said about his mother's desire to travel to a city with street lights, and he swelled with pride as he looked back at the village, where the only thing he could make out besides the sky was the inky-blue mirror of Lake Løsnes.

They turned it off, and he embraced her and knew that from now on the night would be different, that the certainty of light would make the darkness a better darkness.

The Dynamo Master

Jehans stood in the autumn dark at the bottom of the long avenue of hedges that led up to the Gildevollen farmstead. He had passed the parsonage on his way here, and there had been a light in Schweigaard's study window, but it was not the moment to call on him.

It rarely was. But perhaps that might change now.

He shifted the chamber charger on his shoulder and trudged through wet leaves up towards the imposing farmhouse. Here, too, the faint yellow glow of paraffin lamps flickered behind the windows.

Otherwise the village was in darkness. The only visible things on the horizon were the valley sides and the trees that lined their crests.

The dogs were barking before he even reached the courtyard. He leaned his rifle against the outside wall of the farmhouse and climbed the six broad stone steps up to the double doors. The house had been built at exactly the same time as the demolition of the old stave church, and rumour had it that there had been an argument between Gildevollen and Schweigaard about who should have use of the local workforce.

Jehans had never knocked on the door of such an imposing house.

A young boy came out. His face was impossible to see in the darkness. Jehans was led down a long corridor and into a small side room, through a parlour and finally into the large living room, where he found the farmer sitting at the end of the table, a fire in the hearth, reading the newspaper by the light of two smoking kerosene lamps on either side of him.

"Yes?" Gildevollen said, without looking up.

Jehans continued to stand there. He heard other people

294

coming in behind him, but did not turn, he had no wish to see who they were and would gain nothing by knowing.

Gildevollen read on. Turned the page and read a bit more, before finally looking up at Jehans.

"The clock just struck nine," he said, nodding towards a grandfather clock that was ticking somewhere in the corner.

"Aye, 'tis late," said Jehans. "But it has to be dark for—"

"Has to be dark? Only a thief's errands need it to be dark."

"I thought I might show thee sommat," Jehans said. "'Tis outside."

Gildevollen laughed. "I know what's out in my own courtyard. Unless you've dragged a wolverine here that you want to sell?"

"'Tis sommat far away from here," Jehans said.

Gildevollen grunted and rocked in his chair, and for the next fifteen minutes he busied himself with various farm matters to demonstrate that he wouldn't be bothered by folk who turned up at such a late hour. But Jehans could see he was curious, and they were soon out in the courtyard, where the flagpole stood like a delicately shimmering line between the indistinct contours of the house and the roof.

Many of the household followed them out and more joined them. Among them Gildevollen's eldest sons, two youngsters who laughed between themselves, and a little girl who came dashing out, a voice shouting after her that she should be in bed and asking what the commotion was.

Jehans pointed further up the valley.

"'Tis up there," he said. "Up at Hellorn."

"You want to show me something that's up at Hellorn? Lord help us, Jehans Hekne. You should have gone to the doctor in Vălebrua. Not come here."

"I mun only give the signal."

"Ooh, that too? And who's going to hear you shouting from this distance?"

"I have my rifle," Jehans said, reaching for the gun. He cocked the rifle and lifted it.

"If ye can all cover yer ears?"

Ole Asmund Gildevollen laughed aloud. "This is getting to be fun. I was pretty bored in there, but not anymore. Just wait a minute. Oddvar! Run and tell Aud and Odveig to light the hurricane lamps and go into the barn. So the cows don't get scared. We're going to have a bit of shooting here."

Two indistinct figures carrying paraffin lamps trotted across the courtyard and up to the barn doors. The glow of the lamps vanished with the sound of the doors being slammed. Jehans put the percussion cap on. He felt a knot in his stomach.

"Well, shoot then!" Gildevollen said.

Jehans pulled the trigger. The chamber charger clicked.

"Damn," he said. He thought folk would laugh, but they went quiet.

His hands were sweating so badly that he could barely put on a new percussion cap. Again he aimed the old gun at the night sky, assumed that nobody lived up there, and fired again.

The shot rang out over the courtyard, and everyone looked in the direction towards which Jehans had pointed.

But the darkness was no less dark.

"Well?" Gildevollen said.

There was the quiet creaking sound of *wadmal* as someone pulled their jacket about them. Gildevollen smacked his lips, as though trying to decide which caustic comment would be caustic enough. A nursemaid told the little girl who ought to have gone to bed that it really was time to go inside and go to bed.

"No!" screamed the girl. "I want to see the Christmas star!"

"Star?"

"Look there! And there!"

Jehans lifted his head. Up in the darkness was a soft point of white light. It looked as though it was hanging there in the air, and then another lit up and hung in the air. Then a third and a fourth, all glowing like tiny stars.

Gildevollen was deafeningly quiet.

The four lights continued to hang there, their strength began to vary, then three of them went dark in quick succession, and the fourth began to blink on and off. But suddenly all four lit up again, and the little girl declared that Jesus must have lit all his Advent candles up in God's House now, which meant it would soon be Christmas.

But Jehans was no longer looking at them. His gaze had turned towards the real stars, as he thought: *Mother, do ye see me now?*

Next day Ole Asmund Gildevollen went up to Hellorn to inspect the electricity station. He had brought a farmhand with him to carry two picnic lunches and six bottles of root beer, and taken many breaks on his way up the steep path, so he was well fed and watered. The spray from the Breia mixed with his sweat as he nodded and examined the water channel, the waterwheel and the shed containing the dynamo.

Gildevollen turned towards them and Jehans knew what he saw.

A man and a young woman, both emaciated, with calloused hands and patched clothes. It had been two years since they had started to break up the land on Hellorn, and in those two years Kristine's face had grown more gaunt, her skin browner and her answers shorter.

"'Tis just temporary," Jehans said, loudly, so as to be heard over the roar of the river. "'Tis a wide enough channel for now, but we can take a good deal more water later."

"That's easy," Gildevollen yelled back. "'Tis just a matter of setting folk to work. Of sawing more planks and forging more nails."

Jehans said they needed to buy a Pelton turbine and a marble plate on which to fix the couplings. Three measuring instruments and fuses.

"The dynamo should be no less than ten horsepower," he said. "Preferably thirty. We can start with a direct current dynamo, 'tis simpler and less costly. But if many villagers want to connect and we start to operate machinery, then we mun have an alternating current. 'Tis all standard ware."

"And the wires down to the village?"

"The price of wire by the metre be high. Though it went down last year. And 'tis so precipitous here we could almost throw the wires straight down to the first post in the village. But we mun strategise wisely so we can use the same wire even if we change the dynamos. In Lillehammer they had to lay new wires to all the houses when they went from one hundred volts to two hundred."

"How much does the electricity station in Lillehammer provide?" shouted Gildevollen.

"The waterfall on the River Mesna produces around six thousand horsepower."

"You what? Let's walk further from the river. I need to hear this."

"I said there be about six thousand horsepower in the River Mesna. They get around five hundred with each dynamo."

"And how many dynamos do they have?"

"Two."

They continued to walk up towards the farm.

"How strong is the Breia?" Gildevollen asked.

"She has as much water as the River Mesna, but a steeper drop. I borrowed the pastor's pocket watch this June and calculated the water mass. Kristine and I threw pine cones down the river and timed them. We stood out in it with measuring tape and measured the width and depth in four places. We think the

Breia can provide at least twelve thousand horsepower. More during floods. 'Tis almost enough to run a whole ironworks."

"But we don't have any iron round here," Gildevollen said.

"Nay," Kristine interrupted. "But we do have milk. And I have plans."

Gildevollen nodded slowly. They were almost up by the farm, where his farmhand was sitting on a rock. Jehans could see that Gildevollen wanted to talk to him one-to-one. They slowed down on the last slope and Kristine walked ahead.

When they had a view over the village, Gildevollen said:

"I saw you down there on Lake Løsnes many years ago, Jehans. On that raft you built yourself. I know Kai Schweigaard, of course, and met your father briefly too, and knew your mother quite well. And I heard the Sister Bells every Sunday, but after the Silver Winter I never heard them again. And yet I always felt that one of them was there. Down in Lake Løsnes. Under all that water that flows into it from the Breia. Well. That was all I wanted to say. Although there was something else. It's not good to wear out your womenfolk."

They walked back up, and Gildevollen asked Kristine what she had planned.

"We shall begin with the villagers so they get electric light," Kristine said. "Maybe five lamps to each farm. Everyone sees the value o' that. Just imagine – ye can leave it to stand alone inside a barn wi'out danger of fire. Indoors the light be so good ye can wash your dishes at night and be sure they be clean."

"Yes, the dishes and such, they'll be done whatever, but – tell me about the milk?"

"Think o' cheesemaking. Of the endless work. We dairymaids work wi' our hands for hour upon hour. We churn the butter and crank the separator till our arms ache. We mun stand and stir the cheese till it be cold through, otherwise it turns grainy. 'Tis dark by the time a dairymaid be done wi' her work and she be quite outspent. All this dreary, tedious work can be done for us by electricity."

"So what you're planning, Kristine," Gildevollen said, "is to build a—"

"A dairy. Butangen Dairy."

"Butangen Dairy?"

"Wi' myseln as manager."

"I see. Up here on Hellorn?"

"Down in t' village. We can use a building deemed poorly placed. Sawmills and flour mills mun lie close to the river. But electricity can go uphill, downhill, round corners. So an electric dairy can be wherever we want. Happen one of the farms might rent us an old outhouse? I need two large rooms that can be kept clean. Nowt else."

"Look," Gildevollen said. "We'll get the dynamo. It's not too important whether we have a direct or alternating current. I'll get at least six, probably ten, farms running on that. But a dairy? I'm not so sure. We'll need to do a few calculations."

"In't too much calculating ye need to do," Kristine said. "This be sommat altogether different. The dairymaids up at the *seters* mun fetch water from the stream, and then stand with a ladle t' cool the butter. But with electricity we can pump the cold water, and hot water too. In the dairy hut we have to burn aspen and keep watch all the time for an even heat, and we'll get in such a sweat 'tis beyond endurance. But with electricity? We can turn a switch and regulate the heat in little steps till we get it just right."

"The dairy be non-negotiable," Jehans said.

"But my dear people," Gildevollen said. "Just the light – it'll turn this whole village upside down. Folk need time to get used to change! But alright. We'll discuss it."

"And one more thing," Jehans said. "There be *one* farmer who shan't have any electricity."

Gildevollen laughed. "He'll try to make your life hell. He'll store up anything that goes wrong and slander you and get others complaining."

"Let him."

Gildevollen wiped the sweat with his forearm. "Very well. It's decided. We'll need some sort of cooperative, and I'll be chairman. We must have full control from the outset, or we'll lose hold on any future initiatives. What matters most now is for Gildevollen to be the first farm in Butangen with electricity. The very first cable must run to us, and there must be an outdoor lamp, so as to inspire a little envy among folk. Call me an old schemer, but this is important. My eldest boy back at home needs to start thinking big. His sons will see that it's not just dogged work that's needed to run a farm, but also a certain daring. He'll tell his sons that Gildevollen was the first farm in Butangen to have electricity, and later we'll be the first to have – well, whatever comes next. Mowers presumably. And the next thing too, though we don't know what that'll be yet."

"Aye," Kristine said. "But *Hellorn* were the first farm in Butangen to get electricity."

Jehans shot a glance at her.

"Hmm," Gildevollen said. He rummaged in his trouser pocket and found a piece of chewing tobacco. "Yes, you've got a point." He fixed his gaze on their goat, as she stretched up to nibble on the rowan trees. Then on the scrawny chickens behind the stone wall.

"Fair's fair," he said. "The two of you had the idea, and the bulb did light up on your farm first. But, I'm not so sure that—"

Jehans swallowed back a few swear words.

"Happen there may be a way around this," Kristine said. "Hellorn can ne'er be much as a farm. It could be more like a manager's lodgings, wi' some fields and animals. It were always

Jehans' intention to set up the dynamo. So we could say this were Hellorn Electricity Station from the day the first light bulb were lit. We can wait with connecting electricity up here till everything be in place. That way folk can say Gildevollen were the first *farm* in Butangen to get electricity. But then this mun be an electricity station. And we mun have our dairy."

Butangen Kraftlag was founded two Saturdays later. And the first of many jubilee parties was held that same evening, to celebrate the company's hour-long existence, and the first toast was proposed by its chairman, Ole Asmund Gildevollen. The others who raised their glasses at the long table in the grand dining room were Jehans, Kai Schweigaard and farmers Spangrud, Romsås, Sylte, Norddølum and Fjellstad.

In the hours preceding the party, these eight pioneers had put together their grandiose plans. Jehans was painfully nervous, but managed to present the company with his drawings and calculations. He described the station on the River Mesna, and explained that the Breia could produce far more.

The room went quiet. The farmers looked at each other.

"We have more power than the Lillehammer folk?"

"A good deal more," Jehans said.

"More than the city folk?"

With much enthusiastic nodding, it was decided that the electricity station would be built as planned.

"That's excellent news," Ole Asmund Gildevollen said. "Textile mills and the like can wait. What's important now is that our river can generate more horsepower than Lillehammer's river. This needs to come out. Preferably in the newspapers."

Norddølum's farmer stood up. "I'm thinking of those who paved the way before us. Those who laboured so hard t' break the ground here. On slopes so steep they could barely stand upright as they dug out the roots and rocks, cursing those folks lucky enough to own farms in flatter villages. But now! Finally! Butangen rewards us for its valley being so steep."

"The steeper, the better," said Spangrud's farmer. "That's something I never thought I'd say."

Kai Schweigaard rose to his feet, and told them how he had developed the habit of archiving newspapers. He had employed a carpenter to make shelves in the loft, and in this systematic but alarmingly large library, he had found many articles that showed how other villages utilised their electricity, and he warmly endorsed the plans to establish a communal dairy.

"Yes," said another. "But women ought never to be involved in making important decisions."

"We must look at the facts," said yet another. "We have plenty of milk here, but it can't be sold while we don't have proper transport down to Fåvang and from there to Lillehammer. The road is so bad that the milk will curdle before it arrives."

"That be the nub o' it," Jehans said. "Cheese and butter can be transported and are easier to sell at a good price. The electricity is free! With it we can make goods that be of much greater value than the milk itself. These are the ways we mun think now. There are electric machines that can spin and knit. So instead of selling bags o' wool, we can sell sweaters."

The room went quiet. Initially Jehans thought it was because he had dared to say "we", implying he saw himself as the equal of those around him. But it was the wider repercussions that the others found frightening.

"Spinning and knitting and dairying. They're all women's work. Why change sommat that works?"

"But we can lighten the work of our womenfolk," Jehans said. "Think o' the working hours that could be freed up!"

"It's a question of whether we should," said the burliest farmer. "We can never understand womenfolk. But we can put them to work. Let them manage the cows and the milk and the food. 'Tis the only way to keep them in order. Womenfolk wi' time on their hands start to whinge and talk back, and soon naebody'll get a thing done."

"You may have sommat there," said another.

"I have seen it happen. Truly lamentable."

"A dairy may sound good, but 'tis of no help while the road be so poor."

The muttering spread, together with a general sense of gloom, and in a wise move Gildevollen ordered his maids to put out the glasses and fill them generously with brandy to keep everyone going until the festivities began.

"Right! That's enough paperwork and talk," said the farmer from Romsås.

"But we mun decide on the matter o' the dairy," Jehans said.

"Bah!" said the farmer on Sylte. "That'll have to wait. It's getting late."

"Let's put that aside."

"Here, here!"

"Agreed! To the table! Supper is served!" Ole Asmund Gildevollen said.

"Cheers to the Breia!" Arne Fjellstad exclaimed.

"Indeed," said Ole Asmund Gildevollen. "But first we must raise a toast to Jehans Hekne."

"That be most kind o' thee. But . . ." Jehans felt his voice falter. "But . . . first I want to toast the man with whom all this began. The man who bought books on engineering for the parsonage library. I propose – before anything – that we raise a toast to Kai Schweigaard."

"Yes!" said the farmer from Smidesang, banging on the table. "Quite right! To our pastor! Cheers! To Kai Schweigaard!"

There was no need for appetisers, the guests helped themselves to the large quantities of roast beef laid out before them. The maids kept their glasses flowing with Godtøl from

Lillehammer Brewery, and when they had finally emptied their plates, it was time for coffee and crème caramel, and a box of Sorte Mand cigars was passed round and reckless amounts of tokay were poured into dram glasses, until Schweigaard and Jehans took their leave, giving the excuse of the next day's work, which in the case of Schweigaard was true, with it being Saturday night, and he said in parting that he expected to see a full church in the morning, though this was taken as an amiable joke on the part of the pastor, and the clanking of more bottles could already be heard as the two men put on their coats in the hallway.

In the darkness outside there was a jangling and rattling from the horse's harness, and Jehans heard, rather than saw, the pastor's carriage draw up in the courtyard.

"Jehans, wait," Kai Schweigaard said, placing his hand on his shoulder. "Don't go. Let's drive through the village together."

The conversation between them was strained. No word or phrase ever managing to lift out of the mundane or obvious, as though there were a huge mountain to be scaled and they only ever clambered up a few metres before they slipped back down and tried from another spot, only to fall from there too. They chatted until they reached the parsonage, where Jehans made to get out.

"No, don't move," Schweigaard said. "Let me offer you a lift all the way."

Further along the condition of the road was so poor that the driver got down and led the horse, leaving them to talk more freely.

"I was wondering about Victor," Schweigaard said. "Does he ever write you letters?"

"Nowt that I have gotten, at least. And ye?"

"No. Nothing. I've sent many but never had any response."

"Happen he be gone forever."

"Aren't you curious about him? About how he is? Or what he's doing?"

"Aye. Happen I am. I sense that there be sommat troubling him. Though I canna say what."

"Would you consider asking him to come here?" Schweigaard said. "I think he'd come if you did."

Jehans made some sort of gesture in the dark. And when Schweigaard repeated the question, he said no, he had not thought of asking him.

Moments later Jehans shouted out to the driver that they had arrived.

"How d'you know where we are?" Schweigaard said. "I'd never have been able to find my way here in the dark."

"'Tis the sound o' the brook," Jehans said. "It swings round so that when ye first hear it there be thick forest 'twixt thee and it. But when ye hear it agin moments later, the path wends up to Hellorn on your left."

"All that will disappear soon," Schweigaard said. "With electricity. Our ability to navigate in the dark. But something must die for something else to grow. That much I've learned."

They stepped down. The driver led the horse a little further in so as to turn it around, leaving them alone again for a moment.

"One thing," Kai Schweigaard said. "I've signed up for seven electric lamps."

"Oh?"

"And you're to install them. We'll have three in the parsonage and three in the church itself. But I want one lamp to be placed outside. On the wall of the church."

"Over the door?"

"No. I don't quite know how to say this, but Astrid, your mother—"

They both cleared their throats.

"She dreamed, as you know, of visiting cities that were lit with gas lamps. Where people could see each other when they were out for an evening walk."

They cleared their throats again. The driver had turned the horse, and they could hear his approach through the darkness, with the creaking of the harness.

Schweigaard continued: "I think more and more about whether there is life after death. And I find myself thinking more and more that the dead are here to guide *us*. So I'd like to find a way – a way to express that. I want a lamp on the west corner of the new church. A light that shines out over the cemetery all through the night. Yes, you know whose grave lies there."

Go in the Milk-Shed Yerseln, Herr Gildevollen

The next five years brought greater change to Butangen than the past five decades. The electricity station was already in operation the following summer. Despite its makeshift nature its output was always steady and reliable. No houses burned down. No cats chewed the wires. It simply functioned as it should. Night after night, month after month. Light in more and more houses. Light over an old, well-tended grave.

By 1908 eighteen farms had signed up for electricity. The River Breia supplied them all with power.

While Hekne was excluded.

Osvald kicked and screamed, protested that Jehans did not have sole ownership of the river, which was right, since they did not own the water itself, but then the new term *fallrett*

– waterfall rights – came on the table, he even refused to bow to that, and issued a litany of threats and accusations. But then all of a sudden he seemed to lose any interest in electricity, he could manage without, and he started instead to stir up rumours that it made folk forgetful.

Schweigaard laughed to himself. He had noticed that his eyesight was getting weaker, and each time he reached for the Bakelite switch by his study door, he sent a thought to Jehans. But he often felt a certain melancholy, as he realised that the old times were coming to an end, and with that his near-absolute influence would be diluted. And perhaps another source of this melancholy lay in Ingeborg's words, which he had never quite forgotten.

That the Hekne Weave showed how Butangen's pastor would die.

Perhaps they were careless words, mere superstition, but superstition was gaining an ever-stronger hold over Schweigaard's night-time thoughts. The first thing Schweigaard studied under an electric light was not a book, but the Hekne sisters' pillows. He allowed them to see the new times in the hope of wresting a hint from them about where the weave itself might be found.

But they did not answer him.

And no matter how bad his night's sleep was, the morning sun rose and made his worries fade for a while. Electricity gave the village a desire for more, and Schweigaard was not exempt from such desires. A path was cut through the forest, tall poles were erected across the Løsnes Marshes, and the telephone number Butangen 1 went to the parsonage. Not long after, Butangen 2 went to Gildevollen. The strong odour of creosote that came from the poles lasted for years and lodged itself in the memory of every villager, so whenever they passed one later in life, they thought, here, right here, it smells of telephone.

New plans were constantly being discussed. The most crucial thing was to sort out the road to Fåvang, but that would take years. Besides, the village's pulse lay closer to its neighbours. Being so remote, Butangen had been a separate parish from ancient times, but had been brought under Ringebu's jurisdiction soon after Schweigaard arrived. For the most part, however, the village had continued to look after its own affairs, since the journey was so long and hazardous that seats on the council were often left empty. But now no fewer than three men from Butangen had been voted in.

Oldfrue Bressum could no longer follow much of what happened. She floated about in a state of confusion, constantly moaning about the ringing in her ears, able to do little but darn socks and make coffee. But she was dangerously quick on her feet and had to be locked away with a bottle of apple wine when visitors were expected at the parsonage. Although she generally stayed in the scullery, being suspicious of gadgets, especially the open socket in the kitchen, from which she was convinced electricity might spill and flow across the floor.

The really big change, however, came not in the form of mechanical contraptions, but in a new way of thinking, and that came with Kristine Messelt. The power of electricity would prove tame in comparison to what she could demonstrate when decisions for the new dairy were strung out.

The story told afterwards was exaggerated, of course, the timing of events being less dramatic and her tongue not as sharp. But that didn't worry the gossips who held firm to their version, in which the Gildevollen household had just got used to having a regular supply of electricity and light when the house suddenly went dark one night. Confusion spread in the kitchen and living rooms, and when Ole Gildevollen finally managed to find a paraffin lamp that everyone assumed had been put away for good, it was revealed that a stranger had entered the house. And out of shadows stepped a woman, who told them she had come to make them aware of their frailty. It was Kristine Messelt. She said it had been a condition of business that Butangen Kraftlag would help her procure a building in which to establish an electric dairy. No, said Gildevollen, she was wrong. Kraftlag had said they would *discuss* it. And they, Jehans and Kristine, had received a generous commission from the electricity station.

He was not an unreasonable man, he was merely stating the obvious, and, as he ought to have mentioned when the plan was first mooted: weren't the cows up in the *seters* during the summer? And wasn't it only in the summer that they produced milk?

Kristine was clearly prepared for this, and said at once: "Aye. But nay. It be quicker to collect the milk from the *seters* and send it down here than for each dairymaid to sit in her *seter* and work herself to the bone making cheese and churning butter. Let the dairymaids collect their milk in clean churns, marked with the name o' the farm, and then leave them on a stand along the roadside at a fixed hour so a driver may come and take them away. The trip down to the village takes no more than an hour by horse."

"Carry the milk down from the *seter*?" Gildevollen said. "You're turning the whole system on its head! Our dairymaids will have nowt to do! No more than sleep and preen themselves and ogle the boys!"

"Go in the milk-shed yerseln, Herr Gildevollen, and ye shall soon see. Feel how tired your fingers are after milkin' for two hours at dawn. Follow that with cheesemaking. And two hours' more milking in the evening. Day after day."

"It's not that simple. Folk are poor round here. And poor folk need jobs. It may not be much, but everyone has something to eat. Just think about where you came from, Kristine Messelt!"

"I have thought 'bout that, ye may be sure. Naebody shall go wi'out work. Indeed, we shall get more done. And right away too. Or else some man shall step forward with the same plan as I have put to thee now, and somebody will have the nouse to answer him aye."

The lights came back on.

"Be warned now," she said. "I can turn 'em back off."

Those were her words, according to local folklore. A more likely version of events, however, was that she and Jehans had gone down together, since it was unheard of for a humble woman to barge in and start laying down the law. But what is certain is that she gave him a neatly written sheet of columns that showed the purchase price of milk, the sale price of cheese and butter, and the repayments on a loan. At the very bottom of the right-hand column, underlined twice, was the profit they hoped for after two years of doing business.

"Then more farms will join up. And *I* shall pay them the litre-price for their milk and pay thee rent," Kristine said. "I intend to sell cheese, butter and soured cream. Both here and down in Fåvang. My own cheese."

Butangen dairy was opened in 1909 and Kai Schweigaard made sure he was one of the first to buy his butter there. They had been given the use of a small barn on the very top of an area of scree. Schweigaard was careful not to say anything untoward when Kristine showed him the "production hall". It was somewhat makeshift and crudely put together, still just a barn, but spotlessly clean and far better than any dairy hut on any *seter*, and from the ceiling hung four powerful light bulbs. The most important thing, however, was the row of machines, two bought second-hand, the others home-made with the assistance of a local blacksmith: a cooler, a pasteurising machine, a separator and preheater. She was getting milk from three farms, and what pleased her most was that she had secured a large and reliable supply of goat's milk.

A steady hum filled the room. It seemed to come from both

the floor and the walls. Looking up he saw the source of the sound. Suspended beneath the roof of this extremely rickety barn was a long iron axle that rotated without stop. By pulling levers and tightening or loosening drive belts, Kristine could connect each machine as and when.

Schweigaard recognised Jehans in all this. It was like unfolding one of the sheets of squared paper he had drawn on as a boy.

"Look at this," Kristine said, pulling a lever so that the separator was connected. The humming noise changed pitch and was replaced by the buzz of the machine.

There it was. The power of the River Breia. The power of rain. The power of a steep slope. And she let it replace all her gruelling dairy work without a minute's grief over the old.

Though she had only just begun; this was, she said, just the start. A purpose-built dairy was needed, with a concrete floor and larger windows. A real dairy with electric coolers was what they wanted.

"And Jehans?" asked Schweigaard. "Is he here?"

"He be away in Tretten. Likely he were asked to help with the installation of another electricity station."

Just as the building produced a vaguely dissonant and unsettling hum, Schweigaard picked up a similar tone in the way she said this. A little too fast, a little too glibly, relishing the freedom perhaps to concentrate on her own things.

"Look at this, Pastor."

She pressed a lump of butter into a wooden mould and put it to cool. The moulds were made by Adolf, they were carved with rose patterns that made each pat of butter look like a little jewellery box when the sides were removed, and each was decorated with a cross on top in accordance with the old dairy traditions.

"Costs nowt to make them pretty," she said.

He had never had better butter. Though it had the aftertaste of a faltering marriage.

Schweigaard had never been particularly close to Kristine, but he glimpsed Astrid Hekne's will in her now, and he knew Astrid would have been proud to have her as a daughter-in-law. Kristine's strength had blown invisible mountains open, and Astrid would have defended it even when Kristine put her own happiness before pleasing Jehans.

Whether or not they had children, these two. Astrid could say from the grave that this was where it turned.

With electricity and a pat of butter.

During the spring of 1911 Schweigaard saw more signs of cracks in their marriage. They moved down to the village, sectioned off a couple of rooms in the dairy building and made themselves some sort of home, allowing a couple who had recently returned from America to work the land up at Hellorn. The dairy was taking deliveries from more and more farms, which in turn increased Kristine's workload. She hired the young Ada Borgen and Widow Fløter to help.

Meanwhile, Jehans regularly took on work away from the village. There were steep tributaries throughout Gudbrandsdal and every village wanted an electricity station. Despite his lack of any formal education, Jehans Hekne had become a much sought-after engineer, he was *the* man everyone wanted to wade through their waterfalls and steep rivers. He worked as the right hand to a very experienced but gout-stricken engineer, and when the technical drawings could not be taken nearer the river without getting wet, Jehans Hekne took charge. He oversaw the building of dams, the sinking of electricity poles, and eventually the use of dynamite. He was dripping wet most days, and older folk often chuckled and said he looked like the creature they called Vasslos, who leaped from rock to rock and led the spawning fish upriver.

On the rare occasions Kai Schweigaard saw Kristine and

Jehans together, he could see they were no longer the young couple from Hellorn. They were a work team, an excellent work team, but it was difficult to imagine them as parents. After just a few years, they had left the farm into which they had put so much work, which few people would have had the heart to abandon. They both possessed a will so strong as to be ungovernable, and a shiver brought them close only for the briefest moments.

Schweigaard found comfort in the Røhme family, who now numbered five since Fru Røhme had given birth to a girl and another boy with just a two-year gap. They had electricity in their rooms too, and little Simen was at an age to start reading, and Schweigaard sat with him, taking pleasure in how fast he learned his letters. Then, when the boy had gone to bed, Schweigaard would stroll back to his wing, where it was very quiet and too many thoughts would come to him too fast.

Kai Schweigaard still sent letters to Victor Harrison every summer and Christmas, telling him about the village and what Jehans was doing.

Until now he had received no answer.

Up Where Church Bells Ring

Victor Harrison stood in a turbulent whirlwind of engine noise, petrol vapours, oil spray and exhaust fumes. The engine picked up speed and the propeller turned into a transparent grey circle with a little black dot in the middle.

Like the water rings around a sinking church bell.

Way back when.

The plane was a Blériot XI-2. His father had said that any-one who got into that damn thing must be a lunatic. "I mean *a lunatic*," he had said. "Have you lost your mind? You have responsibilities, Victor. For Finlaggan! For the plantation!"

Robert Harrison slumped into his chair. "We'll both die, Victor. You when your plane crashes, and I from heart failure when they bring me the news."

Victor looked at his father. He was getting old and fearful.

But there was no going back, he had made his decision long ago. Fly? Of course he would fly! The desire had been kindled, and it was now fully ablaze. He felt his whole life might come to a standstill if he let this opportunity pass by, he felt he was behind already, and saw the dark shadow of disappointment looming if he let the chance slip. Which was why he had to go up, why he had to buy a plane, and why he was here.

At Louis Blériot's flying school in France, with its view towards the Pyrenees. The school was located here because it consistently had the lowest wind speeds in the country. It had been advertised as a two-week course, yet Victor had already been here for three, ironically because of bad weather. It was forbidden to fly in anything more than a light breeze, since the planes were so sensitive that just one gust of wind could throw an inexperienced pilot into a spin.

And so: No guarantees, *Monsieur Harrison*, full payment in advance, *Aviateur Harrison*, twenty-eight thousand francs for the XI-2, and another three thousand for your instruction. *Bon.*

And here it was. His very own plane. Standing before him. Just eight years after the Wright brothers had lifted into the air.

Yes. It had cost him a small fortune. He could have erected a fine new building at Finlaggan for the money. But what were mere francs when measured against something divine? Its wings were shaped like a bird's, he sat up high, with an unre-stricted view, it was *feather-light*, with a dry weight of under

315

three hundred and fifty kilos. The pilot sat in an oblong box of thin wood, behind a three-cylinder engine of a full twenty-five horsepower. The wings were made of taut, parchment-coloured canvas stretched over a frame of thin ash, and behind him there was almost nothing, just slender wooden struts leading to a tail rudder which he could control to some degree with a lever and thin steel wire. Elegant indeed, but no less French, since, on closer inspection, the Blériot was a charming mongrel. Each of her instruments was made by a different manufacturer, and of different proportions. The clock was a standard Jaeger desk clock that had to be wound up before each flight, and next to it was an ordinary window thermometer.

He had been allowed to take the plane up a couple of times over the last few days, and the first thing he had learned was that the engine had no means of collecting the lubricating oil – some kind of vegetable oil – so that it splashed straight out. He got used to wiping his goggles with the back of his leather gloves so he could see. On his next trip one of the drain valves got caught up, and he and the plane were instantly doused in hot oil. His instructor burst out laughing, saying he mustn't get in the habit of licking his lips, this was castor oil, and a mere drop would force him to make an emergency landing to empty his bowels.

Despite all this he felt calm. Calm for the first time since leaving Butangen.

A few months after returning from Dresden, he had left for Ceylon and stayed there for two years. Two years of red mud, chill mornings and green mountains. Kumara had assembled a team to burn fields of stubble and shrubs, and they extended the plantation, installed modern drying equipment and, not least, good, rain-tight living quarters. Victor wore his clothes threadbare, smoked a lot, drank more than ever in the evenings, and worked himself into a dripping sweat, and when he finally saw shoots appearing on the bushes, he thought: *We created this.*

Kumara's wound began to hurt again, his youngest son took over from him and Victor said: "Come back to England with me. Forever, if you want."

Back at Finlaggan Victor brought some order to the outlying pastures. They burned the heather on the hills, and the grouse returned to the hunting grounds, which looked across the Cheviot Hills. He walked past the ancestors' gallery avoiding the gaze of his fifteen-year-old self. Kept himself occupied, like an eternal guest in his own house.

Suppers with his father as always. Delighted that *things were getting done! Tip-top, my dear Victor! But don't forget the hunt for a young woman.*

He was not a success in that hunt. It seemed to have been abandoned in Dresden along with everything else he had left there. He occasionally took out Elsa Rathenau's photograph, but her face belonged to that long autumn he wanted to forget.

He had bought one of the very first motorised cycles in 1908, a Matchless, and had travelled north into Scotland with a fishing rod and tent. In an overgrown river where mayflies hatched, he heard a humming overhead and looked up and saw a parchment-coloured Blériot. He saw a similarity between it and the mayflies. Nothing more was needed, other than twenty-eight thousand francs and a tumultuous quarrel with his father.

"This is absolute *lunacy*, I tell you! Are you planning on being some kind of circus acrobat?"

In fact, Robert Harrison had investigated the matter quite thoroughly. The best engineers in England and Germany had dismissed the plane as nothing but a plaything for egocentric, wealthy risk-seekers. Flying in such a machine was a technical impossibility, air was simply too porous, only a Zeppelin could lift passengers or cargo, and only a hot-air balloon was suited to observations. And the only people to think otherwise were the French, in other words: madness from all sides.

317

"You were in the Transvaal, Father! Are you saying that wasn't dangerous?"

"That was very different. An altogether different sort of risk. There was some meaning to it."

Victor shook his head. Said he wanted to see Finlaggan from the air. Finlaggan, the Cheviots and the coast.

"No. I've said no."

"You can't stop me doing anything!" Victor said. "You, least of all!"

"Me, least of all? What do you mean by that? Least of all?"

Victor glared at him. It was the first time any cracks had opened up in their relationship. And what he saw behind them was the big question.

Did he know? Or did he not know?

Or was he like Victor himself? A man who preferred not to know?

Victor swallowed hard and stared at the floor. There was too much at stake. Too many years had been allowed to pass. He suddenly seemed so old, so frail, this kind and generous man to whom he owed everything. Who now repeated that it would break him if Victor were to risk his life for anything as pointless as a pilot's licence.

Victor felt close to him in that moment, very close, but knew that he would defy him. And thought: It makes no difference, Father.

No difference at all.

Whether I fall down from the sky or down from the ancestors' gallery.

It was quarter past four in the morning and he was standing alongside his flying instructor, Carax. A short-tempered little man with a handlebar moustache who gesticulated wildly, and shouted corrections at the slightest error. Victor had inspected the plane earlier that morning in the half-light, checked that the bracing and warping wires were all evenly taut, that the oil and petrol pipes were free of cracks, and that no unusual noises were coming from the engine, *because one cannot leave everything to mechanics, not when it's a matter of life and death, Monsieur Harrison!*

There was no end to what Carax had taught him. A pilot must carry at all times a leather bag containing a needle and thread for the wings, a saw and glue for the frame, and spare ropes and wire in case the cross-bracing wires came loose. More important still, he must carry wads of cash in small denominations, because they had to pay for any damage caused when they landed in a field – speaking of which: he must *never* land in a field full of cows, they created large tufts as they grazed, which would break the landing wheels. Sheep and horses were what he should look for.

They had already gone up, quite high even, but Victor had always sat behind Carax and been careful to remain slightly detached, wanting to savour the moment when it came.

And that moment was finally here. Carax climbed into the back seat and nodded.

Victor took the front seat and forgot all about Carax. He set the propellers rotating, they gripped the everything-and-nothing that was the air, they picked up speed and soon the tree trunks and landscape started to race past him.

He was reminded of his motorcycle as the aircraft accelerated and the wind caressed his face, saying: Give the engine more and you shall receive more. Give even more and you shall receive even more. And as his speed increased, he sat in a marvellous cauldron of air currents, engine vibration and trembling wheels, but then suddenly the propellers changed pitch, they gained control of the air and the wings found a mass on which to float, and a second later the shaking stopped and he was riding on another material, he grabbed the lever that controlled the wings, making them curve and lift higher, and the sun shone in through the fine sailcloth as he lost sight of the wings, like a bird that neither sees nor considers the beating of its wings.

At last.

At last he was up.

Up with the wind and the sky and the infinite view across the landscape. Followed by the hum of the engine and the occasional spatter of hot oil.

He had barely looked down during his test flights. But now he was up here, free from everything. In a world that was entirely *his*. High above Finlaggan, high above the madness in Norway, high above Ragna's equivocation.

The Blériot was as fickle as a butterfly, but he felt a unique *contact* with it, it put his every nerve on alert, and he adjusted the ignition and fuel as though he were offering treats to a horse. He tried to anticipate the little gusts of wind as they came, riding them out until the plane responded, careful not to overcorrect, but to rest on the air currents and follow them.

He looked down now.

It was as though everything down on the ground – the houses, shops, fences and even the miracles like the petrol-powered trucks and telegraph stations – all became insignificant and small from here. Up here, the world seemed to sort itself out. Everything seemed so clear-cut, the result of major battles and not minor ones. Straight roads, canopies of trees, irrigation canals, red-tiled roofs.

And there, something to the right, a strange, dark-blue shadow – the sea!

And he knew he had finally found it. Found it up here.

Calm.

They landed and he wiped the oil from his face.

Behind him, Carax was very quiet. Eventually he removed

his helmet and said Monsieur Harrison was *un aviateur magnifique,* and something that Victor initially took to mean that he was a born pilot, but understood later to mean that he had the *spirit of flight* within him.

He was soon up again. Enjoying the unique calm some people find in danger.

This time, Victor flew near a village. He could see a large stone church, and in front of it a group of people. A white bride entered the church, and he turned the plane so as not to disturb them. But the sound of church bells caught up with him.

A swift came and flew alongside him.

The bird did not miss having someone to tell.

But *he* felt it, felt the urge to land and go to a fellow human being and tell them how it was to be up here. To tell it to someone who would be neither frightened nor anxious. To someone who would understand what had not been said. To someone who would tolerate getting hot oil in his face. A man who might notice that the plane he had bought was a two-seater.

A man who had built a raft when he was twelve.

He decided then and there to start opening letters that came from Kai Schweigaard.

Dress Warmly, My Boy

It was 1914. In late November, Kai Schweigaard and Herr Røhme went to Lillehammer to buy supplies and stay the night. Schweigaard stopped at the Narvesen Kiosk in Lillehammer station to buy all the latest national newspapers; events seemed to be moving fast. It might have been far away, but even the villagers of Butangen were fearful, since wars could spread like the plague. It was as though they could hear the din of cannons on the other side of the Løsnes Marshes. Everybody thought it would be decided in a few months, with cavalry and bayonets, those involved were civilised nations after all. But hundreds of thousands had already died, the generals had sent out hordes of soldiers using Napoleonic War tactics, but they were met by the invention of the new century, the machine gun, which mowed them down like weeds with a scythe.

On their way back to Butangen, snow hung in the air and there was a bitter, ice-cold wind. The horses were waiting for them at the station, and they managed to come round Lake Løsnes before sunset. Up by the parsonage, Simen stood with the gate wide open. He waved them down towards the courtyard, and Schweigaard realised that he had been standing at the living room window, hoping they would come back soon.

"'Tis Old Margit," he said. "Old Bressum. She took ill. Right after ye left."

Schweigaard dashed across the courtyard and opened the front door so fast that the kitchen cat arched her back and hissed. He mounted the stairs two at a time to her bedroom. He had rarely been inside, and had no idea whether it had always smelled like this: a sharp odour of medicine that floated over the damp, cloying smell of a confined human being. She had always had a horror of draughts and closed all the windows the minute she entered a room, a habit that had irritated him beyond measure. No lamps were lit, and he could only vaguely see some movement near the headboard.

"Nay! It mun be serious now," peeped Oldfrue Bressum. "When the pastor do come."

It was typical of her to say something that rendered any answer impossible. All he could do was to walk over and ask if she was in pain. On her bedside table was a brown bottle, a coffee cup and a bill from the doctor.

"It gurgles mighty queer in my chest. And my head. It be throbbing."

Schweigaard looked at her. She seemed clearer than in years. "Hmm," was all he said.

"It mun take its course now," Bressum said. "The doctor said there in't long to go."

"He said that to you?"

"The doctor? Nay. He just gave me the medicine bottle there. He were down in t' village and that Røhme woman went and fetched him up. I didna' want the doctor. What would I do wi' a doctor? But I drew myself up from my bed and went over to the door and I heard him say it. 'Tis the only way if ye want to know anything 'bout anything."

"You're sure you heard right? You seem quite bright today."

"Nay, Pastor. 'Tis soon."

"The ringing in your ears? Is it the same as ever?"

"Just as bad. I only hope it doesna' follow me when I cross over."

She was unusually clear-headed. He had, in fact, hoped that she might slip away in her sleep during one of her blurry, forgetful weeks. He should have known it. That Oldfrue Bressum would meet Death with arms crossed, feet square, and snarky. *Oh, so ye have come!*

He unlaced his boots and sat in his stockinged feet.

"Yer feet didna' get damp where ye went?"

"No," Schweigaard said.

"It smells o' wet sheep from them feet o' yorn. So ye have gotten wet. Go 'n' get dry."

"Alright. But let me sit here a while."

The door opened, and Fru Røhme asked from the doorway if they needed anything. Simen was behind her.

"Be sure t' make sommat for the pastor," Oldfrue Bressum said. "Ye can see he has just got back. Three slices with eggs and anchovies and plenty o' salt on top. He likes that. I know."

She went on badgering Fru Røhme, and Schweigaard turned and rolled his eyes so that Fru Røhme could see, but they let her have her way. He interrupted Bressum and said: "And you? Won't you have something too?"

She shook her head. "Me? Now? There be more left in the *stabbur* if folk learn to die on an empty stomach."

Schweigaard agreed. He asked her about any relatives and whether she wanted anyone particular to get what she had in the bank.

"I have nowt in the savings bank. 'Tis up there," she said, nodding towards a jar in the window.

Fru Røhme came in with a plate of open sandwiches. The kitchen cat had smelled the food and was weaving in and out of her legs. It jumped up onto the bed, and Margit Bressum buried her fingers in its fur. Schweigaard ate one of the sandwiches, and then, pretending to be absent-minded, left the plate and went off to change into something dry. On his return everything was eaten and Oldfrue Bressum was holding a piece of anchovy out on her finger, which the cat was licking.

"Oldfrue Bress – Margit. I hope things have been tolerable for you over these past years."

"I have got by. And I have, in my own way, tried to look after the pastor."

"I know, Margit. For more than thirty years."

"Aye, and the old pastor afore that."

"Yes."

They fell silent.

"It were too bad for thee and the Hekne girl," she said. "I have often thought about it. Though I have nay said much."

Schweigaard cleared his throat and nodded.

"I came here in 1859," she said. "Much has changed. More than were good for me t' see."

"1859. Was that when your husband died?"

"He did nay die. He took off one day."

"I always thought he died."

"Nay. And no man ever offered me company agin. I were too cainjy, they said."

"People are different."

"I were never so cainjy or cankery as a young 'un. But I were big sister to six brothers. Mother fell ill after the last boy."

"Ah."

"So I had to take care o' them. That were why I got so cainjy, Father said. A shrew and a scold. Said it so often, I got used to it."

They were silent even longer this time. Schweigaard's thoughts drifted to his mother, whom he had failed to visit when she lay dying. For a long time, he'd had a bad conscience about not having a bad conscience about it. It was niggling at him again. He worried that he was emotionally numb, but sitting here now with Fru Bressum, he knew he was not.

He could hear Fru Røhme moving about downstairs, and the clock ticking high on the wall. It was the only object in the room, besides her clothes in the cupboard and the jar on the windowsill, and it struck him that she owned barely anything. He got up, went over to the jar. It was full of banknotes, all folded in half, exactly as he had always folded her wages.

"When I die, Pastor," she said, "be the ground frozen so hard that I mun lie out in the bell tower now till spring?"

"No. It's not so hard that Røhme can't dig a hole."

"Ye be lying now, Herr Pastor. I got up last night and looked at the thermometer."

"Didn't the doctor tell you to stay in bed?"

"Aye. But 'tis no good for a body to lie abed when they be

dying anyhow. So I went out on the doorstep. The wind blew through my nightgown. 'Twere minus fifteen. By the new measure. By the old measure, minus thirty. By Herr Farenhouse's scale."

"Fahrenheit. Anyway, we've never had a colder November. Not that I can recall."

"I liked the old scale best. But no matter, the ground will be hard wi' frost. And I do nay wish young Røhme to work any harder on my account."

"Margit. We'd be *happy* to work harder for you."

"For me?"

Her voice was fainter now.

"Yes, for you. It would be a pleasure."

She grew weaker during the night. He held her hand and the cat lay at the foot of her bed. When she spoke again, her voice was frail.

"I shall die very soon, Pastor."

"We must take it as it comes, Margit."

"Stay, then. And open the window so I be not caught in this room. Air me out. And carry me out through the corpse hatch and walk me agin the sun."

He nodded. It was a custom he upheld at deathbeds in Butangen. The instant somebody died, a window or a door was opened so their soul could leave. Otherwise it would settle in the walls and turn into a ghost that haunted the room, and for a similar reason they had to carry the coffin out through a special hatch and walk around the house in the opposite path to the sun, to confuse the spirits. But as far as he knew, there was no such hatch in the parsonage, the veranda door would have to do when the time came. But he really did not mind walking with Bressum a little further. Alive or dead.

"It shall be cold for thee when ye lay me in the earth, Kai

Schweigaard. Ye ought t' eat more fat. More pork. It helps wi' the cold. Ye have grown too thin. Promise me to eat more pork, Kai."

"I promise you, I'll eat more pork, Margit."

She dozed off and he pulled the chair closer to the bed and took her hand again. He waited as he had waited beside so many deathbeds in Butangen. The candle on the bedside table fluttered restlessly, and a sharp odour came from her mouth.

Her breathing slowed and her pulse grew weaker and weaker. Her hand grew colder and then her gaze slid inwards. There was a rattling in her throat, and after a deep sigh the breathing stopped and her muscles went limp. He folded her hands, got up slowly and went to the window and opened it.

But he did not feel any soul escape. It was only the night that came in.

Suddenly the cat hissed and sprang off the bed.

"*Happen ye may not ha' seen it,*" said a voice in the room. "*But ye were allays my boy.*"

Schweigaard swung round and felt a shiver down his spine. She was lying there with her eyes wide open. He found it hard to grasp that it was her voice, but there was nobody else in the room, and she repeated that he was her boy.

She blinked.

The cat jumped quietly back onto the bed and began purring.

Schweigaard swallowed and said:

"Thank you, Margit. Thank you. I did see it, but—"

"'Twere difficult to be someone's boy. As it be for the Hekne boy now. So difficult for all of ye to take from another."

She was so gentle, so altered. And it struck him that this was how she had been before she grew so *cankery*.

He sat on the edge of the bed again. "I died," she said. "Just now."

"Margit. You're still alive."

327

"Nay. I be dead, for it no longer rings in my ears. But I have come back to thee to tell thee sommat."

He took her hand.

"It were nowt but grey out there. Just a mist. There were no mountains or forests or rivers. Only folk who hung in the mist and were made o' mist. And then two folks came out o' the mist and were made o' mist, and said ye mun dress warmly when ye lay me in the earth. That ye mun wear the Crucifix Robe."

"Crucifix Robe?"

"Aye. The pastor's red and gold robe. The one wi' the cross on the back. The old one that be lined wi' reindeer skin. For it shall be bitterly cold the day I go in t' the ground."

There was no more breath left in her, and Kai Schweigaard gave way to tears as the grip on his hand loosened, and she said:

"*Dress warmly, then, my boy.*"

The Crucifix Robe

They stood around the grave and sang. Schweigaard. The bell ringer. The parsonage farm tenant and his family. Herr and Fru Røhme. Simen, Lilly and Johan Røhme, ten, eight and six years old. Adolf and Ingeborg. Jehans and Kristine. And on a tombstone sat Oldfrue Bressum's cat, huddling against the cold wind.

Christianity's shivering representatives in Butangen.

They had remembered her with absolute honesty in the church, knowing that by mentioning all the times she had been irritating or snarky with them, the good memories would stand true. Even her supper of rancid shark's liver was memorialised, and young Simen Røhme approached the coffin and cried and told them about a time she had received a letter and went in to him and asked him grumpily: "So d'ye want the stamp?"

Schweigaard himself had no recollection of Bressum ever getting any letters, but it was on that day that Simen had started to collect stamps, showing her every new stamp he was given.

As Bressum had predicted, it was even colder. Much colder. One of the coldest November days Schweigaard could remember. The thermometer showed minus twenty-three degrees, and the wind howled as though it had decided to tear the church down, but what made it really cold was that it had not yet snowed. The ground was grey, the grass was frozen stiff, and the trees looked like cast iron. When the time came for him to scatter the earth, it froze as it tumbled through the air, and sounded like a shower of pebbles when it landed on the coffin.

Nonetheless, Schweigaard did not feel the cold because he was wearing the chasuble. Out here it felt like a bear skin, and as always he seemed to radiate greater faith when he wore it, much as the heat from an open fire penetrates deep into the body. It was a violation of all the liturgical rules, and if the bishop had seen him, in this blood-red robe flapping in the wind on this greyest of November days, he would have been instantly removed from office.

But he thought: What wouldn't we do for Oldfrue Bressum?

They ended their moment of reflection at the graveside, and he seized a rare opportunity to invite Jehans and Kristine, as well as Ingeborg and Adolf, to come back to the parsonage for some food.

He changed clothes in the sacristy and hurried back up. It felt as though he was still wearing the Crucifix Robe. Not in terms of weight or shape or bodily sensation. But as an invisible, but agreeable, warm and enveloping layer.

The conversation at table was distinctly awkward. Kristine

was wearing a formal dark-blue skirt, a white blouse and blue shawl, Jehans was in a greyish suit and poorly polished shoes. They sat closely side by side, but both talked as though the other wasn't there. They seemed so uncomfortable.

Fru Røhme had put the food on the table and then withdrawn, since when ordinary folk came to the pastor's table they generally helped themselves. Making everyone equal. As the dish was being passed round for a second time, the silence became too much for Ingeborg.

"Well, out wi' it!" she said loudly. "Tell the pastor right this minute!"

Kristine straightened up and explained that the dairy inspector for South and Mid Gudbrandsdal had visited the dairy unannounced. "To carry out an inspection." She had been busy stirring a vat of rennet when she was told that there were two men outside who claimed to be from the authorities.

The dairy had been expanding steadily since it opened, and Widow Fløter and Ada Borgen were now employed full-time. They had also entered a contract with Herr Paper Cone to sell dry goods on commission: coffee, sugar, small grocery items, gun cartridges and matches. These were sold from a room near the front door. It was not quite a shop, but more of a shop than not, and the accounts were always correct to an øre.

"Aye, so in they marched," Kristine said. "Put on their white coats, took out a mighty great protocol and began poking about in every corner."

Generally, in the past, the only outsiders to set foot in Butangen were the doctor, the postman and taxman, but now these strangers had come with their endless checklists to mark their approval or disapproval of everything that took place in this old, windswept barn.

The inspector had pointed out that the electricity connections were makeshift, and that most of their pots and pans were home-made and partly of wood, but then he let something slip. Something that only a local could know, about the supply of goat's milk, and Kristine began to suspect that Osvald was behind this. But, no matter how high the inspector's assistant clambered to find dust, or how deep into the corners they searched for mouse droppings, or how minutely they studied everyone's overalls, the only possible conclusion was that the cleaning was impeccable.

It was Ingeborg, not Kristine, who supplied this last detail with a flourish.

"But?" Schweigaard said.

"It seemed to make no difference, no matter how clean it were. They didna' seem at all interested. The problem was that we took in more milk than were permitted for a farm dairy."

Schweigaard noticed Jehans shift in his chair. He seemed both proud and uncomfortable.

"They said I mun either take in less milk," said Kristine, "or hire a publicly approved dairy manager. 'Aye,' I says to them, 'and where might we find one o' these publicly approved dairy managers? Do they arrive at the railway station in a chest?'"

No, the inspector had replied. They were trained in Levanger. Problem was, they only allowed men. Women could be trained in dairying, yes, but not to become dairy managers.

"They stood there, in Kristine's own dairy," Adolf said, "and told her she had to hire *a man* to stand and watch her making her cheese 'n' churning her butter!"

Kristine blushed and looked down at the table. Ingeborg took over the story from there.

The inspector must soon have realised that Kristine Messelt was the wrong person to order about. She had grabbed his arm and showed him how she directed the whole process, from when the milk came out of the udder to when the cheese and butter were packed and cooled. He was given a stiff lesson in cleaning, working methods and recipes, and she explained how they maintained standards among the farmers so the milk was pure, and shared insignificant details that weren't insignificant because they affected the taste, keeping qualities and the like, and she lectured the two men on three centuries of dairy tradition, exceeding the inspector's own knowledge again and again. And when they finally got to taste the butter and cheese and soured cream, the dairy inspector for South and Mid Gudbrandsdal and his helper just stood there licking their lips.

"Well – anyhow," said the inspector finally, "your production levels are too high!"

"Clearly!" Kristine said. "Do ye not think I have thought of a solution t' that?"

She disappeared into another room and returned with a pile of neatly folded papers she had been working on for over a year. They were the working drawings for a large dairy with twelve employees, together with financial forecasts that showed a profit after four years. With free electricity.

Just one week later a letter was sent to the Levanger Dairy School with the inspector's *urgent request* that Kristine Messelt be permitted to train as a dairy manager.

"And?" Schweigaard said.

"A letter came the day before yesterday. I start after Christmas. There'll be two of us. Two womenfolk in the class."

Now Jehans chimed in. "And," he said, "we talked with the director of the bank. We can get a loan of six thousand kroner. With the calculations Kristine showed him. To build a new dairy with a little shop. With my machines. We can buy a plot of land at the crossroads right up here. Along the road down from the *seter*."

Ingeborg sipped her coffee and chuckled. "Answer me this, Herr Pastor, can ye think o' a farm the big new dairy should nay take milk from?"

*

It was bitterly cold as Schweigaard's visitors crammed into the carriage later that night, and Herr Røhme climbed up onto the driver's seat to take them home. Adolf and Ingeborg snuggled up together under their sheepskins, and the snowbells rang out as Schweigaard waved everyone off. He felt great pride for Kristine and Jehans, but would have liked to see more warmth between them.

Schweigaard lingered out in the courtyard, despite only being lightly dressed. He occasionally liked to allow the icy cold to sink right into his body, and then to go back indoors to the stove and tell himself that nothing lasted forever. Not even the cold November weather.

A shiver went through him.

The extreme cold reminded him of something long ago. More than thirty years ago.

His body's reminder of the New Year's Mass when Klara Mytting froze to death. It had been so horrendously cold in the church. He had only held out because he was wearing the chasuble. Past impressions came back to him, from a year of misunderstandings and lost opportunities. They mingled with Margit Bressum's final words on her deathbed.

Other words too came into his head. Things that older villagers had said. Adolf who told him about the portal. Turned so the carvings faced in towards the sheep. Widow Framstad. *Folk could see it wi'out seeing it.* And finally Pastor Nilssøn's strict orders. A chasuble lined with reindeer skin to *warm his frozen limbs.*

Schweigaard went inside and fetched a pair of scissors and a knife. He hurried down to the sacristy. Locked the door and turned on the electric ceiling light. It was in here that he had once opened the coffin containing the Hekne sisters' pillows, and he now felt the same, slightly unseemly, sense of anticipation.

He took the chasuble out of the cupboard. The cloth was impressively weighty, it smelled of old wool and olden times, and very vaguely of the old stave church.

It had to be here. If he was right in his understanding of the Butangen psychology, it had to be hidden here. Pastor Nilssøn had invited a few craftsmen to work on the church. It was quite conceivable that a seamstress, a girl from Hekne perhaps, had crept in. Hidden herself in the one place nobody would dare to go. The bell tower. For it was said that if anyone other than a member of the Hekne family saw the bells, they would die of a stroke or some terrible disease. And one night she took down the Hekne Weave and sewed it into the chasuble. Into the front, so it faced the congregation. Just as the old and new faith stood face to face in the stave church.

Where should he start, make the first incision? He knew more about Mars and Jupiter than about a needle and thread.

Try anywhere. It's just a bit of old cloth! No, it's more than that. It's a chasuble. One of the church's most sacred objects.

The crucifix gleamed gold towards him on the scarlet background, and he hesitated at desecrating it. For he had learned that it was possible to respect the cross even if he was angry with God. The robe was not consecrated, only Catholics did that, yet he felt that what he was about to do was so unseemly that he said, "*I hereby release this chasuble from its Christian duty.*"

Kai Schweigaard took the knife and nicked a seam. Tugged on some threads. Made an opening and slipped his hand inside a furry compartment.

There, under the contours of the cross, he felt nothing more than ordinary reindeer skin.

In a fit of disbelief and dismay he slashed the front of the robe. Was there anything else inside? A smoother cloth, with little ridges?

He grabbed the chasuble with both hands and tore at the

cloth and cut more seams and tore at the cloth some more and then stuck his hand in again.

But as the torn cloth crumpled in a hopeless heap around him, so did he. The chasuble was a complete wreck now. This was the work of a vandal, blasphemy in a sacristy.

There was no tapestry here. Just a scrap of dark-grey woollen lining, folded double. He gave it a dejected slap and a cloud of dust rose under the electric light.

When he took his hand away, it was no longer his own, it was as black as if it had touched the inside of a stovepipe, and on the dark-grey lining was a hand-shaped mark, and in this imprint he thought he glimpsed hints of an orangey-yellow colour.

It had been coated with soot. To stop the colours shining through.

From all his years of searching, all the years of discussion about looms and weaving, wool and cloth, he knew it had to be cleaned the way tapestries had been cleaned throughout history. By pressing it into fresh, very cold, dry snow. Warm water would cause the wool to shrink and be ruined.

Until now the window had been filled with the reflection of the ceiling light. He went up close to it, and looked across the cemetery. A powdering of snow over the tombstones.

It had been one of the longest nights of his life.

As the morning dawned he went behind the *stabbur*. He could hear the bellowing of cows in the barn below, but otherwise the parsonage was quiet. There, in the first snowdrift of the winter, he unfolded the fabric and patted it gently into the snow. When he lifted it, a black square was left behind. He thought he saw hints of colour and moved the fabric to another patch of clean snow. He became almost heavy-handed as he continued to press it repeatedly into the snow, until he was surrounded by black squares, and each time he did it, the colours grew brighter.

It was not only soot. The weave had hung in the church since the early 1600s, and the snow now took on a brownish colour, from centuries-old church dust. The weave was generally tight, but one corner was significantly frayed, and here and there it was showing signs of wear.

He went on until the snow no longer got dirty.

Then he finally turned the weave over.

Snowflakes settled gently over myriad colourful patterns and human and animal forms.

Kai Schweigaard looked up at the sky and at the snow-flakes that tumbled so infinitely slowly towards him. They fell like human lives towards Earth, each flake visible for just a split second before vanishing, and those that let his gaze catch them landed on his forehead.

"Thank you, Margit Bressum. Thank you."

He hung it on the wall in a little side room in his bedroom, a room with a window but with no electric light, wanting to see the Hekne Weave as the villagers had seen it in the stave church.

It was larger and more highly coloured than he had imagined. A rectangular riddle set against an inky blue background. In the centre a large wreath of vibrant red-orange, and, flickering within that, something of copper green.

Some of the patterns were woven in a yarn so bright it was almost luminous, and he got a sense of how the weave must have looked from the pews. From a distance, the wreath was an eternal flame in a dark, tar-smelling haze. A rising sun or dying fire. When the room was dark the wreath seemed to be on fire; in the daylight it was more like Christ's crown of thorns.

As the carvings on the stave church's portal wound about each other, so too did the patterns in the weave, a stream connecting life and the end times, a study in unfathomable mystery.

It was easier to understand what was depicted inside the wreath.

Skråpånatta: the Night of the Great Scourge.

The wreath was night, fire and sunrise in one. He had to go right up close to see the figures inside the circle clearly, and in doing just that, in venturing all the way up to the weave so his entire field of vision was encircled by patterns and creatures, he became more open and receptive, and he *did* in fact think it was scary to look upon them.

For there they were.

The birds that spat fire. Wings outstretched over a sea of flames. Frenzied human faces with huge, wide-open eyes. Below them men with swords. Burning houses and fleeing people. The birds were the same red-orange as the sea of flames, their wings also being aflame, so they too were part of the fire, as though flames cast flames upon flames.

Was there wisdom or punishment in these flames?

The pattern outside the wreath was different, more like that of the pillows. Humans, animals and shape-shifters, everyday life intersecting with catastrophe. Cows and people floating in water. Was this the biblical flood or the terrible Gudbrandsdal flood of 1789? A white streak over a house. Lightning, or was it perhaps the coming of electricity?

He took a step back. How unthinkably *old* this was. Started by two girls in the early seventeenth century, completed after one of them had died. Despite the vivid glow of the plant-based dyes, the sheep wool seemed ragged and worn, especially in the corners, and he could not find the place where they were said to have woven a picture of themselves. Many of the images were hard for him to interpret or understand. Though it evoked in him a distinct feeling of the end-times. And there – a skeleton riding a wagon, with dead human beings in its wake, might that be the Black Death?

He collected himself.

Did he see what he saw? Or just what he hoped to see? Were these not just cryptic depictions of events that were bound to happen sooner or later? You only had to wait long enough, and a war, a forest fire, a flood, a plague would come.

He remembered the story of Jenny Stueflaaten's tapestry that had fallen apart when it had said what it was meant to say. This one was generally tight and doubtless still had a long life ahead of it, and, if he believed all that was said, there was still a long time left before Skråpånatta.

Kai Schweigaard shook his head, both at himself and the Hekne Weave. Nobody should be allowed to look at this tapestry, not without very good reason.

Nowhere did he see any sort of hint at how the last priest in Butangen might die. That was the only thing about the weave that offered him any comfort. He stood there and looked at the birds that spat fire.

At the end of the world.

We'll Drop Bombs Tomorrow

"One more?"

"No thanks. I'd stop now, if I were you."

"What else can a fellow do?"

"Stop after the second and then go to bed. Try to get some kip."

"Pretty boring, wouldn't you say?"

"Perhaps. But that's why our pictures hang *there* and not *there*. Thus far."

The other pilot shifted his gaze from the western to the eastern wall of the mess. They were photographed when they arrived at the squadron, and their portraits were displayed on the west wall, over the table with the gramophone. As they fell or went missing in battle, their portraits were moved over. The east wall was now almost full of pictures, and a new row had been started the day before yesterday.

His drinking partner was Arthur Harris, a twenty-five-year-old pilot who had grown up in Rhodesia. They had met very briefly back in 1915, when their names were called out one after the other because they were consecutive in the alphabet. Victor wondered how many such alphabetical friendships had been formed during the three years since the start of the war.

It was the autumn of 1917, they were sitting in the airmen's mess near St Omer in France. In the two years they had been here, both had adopted the military man's phlegmatic demeanour, a tendency to sit askew in their chairs, a languid indifference when they were indoors, but outdoors it was impossible to hide their nervous, hurried gait.

Earlier that day, they had test-flown the new planes, which had arrived in crates and been assembled on site: six heavy de Havilland DH-4 bombers, with engines from a small car manufacturer by the name of Rolls-Royce.

He remembered the start of the war as a time of comparative ease. He had obeyed a sudden impulse to join up, since neither Britain nor France had any real air force, and he and some other pioneering airmen had flown to the front on the off-chance, many in their own planes. They carried out reconnaissance missions, dropped the odd message bag, needed nothing more for communication than signal pistols, and when they met German pilots on similar missions, they waved at each other.

Until, that is, the first shot was fired in the air. Nobody knew who fired it, only that it was shot from a pistol a couple of months into the war. German co-pilots were soon armed with Mauser rifles. A little later, the first machine guns were installed. But everyone was shooting at everyone, from the air and the ground, because nobody had thought to mark the planes with any insignia. In the end the Germans marked theirs with the iron cross, and the Allies hastily collected red, white and blue house paint, and decided on the three-coloured roundel as their symbol.

Now, three years later, Victor had got used to 375-horsepower engines, 500-pound bombers and front-mounted machine guns. He had only been at war a few weeks when three of his comrades had crashed, and he realised that the restless determination that had prompted him to join up also gave him unique abilities as a fighter pilot. Although this was only because he had a companion, the shadow of an invisible co-pilot that was always alert to danger. Not that he had a sixth sense, but something beyond the fifth.

He brought death and saw death. Every day.

But he was affected less and less by what he saw. Only occasionally did he acknowledge what he and his plane had become. This erosion had begun sometime in 1915 or 1916, somewhere over the front when he spotted a strange, black cloud just above the ground, and realised it was a host of flies, eating the soldiers who had been caught on the barbed wire. The two things he had most admired before 1914 – the rifle and the airplane – had combined to form an abominable flying beast.

Today he had test-flown the new plane. Feeling cold and rather indifferent he had driven it up the runway, tested all the levers and checked the instruments, fired a few rounds from the front-mounted machine gun, then landed it, removed his helmet and walked back along the runway. But as he passed the plane that Arthur Harris was about to board, he seemed to hear Carax's voice from many years ago.

Wasn't there a certain dissonance in the hum of one of its propellers? Didn't it have a slightly odd tone as it cut through the air? The mechanics turned off the engine, and it did indeed prove to have a minuscule crack.

"I'll be forever in your debt, Victor!" Harris said. Victor felt a vague sense of foreboding, a glimpse into the darkness. As he did sometimes.

"I expect you'll get the chance to repay me. But not yet."

"I hope I'll have to wait a very long time!"

"Me too," Victor said. "As long as possible."

They both knew that this didn't necessarily mean much. Pilots survived twenty-six flights on average. Early tomorrow Harris would set out on his sixth flight and Victor Harrison on his thirty-second.

One of the other men went over to the gramophone and put on another interminably cheerful wartime song that was meant to keep the men's spirits up. The record crackled.

"So, is it true that you were in Macedonia?" Harris said.

"Only very briefly. I was there after my first year of the war in France. Later they called me back to England as an instructor. But yes. I was in Macedonia for a while after we met."

"What were you flying over there?"

"Any planes that would go. I had an Armstrong Whitworth."

"Did that stand up well against the Fokker?"

Victor shook his head, saying that almost nothing stood up against the Fokker. "Except the Sopwith Camel, in the hands of a good pilot. Tell me something. D'you believe all the rumours about the long-range bomber? The one that can get all the way to Berlin?"

"Certainly. I think it'll come. Four engines. Fifteen hundred horsepower."

"My first plane had twenty-five," Victor said. "And that was just seven years ago."

"Did you own your own plane? I didn't know that."

"Still do. She's back at home. A Blériot."

"The one they crossed the Channel in? Or was that a Farman?"

"No, a Blériot. Louis Blériot flew it himself. I met an American youngster once. He pointed to a photograph of a Blériot and said that there were several laws and principles of physics and aeronautics which its maker hadn't *understood*. I asked this youngster if *he* would have understood Newton's laws if it hadn't been for Newton. But yes, the Blériot is a bit dodgy, although some crazy fellow from Norway managed to cross the North Sea in one, too. Tryggve Gran."

"Gran?"

"That's right. I met him a couple of times. He's fighting for us now. Crash-landed in a DH-9. Survived that too, no doubt!"

"I've only heard of the Channel crossing. They said it was the greatest achievement in aviation. Until that point, at least."

"Gran flew six times the distance. Through stormy weather and fog. Such bad weather it would have been hard nowadays in one of our fighter planes. Didn't break the chassis either when he landed. But nobody's ever heard of him."

"Because . . . ?"

"He flew on July 30, 1914."

Harris whistled and shook his head.

"Quite! He had agreements with German and English escort ships to pick him up if he crashed, but they were called home the day before Gran took off. War was declared while he was up in the air. None of the British or European newspapers reported it."

The two men drained their glasses and were silent for a moment.

"It's strange," Victor said. "The Norwegians have something called a *vardøger* – a premonition in which they think they see or hear a person before they actually arrive. Gran said a Norwegian fisherman had heard the *vardøger* of his airplane before it appeared over the horizon. A man who'd never even heard an aircraft before."

"You really must make that your last *now*, old chap. We've got bombs to drop tomorrow."

"Indeed." Victor put down his glass. "We've got bombs to drop tomorrow."

He rose to his feet. He was about to say something, but changed his mind, and said only, "Take something that'll bring you luck. Something or other."

"D'you have something like that?"

"Yes. I certainly do."

"And it brings you luck?"

"Nothing brings one luck in itself. What brings us luck is our *belief* that something brings us luck."

The Hammer Comes Down on Hekne

Jehans was standing near the barn. He wondered when he had been here at Hekne last. Twelve years? No, thirteen. The farm hadn't changed much. But back then, during the angry years, the days of hatred, he had never noticed the beauty of the ancient timber buildings, never allowed himself to feel awe at the beautifully crafted staircases, never considered the toil of womenfolk that had been so crucial yet barely left a mark, invisible as women's toil always was, like footsteps down to the stream, swiftly overgrown if nobody walked there anymore, a mere memory of a water yoke borne on shoulders and monotonous workdays.

Everyone who had ever lived there would be forgotten in a world without heirs left to remember them.

But now, today, *he* thought of them. The Heknes. And he thought he saw his mother, or a kind of reflection of her, a restless figure walking between the *stabbur* and the farmhouse, a girl much younger than he was now, a girl with an innate goodness and strength of will, qualities that would be converted after her death into something she could never have guessed at. And this vision of her took on the weight of sorrow and all eternity. She had walked here, surrounded by her own everyday reality, with no way of seeing into the future or the generations to come, without any idea that she would give birth to *him*, that he would stand here, knowing more about her than she would ever know about him.

It hadn't troubled him much. The question of whether *she* had been the one to decide that Victor, and not him, should live outside the village. Perhaps the choice hadn't been hers at all. But he would like to know, and he wouldn't blame her no matter what.

He walked over to the grindstone and looked out. He had never expected to feel any sense of grief here.

But right now, today he was here to take leave of Hekne. The farm was facing a forced auction.

Things had already started brewing five years ago, in 1912. A young cottar had died suddenly when working for Osvald in the timber forest, and all the cottars were at his funeral. The dead man had contributed hugely to the village's communal efforts up at Hellorn, so Jehans would have gone to his funeral no matter what.

Osvald, however, did not go.

Jehans observed it in the other cottars as they stood around the coffin. That something was brewing. That they were about to draw again upon the strength they had shown in Hellorn, but that Osvald was about to be hit from an altogether different direction than he expected.

It had happened in the spring, in April, on a bitterly cold day that Jehans remembered because of the wind and huge snow-flakes. A shift in the weather had chased away the mild air and with it any hope of an early thaw. It was, in fact, a good day to stay indoors.

But it was also a good day to leave Butangen.

Very few families emigrated to America nowadays, but one of the cottars had recently heard that huge areas in the Cana-dian province of Saskatchewan – which was "as flat as the ice on Lake Løsnes" – were now open to new settlers. Each family could get an incredible sixty-four hectares of land for free, and the neighbouring land would be put aside too and given to them free of charge if they stayed on for good. But Saskatchewan was largely uninhabited, and it was far better to have people you knew around you. Thus the plan was hatched. Six large families. Friendship founded on injustice. Six households, as independ-ent, property-owning neighbours in a new country.

Jehans had been warned of what was happening, and had walked down from the dairy to say his goodbyes. He would often wonder later if they had expected more from him that morning. They were gathered outside the church, a darkly clad, bedrag-gled crowd. Each family pulled sledges loaded with large cases, and stopped in the whirling snow to look around. They said little. He remembered how two children broke away from the crowd in tears, screaming *hematt* and trying to run home before they were swiftly pulled back among the dense mass of overcoats and shawls, where they disappeared from view and earshot.

It was the cottars who left Hekne that day, and it was Jehans who waved them off.

Contracts were terminated, and, in one night alone, Osvald lost nine good farmworkers and twelve strong girls, as well as eight or nine able-bodied children. They left the keys in the middle of their kitchen tables and let their stoves burn out.

Halvfarelia now stood empty. As did five other smallholdings.

From then on everything was a struggle for Osvald. He failed to get new cottars, and found it increasingly difficult to keep control of his band of hired farmworkers. The following year he had to sell some of his cows because he was short of fodder for the winter, and in January he swallowed his pride and went to Vålebrua to order a mower and binder. But since nobody could deliver the machinery before June, and it was too heavy to take over the Løsnes Marshes during the summer, he ended up buying newer, more expensive models that he could get straight away. The Great War led to rises in interest rates, and no matter how hard he tried to flog more out of his workforce and machinery, he needed more money, and then more money, and pretty soon he received the first letter from the bank informing him that his payments were in arrears, and a reminder that he had used the farm as a guarantee. That had been in 1916, during what had been a very fine summer. It was now 1917 and the bank was finally holding an auction, and Jehans was there to see the Hekne family history run to its conclusion.

Truth was it already had. Butangen was an entirely different village these days, and Jehans knew that he and Kristine were largely responsible for this.

They had a marriage of sorts, these two. She had attended the Dairy School, leaving Widow Fløter and Ada Borgen to run the dairy, and two years later she had come home with a framed certificate and new overcoat, and all they talked about was construction and the installation of machinery.

They ate together, drank coffee together, slept in their bed together, but never went anywhere together, they never danced together, and their embraces were fleeting. And when they spoke it was about practical day-to-day matters, indeed their conversations resembled those he and Kai Schweigaard had in the difficult years, awkward and distant. He could admire her, most certainly, but the ferocious determination they had shared in their little one-room palace was gone, as was the desperate, raging desire they had felt up at the *seter*, his urge to run up into the mountains after her, in pursuit of the one and only Kristine Messelt in the whole wide world. In the last few weeks they had lain with their backs to each other, and she rarely ever nudged him to see if he was asleep.

What has become of me? Jehans wondered.

Is this all there is?

Dynamos and water channels?

Their room was cramped and miserable and he was restless. He had redeemed the Krag long ago, but had not shot any reindeer for years, choosing instead to take on additional work in the autumn. He had considered buying a hunting dog and a double-barrelled shotgun, but realised he had no hunting companion to join him in the chase.

A face would come to him now and then in his sadness. The face of a man who could advance with a shotgun, its safety catch off, on the right side of the dog as it retrieved a bird, without a word needing to be said.

This was what things had come to.

He was ashamed to think this way. Disgusted by his own vapid resignation.

Still, things had turned out as they had, and were as they were, and they could have been worse. There was a fair bit of money in their bank account. They had been offered a loan for a new dairy with modern equipment, which would require all they owned as security, plus two years' work, but even in the icy air between them, Jehans thought: I shall do it for her. *We* will build it. It will come into being through us.

He had signed the loan papers. But then one of the bank

employees beckoned another over and whispered something. Oh well, he thought, it's going to come to nothing after all, they clearly don't trust me. The bank manager came back with the large handwritten protocol and asked why he did not redeem the security in Norsk Kvælstofaktielskab that was in his name. Transferred to them by Pastor Schweigaard with instructions to make "sensible investments", with the result that ninety kroner had grown to nearly two hundred.

The auction was set to begin in an hour. Potential buyers from outside the village, grouped in twos or threes, farmers in their prime, with enough years behind them or heirs ahead to take on a new venture.

Three men came towards where he was standing, but did not acknowledge him. They had probably mistaken him for a farmhand, which was fine by him.

How much the bailiff was demanding from Osvald was unknown, and nobody had any real idea of what the farm could go for. Inflation and the Great War had upended everything, and the only reference folk had was that farms in Brekkom had been sold for between six and fifteen thousand kroner in recent years. But interest rates had gone up even more since then, and Hekne was likely to be sold for just ten thousand, twelve at best.

He wished Kristine was here now. So she could see him.

And see the place that had made him who he was.

But she was in Kristiania on a course about some new pasteurising machines.

He looked up at the windows. No movement. Osvald had probably forbidden the children to go out.

A stranger began to set up a table for the sheriff near the grindstone. The slope meant that everyone in the crowd would be able to see. The man laid a few rocks down to make the table level, and when it was ready, the sheriff put his briefcase on it and took out a brown wooden hammer.

Jehans wondered if he was partly to blame for this. Hekne was now the only farm without an electricity pole and one of the few from whom the dairy took no deliveries. In many ways the farm was just as it had been in the time of the Hekne sisters.

He had never given them much thought before, but now he looked out over Hekne and thought: They actually lived here. Right here. They had their loom in one of those rooms, and perhaps they slept there too. And their father, Eirik Hekne, was also here somewhere. The man responsible for the legendary deed, the man who cast the Sister Bells at such enormous expense that Hekne had almost gone into foreclosure back then.

The man he himself was descended from.

His thoughts went to his brother again, and to what he had said that night on the shore of Lake Løsnes.

"What would you know about what it might cost me?"

Had Victor perhaps felt what he felt now? A duty towards a place? A duty to all those who had once lived here?

The farm was nothing but earth and timbers. Yet there was something more. Something invisible that *demanded* something. Something that had been in hibernation under Osvald's rule. Was that what he felt now. The ancient *Hekne Way*? That dared and lost, and still won?

He began to play with the thought. Played with it so long he failed to notice that the thought had begun to play with him.

"Silence!" called the sheriff, before declaring the auction open. The Hekne farm, with fishing rights, *seters* and cottars' small-holdings, would initially be offered in its entirety. If, however, the bids were too low, it would be divided up. The mower and binder would be sold first, followed by Halvfarelia and the other cottars' farms. They would continue thus until the debt was covered, so that Hekne could still function as a working farm, albeit on a simpler basis.

This was unexpected. It indicated that the bailiff was demanding a large sum, and also that Osvald had grown tired and would prefer to get rid of the entire farm.

"So, we are offering the whole Hekne farm," the auctioneer said. "A bid has already come in for six thousand kroner."

A murmur went through the crowd. It seemed that one of the outsiders had placed this bid in an envelope. Some said it was a shamefully low bid, others that it was extraordinary that folk had that much money at all. Everyone held their breath to see if anyone could better the maiden bid.

Lars Romsås was standing right at the front. It was common knowledge that he was considering buying Hekne. He had two sons whom he wanted to have nearby, and there he stood, a wealthy man with a plan. He looked around, put his thumbs in his braces and tugged them a little, prepared himself to shout out a bid.

Suddenly Jehans worked his way through the crowd. A wild, uncontrollable urge gripped him. Not unlike the feeling that had gripped him when he bought the Krag and Hellorn. An urge to spring forwards to the smelting pot with all he owned. An urge to be himself again.

"Seven thousand!" he yelled.

Astonishment and the rustle of clothes. Folk turned to see who was bidding. Lars Romsås leaned forward, and Jehans met his gaze.

Everyone waited.

Romsås bit his lip. He shot a glance at Jehans. Gave a slight bow. A signal of retreat, or at least temporary withdrawal.

There were no further bids.

The sheriff cleared his throat and shouted: "Could the bidder come forward?"

Jehans stepped out of the crowd and walked up the slope towards the grindstone. Behind him the crowd had fallen silent.

"Seven thousand," the sheriff said quietly. "Are you aware you've made a bid of seven thousand kroner? It's a binding offer."

"Will it be enough t' cover the tax demand?" Jehans asked.

The sheriff did not answer the question directly, but said: "That is never settled on the day. Not on a farm. But you'll need to show me that you can raise that much money."

"I have a loan of six thousand. For the new dairy."

"Do you have the agreement with you?"

"Nay. 'Tis at home. But Gildevollen has seen it. He be right there, at the back."

"I can see. And you'd prefer to spend the money on a farm now?"

"The farm has only just come up for sale."

"And the loan? Can you change it just like that?"

"For Hekne, aye. We can take one of the outhouses and turn it into a dairy."

"Then you'll be short of money for – but, that's your concern. You say the loan is for six thousand. And the last thousand?"

"I have a fair amount in the bank. I'll manage seven."

The sheriff beckoned him to come close and said: "If there's any jiggery pokery, any at all, then you'll go to debtors' prison. I'm the sheriff. I repeat, I'm the sheriff. The whole village is watching. Seven thousand kroner must be paid inside a week. After that, I shan't give you even two days' grace. It'll be handcuffs and jail. So you can withdraw your bid now."

Jehans said that his bid stood firm. He stepped back into the crowd. Their eyes travelled between the sheriff, Jehans and Lars Romsås, who smiled and put his hands behind his back.

"So seven thousand kroner is bid. First time!"

It was so quiet that folk could hear a dog barking up in Fjellstad.

The sheriff called out twice more.

Silence again. This time the same silence as when church bells have fallen still.

The hammer fell, hard wood against hard wood, a knocking that flung itself against Hekne's walls and over the crowd, past the new church and over Lake Løsnes.

We Were a Pair Once

"We can build it in the farmhouse," Jehans said. "Take the whole ground floor. Then we shan't have to build anew. And we can sell the harvester to get money for the dairy equipment."

"Ha! So we can sell the harvester, can we? Happen ye can go out on yer own and mow all the fields wi' a scythe?"

An unlit electric lamp was above their heads, and on a hook hung his jacket. She had not yet taken off the overcoat she had bought in Kristiania. They were standing in the narrow corridor between the kitchen and the living room, above the dairy, the rooms they had inhabited for several years now without ever really bothering to decorate or care for them.

"We *agreed*, Jehans! Agreed to build from new! With new machines! And a concrete floor that were easy to keep clean! Wi'out crooked timbers from the year 1600. We were going to build a *community dairy*! Nowt temporary. One that would stand alone, wi' a street entrance! So folk can come to the shop wi'out thinking they be walking in on a private house!"

Her voice was steady and calm. Which told him that she had something brewing. Like the invisible, rumbling force he felt when he placed his hand on a large water pipe.

"Every evening up there in Levanger I worked on those drawings. Three big rooms with good light. A row of machinery with a large pasteuriser. A separate room for cheesemaking. A cold room for the finished cheeses. A changing room wi' a sink for us womenfolk. I imagined little name plaques. Brass signs. So as to say that here, here we have permanent work."

"Aye, but – the price, Kristine! Seven thousand! For the *whole* farm. It'll mean nowt more than a little delay."

Kristine scoffed.

"And apart from that, we have two hundred kroner more in the bank."

"Where from?" said Kristine.

"A picture that my father painted. That were sold in Germany for ninety kroner. But it were Victor who – well, Schweigaard put it into securities so it gained interest."

"Ninety kroner?" cried Kristine. "We had a whole ninety kroner back then?"

It was the first time she had hit him. She had her wedding ring on, and the sharp tips of wire scratched his cheek.

"Good God, look at us. Ye let me wear myself t' tatters up in Hellorn. I grew five years older in one year, Jehans! But this, this be worse still. I have never wanted Hekne! I wanted my own place. Truth be told, ye have never offered me owt but drudgery."

"When ye say it like that, then."

"Ah, there we have it! The whole problem. 'When *ye say* it' indeed! That be the nub o' it. *For 'tis only when I say a thing that ye understand it!* Ye mun talk to me first, we agreed upon that!"

"But Kristine, 'tis *Hekne*! My mother's farm! Hekne! And Halvfarelia comes with it! I can bid Adolf and Ingeborg move back on the eighteenth!"

"Ye should have asked me, Jehans. Ye *had* to ask me. What have ye been to me these last years? Near nowt. A man in my bed. An engineer and dynamo master. And aye, I have gone and done things o' my own too. As womenfolk allays have, wi'out anybody noticing. And now ye are gonna try to rope me in? Watch me take care o' Hekne? So ye can sit there on yer wooden stool, gaze about thee and feel satisfaction that Osvald were finally chased out?"

"But Kristine! Look at what we have achieved. Look up at the ceiling. Look. I press this switch. And there be light. And ye? Ye run a modern electric dairy!"

"Aye! I do indeed! I run a dairy! And now ye will have me run a farm? We mun find workers, dairy maids, milking cows, there be houses to repair. How many houses? Nine log houses with crooked slate roofs?"

"Twelve. And two summer farms."

"We mun buy seeds, industrial fertiliser, the list goes on. Inside there be glass and floors that be impossible to clean. If the farm cost seven thousand, ye mun spend a thousand in the first year to get things running. But, my dearest, now I think on't – there be no cows in t'barn now?"

He shook his head. "All the barns are empty. Osvald sold the livestock separately."

"'Tis better that way. That there be no animals. For then we mun get started straight off."

Things were a little calmer between them now.

"Osvald has got work running a farm in Biri somewhere," Jehans said. "He won't even greet me. They leave the day after tomorrow."

It blew up again.

"I should ha' known. It be just like ye Hekne folks to rush in wi'out seeing the risks!"

"But Kristine. S'wounds. Look at us! We live in two tiny rooms and work till late. Hekne may in fact be—"

"S'wounds? Did ye get that word from Osvald as part of the

deal? When will ye understand, ye were not made t' be a farmer? A reindeer hunter, Jehans, that's what ye be! More than anything, a reindeer hunter! And times have changed. Hekne is not as ye remember. When there were thirty men and women of all ages as knew what t' do and did it wi'out a murmur. We mun hire folk now and buy tools. Ye know sommat, Jehans? Osvald has won out again."

"Nay. He has not. I own Hekne, Kristine. Happen it'll take us a few years, but then we shall have a farm *and* a dairy. But I should ha' known. Known how ye would be."

"How I would be?"

"Aye, for I know one thing for sure. The minute the new dairy were ready, Kristine, d'ye know what ye would ha' wanted? One that were yet bigger! Ye'll be moving out t' village soon."

"And when were that wrong? To want sommat bigger? We go up in the world, and then we want to go higher! In't naebody wants to go down! And Hekne will only weigh us down! We had nowt but drudgery up at Hellorn. I have more drudgery in the dairy. But ne'er this constant didderin'. The drudgery were real enough, but we could tackle it wi' our hands. Am I meant t' be stuck now in didderment?"

With that Jehans saw her distaste for the deal. To stuck in *in didderment* was worse than any backache. It was like waking up every night with a toothache. A farmer's worries about everything that ought to have been sorted, the rotten wood and leaking roofs, fears about the harvest, about debts, about frozen crops. It was a word for farmers and priests. A word for Osvald Hekne. And now he had bought it from him and paid seven thousand kroner for the honour.

Suddenly he saw something else. Another concern. About something they never put into words.

How things would look. A woman in a manager's position with no children was one thing. But a farmer's wife? That was something else. A house with twelve bedrooms. She would be seen as the childless farmer's wife. In the old days this would not have been as visible, since farms were always heaving with folk and relatives. But now. With just the two of them. On a huge farm. With all those empty bedrooms.

She went into her room and he heard her pull out a drawer. She closed the door, and when she finally re-emerged, she was wearing rough clothes and shoes, and had filled a grey knapsack.

"I warned thee many years back," she said. "Up on Hellorn. That ye mun never do owt like that again. Ye gave me yer word but now ye have broken it. So ye can stay here with yer Hekne farm. We were a pair once, Jehans, and didna' do badly, but now we are one and one."

If only she had slammed the door. But she closed it very calmly, so that he would always remember the click of the lock as she left for good.

But Not in Flames

These mornings when he was alone with the clouds. When Finlaggan slept behind him and he walked across a freshly mown field with his helmet in his left hand and a cigarette in his right, a cigarette he would stump out well before the plane's odours reached his nostrils. From the petrol, the lubricating oil, the waterproofing of the canvas on the wings. The leather of the seats. An olfactory mirage that already came to his attention at thirty metres' distance. The smell almost made the aircraft more real than seeing it. And as the Blériot took off he smelled the damp of rivers and on occasion the ozone after a thunderstorm, until he reached the loftier, cooler air streams, where from minute signs he could predict the weather changes that would come in a couple of hours, before he landed and warmed his hands on the engine and saw his father waving his walking stick, an old man who'd been awoken by the hum of a plane.

These mornings when he ascended into the sky.

Distinct from this morning. 3.50 a.m. In an officer's tent south of Peronne.

Sometimes he was woken by the rain drumming on the tight, brown canvas. But tonight it was the nightmare about the dead soldier that woke him.

Like most of the men he closed his eyes or looked away when the bombs exploded or bullets hit. Which was why everyone always had such vastly different versions of what happened on the battlefield. But last year he had, on one occasion, kept his eyes open. They were flying Sopwith fighters and were under orders to chase any German troops in retreat. None of the pilots were happy about this. Early one morning they flew over an entire unit and managed to kill most of the soldiers, except one, who was left standing in the middle of the road, holding a Mauser rifle. He aimed upwards, fired without hitting anything and tried to reload. Victor turned, found him in the machine-gun sight, and came so close he could see it was a young boy in an oversized uniform. He wanted to turn away and let him go, but his finger pulled the trigger on the machine gun and he watched the lad quake with bullets, fall to the ground and lie, legs trembling, while his helmet rolled in a semi-circle around his head and the blood flowed.

Perhaps I was related to you, thought Victor. I am, after all, half-German.

The boy's face penetrated his memory and stayed, except when he took lots of Veronal.

*

Victor sat up. The ground was quaking under him, and he heard the roar of cannons. The dew that had gathered inside the tent trickled down in narrow paths.

The grenades were close, but would not reach the airbase.

As a fighter pilot he had his own tent with a wooden floor and a good camp bed. He went over to the tiny folding table with its washbowl and glass, brushed his teeth by candlelight and looked at his face in his small mirror that was lying flat on the table. It had fallen from its hook the day before and had a long crack across it, and he moved his head so the crack distorted his face. He was many years older now than his real father had been when he died, and if he went back to Norway now, the pastor might no longer recognise him as Gerhard Schönauer's son.

The pastor. Victor received a few letters from him each year, always forwarded to him from Finlaggan in Kumara's handwriting. Meanwhile his father's letters came every other week. Victor regularly answered these, but never the pastor's, even though his father only described everyday life at Finlaggan and gave the odd snippet of news about his mother and Joseph. More than a year had passed since Victor had last been home on leave, and his father had been frail. He could no longer follow world events so closely, but Kumara took him out for walks so that he lived in rhythm with the seasons.

Autumn has arrived here at Finlaggan, Victor. Went fly-fishing, but my shoulder has started acting up, so my casting technique isn't what it was. (Nobody will ever catch me fishing with live bait.) But I'll catch them, never fear! (The trout are always kind to old farts.) And I can still swing a shotgun. The day before yesterday I even shot a pheasant (missed the first three, shh).

Victor. I know you must do what you must. But try to do what you must and come back in one piece.

I beseech you.

Your Papa

Kai Schweigaard's letters, by contrast, contained outwardly straightforward news about the village and Norway, but between the lines was a wisdom Victor valued increasingly. He always made some mention of what Jehans was doing, although he no longer nagged Victor about any possible reconciliation. In the last couple of years his letters had become strikingly intimate, describing how he struggled with *old man's angst*, as he called it, an indefinable fear of the end-times, there was a sort of religion in it, not moored to any sort of crucifix, but to a hope for the world.

Victor often reread these letters. They eased an ache inside him that seemed to be growing ever more painful. Everything he had done thus far in life was in reality utterly insignificant. Most people's lives were insignificant. It was so clear to him when he took the plane up and saw the madness from above. From up there, he no longer understood human beings, any more than he understood the activities of ants when he stood and looked down at an anthill.

The bombing continued. His toothbrush began to rattle in its glass on the folding table. Far away, several loud bangs could be heard, and the glass moved. These were the cannons they would bomb in a few hours. More grenades followed. And his razor clanked on the tin dish.

It felt so close. Might they now have even longer-range artillery? No. It always seemed worse than it was. Once, in 1916, when a fortification had been mined and then blown up at the start of the Battle of the Somme, the shock waves were felt in London.

The grenades were probably neither closer nor further away tonight. He had merely forgotten the details of the previous night.

Victor noticed that his hands were shaking, and when the cannons started up again after a brief pause, he thought it was not the roar of artillery he could hear, but church bells. He told himself it was his imagination, but from the third year of the war he had started to confuse sounds and attribute them to different sources. Reality itself seemed to falter at times. A battlefield might change into a Norwegian landscape, or he might find himself in Ceylon, or believe that the bombs that were dropping on France were dropping on Finlaggan, that the Germans' mascot dogs were in fact Pidge, and occasionally the boy soldier of his nightmares took on the features of Jehans or even Elsa Rathenau, and, increasingly often, when he flew over a body of water he would mistake it for Lake Løsnes.

Yesterday he had heard the church bells ringing in Peronne, but had thought of the stave church in Dresden. There was such a shortage of metal in Germany that half the country's church bells had been melted down to make cannons.

The cannons roared again. He suddenly felt frightened. Far more frightened than usual.

What if they had melted it down? The church bell he hadn't dared to climb up to? Perhaps it was *her* he heard now? Perhaps it was Halfrid calling him?

He was up again with the hum of a 375-horsepower engine in his ears. Captain Harrison at the controls. A talisman in his inside pocket.

Co-pilot Thorne behind him, a highly driven man who knew exactly when to drop a bomb or fire the machine gun.

One of six bombers going out. Four fighters would follow. Suddenly the squadron leader turned his plane. He had the sharpest mind of any man Victor had flown under, with a unique flair for surprise attacks. Presumably he had found a better target than the cannons they were supposed to take out.

Below him, there in the morning mist, he saw them.

Soldiers and horses and trucks on the move. As a rule, the Germans moved their troops under cover of night, but there must have been some delay. It was a huge column, over half a mile long, and the fighters lined up to bomb them. He heard the firing of machine guns, but was unable to work out whether it was enemy fire or their own. The first plane dropped a bomb on a truck. It must have been carrying grenades, since it exploded so violently that the flames licked the belly of the plane in front of him, and when Victor then flew over it, his plane shook in the rising hot air.

Victor was waiting for Thorne to drop some bombs. But nothing happened. Below them soldiers were scrambling over trenches and towards their machine guns. Two mounted officers set off across a field. A Sopwith followed them and one of the horses came crashing down.

As the planes lifted higher into the air to head back, he smelled the acrid odour of smoke rising from below and glimpsed the movement of dying men and scorched horses.

God help us. What have we done? Great God. What have we done?

Doubtless we have only done to them what they did to us.

Suddenly the glass on the altimeter was smashed, a split second later and he saw three holes in the hull right next to his arm. Behind him he heard machine-gun fire, and as he turned he saw a group of Fokkers flying out of the sun.

He glanced over his shoulder towards Thorne. "Look!" he yelled. "Can't you see? To our left!"

More shots rang out behind him.

"Thorne! Return fire, damn it!"

He turned again and saw Thorne's hunched back. He was holding the machine gun, but wasn't firing.

Hell. The man was dead.

Any other thoughts vanished from his head, his mouth went dry and his heart pounded.

The sky filled with red streaks. Searchlights from a field cannon below. They rarely hit him, but searchlights were easier to see than the plane itself, which meant he would attract the attention of even more Fokkers now.

On his left he saw smoke coming from a bomber. The pilot must have been hit, since there was no evidence of him trying to right the plane, there were no kinks or curves in the ribbon of smoke, the pilot only followed the line that pointed to his death.

Where were the others?

From below he heard a rumbling, and a huge shadow rose in front of the propeller. A new kind of anti-aircraft gun perhaps. Quick to zoom in, accurate. Intended for only one thing. To hit him.

Where *were* the others?

Far away he spotted two more planes being shot down, and there were now no others in the air space around him.

They had been six, and he had been the sixth out.

Suddenly his whole control panel burst apart, a burning sensation went through his arm, as though a red-hot iron bar was being pushed under his skin, and everything around him seemed to take on a red hue.

They'll get me now. They'll take me.

His entire field of vision was filled with sky. Then ground, then sky again, then ground and he realised the plane was spinning. The artillery on the ground had stopped firing, and a wild idea came to him, that this might be what a pheasant thought when it was shot down, that the hunters held fire and stopped to admire the bird as it fell.

The plane started to burn.

Dear God. Let me die from a bullet or blow, but God, don't let me die in flames. Not in flames.

He saw the cannon. The long-range avenger. And believed he had been shot down by his own recast family silver, by the sister of the church bell he had forsaken at home in Norway.

In the next second he thought of a brother's eyes and a reindeer's eyes. Of a tombstone near a white wooden church in Norway and of Elsa Rathenau's gaze, and as he rushed towards the earth, he saw Finlaggan again, and Pidge lying with one paw over his nose and opening one eye in the hope that it was *him* coming in, he saw the Cheviot Hills, and standing by the stable doors were his father and Kumara, shading their eyes to see, and the Norwegian pastor came to join them, and all three stood and watched him fall.

Then he was back in reality.

Beneath him the ground was completely churned up. Bomb craters, which at the beginning of the war were individual rings, now merged. But the edges of the craters had been torn down by new grenades, and there was no water to smooth them, and now they formed a pattern of overlapping circles. It looked like a lake in heavy rain, but only Lake Løsnes could quench the flames that engulfed him now, and the only trace of his life would be a ring in the water that would soon come to rest.

The Last Thing We Do Together

Jehans had thought she just needed some time to herself. To sit on a warm rock by flowing water well away from any stupid men and Hekne and seven thousand squandered kroner.

363

He stood staring at the door that she had closed behind her, turned and paced about a little. They had a small electric hob and he made himself some coffee, but his cup was barely half-empty when he felt an unbearable distaste for these wretched rooms in which they lived, and he ran out to find her.

She wasn't by Daukulpen or by the stream she liked to walk along to stretch her legs after a long working day. She wasn't at the lookout on the way up to the *seter*, and when he turned and came back down he didn't find her by Lake Løsnes, and he knew she would not be at Hekne.

Folk must have seen her, that was certain, since it was late autumn and everyone was out on errands, going this way and that with cows or sheep or carts of hay. But there was nobody to ask about a thing like this. Least of all for a man who was talked about as much as he was: the son of the Silver Winter, the scythe chaser, the pioneer, the dynamo builder. Here he was, for all to see, the harum-scarum master of Butangen.

But yes.

There was someone he could ask. The man who had always been there and waited for him.

But later, when Jehans left the parsonage, she had not been there either. Schweigaard stood on his front step and watched him leave.

Of course, she had not gone away to reconsider. It was ridiculous to think that anyone from Imsdal would merely go away to *reflect* upon things. When she was angry, she was like a big bird in the forest. She put all her strength into flapping her wings, rushing through the branches and treetops until she exhausted herself and was forced to land.

Later that afternoon he passed Saubua. Kvia towered against the horizon.

He was carrying the Krag on its strap over his shoulder, a

man in the mountains had to be seen to be on a mission. But if a reindeer were to appear now, it would be allowed to pass. It was up near Kvia that he had shot his first reindeer with the Krag. A young buck which he had strained every muscle in his body to shoot, and which he had carried down to her, only to have to take him back up.

He had felt a remorse and doubt that day. Perhaps the Krag was meant for greater men than he. Now, carrying the same weapon, near the same place, he felt something similar. That the life he had ventured upon was meant for a greater man.

It had turned cold. Not wintery-cold with snow on the air, but October-cold, the kind of cold that made the skin on his face numb, and made the sweat on his spine go cold the instant he stopped walking.

It was then that he spotted a female reindeer.

She was standing on the edge of a marsh, and seemed unwell. Bowed over. Walking in circles.

He shifted his grip on the Krag. He had no time for this. No time at all. To shoot it and gut it and pin it down with rocks.

Still. She was behaving so strangely. And now she lay down. Despite having probably caught his scent.

She was clearly in pain. A lot of pain. And he remembered Adolf's words.

When we must, we must.

He held the Krag near the ground, and moved forward, low on his haunches, the heather and juniper bushes grazing his fists. He was purposely careless as he moved, because if she was healthy, she would be startled and run off.

But she just lay there. Only when he came closer did she get up. Turned, sat on her haunches, turned again, then lay down again.

Jehans stopped some forty metres away and waited. She continued to behave as before. Walking in circles without ever quite getting up, and then lying down again. He crawled over to a ridge that gave him a clear shot path and pulled back the bolt. The Krag clicked smoothly as it fetched a lead-tipped bullet from the magazine, and he sat up with the rifle unlocked and made himself visible.

When she got up, he recognised her.

It was the same female he had stumbled across after meeting his brother. She had the same unique streaks in her coat, and stared at him with the same eyes.

Could she really have lived that long? Almost certainly. They could reach fifteen or twenty years.

She was in pain, and he felt pain just looking at her. He lifted the Krag and took aim. There was no hunter's fever in this moment, nothing but cold blood. He felt the painful decisiveness of *when we must, we must*, and fired. The shot rang out and as she came crashing down to the ground the pain continued to swell in him and he felt the tears well up.

Jehans got up and walked over to the female. But as he reached her his stomach knotted and he threw up.

Two very wet, grey-black creatures were scrabbling and kicking in the heather. He tried to believe they were something other than reindeer, but they moved. Two gangly, newborn calves. One had crawled to its mother and sucked on her udder, while the other gazed up at him and tried to get to its feet.

Mucus and blood flowed from the female's rear.

Christ. Christ, forgive me. She were calving. That's what she were doing. But what reindeer calves at this time o' year? 'Tis impossible. Goes agin all natural lore. Surely, no reindeer calves now?

She lay with her legs straight out, but no blood came from her mouth as was usual from a lung shot, and it was in her lung he had shot her. The first calf let go of the teat and floundered away. Jehans crawled up to the female and ran his fingers over her side but found no gunshot wounds or blood. Suddenly he felt warmth from her nostrils and heard a loud snort as she got up, and he keeled over into the undergrowth and found himself lying under her belly.

She looked down at him and snorted again. And as she stepped over him he looked straight at the crescent moons in her hooves. And the moss came loose from her hooves and scattered on his face. She walked over to her calves, and they staggered up and began to drink.

Thus they stood and gave and received milk.

The reindeer fixed him with her gaze, then suddenly all three disappeared into the tall thicket.

He was sure. It was the same reindeer. As alive as ever. As if the Krag had refused to kill her. Or as if she had risen from the dead.

This episode lodged itself in him and added to his self-reproach over Kristine and the farm purchase, and he was both troubled and terrified as he hurried on.

He was not so strong these days. When travelling distances he once took at a stretch, he now had to stop to rest. He reigned supreme over water channels, gunpowder and dynamite, all of which shepherded the forces of nature, but none was of help to him here. Going uphill he had to hold his sides, downhill his knees hurt, and heading for the *seter* now he realised that even if she wasn't there, he would not have the energy to walk to Imsdalen to find accommodation.

He stumbled sore-footed down the hill and reached the *seter* as evening fell. The *seter* had always been a vision of farm animals and ribbons of smoke rising from chimneys. But not today. The air was cold and raw and yellow leaves clung to his boots. Folk had left for the valley, all the dairy sheds had their windows bolted, everything was rain-sodden and forlorn, the meadows had been grazed bare, and the nettles lay flat on the ground.

During the second autumn of their acquaintance, he had shot a female reindeer that was alone, and she had hung its antlers under the eaves of the log cabin. They were still there. But one of the nails had rusted away and it would not be long before they fell down. He was struck by a sense of hopelessness, laid his Krag flat on the grass and sat on the doorstep as the light faded.

His back hurt as he drew open the hatch of the *finlands-bu*. It was close to collapse. Certainly nobody had been in here in a long time, there were no traces of smoke inside, just darkness and a vague odour of earth and age. He went out into the forest and broke off some branches. It was impossible to see in the twilight which were dry enough to burn, and he bent them to check if they cracked, rejecting those that did not, and he thought to himself that this was how the blind get by in the world.

Soon the darkness was so dense that it made no difference whether he was inside the *finlands-bu* or not. He lit some twigs inside the hut, then sat outside. He hung up his sweat-drenched clothes and put his mind to surviving the night.

Now, in the darkness, he felt a greater sensitivity in his fingertips and senses, and he sat with the smoke enveloping him in rhythm with the wind. Then he opened the hatch again and crept inside. And in the glow of the embers he stoked the fire. The flames flickered into life, and he remembered the night in the mountains with his brother. As always when he sat by a fire, he saw shapes and creatures emerge, like pictures of old events or suggestions of new ones, and all at once he saw his brother's face. He was in the flames and created by flames.

Suddenly Jehans heard a rustling out in the thicket. He sat very still, his senses on alert. Whoever it was had reacted to his silence and stopped, but then moved again. A hand brushed against his ear, then two hands held his cheeks, and he knew there was only one person who touched his body like that. And he knew her body well enough to return her touch, but as he stroked her hand, he noticed there was no longer a ring on her finger, and he investigated no further.

Next morning they lay close together on the dirt floor. Warming each other out of necessity. She had passed the *seter* that evening on her way to Imsdalen, and, hurrying to get there before dark, she had fallen and twisted her ankle. It was so painful she had been forced to turn back, not wishing to perish in the forest. She had intended to break a window on one of the huts, but then she had smelled smoke. Unlike Jehans, she had had enough sense to bring food with her, and still had a couple of cans of peas in pork fat. She shared one with him as they sat in the dawn light, looking at the autumn and the *seter*.

But the *seter* and the autumn were no longer theirs. He did not even tell her about the reindeer that the Hekne Krag had refused to kill. All they shared now was a ghastly sense of the impossible, and it bore the names Jehans Hekne and Kristine Messelt.

"Happen ye plan t' walk on to Imsdalen," he said.

She did not look at him.

"'Tis not that I wish to, but that I mun. The Hekne in thee always breaks through. And tonight I have seen 'tis wrong to blame thee for that."

"Ye have every right t' blame me."

"But it comes to nowt! Ye shan't ever understand it of yer own accord. All ye do, Jehans, ye do for yer mother. For the dead need not be asked what they think. Because the dead can never be owt but pleased and amazed. And I canna' bear to be the one who blames a man for being as he be cos his mother be dead."

The sun came and offered them a drop of warmth.

"I shall do thee one last service, Kristine. I shall carry thee

369

down to Imsdalen since ye canna' walk. The last thing we do together shall be to stroll easy downhill."

She limped over to a large rock and clambered onto it, then he leaned forward and she wrapped her hands round his neck and clamped her knees around his hips. He was incredulous at how light she was, it made him realise how much had gone to waste when he had not lifted his own wife for so long.

"'Tis I who have made thee so thin, Kristine."

He was stiff after the strenuous walk yesterday, and when he grabbed the Krag he was unable to get it over his shoulder, because she sat on his back.

"Hold it in your hand, Jehans."

"Hmm."

"Ye mun take yer Krag with thee. Ye shall manage the both o' us."

Jehans took the rifle in one hand and they reeled towards the cart road. To their right was the slope down towards Imsdalen. They would be there in just a couple of hours. To his left were the unforgiving slopes up towards Kvia and the surrounding mountains. He could get back up there that afternoon if he managed to get some food down in Imsdalen.

When they reached the fork in the road, she suddenly pressed her knees into him as though he were a horse.

"Jehans Hekne. Ye mun choose now."

"Choose?"

"'Twixt Imsdalen and Butangen."

He did not move.

"Ye mean – ye shall come home wi' me?"

He heaved her a little higher onto his back. Stared up the endless slope that was just the first portion of the long homeward journey. Beyond it were bare mountains and rain-heavy clouds.

"Carry me home to Butangen, Jehans, and I shall forgive

thee. Carry me from the *seter* to Saubua and from thence to Butangen, and I shall move with thee into Hekne."

Just half an hour later his head was pounding, his knees ached, and as the slope grew steeper he stumbled blindly forward with the same gritty determination as when he had carried the reindeer kill back home all those years ago. She gripped his shoulders and he was panting hard, mouth gaping, trying to get a rhythm to his breathing and steps. He stopped at a boulder occasionally, set her down and stretched out flat on the ground, sweat running and heart pounding. Then, leaning on the Krag, he got up again and let her climb back onto him. Eventually he had to take breaks even when there were no boulders in sight, and when they reached a stream he lay on his belly to drink, filled a bottle and offered her some, and still not a word was said.

Five or six hours later they had finally reached the top and could start on the long walk down towards Saubua. His neck and shoulders were stiff, and there was a stabbing in his kneecaps. They had run out of food now, and started to cram their mouths with old, wrinkled crowberries as they went. There was nobody else here in the mountains. The Krag weighed more and more and he shifted it from his right to his left hand.

"I can take the Krag, Jehans."

An hour later he stopped to vomit. Another hour after that, she spoke for the first time in so long that he jumped.

"There be a difference," she said, "between some grand folk and others. Romsås, he be one o' the gooduns. Ye said he were at the Hekne auction."

"He – he were after a farm for his son."

Jehans lurched around a boulder, nearly bringing them both down. She waited until he was steady again, and then said: "Aside o' the electricity station and the sawmill, nobody in Butangen has ever agreed upon anything. 'Tis a leftover from the past.

No farmer sleeps well at night except he has at least one dispute in the offing, over land or forests, or fishing rights. There mun be an end to all that. We can let other folks use the machinery that Osvald purchased. Share the equipment."

Jehans was stomping along more than walking now. Breathless, he said:

"Ye mean – that we – can rent it out?"

"Or share out the labour. Folk from Romsås or Gildevollen can help us for the first couple o' years. 'Tis a mighty big cowshed and there be ample fields too. We'll come to some agreement among us. Offer folks space in the barn and the use o' the machinery. While we build the new dairy. On that plot we talked of. Happen we may have to sell some o' the farm to raise a skilling. Sell a few smallholdings."

All this talk of the future was tiring. He stumbled more and more, increasingly unsteady, and his breathing whistled. The blood pounded in his temples and his eyes flickered. And he answered with the occasional nod as she continued to lay plans for Hekne. And he recognised the same folk wisdom in her as when she had brought the piglets up to Hellorn, but on a grander scale, and he sensed that she might now, unless he keeled over and broke both their necks, begin to call herself Kristine Hekne.

As evening fell he lost all sense of time and reeled onwards. His eyes felt too big for his head and he could barely see ahead of him. Kristine existed only as a god-like voice above him and a god-like burden on his shoulders.

"'Tis there," Kristine said. "I see Saubua."

His strength returned enough for him to straighten a little. His tongue was swollen and the taste of blood filled his mouth. But there it was. And he noticed only *one* thing.

That everyone is lighter in their step when they see Saubua. No matter how weighed down they may be by duties or actions.

She cleared her throat.

"Jehans?" she said.

A nod was all he could manage.

"I have sommat to tell thee."

"Oh?"

"Aye, I do."

"Oh."

He lifted his head, gazed at the surrounding mountains and shook the sweat from his fringe.

"I have na' twisted my ankle at all."

He finally stopped. But did not put her down.

"I had to take revenge, Jehans. For thee and for me, my sweet."

A sense of relief came over him. He felt a wonderfully expansive tingling inside him.

Kristine was about to slide down to walk on her own, but he hoisted her back up and gripped her legs more tightly. She reached her hand down, and he felt that she was now wearing the ring he had made all those years ago. He quickened his pace and the way he held her thighs was a hint of what was to come when they got to Saubua. And she locked her arms about his chest and breathed into his hair, and as they walked on she began kissing him, and he turned so she could nibble him as she breathed more heavily, and soon her lips played near his ears, and they stumbled through the door of Saubua and rendered each other naked.

Third Story

Her Name in Bronze

The Poor Bells We Have

KAI SCHWEIGAARD SAT IN THE ORCHARD ON A WOODEN
bench that had once been white, reading yesterday's *Lillehammer Tilskuer*. The quality of this newspaper had been in decline
throughout the war, disorganised and inaccurate, and filled with
commentary telegrammed from abroad. He also took *Laagen*,
but the problem with that was its strident tone and hopeless
printing errors.

It was late autumn 1918, and the war seemed to be drawing
to an end. The sons of a few Butangen families who had emigrated to America had fallen, two in 1916 and one in 1917.
Only children played at war, they divided themselves into Brits,
Frenchmen and Germans and shot each other with wooden guns
and threw pine cone grenades. Doubtless that's how we survive,
thought Schweigaard. By not comprehending something in its
entirety and adapting to it, however wrong that might be.

"Pastor?"

It was Simen. Simen Røhme. A quick lad, with a shock of
blond hair, without any big blots on his copybook beyond the
time when he and his friends stole apples during Sunday Mass.
He was a brilliant young scholar and his parents were greatly
relieved that their defects had not been passed on.

"The post is come," Simen said. "Shall I bring it out to thee?"

"Is there much?"

"The newspapers and six letters."

"You'd like the stamps, I expect?"

"Yes, please. Father made me a new album yesterday. Sewed some sheets of paper together and made covers. I stick the stamps in with rubber glue. Ye may look at the album. 'Tis covered with red cloth."

Schweigaard nodded. "Fetch me my post then. Bring me my letter knife too. And go to the kitchen and ask your mother if I can have a drop of coffee out here."

Simen rushed into the house and Schweigaard gazed after him. He was fourteen years old now. Conceived in some chamber in Jenny Stueflaaten's house in Dovre. Schweigaard laughed to himself. Yes, that had been his heyday in some ways. Better times, even if they were hard times.

It was so weak these days. The coffee. And bitter. They couldn't get hold of anything better.

Kristine still ran the shop from a room at the dairy, but folk had to use ration cards. Most could get by with a kilo of sugar per month, it was worse when coffee was limited to a quarter of a kilo each month. Whenever Schweigaard had to go outside the village on business, he always arranged it for any day but a Tuesday or Friday, as raw-food shortages meant that the government had declared these "meat-free days", and the cafés and restaurants served only the dullest vegetable soups.

And yet.

What brought Schweigaard peace of mind was something that would happen next summer. Nothing had been said, but Kristine had a glow about her lately. Admittedly, the foundation walls for the new dairy were in place at the crossroads, but the soft smile at the corners of her mouth was attributable to something else. The kind of little secret Kai Schweigaard could see right through. After officiating at weddings for forty years, he could see from early on when a woman was with child.

Joy and disquiet in turn. That was how life rocked him to sleep now.

378

His nights had been sleepless and fearful that spring. There was a new strain of influenza that had started in the trenches. The papers called it the Spanish flu, a misleading name that only came about because Spain had kept out of the war and had an uncensored press, so that when the Spanish king and prime minister were struck down by a terrible flu, it was soon on all Europe's front pages.

Fortunately, Butangen was almost untouched by the disease. But it was ravaging Norway's cities, and at its height a hundred and fifty people had died in one week. By late summer it seemed to have disappeared from Norway, but Schweigaard was not sure it would not return. Hundreds of thousands had died from the disease across Europe, and it was a truly horrifying disease. People's lips turned blue and they died in the grips of a torturous delirium.

Schweigaard never felt like a mere spectator to such things. When a major event struck, he thought of the consequences for the villagers, rarely himself. Despite all the developments in recent years, he was still Butangen's only real *authority* figure. The old systems of local governance were gone, but, as with the local midwife, his status here in the community would remain unchanged until he died.

"Here, Herr Pastor!"

He turned to Simen. Beaming, glowing like a rosy apple. Carrying a small coffee pot and cup, with the newspapers and post tucked under one arm. The lad took too big a step forward and a small, grubby envelope slipped from his grip, and as it tumbled in semicircles to the ground, Schweigaard glimpsed a foreign stamp and numerous forwarding addresses. He leaped up and seized it. Densely stamped. By the Reichspost, the German censors, the Red Cross and a French field post office. He was shaking as he inserted his letter opener.

> *The man who once visited you is alive. I too am alive. At times*
> *I feel regret. But he is, more than anything, alive.*
>
> > *Holzminden, 1918.*
> >
> > *Harrison*

"I don't think you can have this stamp, Simen. Not yet. And when you do get it, you must take care of the whole envelope."

Simen gave some reply, but Schweigaard was not listening. He lost track of how long he sat reading those lines over and over, but when he finally sipped at his coffee, it was cold.

The sender was a *Capt. Harrison, No. 56 Squadron*.

The Flying Corps. It came as no great surprise.

Schweigaard had long since given up on receiving any answers from Victor, but he had felt that his letters were being read. When war had broken out he felt anxious about him and sent shorter letters slightly more often.

He must be a prisoner of war now.

I too am alive. But he is, more than anything, alive.

Schweigaard scowled and pondered what this might mean. The German postmark was March 6, the French postmark was June 12. Maybe he could find Holzminden in the atlas. Presumably there was a prisoner-of-war camp there. But who could help him find out more?

He had always been careful not to intrude on Victor. No doubt his family would have had a telephone installed by now, but he had never tried to call him. It was impossible to know what it might trigger if a voice from Norway came on the line. Victor had probably got married years ago, to a woman who had for as many years assumed he was a true Harrison – the rightful heir to the estate.

But now – now that Victor had answered him? Now he had to find out more. Where was he? Was he still alive? Had he ever mentioned anything about Norway?

Schweigaard had his address of course: Finlaggan, Kirknewton, Northumberland. Surely, as here at home, the exchange could connect him using only the estate's name. And if the family had moved, the new residents would probably know where they had gone. It was time to break his silence. Ask the international telephone exchange for a line to Great Britain.

But first he should perhaps get a message up to Jehans. Enquire whether greetings should be conveyed.

Schweigaard sat back down on the bench. It was turned towards Lake Løsnes, and had sunk firmly into the ground over the years. Moving it now would entail rocking and wrenching loose.

He felt a growing impatience as he searched for the right words to say in English. Then he heard the sound of hurried footsteps behind him.

"Schweigaard! Schweigaard!"

It was Herr Røhme. He ran straight over to Schweigaard, and shook him by the shoulder, although he must have seen he was awake.

"Ye mun come, Herr Pastor. At once."

"Where to?"

"Down to Lake Løsnes. I were repairing the wall nearest the bell tower when I saw it."

"Saw what, Herr Røhme?"

"W-we canna' tell. Just come. Afore it stops."

Schweigaard got up, but as he followed Røhme his thoughts were with Victor.

These thoughts vanished the moment they arrived. About forty villagers were crowded together near the bay, all pointing at something further south on the lake. A group of youngsters had started to walk along the shoreline to get a closer look. It was a chill, clear, windless morning, and nothing could explain such a phenomenon.

But Kai Schweigaard had seen all he needed to see. A huge circle in the middle of the lake, clearly defined, tranquil, constantly renewing itself.

"It h-has been there for nigh on qu-quarter of an hour," Røhme said. "That ring on the water. From a fish or whatever. Like sommat were b-boiling beneath the surface. Like it wants to come up!"

Two men were putting out in a boat, but an old woman stopped them. Whatever it was, she said, it must not be disturbed. There were no birds in the air, the cows up in the fields did not bellow. Butangen was silent, the villagers were silent.

Then it began.

The circle in the water slowly increased in size. Quivering rings spread across the watery surface. A rumbling sound could be heard, but Schweigaard could not detect its source. He turned to the new church, but there was nothing there but – a church.

The sound grew in strength, and in clarity and breadth, but still it was impossible to place. Ever-changing, it was as though it gathered fragments and smelted them together into what was to be one fixed, clear sound. And all at once it broke free from the water, the sound of a bell that quivered with silver.

It rang out fourteen times across Butangen, fourteen chimes in groups of two, as loud as only a Sister Bell could be.

Later Kai Schweigaard stood before the Hekne Weave.

Some said it was an impossibility. To hear a bell from under the water. But since everyone who was down there had heard it, the bell must somehow have rung in them all and for them all.

One or two villagers had claimed over the years to have heard Gunhild ringing deep in the lake. But the last time the village had gathered in response to a warning from the Sister Bells was in 1880, when the stave church was about to be demolished.

Grudgingly he had to revive the old legends. The Sister Bells could ring of their own accord to warn of danger. But what could Gunhild want, having been silent for almost forty years? Was she announcing the death of one of the chain-brothers? Had he died today, a few months after sending the letter?

He frowned.

No. It was unlikely that this was solely about Victor. Church bells seldom ring for one person. They ring out for all of us.

He moved closer to the ancient wall hanging. So close he could smell the faint odour of the tarred walls of the stave church. Studied the figures that represented everyday life and the disasters leading up to Skråpånatta, the Night of the Great Scourge.

Was that how it was long ago? When they sought to understand the warnings of the church bells, did they consult the Hekne Weave?

But how could they see what was coming from looking at this? He could see no clear order of events or signs of *when* floods or landslides or forest fires might occur. And the only thing he thought he could pinpoint for sure was the Black Death. A skeleton rode a wagon and in its wake lay the dead, woven in blue-black thread.

He was astounded.

Unlike the other events represented here, the Black Death had taken place *before* the Hekne sisters' time. Why show an event that had already happened?

But then he noticed something else. The weave showed two other similar carts. Both pulled by horses.

But the cart that Death drove was not pulled by a horse or an ox.

Surely that was strange? How could two girls, brought up in a place where farming was their whole life, make such an omission? Then he remembered Astrid's description of herself as a young girl who had dreamed of the new railway trains. What had amazed her the most was that there were draught animals that never needed to sleep at night.

The Spanish flu had been spread that summer by the railway.

Two sisters in Gudbrandsdal in the early 1600s. With an ability of sorts to see beyond their own lifetime. They saw something beyond their comprehension. How did they choose to communicate it? They wove the strangest thing of all.

Kai Schweigaard turned away and shook his head. *No!* he muttered, *I'm seeing what I want to see.*

He shook himself and went outside into the daylight.

But even then he stood and pondered.

The bell had chimed seven times in pairs. This bore no relation to any church lore.

A light breeze swept up from the cemetery, and a memory glowered, a memory from 1880. Diffuse and incomplete to begin with, words spoken in German, related to the new church.

Is this how it is to be over sixty? he thought. With an increasing number of dead people talking to you? He walked down to the church. Stopped at the stone steps and grabbed the brass handrail. It was worn shiny by the many villagers who, for nearly forty years, had used it to climb up and down these steps, and now he too had to lean on it heavily. It felt as though Gerhard Schönauer was right next to him, struggling to make himself understood.

It was usual to make handrails and door handles of wrought iron to save money. But Schönauer had told him that brass was far superior since diseases were spread when people shook hands and German metallurgists had found that a faint electric current was created when hands touched brass, and that this killed any diseases that clung to the skin. It was Schönauer himself who had recommended and ordered the handrail he now held.

So many thoughts and impressions whirring around in his head.

Adolf had said something once.

It were the art, in the olden days, to know how to read signs. All kinds o' signs.

It was impossible to identify one definitive reason for the bell to have rung. Whether it was for Victor or Jehans or others. There were too many possibilities. Not least the possibility that it was just a random occurrence and that the images on the weave were merely decorative.

Unless there was one possibility that encompassed them all. That would relate to the whole of Butangen. As well as to Jehans and Victor Harrison.

That the skeleton was on its way here. Right now. In 1918.

Kai Schweigaard gripped the handrail, feeling heavy and old. He let himself into the church and put on his robes. Then, muttering to himself, he went back out and walked along the stone wall until he found the churchwarden.

"Herr Røhme, you must ring the bells. Then send Simen and the young farm lads to spread the word that people must meet outside the church. One from each farm."

"Mass on a Thursday?"

Kai Schweigaard cleared his throat. "There's a sickness coming here, Røhme. The same influenza we had last time perhaps. Or something similar. I'm going to talk to everyone from the church steps."

"Did the doctor tell thee this?"

"No. I've just – seen signs. Go in the church and ring the bells, Herr Røhme. Three times three chimes. Ring those wretched bells of ours."

Frau Kreis

"Goodwin?"

"Died last night. If you mean Albert Goodwin."

"A corporal, right?"

"A corporal while he lived. I wouldn't know now."

There was a scraping of gravel as the cart was drawn across the large exercise yard of Torgau prison camp. The sound flung itself between the barrack walls. There had been no wind all day, but now a warm breeze had picked up the smell of the latrines and hospital.

The medical officer was ticking something off and shouted: "Gowers?"

"Here."

Five minutes later: "Haddon, Anthony Haddon?"

"He's right here. I'm answering for him. These bandages. He can't talk."

"Does he have any papers?"

"Yes."

"Very well. Harrison?"

"Here!"

"Henders— What's the problem?"

A man limped out of line. "There are two Harrisons, sir. The man who just answered is Samuel Harrison. I'm Victor Harrison."

"Hmm. You're not on the list."

"They transferred me here three weeks ago. I was in Holzminden. No. 56 Squadron. I've got my papers."

The medical officer took out another list and showed it to a civilian who shook his head. "The train's already packed full, I'm afraid. You'll have to go on the next one. In four days."

*

He ambled back into the barracks and sat down. Sergeant Abrahams had left behind the chess set he had made out of wood chips glued together with soaked barley flour. The Red Cross had given them some cans of flea powder that looked like big sugar-shakers, and he found two cans on the other beds and doused his own bed in powder.

Four years of torture without achieving anything worthwhile. As though they had taken a perfectly healthy cow to the slaughterhouse and snipped a little bit off her ear and then a bit more and a day later smashed one of her hooves and begun sticking knitting needles in her muzzle. Four years of this torture, and here they sat with absolutely nothing to show for it. Except that every man in Europe born between 1880 and 1900 had forgotten what it meant to live.

He went up to a guard to ask if he could have a shave, but was told he could not. They still had to keep account of all the knives. So the routine remained unchanged. Sit in the middle of the exercise yard and shave each other, while a guard sat at a distance with a loaded Mauser and made sure the knife was back on the table when they were done. He could have a shave tomorrow. Along with men from the other barracks.

Ah, well. He had no wish to turn the barber's knife on the guards. Not here, not now, in Torgau, deep in Germany, in November 1918. They had treated them as well as they could. Given them some food at least. Whatever there was. Which now, at the very end, consisted only of beetroots.

He never wanted to eat a beetroot again.

He had been a prisoner of war for one year. The night after the plane crash he had come round in an over-crowded field hospital to the sound of groaning soldiers. He believed he was among his own, until he saw that their bloodied uniforms were grey rather than khaki, and realised that the groans of the wounded were identical, whether in English or German.

He had crash-landed in a field right in front of the anti-aircraft battery. A German had leaped forward and dragged him out of his plane, as though wanting to see exactly what he had shot down from the heavens.

Nothing was known about his co-pilot, Thorne.

Victor had heard that the Germans cared well for British prisoners, but assumed this was propaganda. A German doctor found a massive haemorrhage on his brain that was steadily spreading and sent him reeling between panic attacks and unconsciousness. In one lucid moment he saw a doctor holding a drill, felt something spurt out of his temple, and the next day he was clearer in his thoughts. He had lost his hearing in his right ear, had burns covering his left arm and hand, patches of missing hair, and a knee doomed to be forever stiff.

He would have liked to meet the soldier who had pulled him from his plane. He had still been conscious then, and vaguely remembered the face of a very young boy. Then flames and something that went black.

And he remembered something else too.

Astonished laughter and the German words for "madman" and "travelling", and when he forced his eyes open, he saw several German soldiers standing around him laughing. He thought they were about to kill him, but then he heard the German for "daredevil" and "tourist" and someone shouting for the medic to hurry.

On ransacking his jacket pockets they had found a small, forty-year-old book with a brown cardboard cover.

Meyers Sprachführer für Reise und Haus.

The next day the gates stood open and the guards had removed their bayonets. A truck drove out and still the gates were left open. He went to the liaison officer and asked if he could go out on his own now.

"We don't know. We haven't received any official information. But I wouldn't go too far in that uniform."

"But it's over?"

"Officially it's just a ceasefire. But yes. The war is over."

Victor went inside and fetched his letters. His father still wrote every fortnight, but with the forwarding process being so slow, he often got three at once. Aware of the censors, his father never commented on what Victor wrote, which he generally preferred since it meant his father's letters reminded him of a world without war. Among the envelopes he now put in his inside pocket were some from Kai Schweigaard. He seemed to remember having sent him a few lines from the hospital, stuffed with morphine, but *what* he had written, he couldn't recall.

Victor pulled on the heavy leather coat which had been scorched when he was shot down, and which had saved him from the glacial temperatures when flying at high altitude, and from the damp cold of the bunk-beds in two prison camps. Between the pages of *Meyers* he found some German banknotes. Every pilot carried some cash to bribe civilians if they were shot down, and nobody had taken it. He went to the guard and asked how much the German mark had lost in value over the last year. He was a young soldier, who, either from injury or fatigue, had such a bent back that his Mauser almost slid off his shoulder.

Not understanding Victor's question, he shouted something out to another soldier, who shouted back that prices had quadrupled since 1917. If that was what was being asked.

Victor said that was indeed what he had asked, and would they shoot him if he went out on his own and headed for the bus station in the centre of Torgau?

Later that evening he got off a bus in Dresden. The buildings and statues were as magnificent as ever. Yet it was not the

Dresden he remembered. The women were dressed in grey headscarves, there were no children out playing or couples holding hands or any sound of laughter.

He continued along a pavement lit by street lights. Only a few were working, and the length of his shadow changed as he walked along.

There, still standing in the Großer Garten, was a stave church from the year 1170. Lake Carola glinted inky-black in the evening light, and he saw the church reflected in its surface. The jagged wooden roof tiles reminded him of the back of an ancient lizard.

The door to the weapons porch was open, but the main door to the church was locked. Victor stood for a while gazing at the portal, and the carved serpent that was snarling at something over and behind it. He went back out and around the corner, where he knocked on the sacristy door. Nobody came, and nobody seemed to be looking after the church. He gave a little shiver and coughed.

Walking back again, however, he found the church door was standing ajar. He hunched his shoulders and stepped into the ancient twilight cool, walked along the rows of pews, sat down on *die Fröstelstelle* and looked at the altar. He took off his brown leather coat, and sitting up straight he let his eyes roam. He looked up at the ceiling and at the Andreas crosses, and wondered for a moment how the church had been constructed. His gaze drifted over the rough-hewn pine columns and pictured the forests of Butangen where they had once grown, then he closed his eyes, let the ringing in his ears, the echoes of war, melt away, and breathed in the smell of ancient wood. Suddenly he felt the cool air shift to cold, and thought he heard somebody nearby mutter something. It seemed to be in Norwegian but the dialect was too strange, or too ancient, for him to understand. He thought he heard the words *Yorn two bairns shall take us hame* and it was as though the entire war rushed through his head.

It was morning when he woke up to find himself lying on the church pew with his coat over him. And standing in the aisle in a dusty shaft of light was the churchwarden, Emmerich. Older and leaner now, but wearing the same overalls as before.

"Did they take it away?" Victor asked. "The church bell?"

"Come with me."

Victor got up and followed Emmerich to the sacristy. Some blankets and a pillow were hidden in the corner, the only thing to reveal that the churchwarden slept here. He offered Victor some rye bread, but ate nothing himself. He said that two men had turned up from the War Department in 1915. The rule was that they could take one bell from any pair.

"We only have one," Emmerich had said, showing them an inventory filled with official stamps.

But then, in 1917, two more men had turned up, saying that they were now, unfortunately, obliged to forcibly requisition individual bells. Every bell would be given a serial number and the cannon that was cast from its metal would be marked with a matching number. When the war was over, the cannon would be melted down and recast into a church bell, so that the congregation would get at least some of the same bronze back. This had been done in previous wars, and would be done again.

But Emmerich had told them about the legend. That only unmarried people from a particular family in Norway could lay eyes on the metal from which it was cast. Anyone else was sure to die. Taken by a sudden stroke or illness.

"And?" Victor said. "Did they take it?"

Emmerich did not answer. He led him to the little side door that he had held open for him on his previous visit.

This time, Victor did not stop halfway up. Dust danced in the scattered light that came through the gaps in the timber walls, and he found the ladders and climbed up to the top. Soon his head struck the hatch. He lifted it and climbed into the bell tower. He stayed on his knees for a long time, not quite daring to look up, before he finally raised his head.

There she hung. A massive, dark silhouette.

Halfrid.

He lifted an iron clasp on the wall and opened a small shutter, letting the morning light stream in.

It was then that he saw some words scratched on the bronze in thick pencil. Neat, elegant lettering. An artist's script. His father's script. A message from 1880 to his two sons.

Edgar und Jehans. Schön ist, was wir sehen. Noch schöner—

The rest was indecipherable, but he recognised it. *Beautiful are the things we see. More beautiful still the things we understand. But the best of all are the things we do not comprehend.*

"Welcome me in now," he muttered.

The bell began to vibrate. First with a faint, inaudible tremor, then with a low-pitched clang. He ran his fingertips over the bell. The ringing disappeared, but the metal continued to vibrate, and the sound of silver filled him.

He found a street vendor in the town centre and waited until the other customers had gone so that nobody could hear his accent.

There were only beetroots.

He found his father's grave and, standing beside it, he ate his beetroots. Leaving the cemetery he passed an elderly man with a cane who had been watching him. They recognise me, he thought. Soon someone will recognise me.

The shop sign for the Galerie Apfelbaum had been removed and all the windows were boarded up. Behind the glass in the front door hung a handwritten note. The street lighting was very dim, so he lit his tinderbox, and in its bright flame he read that stored artworks could be collected by ringing telephone number 627.

Her handwriting.

There were too many people crowding around the telephone exchanges. He went into a café and asked if he could borrow their telephone. The waiter glared at him and quoted him a price. He could have two minutes to talk, but the café staff would give the exchange the telephone number and a time limit, so he couldn't cheat them by making a long-distance call.

The address he was given was in Zittauerstraße. She opened the door just a crack, and did not recognise him until he said his name was Gerhard Schönauer. Standing opposite him in her hallway she studied him like a map of some foreign country, then shook her head and studied him some more as he unbuttoned his leather coat so she could see the British uniform underneath.

"Have you come to fetch the painting?" Elsa Rathenau said.

He turned his head, saying he had partially lost his hearing, and she repeated the question in his good ear. He said he had not. He had simply wanted to see the one person not associated with war and strife.

She seemed not to hear his answer. "It's too late," she said. "The deadline for reclaiming paintings is six months."

Yes, of course. He'd known that. But thank you anyway.

"Not too late for the painting. Too late for me."

Victor looked at her.

"I am Frau Kreis now. We were married in 1913 and had a daughter in 1914."

"I'd better go then," Victor said.

"No, don't," she said, suddenly taking him by the wrist. "It's in here. Your painting. No, there, over by the piano."

He entered her living room. A piano, a mirror, a wooden chair and a table were all she had in her apartment.

"I saw the banker's order," she said. "From the Bank of Scotland. You'd never told us your name, but I realised it was you who bought the painting but wanted it kept a secret. And that you wanted the money sent to Norway. I was seventeen. I can still remember their names too. Je-hans Hek-ne. Kai Sch-wei-gaard. Impossible for me to pronounce. A country and people I knew absolutely nothing about. I had to go to a very big atlas to find the place where they lived. Butangen. And this strange request to falsify the date of sale. To backdate it twenty-five years. To April 1881. I wasn't even born then. Father refused. So I did it myself. And I looked at the painting again and found myself completely bewitched by it. And by you too. You've probably no idea what such a thing can do to a seventeen-year-old girl. I've never had the heart to sell it."

"Not even now, when things are so hard?"

"I've made a living selling uncollected pictures. One by one. Art is probably the most unprofitable business in wartime. I've barely had enough money for food. Gisela, our daughter, lives with her grandparents. They own a little farm."

"And your husband?"

She shook her head. "Eugen was reported missing at Marne in September 1914. Were you at Marne?"

"I've flown over Marne."

"Did you kill anyone when you flew over Marne?"

"'No. I can say that with absolute certitude. Nobody in Marne."

She offered him coffee, rather weak, but stronger than any he'd had in months. He told her how he had come from Torgau, and that he would be sent back home to England the next afternoon. Then he took *Meyers Sprachführer für Reisen und Haus* from his inside pocket, and from between the pages of words beginning with K he took her photograph.

Elsa Rathenau had a bar of soap and he was able to wash himself from top to toe, after which she pulled the chair into the middle of the room, put a towel over his shoulders and cut his hair, then gave him a shave with her dead husband's barber-knife. Eugen Kreis was his size, but she had sold all his clothes except the suit he had worn on his wedding day. She went over to the piano and fetched the painting. It was rolled up and covered with grey paper held firmly in place by two rounds of threadbare twine.

He asked her to keep it.

"And will you come back this time?"

"I'll come as soon as I can. If I don't, you must sell it!"

She did not unfasten the twine, and he knew that he no longer resembled the man in the portrait, who was rolled up in there with the woman in red.

Elsa Rathenau sat down on the piano stool.

"I'd never had a proper boyfriend back then. But I realised you might like me. In *that* way. You were the first man to look at me like that. And then you just disappeared. Eugen was a good man. But he was flesh and blood. *You* were the man who had come with himself in a painting to sell to himself. I kept it because I thought you intended to come back one day."

She opened the piano lid and hit a low D.

He stayed with her that night, and in the morning he put on Eugen Kreis' wedding suit. As they stood together in front of the mirror, he asked if she still had her wedding dress.

"Yes. But I'm much thinner now than in 1913."

"We're all thinner than we were in 1913," Victor said.

He was leaning against a wall in the bus station when he heard the bells.

Seven chimes from the Großer Garten. As loud as only Halfrid could ring.

He stepped away from the wall and shook his head. Then he thought he vaguely heard another church bell, this one ringing with a purer, more naked sound, as though the top harmonies had been left behind on their journey here so that only the keynote reached him. Its tone bore a sisterly likeness to Halfrid, and seemed to come from the far north.

Stand at the Door and Listen

It went so fast. He was ill with a fever for just four days before he died in his bed, holding the red stamp album in his hands. The sobs travelled down the hallway from behind locked doors, and nothing Kai Schweigaard could say would help, other than that the grief he himself felt for Simen took him back to the moment when he was forced to acknowledge that Astrid was dead. He was unable to eat, had a persistently bitter taste in his mouth, and felt as though a giant pair of forceps was squeezing his body. Yet, this was nothing. Nothing to what the parents felt.

Simen was the life and soul of the parsonage, then he faded away and his lips went blue. They kept his siblings in another house, but his sister ran to him and refused to let go of his hand. His father was grief-stricken beyond recognition, and when Schweigaard offered to get him some help to lighten his workload, he was moved to anger for the first time ever. He would, Røhme said, dig Simen's grave himself.

They laid Simen in the ground next morning, and for the next two days Schweigaard did nothing but grieve. He did not sleep or eat, and in the end he just keeled over, and when he woke up he was fit only to enter the death in the church records and read the newspaper.

It had twice as many obituaries as the week before. Almost all were for victims under the age of twenty-five, and many were for siblings who had died the same day. *A dear son and brother,*

Halvard K. Lokvam, 20 years old. Ivar K. Lokvam, 18 years old. Beloved wife and mother Jørgine Avlund, aged 20. Our dear daughter and sister, schoolteacher Anna Lindsehaug, 21 years old. Our dearest daughters Gudrun Simensen and Ada Simensen, aged 22 and 15. My darling wife Kari Havn, 26 years old.

And still, he had read only half the obituaries for the district that day. There were even more the following day. The Spanish flu preferred to take the young and strong. Doctors calculated that, at this rate, more people would die from the flu than the millions of soldiers who had died in the Great War.

The liquor ban had been partially lifted, and every household was given a ration of a half-bottle of medicinal brandy per month. In the *Lillehammer Tilskuer* Schweigaard read one dubious piece of advice after another. *Stick glowing knitting needles in tar and inhale the smoke. Boil half a cup of water and pour in as much sugar as will dissolve in the water, pour into a glass, top up with alcohol and drink as much as you can.*

He was deeply troubled. Not once did he see a newspaper declare on its front page what a catastrophe this really was. They all preferred to discuss politics and war and trade, with little care for the poor. And in the Lillehammer newspapers there were just a few notices, reporting that *The Spanish flu rampages in the valley again.*

Kai Schweigaard went down to the kitchen and dug out a few crusts of bread. Fru Røhme was not to be disturbed now, and he needed sustenance to get through what lay in store for the village.

He had hoped to save Simen. He had hoped to save them all.

On the day when Gunhild had rung in Lake Løsnes, folk had come down from every farm, and he had stood on the church steps and told them he had received a message that warned that a danger was on its way, likely a disease, and lifting his voice he pronounced there were ways to avoid it.

Truth was, as a man of the church, Schweigaard knew a great deal about the spread of diseases. He had followed the debate for decades in the *Luthersk Kirketidende* over whether tuberculosis might be spread at holy communion, when the congregation drank the blood of Jesus from the same chalice. For centuries it had been forbidden to do anything else, the ritual was the very symbol of the Eucharist. Moreover, argued the zealots, true Christians ought not to fear death at all, leastways not in the banquet of eternal life. In 1914, however, medicine had finally won the day, so every man and every woman would receive the holy wine in a chalice of their own.

There, on the church steps, Schweigaard had put all his accumulated knowledge into his advice. Mass was cancelled indefinitely. Auctions and public dances were best avoided. Folk ought not to visit other villages. They should maintain a distance from strangers. And always veer on the side of prudence.

He knew that for the folk of Butangen the last three pieces of advice would come easy.

Still, he had expected some questions. Where had he learned all this? What kind of disease was it? When would it come?

But not a single question was raised.

They would not, he thought in his surprise, have accepted this if I were aged twenty-five and new to the village. But now that I'm sixty they listen to me. I am the *pastor* here.

But he knew it was a far greater power than himself to which they listened. Even now, in the twentieth century, the legend held sway in Butangen. There were old folk who still rose bent-backed from their beds and their stools, and said: "Take good heed! The bell has rung."

But this had not saved Simen. It was now November and four villagers, counting Simen, were dead. Butangen had fared better than other villages, but whether this was down to his advice was impossible to say.

He opened his newspaper again. All over Norway lectures were cancelled, meeting rooms, schools and public libraries closed, trains went without conductors and telephones stopped working because the switchboard ladies were sick. Family portraits lay unclaimed in photographic studios because the photographer was dead. No cure existed, and the doctors themselves fell ill.

Schweigaard got up and paced about restlessly. He could not do what he wanted most, to sit at his parishioners' deathbeds, for as folk said: "Then the pastor shall die, and who will bury us then?"

A week later the disease came to Hekne.

It was Kristine who brought Kai Schweigaard the news. She told Schweigaard that Jehans had been meaning to come down and tell him something, something that had been weighing on his mind. But that he'd got a headache and sore throat, as though he was getting a chill. He'd felt so groggy that he decided to wait until the next day, but only got worse overnight.

"'Tis hard," she said, gathering her shawl about her. "I wants to put my arms about Jehans, but canna'. He has gone t' bed in the big room upstairs."

Under her apron he could see that her belly was perfectly round. She told him they had been sleeping in separate houses for some time, and when Schweigaard looked uneasy, she quickly added: "We did so for fear o' the Spanish. Jehans read in the paper that it strikes at womenfolk wi' child. So he said it were for the best."

"Most wise," Schweigaard said. "Most wise. Is he very ill?"

"Nay so much. But 'tis this baleful influenza for sure. He were ranting o' late and said he wanted to go down to Lake Løsnes. I said I would fetch thee. I knows ye canna' go near him. But happen ye may stand at the door and listen to what he has to say?"

Schweigaard walked back up with her. He found his way through the farmhouse and eventually reached a rather large, low-ceilinged room at the furthest end. It had daylight from two sides and a view of Lake Løsnes.

But Jehans was fast asleep, and Schweigaard dared not stand there too long. He waited outside for an hour, then went back in. This time Jehans mumbled a name.

"Your brother?" Schweigaard said. "Are you asking for him?"

Jehans tried to sit up a little and nodded faintly.

The dairy had to close the next day because Ada Borgen had fallen ill. The new creamery was only half-finished, but they had already started to use the new machines and took delivery of milk from most of the farms now, too much for Kristine to handle alone. A few years ago this would not have been a problem, since the farms still processed their own milk, but folk had grown accustomed to sending it away, and were used to the cash it brought them. Schweigaard took a walk up to the dairy and found Kristine all alone, frantically scrubbing pots and lugging milk churns about.

"This can nay go well," she said.

"You shouldn't be lifting anything heavy," Schweigaard said. "Not now."

"I canna' sleep. We took it upon ourselves to handle other folks' milk! Argh! How could I have been so hare-brained! If more womenfolk fall sick, the cows'll burst wi' milk and there'll be nay choice but to shoot them!"

"You mustn't think like that, Kristine. Really you mustn't. You're not alone in this. Folk must do the best they can."

"Ye mun go up to Jehans now, Pastor. I put a platter o' food in the hallway and waited and tinkled the glass. But I did nay see if he rose from his bed, for I had to come down here."

Schweigaard hurried up to Hekne in the bitter wind. Once

again he found himself standing in the doorway, but this time Jehans lay sweating beneath the bedsheet, muttering something incomprehensible.

To be so powerless! To have to stand there! While fate ravaged another man's body!

To keep his nagging thoughts at bay he decided to take a look around the huge old farmhouse. He wandered into the entrance hall and saw that nothing had changed since Astrid was alive. He had stood right here, at the bottom of these stairs, watching her as she descended with some knitting in her hands, when she had finally agreed to *take a stroll* with him.

He was a very different man now in a very different time. But she would always remain in that moment in time.

Schweigaard fell into thought about the room in which Jehans now lay. It could hardly be classed as a sitting room, being right next to the scullery. Neither could it be an ordinary bedroom, since these were always on the first or second floor in farms, to avoid the dung flies, which rarely flew that high. Being lit from two sides, however, it seemed more like a workshop of some kind. He went back outside and looked up at the founding lintel over the main door.

The first thing he saw was the mark of Lynstuten. Carved deeply into the wood, an ox with angular horns. Under it the date: 1613.

He imagined old Eirik Hekne. A man who owned a vast pine forest and had a boundless love for two daughters. Naturally he had set aside a room especially for them. For two girls who were unable to climb the stairs. The farmhouse was built of heavy timbers, so its layout would not have changed since 1613.

Kai Schweigaard was now sure.

Jehans had lain in the room where the Hekne sisters had once worked and died.

*

Her Name in Bronze

Back at the parsonage Simen's mother was in the kitchen.

"Please don't bother making anything," he said. "Look after yourself. I'll find myself something to eat."

She shook her head. No, she must keep busy. To hold the pain at bay.

She took out a jar of preserved pears, and he knew she was planning to make one of her delicious, colourful compotes.

A little later he smelled roast pork.

Simen's favourite. His too.

Schweigaard ate alone and then sat poking the sugary pieces of pear. It was said that Gunhild completed the Hekne Weave after Halfrid had died. And since they shared each other's senses, it was presumed she had seen into the realm of the dead. But whatever she had managed to weave in those last hours, it could surely only be a tiny fragment of the whole?

He got up from his half-eaten dessert and went over to the Hekne Weave.

Her final contribution had to be at the edge of the weave. He had, of course, studied every corner minutely, looking for the slightest colour difference, all excepting the corner in which the fabric was coming apart, where it seemed hopeless to look for clues.

It was to this corner that he returned now. He took the loose threads in his hand and tried to comb them out. They were in a complete tangle. He lifted the weave down very carefully and carried it into the sewing room where he and Astrid Hekne had once folded an Advent tablecloth. He spread it out on a table and turned on a switch. For the first time ever, the weave was flooded by electric light.

He sat for over an hour trying to straighten the threads. It was impossible to keep them all in order at once. The moment a pattern seemed to emerge, it disappeared again and turned back into a mass of threads. Eventually, however, when he had

402

finally flattened all the threads against the tabletop, an image took shape.

Ye too shall see the sign. Ye, in partic'lar, Pastor.

Gunhild's time was neither limited nor measured on that last day. Death was present in that room, but sat himself down and waited. Giving her all the time she needed to fulfil her task. A small, but perfect motif. Woven in a different style from the rest of the tapestry. Woven by two hands, not four, from a life that was ebbing away.

The last thread of the Norns.

It was not a vengeful omen. More a whisper in another vocal register.

He did not find out when, and he did not find out why.

What Kai Schweigaard found out was how he would die.

An Old Blériot

The gatekeeper's house was locked. Inside the dusty window was a spindle chair and nothing else. The wrought-iron gate creaked as he pushed it open, and he limped up the tree-lined driveway and came into view of Finlaggan.

It was still extremely early, and yet.

Where was everyone?

The house looked gloomy and deserted in the cold November light. The ivy had not been cut, and the windows on the first and second floor were overgrown. The fountain was dry, the gravel paths were covered with old leaves, and the guttering was loose in places and dangling down. Nettles were growing in front of the stables, and he realised that the horses had been sent to the front long ago.

Still. Finlaggan was built of solid brick. The nearby rivers would continue to flow, the fields would be green again, new foals would be born, good people would need work, and they still had a view over the Cheviots.

The entrance hall was dark. Colder inside than out. Victor was back in uniform. He put down the parcel containing his airman's clothes and the German suit and went over to the staircase.

"Father! I'm back!"

No answer.

"Father?"

Then, from the left, the sound of light footsteps. The steps of a man who had walked barefoot all his life, but had finally put on shoes.

It was the first time he had touched Kumara, but now they clung to each other like children.

"Are you well, Mr Victor?"

"Not too bad," Victor said, looking across the hallway. "But where's the Wilkins boy, and the others?"

"They were called up one after the other towards the end of 1916. It was the same on all the estates. There are no young men left here."

Kumara pointed at him. "What happened to your hair? And your leg? No. Don't answer. You need food."

Neither man moved, and Victor knew there was something that had to be said before they ate.

Kumara shook his head slowly.

"Your father passed away four months ago. Peacefully. He didn't suffer. I was with him."

Victor looked up the stairs.

"But I got a letter from him just weeks ago!"

Kumara described how his father had fallen ill in the autumn of 1917. When the doctor had told him that the end was close, he had spent days writing post-dated letters.

"They're all up in his room. A big pile. I was to send them every fortnight. And if they ran out, I was to write them myself and pretend he'd dictated them."

Victor sat down on the stairs. Any sense of urgency drained from him, but the feelings of grief that he hoped might fill him did not. Not strongly enough. It was as though his father's portrait had simply been moved to the wall of the fallen.

"He's buried here, I take it?"

"Yes. He is lying in the memorial garden."

He nodded.

"And Mother and Joseph?"

"They didn't come, Mr Victor. They were afraid of the submarines."

"And since?"

"They're still afraid of the submarines."

"Hmm."

"Mr Victor. When you were reported missing, a lawyer came with a letter from your mother."

Victor got up. "They haven't sold Finlaggan, I hope? Don't tell me they've sold Finlaggan!"

"No. I gave the lawyer a letter from your father. A letter that stipulated categorically that there would be no funeral until they had a body to bury. That you had to be missing for four years before Joseph and your mother inherited the right of control. In case you were being held in a prison camp somewhere or other. And on your return, I was to tell you that Finlaggan was put into your name five days before you were born. It became yours on March 23, 1881."

"Five days before I was born?"

"Your father insisted I say those exact words. Precisely. He even had me repeat them every day. But she's sold the plantation. And the Edinburgh apartment."

Victor sat down again and put his head in his hands.

"Listen, Mr Victor. We've got three hens left, but one of them has stopped laying. I'll cook it the way you like. I've saved a few spices."

Victor looked over the desolate entrance hall and the dark wooden furniture that Kumara had kept polished.

"That sounds good, Kumara. So long as we're sharing. I don't want to eat alone. Especially now."

He got up and they wandered about. They passed the telephone, and Kumara remarked that it only worked now and then.

"Though a man called three days ago. From *Norway*."

Victor stopped suddenly.

Kumara said he hadn't caught his name because it was a crackly line. But it was an older man with an imposing voice. He had called once before, but then Kumara had not understood what he wanted.

"But this time?"

"He said a man you know in Norway is close to dying. Something like Jonas or Johann?"

Outside the window he saw Kumara walking back with a decapitated hen. He was holding it by its tail and it dangled back and forth so little drops of blood splashed on its feathers.

Victor cranked the telephone for a third time without getting through to the exchange. He paced about. As restless as when he had waited for his flight orders. He went up to his bedroom and changed into his old hunting clothes. He found himself looking around for the dog, but there were no dogs in the house anymore.

He opened the door to his father's bedroom. It smelled stuffy. On the dresser lay a thick pile of letters, and next to it a cigar box containing stamps.

Victor opened the wardrobe and found his father's favourite worn-out tweed jacket. He seized it and hugged it to him, just as he had Kumara. He held it for a long time, but it had no more effect on him than any old bit of fabric.

He felt nothing, and feeling nothing was, he knew, the worst thing war could inflict on a man.

But he did not put the jacket down. He held it close, searched the threadbare tweed for his father's smell, for the remnants of a life and the memory of a voice.

It was the first time they had embraced each other.

He went on holding and hugging and then something loosened. There was a stinging in the corners of his eyes. His body started to shake. He was shaking so hard he had to sit down on the bed, and finally he felt them running down his cheeks.

"Thank you, Father. I thought the war had taken them."

He sat there, appreciating each tear, then straightened up and went over to the pile of letters. He opened the first, read it slowly, then put it back in its envelope and opened the next.

Spare, always beautiful descriptions of an old man's thoughts and of the changing seasons at Finlaggan. An estate that offered all a man could need. Riding, fishing, shooting and farming, through spring, summer and autumn. Beautiful fortnightly reminders of the joys of living on one's own land. Fantasy and reality intertwined. Forty-three letters in all. Enough to help keep Victor's spirits up if the war had lasted until May 26, 1920.

This last May-time letter ended with: *It's mild and everything's very green here at Finlaggan. But the weather's about to turn, so I'll leave you now, as I must get out for a walk before it rains.*

When Victor came downstairs the dining room was filled with the fragrance of a Kerala stew, but Kumara had set only one place at the end of the long table. Victor went to the sideboard to fetch another plate and set of cutlery, and moved his own plate so they could sit and eat facing each other, and when they had finished he thanked Kumara, and said he unfortunately had to rush off.

They walked out into the morning sun and over to the shed where the Blériot was kept. He had not wanted to see it when he had come on leave, and he had to trample down the vegetation to open the doors. Inside, the entire airplane was draped with bedsheets.

"It was impossible to keep the birds off her," Kumara said. "I tried to mend the gaps in the timber walls, but there were so few materials. A strange sight. All those little birds on one big bird. I was worried that their droppings would corrode her wings. So I took your mother's old sheets and spread them over her. I hope that wasn't wrong."

"Absolutely not, Kumara."

They pulled off the sheets, coughing as the dust and dry bird droppings swirled about. When the dust settled, he could barely believe what he saw.

Only five years had passed since he had flown her last, but compared to the warplanes he had been flying, the Blériot seemed fifty years old. And she was not in a good state. Her wires were rusty and slack, and the canvas over her wings was stained and needed tightening.

Kumara took off his shoes.

With needles, thread and glue they patched the holes in the canvas. They restretched it over the wings and body of the aircraft, and adjusted the wires and connections. Victor took out the carburettors and cleaned the float chambers and needles. Petrol had been rationed, but Kumara had stashed four barrels, which should contain 180 gallons in all. In 1913 Victor had changed the engine to a French Gnome, and he had filled the cylinders with preservation oil before leaving for war. When they heard the engine splutter into action later that evening, it may not have been running quite as smoothly as in 1913, but neither was it much worse.

"Must you?" Kumara asked. "Right away?"

"Yes," Victor said. "The war did that to us. Always out the next day. No matter what."

Next morning, Kumara had slaughtered another hen, made some Kerala stew and spooned it into three small metal dishes. They filled the Blériot's tanks and studied the map. Tryggve Gran had flown from Cruden Bay to Revtangen in Jæren in just four hours and ten minutes, and, being light, the Blériot still had plenty of fuel left.

Victor looked up at the sky and remembered his instructor, Carax. He smelled rain on the air, but was unsure when it would come.

"Kumara," Victor said, "if I don't come back, you must send word to Florence. Thank my mother and say that Joseph should take over Finlaggan. I've left a letter for my lawyer to explain that I want you to manage the estate. There's a sum of money too, so if you want to go back to Ceylon, you can."

"I've waited for you for four years now, Victor. It won't be easy for me if you die today."

"Don't worry. I don't intend to die today."

"But when you do die, d'you think I'll be the only one who remembers you?"

"Perhaps, Kumara. Perhaps. Although I suspect that after what I'm about to do, there will be a few people who remember me."

He put on his hat and goggles, ran the engine until it was warm, lifted the Blériot up into the sky, took a lap over Finlaggan, then pointed towards the coast. He was wearing Eugen Kreis' suit under his leather coat, and beside his knees was his old school atlas. Close to the coast he landed in a field. He had forgotten how sensitive the Blériot was, and almost went into a spin. He had some cans of oil and petrol in the backseat, he refilled and took off again.

Soon the North Sea lay around him in a gentle, grey arc. The wind had dropped. He flew over a fishing boat and a ship, then for forty minutes he saw nothing but calm waters.

Suddenly he saw a German Fokker in the corner of his eye. His reaction was instantaneous and he swung the plane to the side. A second later he realised it was a figment of his imagination. When the Blériot finally reacted to his mistake, it rolled over so hard that he had sea to his left and sky to his right.

He met a bank of clouds and felt a crosswind. The compass needle was not rotating quite evenly. The engine juddered now and then, and he hoped he wouldn't fly into rain, causing it to over-cool.

But the Blériot ought to manage this. He felt sure it could manage it. The real question was whether he would get there in time. He had thought the war had numbed his capacity to feel much for people, but now he knew otherwise. He missed his father and had been sad to leave Kumara so soon, and now he pictured a campfire in Norway many years ago, with dry juniper that flared up and spat and sent sparks in an arc over the night and the mountains.

Carry me over this sea, he said to the Blériot. Carry me over.

It was then that he encountered the first real gusts of wind. He flew lower to check out the formation of the waves below. They were facing in a south-westerly direction and were barely white, indicating a fresh breeze. He corrected the compass for a twenty-five degree wind drift.

Moments later the clouds turned menacingly black. The Blériot began to list dramatically, and he had to adjust the drift to thirty degrees. Banks of fog were building up in front of him. Beneath him the waves were getting continually bigger. The wind must be nearing gale force now, and again he adjusted his course. An hour later he was flying through a thick, milky-white fog, with almost no visibility.

Was this where it would all end, he thought. In salt water. Not fresh water? Whatever the case, all water ultimately flowed back into the sea. Whether you drowned in the North Sea or in Lake Løsnes, you drowned in the same water.

He tried to climb above the fog and instantly felt a drop in the temperature. When his altimeter read five thousand feet, all his instruments went white with frost, and he kept having to wipe the glass with his glove. Soon the carburettor could be adjusted no further, and the engine juddered in the thin air. He was shivering as he gave up and lowered the plane to see if it was possible to fly beneath the fog.

As he began his descent he heard a loud clunking noise in the engine that refused to stop no matter what adjustments he made. Suddenly he smelled gas and the engine cut out.

The Blériot went into a nosedive, and as it hurtled like a lifeless boulder through dense fog, he was convinced everything was over. He brought in the other fuel tank and started pumping by hand while trying to avoid going into a spin. The engine kicked in again, but the altimeter dropped from five hundred feet to three hundred feet and suddenly he was out of the fog and heading straight for the sea below him and a mass of huge breakers. But then at last the Blériot reacted and he was in control of her again. He stayed under the fog, trying to gauge whether the crests of the waves were throwing water eastwards or southwards.

Two and a half hours had passed since he had left England's coast. Assuming he had set the compass correctly, he must be about halfway there.

He was flying in the fog again, and it was even denser than before. Victor didn't quite know what to think.

For the next hour his desperation was fuelled by a fear of loss or of failing to arrive in time. An awareness rose in him of all the things he hadn't known for so many years. Jehans was dying in Norway. Perhaps he was already dead. He wanted to get across this sea, run across the mainland and be there, back among the people of that little village, to talk to the pastor at last and show him that he was now years older, and he wanted to see a brother who had perhaps at least *thought* of writing to him, just as he had thought of doing.

One hour later and the land of Butangen and his brother was still nowhere to be seen.

Was it smoke that filled his nostrils? Coal smoke? Or something burning in the engine? He dived down into the fog again and when he burst through it the plane was heading for a ship. His landing wheels almost grazed its masts and men were shouting wildly below him. All of a sudden he found himself in brilliant sunlight and straight in front of him was solid ground. Soon he had landed in a field and was scrambling stiffly out. Ten or so people ran towards him, as he rushed behind the Blériot to empty his bladder, taking so long that two boys got to him before he was done.

The others were soon gathered around him and the Blériot, full of questions, which he tried his best to answer in the little Norwegian he remembered. When he brought out his school atlas their first reaction was disappointment at not finding their village marked on it. He needed to buy some petrol, but the locals were very sceptical when he pulled out some pound notes. He had brought a copy of the *Financial Times* to reassure people of the exchange rate, but they were still unsure. Only when another villager came along with the previous day's *Fædrelandsvennen* did they realise that the man from the sky was offering them a small fortune for some petrol, and they rallied to help.

His next landing was just north of Kristiania, where he bought some lubricating oil as well as more petrol and ate

Kumara's food. It should have taken him only two hours to fly from here, but then, when he reached the end of Lake Mjøsa and continued up the River Laugen, he lost his way. He was so desperate he could barely keep the plane steady. There was snow in the air, and he was absolutely exhausted and starting to get sloppy at the controls. The Blériot lurched violently. *Don't die now*, he said, *now that you're almost there.*

He wanted to live. And he wanted his brother to live. Jehans was most probably dead already, but Victor wanted to come as close as he could to the possibility that he was still alive. The possibility that they all might live to travel together between Butangen and Finlaggan and Dresden, the five people who were still here on Earth: Jehans Hekne, Kai Schweigaard, Kumara, Elsa Rathenau and him.

Below him he spotted a farmhouse, and then a field with some horses. Flying low, he chased the horses to the end of the field, then turned and landed where the horses had stood.

Looking up at the farmhouse he saw a Norwegian flag at half-mast.

A tall, distinguished-looking man came striding across the field. He held a little boy by the hand and stopped at a fair distance. He informed Victor that he was on Lo farm in the village of Fron, and that Butangen was much further south. They were in mourning because the farmer had died of the Spanish flu two days earlier. He would find Butangen if he followed the river south to a church with a white spire just before the river widened.

Twenty minutes later Victor Harrison landed in another field. As he took off his helmet, it was growing dark and bitterly cold. He left the Blériot standing and limped forward.

In Loving Memory

He had been plagued by hallucinations before. But this was by far the worst. Edgar Hekne or Victor Harrison or whoever he might be was sitting by his bed.

The figure vanished and Jehans sank further into his fevered dreams. When he woke up again, Kai Schweigaard was at his side, feeding him with a spoon. Jehans reached out to check if he was real. He was. Jehans tried to push him away, whispering that he would get infected too if he stayed.

But Schweigaard was calm and begged him to eat. "I'm going to stay here with you, Jehans. Until the very end, if it comes."

They came and went and were either hallucinations or real. Schweigaard, Adolf, Ingeborg, Victor and then Schweigaard again. Then Kristine appeared in the doorway, and he insisted loudly that they must pick a name for the child she was carrying! She burst into tears, saying that they already had.

He slept deeply and felt a bit stronger when Kristine reappeared at his door, and then he spoke and thought he got an answer, but was unsure if he was just remembering something that had already been said.

"Kristine."

"Aye."

"If this should nay go well."

"Aye, Jehans?"

"Ye were all I ever wanted, Kristine. Not this farm. Not the electricity station. Just thee and a little one."

"Little ones," Kristine said. "They be kicking me now."

"It all went by so quickly. So quickly."

"I wish I could take thee in my arms, Jehans. Give thee comfort. But I mun stand over here."

The mists of sleep wrapped about him again, his lips grew stiff, his chest tightened and she disappeared, and he was unsure if he had said what he said or had just thought it.

He heard voices again. Imagined that Kai Schweigaard and Victor Harrison were talking. They seemed so close. But his joints were too painful for him to turn and check if there was really anyone in the room.

"You do realise you'll get ill too? If you take him with you?" Schweigaard said.

"Ill? And what about you?" said Victor Harrison's voice. "You're sitting there feeding him."

Jehans felt a flannel on his brow. Laid there by Schweigaard's hand. The pastor smoothed a salve on his lips. Then he got up. Through half-closed eyelids, Jehans saw a man who resembled the brother he had punched in the face all those years ago.

His brother handed him four tablets and told him to swallow them.

When he woke up again, they pulled back his duvet, grabbed him under both arms and lifted him, and he heard Kristine shouting that she would never forgive them. He was moved onto a hard stretcher. He felt his body jolting, a horse whinnied, then he was in a church. It had to be the old stave church, since the smell of tar filled his nose, and he was lying stretched out in an open coffin. They seemed not to have enough pallbearers, his body was being rocked hard from side to side, and along with the smell of wood there was the rawness of icy water. Night gave way to dawn. He sat up to yell out that he was not dead, but he did not slam into a coffin lid, and when he was upright, he realised that the smell of tar came from the priest-boat and that he was out on Lake Løsnes.

They had dressed him in a heavy brown leather coat. A crunching noise issued from the delicate crust of night-formed ice as the boat pushed its way on.

"It's grown since my last visit," Victor said, nodding towards the forest.

Jehans was unable to answer.

They rowed further out. The lake was ice-free here, and the boat glided silently on. Victor looked up at the sky between oar strokes. "It was around this time of day I learned to fly," he said. "There was always less wind."

Jehans lay with his back against the stern and looked up at the clouds. They were sharply etched across the sky and mirrored in the water below, and as his eyes drifted from one to the other, there was no difference between the sky and Lake Løsnes.

"Can ye – can ye fly that high?" Jehans asked, looking up at the clouds. "As high as the clouds?"

"Certainly. Just as high," Victor said. "Or as deep."

"As deep?"

"Each cloud has another to match it in the water. So long as the water is still. As now." He rowed further, and added: "That's how you start thinking. When you're up there."

When he was next conscious they were out on the raft, and Jehans felt the water wash over his legs. Victor was standing there with an oar, trying to keep it steady. He said that Schweigaard had got a man to tighten the raft and mount a hoist. But the ropes were quite rotten and the logs were constantly creaking and he wondered if they could take the weight of a church bell.

When Jehans came round again, some time must have passed, since the morning sun had grown stronger. Victor rowed towards a white-painted board that rocked in the water. He steered the raft directly over it, and when the board popped up in the hole in the centre of the raft, he grabbed it and pulled on the shoemaker's string that trailed down into the water. He lowered a five-armed dredging hook and dragged it back and forth, the water swirling around the rope.

The rope pulled up higher again. A fresh pendulum movement. Back and forth. The hook down among the rocks and the roots and mud.

Back and forth.

Suddenly everything ground to a halt and the raft started to rotate on its own centre. It was impossible to tell if they had caught something in the depths or if something had caught them.

Jehans fumbled for something to grab hold of and stared at the rope. His brother hooked it over the hoist and some of the sprockets began to click, and as it took the weight, the raft creaked and lay deeper in the water. One of the ropes burst and two logs slipped free, Victor backed towards the edge of the raft to keep it balanced. The grating sound of wood and wet ropes and hoists grew louder and harsher. Under them a great weight swayed from side to side, transferring its movements to the raft. The locking hooks on the hoist clanked loudly, while around them Lake Løsnes lay smooth and vast and infinitely quiet. Jehans collapsed, but his brother shook him awake again.

The hoist continued to clank.

Something seemed to be gathering, something dense, and the water trembled, obscuring the shape of what came up. The raft shook and the hoist clattered while the black area in the water turned blacker than water.

Soon water was spurting up from the hole in the raft. Victor got up and grabbed his brother with one hand and pulled on the hoist with the other. At last the church bell burst free from the water, bringing a blast of cold air with it. Dark and massive it swung before them, overgrown with sediment. The mud ran slowly off, and gradually some engraved letters came into view. An inscription ran around the entire bell, it was impossible to say where it began or ended, and the inscription that made itself visible in the water on Lake Løsnes read thus:

MOTHER ASTRID IN LOVING MEMORIE

The Sacrament of the Old Faith

The next day the Spanish flu got its teeth firmly into Victor Harrison. He came down with a terrible fever and was given a bed in the same room as Jehans. Schweigaard caught sight of his bare torso and shuddered at how emaciated he was and the extent of his wounds. An ugly scar ran across his chest and there were massive burns around his left shoulder. His ribs were sharply pronounced under his skin, some looked as though they had been broken and set crookedly. He had survived the war for four years, only to succumb to it now. And he grew weaker and weaker with each passing hour.

Jehans was so ill he could get no worse. He lay in a silent sweat, staring up at the ceiling.

Next morning Victor had deteriorated yet further. Schweigaard defied Kristine by sitting with them both, trying to get some porridge and boiled water into them. But then he had to go out for some fresh air. This, he thought, is unbearable.

Gunhild had been hung in the bell tower that night. After hauling Jehans back up to Hekne, Victor had wrapped her in canvas and with Herr Røhme's help he hoisted her up into place. Only when he was alone with her had Victor removed the cloth.

It was still early when Schweigaard and Victor had walked

past Astrid's grave and through the November-cold village. They had walked past the dairy and the unfinished building, and then at the gates of the parsonage Victor returned the copy of *Meyers Sprachführer für Reisen und Haus* to Schweigaard, and asked him to write to Kumara and Elsa Rathenau if things should end badly.

"I read in the newspaper that several million people have already died," Victor said. "I sometimes think this plague will just keep coming. That we'll never be rid of it. That it will continue until we're all gone."

Then the two men wandered back up to Hekne. The farmhouse lay as still as a painting. And watching from behind the window of the old annex was Kristine.

Victor tried to disguise his cough.

"Do you think this is the end, Schweigaard? That this is doomsday. What you call Skorp—"

"Skråpånatta."

"Yes. Skråpånatta."

Schweigaard turned his gaze towards the cemetery, thought for a moment, and said, "I did. But I'm not so sure now. I suspect more awaits us."

They parted ways on the stone steps. Victor went inside to see his brother, and Kai Schweigaard stood for a moment in the cold, grey light and gazed across the village.

Two flags at half-mast today.

The flag that we finally won for ourselves. In this land that we finally won for ourselves. Only to find ourselves asking if this is where it ends. With a plague that kills us all off. A plague that lowers all flags in all lands.

He looked down at the bell tower. Was there space for them all in there? For all the villagers? So he would be left to bury them single-handedly come the spring?

*

That evening their coughs sounded even tighter and more pain-ful. The air in their room was clammy. Neither brother ate or drank what he put out for them.

Victor lay there, sweaty and grey-faced. He had kicked his sheet so it lay in a little bundle at the foot of the bed, but he did not even have the energy now to kick. He was muttering some-thing over and over again. At first it sounded like the name of the woman he had talked of, Elsa Rathenau, but it turned into an incomprehensible ramble.

Kai Schweigaard opened a window, so sad he had to grab the sill. No, he thought. No. I can't bear this. Not again. With every-one dying like this.

He sat up close to Victor Harrison. A rotten, sickly-sweet breath from his mouth, spasms constantly running through his body.

Victor opened his eyes wide. Schweigaard was certain it was over. But then Victor mumbled something again. It did not seem to be in English. Rather, its intonation resembled the old Butangen dialect.

Kai Schweigaard got up. What if I go down and fetch the pillows? he thought. One last attempt.

But it would make no difference. The events in the circle would be fulfilled tonight.

He went out into the courtyard and sat on a cold, wet rock. He saw Kristine at the window of the other house. He sent his thoughts through all the events and experiences of a sixty-year life. There was no help. No medicine.

He remembered something a woodcutter once told him. The man had got an axe in his guts. He had never been a church-goer, but there in the forest, when the going got tough, he hadn't taken the chance that God might not exist, and had clasped his hands over his wound and prayed as ardently as any nun.

Schweigaard straightened his cassock and went down to the

church, where Mass had not been held since the day Gunhild had rung. He let himself in, stood in the aisle and cleared his throat, as a man does when he enters his own house but wants to signal his arrival to someone.

When Astrid had died, he had made an agreement with God that they would talk again in forty years. There were a few years left before that time was up. Nevertheless, Kai Schweigaard knelt before the altar and said that he was here now, in case the Lord was also there before the appointed time.

He rose to his feet an hour later. Went outside and stood for a while by her grave. An old memory had come to him in the new church of a conversation he'd had with Astrid when she had come to fetch Klara Mytting's body. Klara, the old pauper woman whom Astrid had brought for New Year's Mass in the stave church. Klara, who had frozen to death during the service. Klara, with her open-hearted, childlike belief in all sorts of magical healing and spells.

He let the word form on his lips. A word he had not heard since Astrid Hekne had sat in the pastor's office almost forty years earlier.

The Holyblight.

He and Astrid had talked about holy relics. About relics with healing powers. The little caskets that the Catholics filled with locks of hair and toenails that cured the sick. And Astrid's question: *Who decides that one counts while the other do not?* Their whole conversation came back to him now. Klara had wanted them to scrape off the Holyblight for her. *Klara said it grew inside the church bells, and that it were a remedy for all kinds of sickness.*

Back in the parsonage he fetched the knife from the Hekne sisters' coffin and an old, battered tin cup that had been in the stave church. He went over to the gutter closest to Astrid's grave and took some rainwater. Her grave was covered with a fine layer of snow. He stopped outside the bell tower.

He had never strayed further from the message of the Bible.

Yet perhaps he had never been closer. What was the difference between the Holyblight and a red-hot knitting needle in tar?

Belief. That was all. The one thing you had left when nothing else helped.

Once again he asked himself whether he could defend what he was about to do. All his powers of reason and education opposed it.

But he had to. He had to *believe*. Just as old Klara had done long ago. But even a thought about the power of belief had an ulterior motive, and he let go of any thoughts as he went into the bell tower.

It was different in here now. A different greyish light. A different silence. More church-like. And in the half-light in the middle of the room he saw the bell rope. Water had dripped from it and left a small dust-coloured stain on the floor.

He climbed up into the belfry.

Sometimes when he was out on Lake Løsnes he felt an irresistible draw to the watery depths below. An attraction and a terror. Vertigo's evil brother. What he felt now was similar, yet utterly dissimilar. Suspended from the middle of the ceiling was the solitary church bell. Massive, dark, heavy, and coated with verdigris. Sister to a sister.

Schweigaard took hold of the rim of the bell. It reacted to his touch with a slight sway, as though it were waking from a doze. He set the knife's blade against the inside of the bell, scraped it and collected the tiny green grains in the tin cup. It was impossible for him to hold the bell steady as he did so, and the metal released a deep vibration. It sounded neither hostile nor reluctant, the bell let him take all he needed, and as he descended the ladder, a faint echo resounded behind him.

Back up at Hekne he sat by Victor's bed and plunged a spoon into the tin cup. Dark specks swirled around in the water, and he forced this gritty drink into Victor. Then he went over to Jehans and did the same.

Pulled a chair into the centre of the room and sat down.

The brothers writhed in the darkness behind him.

There was nothing more to be done but to let the night descend and clasp his hands in prayer.

Reunion

He knelt beside the grave, but this time he rested his knee on a wooden board instead of the Bible. It was August and the blue-bells were starting to fade. He cleared some wizened leaves and prepared the grave for the autumn.

The wind was playing in the silver birches down by the bell tower. As he peered through their branches towards the lake, they cast a green tint on the sparkling waves. The birch trees had been barely thicker than a finger when the bell tower was first built; now their tops reached above its roof.

Fru Røhme was still in mourning, but had surfaced from the deep melancholy he had believed might break her. She sat by Simen's grave each morning, but could laugh with her other children. As to Herr Røhme – he dealt with it in his own way. Schweigaard got a lump in his throat whenever he saw him tending the cemetery. He never paused at the headstone for long, but had adopted a habit of carrying wheat grains in his pockets and scattering a few there each day, so the wagtails and the yellowhammers hopped around Simen's grave.

We all find a way.

However we can.

Earlier that day, Schweigaard had locked away the Hekne Weave and the sisters' pillows. They were laid in a blue-painted chest in a room behind his study, and he did not expect to take them out again for many years. But before hiding them away, he cast a final glance at Gunhild's pillow and studied one of the reindeer. He had assumed it was falling down, but now realised that falling and getting back up had much in common. It reminded him of the inscription that encircled the church bell, it was impossible to read more than half the text at once. Its meaning depended on which word he chose to read first, and any one word could constitute either the end or the beginning of the inscription.

It's good, he thought, and lay the pillows and knife in the chest. It's good, he thought, and rolled up the Hekne Weave and laid it next to them.

It's good.

He locked the chest, crossed over to the wooden sculpture of Christ on the Cross, hung the keys on his big toe, and nodded up at him. It was late summer and it was afternoon, but still there was much left of the day, and of the year, just as he knew there was of his life before his last deed. Next week he would take the train up to Dovre. He was not quite sure what her hopes were for this visit, but there was a liberation just in sitting at a woman's table.

Kai Schweigaard sat on the bench and looked out. He was old enough now to watch village life through binoculars without shame. He liked to scan the opposite side of the lake, where the new road went along the edge of the marshes, curious to see who was returning from a trip to Fåvang. He puffed on his pipe and saw a two-horse carriage appear over the hill. Both horses were from Hekne and he left the binoculars on the bench and rushed, rather stiffly and unsteadily, down to the priest-boat. He rowed across and waited. As soon as the carriage came back into view, it stopped without his waving it over.

"'Tis kind o' thee," Kristine said.

"Such are the pleasures of an ageing pastor," he said.

Settling into the boat, she described the events of her day. She had purchased eighty kilos of coffee, five bags of sago, a large carton of matches and some bullets, but had been unable to get much sugar, with rationing likely to last a while longer. The exciting news, however, was that the fellow who delivered goods to Herr Paper Cone had bought himself a brand-new, bright-green American truck, with shiny bumpers. The children had swarmed around it like bluebottles round a lump of meat, and the driver had let them all pile into the truck bed and given them a ride. Schweigaard laughed and said that they might one day have a good enough road for folk to drive all the way up to Butangen.

"And that shall indeed be welcome," Kristine said. "But however good the road, it shall always be a pleasure t' be rowed over this last stretch."

She looked across the water and smiled. Schweigaard planted his feet firmly in the bottom of the boat and rowed on. Steady and precise. Or fairly at least. He was a bit forgetful these days, and had started to mix up names and dates, but he was still physically tough.

"Have they thanked thee?" she asked. "Thanked thee properly?"

"Yes. Each in their own way. Together and individually. Are you expecting them back today?"

She shook her head. "Who can tell when those two may come? But the wind turned yesterday eve, so the reindeer can have moved at nightfall. They may have spied the herd in the twilight but waited with shooting so they might carry their kill down by day."

"Time in the mountains is the same as it ever was," Schweigaard said. "Folk always seem to have more time up there."

"Oh?"

"I'm just comparing it to when Victor first came here. He said it took eight or nine days from leaving his estate in England to his arrival here. And before the railway it would have taken a good fortnight. But last year he got here in just fourteen hours."

"I were glad his plane couldna go up in the air again," Kristine said. "He talks o' buying a new one. A cargo plane, he said. He has plans."

"He always has plans."

"He comes here of a sudden and goes of a sudden. 'Tis queer he has nay fear o' all this travelling. Nay fear that a boat might sink. Or a plane might drop from the sky. Or a train leave its rails."

"No," Schweigaard said. "He's fearless. It's what he was made for."

They talked on. A late summer breeze drew patterns on the water around the boat, like the searching strokes of an artist's brush, visible only briefly before the wind went a little further south to play upon the water there. She told him that the new dairy would be ready to accept milk deliveries from next June. They had to sell some fishing rights and a *seter* to raise money for the new separators and pasteurisers. Jehans hated dividing the farm, but took comfort from the fact that the fishing rights and *seter* had been sold once before, when the farm was in debt after the casting of the Sister Bells. The opening of the dairy was to be celebrated with a big "give-away" of something she had learned to make at the Dairy School in Levanger, which nobody in the village had ever tasted before.

"'Tis called ice cream. And it shall be to yer liking, Kai. We put strawberries in't. There may soon be motorcars that can keep food cold, and in just a few years we may have an even bigger business. I plan t' name it Døla-is."

It was a bright, sunny day, and he watched her as she sat in the boat with Lake Løsnes all around her and the steep fields of Butangen before her and he saw how at one she was with the place in which she lived.

"There be sommat I have pondered upon," she said. "How ye dared to tend to Jehans and Victor when they lay abed with the Spanish. And how ye dared visit all the other sick folk too."

His thoughts wandered, until he realised she was waving her hand to get his attention.

"What?" he said.

"I were wondering how ye – ye be rowing us onto the shore."

He turned and, rowing with one oar, redirected the boat towards the church. "I must have lost concentration for a moment. What were you saying?"

"I were asking *how* ye dared do it," she said. "Were ye nay frightened o' getting sick and dying too?"

"Ah that. Well now. A priest should never tell an untruth. But a priest may omit to say a thing sometimes."

Kristine nodded, but was not satisfied.

"Although," Schweigaard said, "he may perhaps say that he saw a sign once. And that this sign told him that he would die of neither a stroke nor disease."

They had almost reached the shore, and he took four long, powerful strokes with the oars, before bringing them in and letting the bottom of the boat grind into the gravel. And with that their trip was over. He liked to come ashore at Butangen like this, rather than coming alongside the pier and having to clamber up unsteadily. Here it was as though a big hand reached under the keel, took a firm hold of the priest-boat and drew him gently in, saying: *So ye are come back at last, Kai Schweigaard.*

*

He helped her ashore and asked if she would wait for the carriage, but she said that Widow Fløter planned to go straight up to the dairy shop with the goods.

"Ah, so she was your driver."

"She near runs the whole shop. Getting quite headstrong, but that's all t' the good."

They strolled up the slope and reached the spot from which they could see the bell tower.

"Well, there are only twelve days to go," Schweigaard said.

"I wonder if folk shall believe it true," Kristine said. "Happen they have forgot how she sounded. What shall ye answer if folks ask how she came back to us?"

"There's no guarantee they'll get an answer. I can start to blame my age now."

"So it shall be the same day for Victor and Elsa as for us? The bell shall ring for them there in Dresden?"

"Yes, that's the plan."

"How did he manage that?"

"It was simply a matter of choosing the same day and time. He must have got to know the churchwarden down there. So at eleven o'clock Halfrid will ring for the wedding there and Gunhild will ring for the baptism of your two."

"'Tis well he be wed. I never saw a lonelier man."

"Hmm."

"Shall they ever come t' visit? So we may meet her?"

"That's certainly the plan. Sometime next spring, he hoped."

"And his best man? Happen he met him in the Great War?"

"No, they met in Ceylon years ago. And it seems he wants to see Norway too, so he'll probably accompany them when they come."

"Still. 'Tis sad they shall have naebody from here at the wedding."

"Yes, but . . ."

Kai Schweigaard fell silent.

"What?"

"Oh, just something he said. I don't always understand him. But we were in the sitting room one night and it was getting late and he said there was somebody from Butangen down there in the old stave church. Somebody for whom they planned to play a Norwegian hymn as the bell rang out for their wedding."

They had reached Hekne now, and walked into the courtyard. There were no hunting rifles by the entrance, and they saw the wind direction from the tops of the birches and agreed that the brothers would probably be back much later. The farm was getting busier with folk. They had given houseroom to a family with three children who had returned from America. And one room in what had traditionally been the grandparents' annex was now inhabited by Isumruggen, a famously strong but heavy-drinking man from Hundorp whose nickname meant the Isum Giant. Arrested for violating the Vagrancy Act, he had been sent to Hekne to work for his board and lodging. Ingeborg and Adolf were now even more deaf, but the little comforts supplied by Kristine and Jehans had eased their suffering, not only that but the babies had given them a new lease of life. And when the day was over, Ingeborg would settle in the rocking chair like the old Hekne farm wives, eating sour cream waffles.

Kai Schweigaard and Kristine went into the downstairs room. Ingeborg said they had to be quiet as she had only just got them off to sleep. But the babies woke up the instant Kristine came in, and she lifted the little boy from his crib and said, aye, of course he would have milk. Schweigaard felt it was time to take his leave, but Kristine shook her head, he must hold her babbies today! Carefully he took the little boy, who gently kicked the air and gazed about him. Schweigaard carried him over to the window so he could look out. His name was to be Tarald, after Kristine's father. They stood there a while before Schweigaard returned the child to his mother. Then he lifted the little girl and carried her over to look at Lake Løsnes too.

She was impatient, flaying about with her arms and legs, and he smiled as he thought about the name he would enter in the *kirkebok* on the day when the Sister Bells rang together again.

Astrid Regine Hekne. Born June 8, 1919.

He shifted his hold and sensed her will vibrating through her little body. So soft and yet so strong. Astrid cried a bit and wriggled, and Schweigaard comforted her with a quiet *there, there.* He rocked Astrid in his arms and looked into her eyes, and she stared back and was instantly calm when she recognised him.

LARS MYTTING, a novelist and journalist, was born in Favang, Norway, in 1968. *The Sixteen Trees of the Somme* was awarded the Norwegian National Booksellers' Award and the film rights have been acquired. *Norwegian Wood: Chopping, Stacking, and Drying Wood the Scandinavian Way* has become an international bestseller, and was the Bookseller Industry Awards Non-Fiction Book of the Year in 2016. *The Bell in the Lake* and *The Reindeer Hunters* were for many weeks number one bestsellers in Norway.

DEBORAH DAWKIN originally trained in theatre at Drama Centre, London, before turning to translation. Her translations include *The Blue Room* by Hanne Orstavik and *Buzz Aldrin: What Happened to You in All the Confusion* by Johan Harstad, shortlisted for the Best Translated Book Awards in 2012. She is the co-translator of eight plays by Ibsen for Penguin Classics, and is presently working on a PhD about the life and work of the Ibsen translator Michael Meyer.